*This book is dedicated to Larry, my love,
who stood by me every step of this journey and
whose inspiration, dedication and confidence in me
made this book possible.*

Acknowledgments

As I pursued my dream to write this first book, I was gifted with wonderful people who helped me overcome feelings of being overwhelmed and out of my comfort zone. Their support and belief in me enabled me to accomplish my goal. Thank you, and special thanks to:

Kelsie, my fabulous daughter, for giving a push (okay, a shove) to put fingers to keyboard.

Gary Steinhilber, for his selfless patience and commitment that kept the writing moving.

Pat Goetz, Steve Nichols, and Luke Weber, who so graciously helped along the way so that the dream to write this book was realized.

To Nedler Palaz and Nancy Patacca for giving me the courage to follow in their footsteps to become an author.

To family and friends for their cheering and enthusiasm and for *never* giving up on this book getting published.

To Cap Daniels and Mia Sheridan and others for helping me through the publishing process.

Clarissa Thomasson, my editor, for her guidance.

Cross Ink, Corp., for cover design.

Bookends of Murder
A Bekbourg County Novel

By Sherrie Rutherford

Part I

Chapter 1

Early Morning July 5, 1980

Another July Fourth celebration cloaked the surrounding countryside with the dense smell of burnt fireworks. Though it was well past midnight, the night was marred by oppressive hot and humid air trapped beneath a blanket of damp haze. Only the chirping of crickets and noises of other nocturnal insects broke the stillness.

The house was unique and stood basically alone save for the house across the road and a couple of houses hundreds of yards away. Its flamboyant owner had invested a substantial sum in transforming an 1800's farm house into the luxurious home. Reflecting the late hour, no lights shone through the windows. Outside lights were off, and no light was cast by the moonless sky.

The early morning hour found two darkly clad figures slowly making their way from the woods behind the house—certain of their destination. Their masks made identification impossible yet bespoke of their menacing intent. They approached the concrete patio off the back where a door opened into the house. One of the intruders deftly worked the door's lock—allowing them to enter silently. A hail of gunfire soon erupted inside the house. Brief silence was followed by a blast of more gunfire. Silence was wrenched from death. Eeriness seeped into the still air. Although neighboring dogs had begun barking, gunfire mistaken for teenagers shooting fireworks late into the night failed to garner suspicion.

Inside, the confused voice of one intruder stammered, "Who were all those people? You said only Burkhart was here."

"Shut up!" the second hissed. Both stood frozen—the first assailant waiting for instruction. The headman was resolute. "We'll burn it. Hurry, see what you can find in the garage."

"What about the coins? Ain't we goin' to find them?"

"We don't have time. The cops may already be on their way with all the noise. We got to destroy any evidence. Go!"

Seconds ticked into minutes, but soon, the figures exited the house and vanished into the dark woods. A different kind of smoke began to fill the night sky. The house, dark moments earlier, now emitted a glow from within that grew brighter with ruin. The home was soon engulfed in flames.

Chapter 2

May, 1978

Located where the Appalachian mountain range began to fade in the southeast Ohio region, the small rural town of Bekbourg, Ohio, had prospered from its founding due to its proximity to pioneer trails intersecting north-south and east-west. As the region developed and roads were built, nearby Chillicothe was established as the first capital of Ohio. Paper mills opened in Chillicothe, and Ohio University was chartered in nearby Athens, Ohio. Coal and iron-ore mining, brick-making and wheat and corn mills marked the emergence of lucrative area industries. However, as the global economy changed in the 1970's, like much of the rest of the region, its economy began to languish, and it appeared that Bekbourg's best days were behind it.

Signs of the 1970's economic stagnation were evident in the sparse patchwork of homes in the rural suburb. The houses had large yards, mostly resembling light green carpet with soiled patches that merged with former corn fields overflowing with vines and brush. White concrete flower boxes blotched with discoloration that spoke of years of use were filled with blooming flowers and competing weeds. Lined across the fronts of some houses was overgrown boxwood shrubbery. Propane tanks were common fixtures in many yards. Some of the houses had additions where no effort had been made to synchronize the rooflines. Few trees were present in the front of the houses, but large wooded acreage stood undisturbed behind most of the lots. Separate garages and metal sheds had been added over time on most of the properties. This was the community where Sean Neumann had been raised, and his high school graduation was now two days away.

Sean and his circle of friends were sitting in the long-abandoned isolated barn, years ago claimed as their hangout when discovered on a shortcut to the fishing pond. Billyboy, Sean's old black Lab, was lying asleep up against him. Sean looked around at his friends, who had all started elementary school together. Sean typically never drank more than a couple of beers, but he figured there was something momentous about tonight. The trappings of teen-age boys, rumpled sleeping bags, metal folding chairs, discarded paper wrappers, tattered men's magazines, and countless beer and wine containers attested to the camaraderie spent here over the years.

One in their group had a gun that his dad had given him for his fifteenth birthday, and they had taken turns target shooting out back of the barn. Sean wondered if, like him, any of the others felt despair or an empty void. Certainly, jubilance over the impending graduation seemed to be lacking from the close group of friends. Sean thought it was as if everything was on hold and they were all waiting for something to happen. One thing was for certain, things were about to forever change for this group of friends.

During their senior year, their time together had dwindled due to the pulls of typical senior-year demands. Gary had visited several college recruitment calls, and Danny had spent more time working at the gas station. Mike's time, when he wasn't involved in football activities or doing odd jobs, was spent with Geri. As he nursed his beer and slowly scratched Billyboy's ears, Sean figured this was probably the last time they all would be together at the barn, but was it possible that he might not ever see some of his friends again? Would they each go their own way with childhood friendships discarded like one might toss aside his favorite, but thoroughly worn, football cleats? Would it matter one way or the other?

He wondered if he would miss any of the guys except Mike. He guessed he might feel something if he knew he wouldn't ever see Danny again, but for different reasons. Mike was his best friend. They had always clicked and understood each other, and they were a winning combination on the football field.

Despite being heavily recruited by large universities, Mike Adams was hanging up his football pads to attend the state police academy. He and Geri had been going steady since junior year, and Sean figured Mike would marry the perky, cute blonde, who was never at a loss for words and never met a stranger. He smiled thinking how the petite cheerleader only came to Mike's chest. Hidden beneath Mike's tall, slender physique was muscle and strength. Mike had wavy brown hair, which wasn't as dark as his brown eyes.

Danny Chambers was asleep on the threadbare woolen blanket that he had carried to the barn when they first started hanging out here. Danny was also on the football team, but he didn't see a lot of playing time. Throughout school, Danny had struggled to pass the basic courses, but what he lacked in his school work, he made up for in his uncanny knowledge of cars. He was planning to join his dad working in a gas station.

Gary Werner was one of the best offensive linemen to ever come out of Schriever High School. He wanted to stay close to home, so he was heading to Ohio University in Athens on a football scholarship. He was a mountain of a man. Sean couldn't figure how he could fit comfortably in his older-model VW Bug. He often bragged how he started shaving before any of the boys in their class. Gary put just enough effort into his studies to get by. He was popular with most of his classmates—especially the girls.

Jeff Thompson, the son of a powerful County Commissioner, was swapping stories with Gary about their recent female conquests and the fertile fields they were about to plow in college. All the friends, with the exception of Jeff, had been teammates on the Schriever Warriors High School football team. Where the other four wore jeans and tee-shirts, Jeff wore khakis and collared shirts. He wore his straight, brown hair trimmed neatly and combed to the side. While Jeff had dated several girls during high school, he was never serious about anyone. On his sixteenth birthday, his dad bought him a brand new black Firebird. He enjoyed cruising the local drive-in with a pretty girl sitting by his side. Although Jeff had not decided on a major at Ohio State University, he was already talking about going to law school.

Sean's musings were interrupted by Gary's question about when he was starting his job on the railroad. Sean responded that he would be officially on-call starting on Monday after graduation. Gary asked how he was going to spend time with Becky, his steady since last summer, with him on the road and her attending nearby Hillsrock Community College. Sean responded, "We'll manage."

Jeff, always looking for an angle with the female persuasion, asked in his good-humor teasing, "Think you'll get some on the side when you're out of town?"

"Not likely. Anyway, from what I hear, I won't want it."

Gary nodded his head toward Jeff, "You're not like Jeff here, who'll make it with any skirt around."

Bantering resumed between Gary and Jeff, which left Sean with his thoughts about the turn his life had taken.

Sean had been the quarterback and natural leader of the group, but his promising future in college football was shattered when he suffered a devastating injury in the final game of their championship season. Since his sophomore year,

Sean had led his team to numerous victories flanked by gifted and dedicated teammates. More significant was the fact that Schriever's football coach was Coach Clyde Jackson, whose talents had not gone unnoticed. Despite several offers to coach at small colleges, he remained at Schriever, sending many players into the university football ranks.

Sean didn't know who took it the hardest when he suffered the football-ending injury in the final minutes of the championship game—Sean's dad, Coach Jackson, or himself. Sean had already committed to play quarterback for Coach Jackson's alma mater. Sean remembered the opposing team's two players crashing into him as he scrambled to avoid being sandwiched between them. As one bore into his rib region, the other rammed hard into his throwing shoulder. The searing pain warned of something ominous. He lay on the field with worried players surrounding him while Doc Emerson examined his arm and shoulder. Because Sean objected to being carried from the field, Mike and Gary helped him to the sideline. After scans and X-ray, the bad news came that a complete tear in a shoulder ligament could not be satisfactorily repaired by surgery. His quarterback days were over.

The enormity of Sean's loss left him with any one or combinations of anguish, bitterness, disappointment, detachment, resignation or defeat. His grades suffered, and he withdrew from his friends. His dad's pep talks to "man-up" did nothing but further anger Sean. One day, Coach Jackson called him to his office. "Sean, I know this is hard. I wish I could change what happened. You have so much going for you, so many things to be grateful for. You are an outstanding young man with an unlimited future ahead of you. Don't let this conquer you, Sean. You can overcome this adversity. Don't let it define you. You define it."

Sean and Coach Jackson sat in silence for what seemed like a long time that afternoon. Finally, Sean said, "Thanks, Coach."

After that, Sean started working on his grades and spending time with his friends and Becky. He still had no idea what he wanted to do with himself after graduation. The economy was bad around Bekbourg. He sure didn't want to work at the milk plant where his dad worked, but he also had no money to attend college. He could see the concern in his mother's eyes, and he knew his dad was biting his tongue to stay off his back, which sometimes proved too much. Sean usually left in anger when his dad asked him about his plans after high school.

Chapter 3

Jim Neumann, Sean's dad, was an ex-marine who hated communism and was a true patriot to his country. He was a large, rugged-looking man who wore his hair in a military-cut. He wasn't violent or ill tempered, but he was dogmatic. Where Sean's mother and his sister, Linda, seemed to have no problem with Jim, Sean began to assert his independence around the age of ten and started mowing yards so he didn't have to ask his dad for spending money. Sean tried not to cross his dad, but as he got older, they often disagreed. He continued to do odd jobs, and with the money he saved, he was able to buy an old model pickup truck when he turned sixteen.

This tension between Sean and Jim, however, never overlapped in football. From the time he started playing Youth Football, his father supported him. His father would run patterns and catch for Sean in the afternoons and on weekends. He never missed one of Sean's football games, and he rarely offered advice once Sean reached junior high, because he wanted Sean to respect and trust his coaches. Jim was ecstatic when the first football recruiters started coming around. He saw football as a way for Sean to break out of Bekbourg and make something of himself.

Sean's grandfather, Clarence, had started work with the MV&O Railroad when he was eighteen and retired after putting in fifty years as a brakeman and conductor. Clarence, like his son Jim, had been born in Bekbourg. Clarence was gone most of the time during Jim's youth working the trains between Cincinnati and Wheeling, West Virginia. Clarence rarely made the trip back in one day, so he spent many nights away every week. Also, given the unpredictability of the train schedule, Jim and his mother never knew when to expect him.

But the train schedule wasn't the only reason they never knew when he would show up. Clarence's favorite pastime was spending time at his bar of choice, Knucklepin's Tavern, talking with other railroaders and sipping whiskey. His wife was always nagging him about not being around for his family. Finally, when Jim was thirteen, she left while Jim was at school and never returned. Jim resented Clarence for being gone so much and for causing his mother's departure. By extension, Jim blamed the railroad.

One spring day, his grandfather asked Sean to join him for dinner. When Sean got to the house, they went out to the pond in his back yard and threw in the fishing lines. They weren't getting any bites, but it was like old times when Sean used to spend time fishing with his grandpa. Sean never saw his grandfather through the same lens as his dad did. In fact, in some ways, Sean felt closer to his grandpa than to his dad.

While they were fishing, Clarence said, "Sean, I spent my entire adult life working for the railroad. It pays well. I can get you a job as a brakeman. It'll be a good job for you. You don't have to work your entire life at it like me if you don't want to, but it'll be there for you as long as you want to work."

"Does Dad know you're talking to me about a job with the railroad?"

Clarence snorted, "Heck no. And if you take the job, he is going to be madder than a wet hen. If you're interested, you might wait to tell him until you take the job."

After a while, he and his grandfather put up their fishing poles and went to Frau's Diner. They talked about different things, but knowingly, Clarence never mentioned football. That was a sore subject with Sean, and Clarence didn't want to ruin the special time with his grandson by raising it.

While they ate, Sean pondered his grandfather's suggestion. He knew he had to do something. *"What difference does it make?"* he thought. *"It's as good as it's going to get for me."*

Toward the end of dinner, Sean said, "You're right, Grandpa. I need something to do. It might do me good to get away. My friends all have plans. How do I go about getting the railroad job?"

Clarence gave him the contact information but reminded Sean, "If you decide to take the job, Sean, you need to be prepared for your dad's blow-up. He hates the railroad. He blames it for his mother leaving us. There's more to that story than just the railroad, but I'll leave it at that."

"Well, I'm hoping he might not feel as bad about it since he knows I can't play football anymore."

"I don't know about that," Clarence winced.

About a month before graduation, Sean, his mother, father and Linda had finished dinner when Sean mentioned that he had something to tell them. His palms felt moist when three sets of eyes trained on him. Clarence had predicted correctly about Jim's reaction. Jim slammed his hand down on the table so hard the dishes bounced, and a couple of glasses nearly tipped over. "You did what?" he roared.

Linda rose from the table, "I've got some homework to do." Her departure went unnoticed.

Sean's mom spoke up, "Jim, calm down. It gives Sean a job until he decides what he wants to do. You've been saying he needs a job."

"Look, Dad," Sean said, raising his voice. "Mom's right. It pays good money. I thought you would be happy that I have a job."

Jim was livid. "Not with the railroad! What were you thinking? That railroad ruined our family. Dad should *NEVER* have raised it with you!"

"Don't blame Grandpa! I made the decision. I don't even know if I'll like it, but I'll be making money, and it's something for me to do."

"It's a trap. The money is good. Once you start, you'll never leave it. You can't have a family with that job. If you and Becky get married, what kind of life will you have with her and your kids?"

Sean was glad he had anticipated his dad's objections. Attempting to diffuse the tension, he reasoned, "Dad, I'm not getting married anytime soon, so that's not a problem. I'll figure things out, but I'm glad to have a job. All my friends have their plans. I need something to do."

Sean and Jim sat peering eye-to-eye at each other—like father, like son in their stubbornness. Jim said, "Why didn't you tell me that you were thinking about this? Dad put you up to this. He had no right."

"Grandpa didn't put me up to anything. He knew I needed something to do. All he did was tell me about it, and I'm glad he did. I knew how you felt about the railroad. That's never been a secret around here. It was a decision I had to make for myself, and I made it."

Jim stood and walked out the back door. Helen put her hand on Sean's arm. "Don't be too hard on your dad. He loves you and wants the best for you and your sister. Give him some time."

Sean was exasperated, "Mom, he is never willing to see things my way. Since the injury, he has been even more irritable. Can't he for once see things from my side?"

"He'll come around. Even with his feelings about the railroad, he'll understand you made the right decision."

"Well, if he does, he'll never admit it. He's so mule-headed."

Helen softly laughed, "He is that."

She got up and cut Sean a piece of her homemade apple pie.

Chapter 4

Sean worked long hours that summer and fall. Being a brakeman meant he helped the conductor with the train. He would switch the cars, connect the engine, and walk the train to inspect the connections and brakes before departures. He never knew when he would return home, and he was gone for long hours and many over-nights. He kept a "grip," as railroaders called it, packed for his overnight stays in either Cincinnati or Wheeling. He and the engineer rode in the engine together, and Sean would watch the train to make sure there were no stuck brakes or hot boxes and watch for the signals along the track. To him, the worst part was sitting on the train for several boring hours at a time waiting for the "all-clear" signal so the train was clear to move.

His work clothes were stained with dust and grease. In cold weather, he wore a warm coat since he spent considerable time outside. He wore heavy gloves to protect his hands while handling the heavy equipment and machinery.

Bekbourg was a crew-change point for the railroad. Sean rode about one-hundred-twenty miles west to the Cincinnati terminal and the same number of miles east to Wheeling. On the Cincinnati run, the railroaders typically stayed in the Rivermet Motel in Newport, Kentucky, which was nothing to write home about, but the accommodations at the railroad bunkhouse in Wheeling were in a whole other league. The room was tiny, and a single light bulb lit the room. The sole window was high and could not be opened. Given his size, he couldn't stretch out in the bed, because his head hit one wall and his feet the other. To get the door opened, the bed was shoved up against the wall, and when he reached his arm out to his side, he could touch the opposite side of the wall. The railroaders and other guests on the floor shared a communal hall bathroom. He guessed the food in the cafeteria was passable if someone liked greasy meats and seasoned cooked vegetables. He had to admit though that the cornbread and cobblers were pretty good.

As predicted by his dad, Sean's relationship with his steady girlfriend, Becky Worley, was in trouble. She was in a perpetual bad mood. Their plans were often canceled, or even worse, not even made. She complained about his long hours away from home and that when he was home, he was unexpectedly called out on a job.

A bright spot for their relationship came when Sean learned that he would be laid off during the winter months. He realized this would be a great opportunity to enroll in the nearby Hillsrock Community College with Becky. He saved enough money so he could take a maximum load during the winter semesters. That way, after two winters, he could accumulate enough credit hours to be considered a sophomore. This would be a good way to get started toward a degree.

The first winter when he was a full-time student, his relationship with Becky improved. They often went to school together and were growing closer. Sean warned Becky, however, that by the end of May, he would be back to work on the railroad full-time, but she said she was ready for it. As June rolled into July, it became apparent she really wasn't happy with Sean's schedule. She became even more difficult to get along with, but Sean was too busy to get upset. He thought things would smooth out again during the upcoming winter semester.

It didn't work out that way. Becky's schedule was not compatible with Sean's, and they did not go to school together. Becky also had started going out with a group of friends Sean did not know, and he would often beg off. As the semester drew to a close and summer loomed, their relationship was not working. On top of that, Becky was moving to Athens that fall to finish her degree at OU, and she wanted a commitment from Sean.

Becky was a beauty who had been captain of the cheerleader squad in high school. She caught his eye during junior year. She and her friend, Geri, would flirt with the football players, especially his best friend, Mike, and himself. Sean was attracted to Becky, and Geri and Mike seemed to be the ideal couple. The four did a lot of double dating. Now that Mike and Geri were married, Becky was pressuring him to put a ring on her finger. He had no intention of tying the knot anytime soon.

Sean continued to live at his parents' home. He made enough money to support himself, but his mother didn't want him to move out, and, to be honest, he didn't want a place of his own, because Becky would surely take that as a sign for them to marry. On his time off, he helped around the house, mowing the grass and making repairs. He and his dad had settled into a cordial co-existence, although Sean knew he still disapproved of his working for the railroad but was happy that he was working toward his degree.

Besides the money he was making, the railroad also gave Sean something special in common with his grandpa. They would fish and swap stories about the railroad. Even though his grandpa was retired, he kept up with his railroad buddies, and he and Sean had lots of laughs about the colorful characters that worked for the railroad.

His grandfather loved talking about a character who had started on the railroad about twenty years earlier, nicknamed "Chaw." Clarence told Sean, "He was called that for as long as I remember. I don't even know what his real name is. He got that nickname because he always had a chaw of tobacco in his jaw. He didn't have many teeth, probably because he was always chewing."

Another time, Clarence entertained with more stories about Chaw. "He sure loved his beer, loved hanging out at beer joints and playing cards. It was funny watching him. As wiry as he was, he looked like a spider climbing up over the rail cars. I liked it when he was on the train. He was a darn good brakeman, one of the strongest men I knew. He liked being a brakeman—told me he didn't want a conductor's job."

Sean and Clarence also swapped stories about a man nicknamed "Mule Head." Sean learned quickly that the railroaders were notorious for giving each other nicknames. Mule Head hired on a few years before Sean. "It's easy to see why he got the name, Mule Head," Clarence said. "I never seen nobody so stubborn. He thinks he knows everything and wouldn't take an instruction for nothing. That's the reason he messes things up so much, and he still won't admit he did anything wrong."

Egging Clarence on, Sean said, "There's some other railroaders called 'Mule Head.'"

"Huh." Clarence grinned. "That's 'cause a lot of them *are* stubborn." They both laughed.

Sean then asked if he had ever worked with Dusty. Clarence snorted, "Dusty, now he's an original. He's sure not shy. He talks more than any man I ever seen. Drives a lot of the men crazy."

Sean was grinning, "Well, how'd he get the name, 'Dusty'?"

"Oh, that's because they figure he keeps all the dust stirred up with all that nervous energy he has." They both laughed. Clarence was on a roll. "He and Mule Head are always jawing at each other. They hired on about the same time. Now, Dusty and Chaw get along alright. Dusty's got a pretty good sense of humor and can be fun to be around if you can take all that blame talking. Chaw can be surly, but I got along good with him."

"Grandpa, you get along well with everyone. Someone is always telling me what a good conductor you were."

With a glint in his eye, he huffed, "They haven't been telling you any stories about me, have they?"

Sean laughed. "You never know, Grandpa. You never know what a bunch of railroaders might say."

"Hmmp, I'm going to spread the word I better not hear them passing stories about me to you."

Sean was laughing, and his grandpa was smiling that mischievous smile of his.

Sean knew his grandpa loved the railroad. He once told Sean that after working for a couple of years, it "got in your blood." Sean thought that was probably right, because many of the railroaders he worked with shared his grandpa's sentiment.

One day Clarence and Sean were talking about the railroad, and Clarence said, "They haven't said it in front of me, Sean, but you probably have a nickname."

"Why do you say that?"

"Usually brakemen are small. They have to climb on the cars. They probably never seen a brakeman as tall as you."

They both laughed.

Chapter 5

July 5, 1980

"*Man!*" thought Sean, "*It's going to be another scorcher.*" Sean had worked all night, and daybreak was signaling another hot, humid day ahead. It being July Fourth last night, he'd heard and seen the occasional fireworks on his run from Wheeling to Bekbourg. The train engine had broken down on the return from Wheeling, causing a good six-hour delay in his return home. Life on the railroad was fraught with delays and unscheduled trips. He was irritated and tired, and tired of his job. Having done the brakeman job for just over two years, Sean knew that it wasn't a career for him like the railroad had been for his grandfather.

As Sean drove toward his parents' house, in the distance, he could see several flashing lights from police and emergency vehicles. A police barricade stopped him as he came to the entrance of the road where his family's house was located. His truck windows were down, and he could smell the heavy smoke. His heart started pounding as the cars seemed parked in the front of his parents' home.

As the police officer ambled over to Sean's truck, he hit his palm on the steering wheel out of frustration. Seeing Ben Clark here was the absolute last thing he needed right now.

Ben had been a bully in high school, and he still was. It was complicated now, because Ben was a deputy and could hide his aggression behind his badge. Ben would love nothing more than to invoke his retribution against Sean. Ben had been a senior when Sean was a sophomore. Ben got a warped pleasure picking on kids, and especially on George, a shy, frail-looking boy, whose dad had abandoned him and his mother when George was one-year old. His mother moved them in with her parents, who lived in a singlewide mobile home that had seen better days. George's grandfather was eccentric and collected a mixture of junk that filled their yard. The family stayed mostly to themselves. He was ignored by most students except for bullies like Ben.

Sean happened upon a small circle of Ben's flunky friends in an outside covered area off the gymnasium. Ben was verbally ridiculing George and forcing him to crawl on his hands and knees and bark like a dog. George complied out of fear of Ben. Ben's cohorts were laughing and howling.

Sean usually kept a handle on his temper, but he lost it that day. Sean burst through the circle and grabbed Ben by the shirt and proceeded to roughly drag him off to the side where a large mud puddle had formed from a recent heavy rain. Thinking that Ben needed to be taught a lesson, Sean threw him face down in the mud. A gathering of students had seen Sean dragging Ben and followed to see what was going to happen. Poised for action, Sean dared Ben to get up. Ben wisely knew better than to lift himself out of the mud. The students were laughing while Ben sat there breathing heavily. George had shyly followed and was watching the spectacle from a distance. Sean called George over. George shuffled over with his head down. Second-hand clothing hung on his small frame. Sean put his arm around George's shoulder and told Ben that if he or his groupies ever bothered George again, Ben and the others would face worse. After that day, Sean had seen a couple of boys having lunch with George.

If that hadn't been bad enough to forge Ben's dislike of Sean, the second incident solidified Ben's absolute hatred toward Sean. Ben was second-team defensive end on the football team. He was about 5'11" with a wiry build, but he was strong and fast. One of the main reasons Sean thought he was not a starter was that he played dirty, costing the team penalties. Coach Jackson was forever lecturing Ben about rules, hoping he would not incur penalties.

One afternoon after practice, Sean and Mike had stayed longer to practice their running formation for a couple of the passing plays that they were going to run in the upcoming game. When they returned to the locker room, they saw Ben holding a freshman football player in a choke hold. The kid was pulling at Ben's arm trying to relieve pressure. Ben was threatening, "If you don't get it to me by tomorrow you little shit, you know what's goin' to happen."

The kid was screeching, "I don't have any money, man. My parents don't have any."

23

Sean and Mike rushed Ben and pulled him away from the younger boy. Sean yelled, "What the hell do you think you're doing?"

Ben yanked away from Sean and Mike. "Let go of me, you assholes! It's none of your business." Ben glared at the kid and turned and strutted away.

Mike asked the younger boy, "Are you okay, man?"

Rubbing his neck, the kid was embarrassed, "Yeah."

Sean asked, "What was that all about?"

The kid was looking at the two stars of the football team. It was obvious that he was torn about whether to tell them. Mike urged, "Come on, man. Tell us what that was about."

"If I say anything, he'll hurt me. He's bad."

"We can't help you if we don't know," Sean pressed.

Looking between Sean and Mike, the kid had stopped rubbing his neck and dropped his arms to his side. "He told all the freshman players that they had to give him twenty dollars. If we don't, he told us he will find us alone and beat the shit out of us with a baseball bat. That even our mothers won't recognize us. He gave us each a week when we were supposed to bring him the money. This is my week, but I don't have the money. My parents don't have it, and I don't know where to get it. He told us if we knew what was good for us, we wouldn't tell anyone."

"Let us know if he threatens you again."

The next morning, Sean found Coach Jackson and told him about the incident. Right before lunch, Ben caught up with Sean in the hall. Ben was red in the face with fury. Even though Sean was two years younger, he was taller by five inches and could bench press a hundred pounds more than Ben. Ben grabbed Sean by the arm, and Sean steeled himself for a fight. Ben snarled, "I got kicked off the football team all 'cause of *YOU*, you SOB!"

Sean jerked his arm from Ben's grip and slowly growled, "Don't ever touch me again unless you want your teeth knocked down your throat."

Ben, seething with malice, sneered, "I won't forget this. You better watch your back, 'cause I'm comin' after you."

Sean replied, "Bring it on," and turned and walked away.

That afternoon, Coach Jackson announced that Ben was no longer on the team. He also told the players that he had a zero tolerance for any type of bullying on his team. "If I find out about any of you threatening anyone, you will no longer be on this team. We are here to win, and I won't tolerate any behavior that interferes with that. Is that clear?" he bellowed.

"Yes, sir" could be heard echoing around the locker room.

Ben swaggered up close to the open window. "Well, well, well. If it ain't Mr. Football Stud himself. Or, maybe that's old news. Not the big stud around town now that you can't play football. I bet you can't even get it up anymore."

Concerned about his family, Sean ignored Ben's taunt. "What's going on here?"

Thinking to bait Sean, "Why don't you tell us what kept you out all night, Football Stud? Oh, yeah. That reminds me. I heard Becky's screwin' somebody else. Maybe you're gettin' some on the side, too. Wouldn't be messin' with those underage cheerleaders now would you? I might just have to take you in and question you."

Another officer had walked up and stood off to the side.

"Look, shithead. You know my parents live down there. Now, get out of my way."

Ben raising his voice prompted the other officer to slowly release the holster's grip on his gun, his hand resting on the gun. "I asked you what you're doin' out this time of mornin'. You may be a suspect to this crime we're investigatin'."

Sean made a move to open the door. Both police pulled their guns and pointed them at him. He stopped and growled, "I don't have to answer your damn questions, but I just got off work."

Still pointing their guns, Ben said to Kyle, the other deputy, "Maybe we ought to search him to see if we find anythin' to connect him to this. I don't think he's given us a satisfactory answer."

Ben stepped back from the door and ordered, "Get out of the car!"

Sean was seething and concerned for his family. He sat there staring out the front windshield. They had guns, and he knew that Ben would love nothing more than to get the upper hand. Sean didn't know the other deputy. Thinking he might appeal to the other deputy, he raised his voice, "Are you kidding me? My family is down there."

Ben was hoping for an escalation. He wanted to pay Sean back for the embarrassment he caused him during high school. "Step out now!" he shouted.

Sean figured he'd best step out of the truck. He slowly opened the door. His six-feet-four-inch height and two-hundred-twenty-pound frame dwarfed the two officers. They both took a step back. Out of nowhere, his best friend from high school, now a deputy, walked up. Knowing the history between the two, Mike demanded, "What's going on here? Put those guns away!"

Sean said, "Mike, I need to get down there and check on my family. This jerk here," pointing at Ben, "is abusing his position."

Because he had graduated from the police academy, Mike had recently been promoted to Assistant. Mike turned to Ben and Kyle and ordered them to lower their guns. When Ben started to protest, Mike said, "If you want to keep it, get down there and do your job."

Ben sneered at Sean, "Lookin' forward to next time, Football Stud." He and Kyle walked away.

"Sorry about that, Sean. I don't know why the Sheriff hired that guy. Anyway, your family is safe. It's the house across the street that burned. You can't leave your truck here. It's in the way. Pull it over there, and I'll walk with you and tell you what's going on."

Sean pulled his truck off to the side of the road, and he and Mike started walking toward Sean's home. Mike told him that they didn't know much. They got a call from a neighbor up the street who was watching late-night TV and said out his window, he saw the blaze. When the firemen arrived, they started working to put out the fire, but it had taken a while, because the entire house was burning. One person found near the front door was rushed to the hospital. It was too hot for them to get much further into the house, but they would start their investigation as soon as possible.

As Sean and Mike approached his parents' house, Sean could see that all that remained from the house across the street was blackened, smoldering, charred frames of parts of the house. Mostly, though, the structure had been reduced to smoking debris except for a stone chimney that remained standing. Sean remarked, "Wow, some fire. How could it have burned like this?"

"The house was fully engulfed in flames by the time the firefighters arrived. I overheard some of them talking about it probably being intentional. Well, I'd better get back to work. Oh, I saw Gary and Jeff in town today. I guess they're in visiting their families. They were at Knuck's."

"How are they doing?"

"Seem to be doing okay. No real news. Jeff's still chasing anything that wears a skirt."

"Yeah. Some things never change. By the way, who's that other deputy that was with Ben?"

"Another one of the Sheriff's flunky hires. The Sheriff must be falling on hard times to be making the hires he's making. I don't know what that says about me."

Sean laughed.

"Anyway, his name is Kyle Ramsey. He was two years older than us in high school, and he wasn't on any of the sports teams, so we didn't have reason to know him. I don't know much about him except his elevator doesn't go all the way to the top. But Sean, Ben is another matter. He's mean, and he's got his sights on you. Be careful around him."

Billyboy was lying on a carpet on their front porch and managed to stand when he heard Sean approaching. Sean walked over and scratched his ears, "Hey, boy, looks like there's been some excitement around here." Billyboy plopped down. Sean knew Billyboy's days were numbered. He was fourteen years old. Sean's parents got him when he was a puppy. Sean and he had been inseparable. Sean gave Billyboy's head another rub.

He took off his dirty boots and left them on the front porch. When he entered the house, he heard his mother making her way into the living room. "Oh, Sean, it's so awful." Sean could see that she had been crying. "We're all in the kitchen."

Sean followed and saw his dad and sister sitting at the kitchen table with coffee cups in front of them. His dad looked like he had hurriedly dressed in his old work clothes and untied boots. Helen and Linda each wore house robes and were shaken from the night's events.

As his mom handed him a cup of coffee, Sean repeated what Mike had told him.

of his head, he was bald. Sean remembered his annoying TV commercials—where he tried to sound "down home." Roger's loud, exaggerated voice ended each commercial with, "Drrreeaaamm cars at drrreeeaaamm prices—visit us today at Burkhart's!" Sean said, "Yeah, I always hated those commercials. I couldn't imagine why someone would buy a car from him."

"Well, his dealership wasn't his only business. Several years ago, he opened a pawnshop, and he's run that fireworks business for a long time. You know, Sean, I don't think you want to ask too many questions about this."

"What do you mean?"

Jim took another drink from the coffee mug and set it on the table. "I know Mike is your friend, and he'll probably get the details, but around here, sometimes it's best to not get too curious."

"I still don't get what you're saying."

"Look, Sean. I don't know what I'm saying. There's no future here. That's why I wanted you to leave here, and I want Linda to go away to college and stay away."

Sean didn't want the conversation to veer to his job with the railroad. "Well, Dad, I'm pooped. I need to get some sleep because I've got to take the evening train back to Wheeling. You might want to try to get some sleep, too."

"Yeah, you're probably right."

Sean wasn't that interested in the big fire, but every day his parents would update him on what they were learning. His mom complained that the

Bekbourg Tribune was not reporting much about the matter. The first two days after the fire, the local newspaper carried the story on the front page, but after that, any reporting appeared toward the back of the paper. She heard some information from her friends or in the grocery store, but she and Jim weren't sure how reliable the gossip was. They learned from the newspaper on day two after the fire that five people had died: Roger Burkhart, his wife, Betty, and their son, David. Visiting from Pittsburgh, Roger's brother, Bobby Burkhart, had perished in the fire, and his wife, Carol, had died at the hospital.

A couple of days later when Sean arrived home, his father and mother were sitting at the kitchen table drinking coffee. He walked in as Jim was saying, "I knew there was more to it."

Sean moved to get a coffee mug and poured some coffee. "Are you talking about the fire?"

Jim said, "Yeah. There's big news going around town today. I guess if it's true, it'll be in the paper tomorrow. Even a reporter from a Cincinnati newspaper was seen at the Sheriff's office today."

Sean asked, "What's the big news?"

"Four of the victims had been shot. One of those victims, Roger's sister-in-law, died at the hospital. They think the boy died of smoke inhalation."

Helen said, "I was getting my hair done today, and the women were talking about it. They are nervous that a mass murderer is around here. They're talking about being careful and watching their children real close. Some wanted their husbands to put more locks on the doors."

"Huh. Do they think it was a robbery?"

"The police aren't saying anything, so we don't know. I was telling your mom that I'm not so sure that this goes beyond the Burkharts."

Sean asked, "You think this was only meant for them?"

Helen said, "Roger's brother and his wife weren't even from around here. Why would someone shoot them?"

"I don't know. But you told me that Betty and David were supposed to be gone to the beach and that Roger's family's visit was last minute," Jim said.

Sean asked, "You think they were at the wrong place at the wrong time?"

Jim said, "I don't know what to think, but that's a possibility. What I know is that something is not right in a town of almost five-thousand people when five people are murdered in their house in the middle of the night."

Sean was curious, "But why do you think someone had it in for Roger and maybe even his family?"

"Look, I don't know anything for sure, so I don't want you to discuss this outside here."

Sean nodded, "Dad, I'm not going to say anything. I'm not ever around anyone except the railroaders. I hardly ever see Becky much, with her in college and my schedule."

"I know. I told your mom not to be talking about it. You know, I've heard things and your grandpa has. Roger always seemed to have a lot of money. He loved his old Cadillac convertible and had just bought Betty a new Cadillac De Ville. Last year, he bought himself a big boat. He had to have put a lot of money into remodeling that dilapidated farm house to make it as nice as it was.

"I don't know if this had anything to do with what happened, but about a week before the fire, Roger's fireworks stand burned to the ground. It happened during the middle of the night, and no one could really determine what started the fire. It was a mess from what I heard, with all those fireworks exploding and all. I don't understand any of this, but it's all suspicious, and I think Roger was in over his head, and it finally caught up with him."

Although Sean wasn't that curious, he thought he'd see what he could find out from Mike, if for no other reason, to try to put his mother's mind at ease. Sean was off the following Saturday, so he called Mike to see if they might catch a beer somewhere.

As Sean joined Mike at the table, he asked, "Geri let you out?" Mike laughed at Sean's good-humored greeting. Sean had been Mike's best man in their wedding a year after they graduated, and now, a year later, they were expecting a baby.

"Yeah, she was glad. It gave her a good excuse to go to Athens. I think she and Becky were going to drive up and maybe do some shopping."

Sean said, "Mmm."

"Look man, I know it's none of my business, but is everything okay with you and her?"

Stalling and not wanting to go there, Sean asked, "Why do you ask that?"

"Well, you know, Geri has been asking me if you've said anything about you two. She said that Becky used to talk to her a lot about wanting to get married. Geri thought you were waiting for Becky to graduate from college. But she told me that Becky really doesn't talk about getting married anymore."

"I don't know, Mike. I'm so busy, and I'm gone so much. Becky's busy with college. I guess we're still going steady."

"Geri wondered if you'd found someone else?"

Sean shook his head. "Naw, it's nothing like that. I don't have time for anything but working and sleeping. I barely even have time to help Dad out much around the house. Speaking of which, Mom has been pretty weirded out by that fire and the news about the shootings—with it all happening across the street. She is scared that a mass murderer is on the loose. Linda was telling me the other day that Mom is always telling her to be careful and to keep the doors locked."

Mike took a long draw from his beer. Finally, he looked at Sean, "Yeah, I can see why she'd be afraid. Look, I know that I can trust you and your family not to talk. I'll tell you something. But, Sean, be sure to tell your parents not to mention this to anyone. I don't think your mom needs to worry about anything else happening. I've overheard the Sheriff talking about Burkhart being the target. Apparently, he got on the wrong side of someone."

"Man, Mike. He must have really gotten on the bad side for his whole family to be wiped out."

"Well, the talk around the Department is that maybe Burkhart was supposed to be the only one home that night. Mrs. Burkhart had called her mother earlier in the day and told her that she was going to be leaving with the boy a couple of days later to meet her parents at the beach because Burkhart's brother and wife had called and were stopping by."

"Wow, if that's the case, they sure found the wrong time to visit. Do you know what Burkhart was doing that put a bull's eye on him?"

"No, I haven't heard. But, again, it's just talk around the Department, but there's speculation that somehow his fireworks stand being burned down was some type of warning to Burkhart. Someone checked, and that business was a real money-maker, especially around July Fourth and the other big holidays. I would think that was a big hit to his income. If it was some type of warning, Burkhart must not have listened. Anyway, that's about all I know. How's the railroad job going?"

Sean and Mike ended up eating dinner and catching up. Gary would be starting again in the upcoming football season. Danny got Sally pregnant, and they had gotten married soon after graduation. They had a son. Danny was working at the gas station, and Sally's mother kept the baby while she worked as a hair dresser in the downtown beauty salon. No one had heard from Jeff. He was still in college and rarely came home.

While Mike was growing up, Mike's dad had worked at the local hardware store, and his customers liked him. Mike's mother had been a receptionist at the local dentist office. When Mike was two years old, his older sister by three years, Mandy, died from leukemia. Mike never talked about it when they were growing up, but it was common knowledge you could almost set your watch by his dad's nightly arrival at Knucklepin's, the local bar, after leaving work. It was something that was never discussed, but Mike once told Sean that his mother told him that his dad was never the same after Mandy's death. Feelings of letting her down weighed on him. He thought if he'd had more money, he could have gotten her better treatment. Sean knew that Mike did most of the work around their house, keeping the yard mowed and making repairs—even now.

About six weeks after the fire, front-page headlines ran on the local newspaper and Cincinnati and Columbus newspapers that the police had arrested a suspect in the Burkhart murders. He was a locally known petty criminal, Henry Willis. Rumors were even circulating that he might plead guilty. He purportedly had carried two guns that night. He hadn't planned to use them, but if he did, he wanted to make sure he had a backup if one jammed. He knew that Burkhart kept guns around. Willis told the authorities that he had thrown the guns into an empty coal car in a passing train. The guns weren't located.

However, the news didn't resonate around the Neumann household because a week earlier, Clarence had suffered a massive heart attack and passed away. *"When it rains, it pours,"* Sean thought when his grandfather died. Three weeks before Clarence's heart attack, Billyboy died. Sean and his dad buried Billyboy at the back of their property.

Two days before his grandpa suffered the heart attack, Becky broke up with him. He had not been surprised. They were on a phone call, and he could tell she had something to say. During that phone call, there had been long pauses of silence. Becky finally said, "Sean, it's no longer working for me. I don't feel our relationship is important to you." When he didn't say anything, she said, "I hope you have a good life." With that, she hung up. If he was honest with himself, he was relieved. He would have probably never broken off with her, but he also had no plans to get married.

Sean loved his grandpa and was grateful that he had helped him get a job when things looked so bleak, but Sean knew he didn't belong on the railroad. He didn't want to hurt his grandpa by quitting, so Sean had allowed his life to go into autopilot with the job. Now, since his grandpa was gone, he would not hurt his grandpa by quitting.

Two weeks after his grandfather's passing, Sean drove to Columbus to the Marines recruiting office and joined. His mother took it hard. She hated to see him leave. His father was more accepting of his decision, especially since he was leaving the railroad. Two weeks later, he gave his pickup truck to Danny. His mother prepared a farewell dinner with the family that included Danny, Sally, Mike and Geri. Sean left Bekbourg the next day for Parris Island.

During the third week of September, almost five weeks after it was reported in the news media that the defendant had confessed to the authorities, Henry Willis, age 66, stood before the judge having pled guilty to causing the deaths of five people and setting fire to the Burkhart house. Henry was tall and thin and still a handsome man with a full head of silvery hair and peppered gray and brown whiskers. He had a smoker's cough from a lifetime of smoking, and his teeth were heavily stained from a combination of coffee and smoking.

The newspapers reported that Henry claimed in his confession that he had overheard Roger Burkhart tell someone that he was expecting some silver and gold coins to be delivered to his house on July third, bragging their worth to be around $250,000. The confession was vague about when or where this conversation had taken place. Henry said he overheard Roger saying something about his family being on a beach trip. He knew Roger to drink a lot, and it being a holiday night, he thought he'd be drunk asleep, so he didn't think Roger would wake up, and he didn't think anyone else would be in the house that night.

He broke in to steal the coins, and while he didn't think he'd need them, he carried a couple of guns just in case. Roger Burkhart heard Henry downstairs in his office looking for the coins and confronted Henry. Henry panicked and shot Roger. This woke up the others in the house who came rushing toward the melee, and Henry "just lost it" and killed everyone he saw, but he didn't remember a kid. He was concerned he might have left some evidence, so he set fire to the house, using some gasoline he found in the garage. He fled the house without locating the silver and gold coins. He didn't know what happened to the coins.

During the court proceeding, Henry's daughter sat with her hands crossed in her lap holding a tissue. She was looking down and softly crying. His granddaughter sat stoically observing the courtroom activities. She was only fourteen-years-old, but she knew her grandfather could not have committed such a terrible crime.

The plea agreement was read by the judge, and when asked if that was what he agreed to, Henry Willis, standing as straight as he was capable, said, "Yes, Your Honor."

He had been shackled for his appearance, and as the officers started to lead him away, he turned and looked at his daughter, who was now looking at him. He nodded once, which to bystanders could be viewed as a farewell, but to his granddaughter, a silent message was conveyed. Henry's daughter started weeping. Tears seemed to fill his eyes. As his granddaughter watched him earlier being led into the courtroom, the ever-present twinkle in his eyes was missing, but when he now looked at her, she saw that twinkle one more time. He winked at his granddaughter and smiled a loving smile. That was the last time she ever saw her grandfather.

A month later, the sentencing hearing was held. Henry's daughter and granddaughter were not there. The judge sentenced Henry to forty years with no opportunity for parole. It was not lost on anyone in the courtroom that he would never walk out of prison.

Part II

Chapter 6

Twenty years later

"Captain Neumann, Sir. Come on, work with me. It's time for you to wake up."

Sean was floating. Someone was talking to him. He could detect light behind his eyelids, but they were too heavy to open. He drifted back off to sleep.

A couple of days later, Sean regained consciousness but was confused. He came to understand that he was in the United States military hospital near Landstuhl, Germany, but he couldn't figure how he got there. Many times, his questions went unanswered because his words were too garbled to be understood.

Eventually, he was lucid, but his recollection was still fuzzy. He kept asking about Clint and Tally. He had to be sedated when he was told that Clint had not survived.

Sean's body armor had saved his life. He suffered burns to his arms and hands, and shrapnel had pierced much of his unprotected body. He lost a lot of blood due to a severe wound to his right thigh.

Three weeks after Sean had been evacuated to Landstuhl, Tally came to see him. He was forbidden by the doctors to tell Sean what had happened. Consistently short on words but always speaking with purpose, Tally resolved, "Sean, I'm going to find the mothers that are responsible." Sean had no doubt that Tally would do just that.

A month later, Sean was flown back to the states. The physical pain was intense. But more debilitating to Sean were the recurring nightmares. *It was dark. He and Clint, with guns drawn, were entering a dark cavern. Sean was tense. Something wasn't right. Something evil was surrounding them. His heart was pounding, and cold sweat soaked his clothing. Their legs became immobile. Their frantic escape attempts were futile from an unseen presence closing in on him and Clint. Oh, God! He was screaming for them to run, but no sound was coming from his mouth. Clint vanished from his side. "CLLIIINNT! OH, GOD, NOOOOO!"* The nightmare always ended here with him jarring awake, his body drenched in perspiration and a terror-filled scream.

Sean had no recollection of what happened that night. The nightmares were disturbing enough, but not being able to glean the full truth from them was messing with his thinking. It was hard to reach Tally, but on those few times they connected, he tried to coax Tally into telling him, but he refused to go against the doctors' orders. His PTSD counselor told him that his memory was being suppressed due to the trauma. In time, the counselor thought Sean would remember and come to grips with what had happened.

Once back in the states, he was admitted to a military medical facility where he underwent two months of daily physical therapy and counseling. He was finally released but confined to a desk job.

Sean's career with the Marines had been unblemished. Early on, he had attended the USMC Military Police Basic Law Enforcement Training in Ft. Leonard Wood, Missouri. After serving in the military police, he eventually became an investigative agent in a special criminal unit. He impressed his superiors with his ability to solve cases that many thought impossible to crack. He also gained respect in the civilian federal and state law enforcement circles through several joint investigations.

It had been ten months since Sean had returned to the states. Although Sean had mostly healed, lingering pain and stiffness from shrapnel in his body continued to plague him.

Tanner Bradford, his Commanding Officer, was saying, "Sean, if there was any way I could keep you as an investigator, I would. There's no flexibility on this. You're one of the best investigative agents we have, but your injuries preclude you from staying in this position."

Sean sat stoic. He was not interested in a desk position. Tanner banged his hand flat on the top of his desk, "I hate this!"

Shortly after that conversation, Sean retired from the Marines after twenty years with a pension.

Chapter 7

Tony Pinkston was a hardened man who feared no one other than his dad, Zeke Pinkston. As his daddy before him, Zeke raised his boys not to suffer fools, trust no one other than family, and never, ever cower from anything or anyone. Zeke only had to hand out punishment a few times to his sons, because the memory of his wrath lasted a lifetime. It was not surprising that Tony and Ray's fear and respect for their dad still had them calling Zeke "Pappy."

Tony, Ray and Zeke sat on the front porch of Zeke's house in Tapsaw County. A couple of Dobermans roamed the front yard. Zeke was a wide man, his overalls pulled tight around his mid-section. His short hair was salt and peppered, and his eyes observed everything with shrewdness.

"You boys been hemming and hawing long enough. What you got to tell me?"

Tony knew Ray deferred to him, and so he spoke, "Well, we've got some competition that's moved in."

"What do you mean?" Zeke asked—those penetrating eyes laser-focused on Tony.

"We don't care 'bout others growin' pot. But there's been these two brothers moved into Bekbourg. They started makin' and sellin' meth.

Me and Ray and Victor don't like them cuttin' into our business."

"You boys talk to these men to see if there's some arrangement that can be worked out?"

"Yeah," responded Tony, "but they ain't willin' to move out of the area. Told us they bought their land and they ain't movin'. Suggested we move even though we've been there longer. Kinda high-handed in the way they talked to us. Don't you agree, Ray?"

"Yep. I didn't care for them."

Zeke pondered long enough to spit a wad of tobacco off the side of the porch, "I've been hearin' for some time 'bout a deputy in Bekbourg who has a side business. If they have some help there in Bekbourg, that might make those men act arrogant like that." Zeke thought some more. "It might be a good idea to check this out. If he's in cahoots with them men, you might hire that deputy to help you."

"We'll check him out. Who is it?"

"Name's Ben Clark. He's one of the Sheriff's deputies."

Chapter 8

"You sure 'bout this, Tony?" Ray asked, chewing on a hangnail. Ray and Tony were sitting in the old biker's bar, Koot's, with their cousin Victor Shultz.

"Won't know 'til we ask. Victor's been checkin' Clark out. He's seen him with the Todds. Why would he be with them if he wasn't workin' for them? He didn't arrest them."

Ray asked, "What makes you think he won't tell them that we tried to hire him? Or he might double cross us. How would we know?"

"Pappy seemed to think Clark will do our biddin' for the right price. We're smart enough to know if he double crosses us. I like him workin' for us instead of those Todds."

"Ray, I agree with Tony on this. Let's at least talk to Clark. Tony don't have to raise nothin' if he gets a bad feelin' while talkin' to Clark."

"How'd you know he'll be here?" Ray asked Victor.

"Well, he either goes here or Knucklepin's. If he ain't show'd up here soon, we can go to Knuck's."

Sometime later, Ben Clark walked in, looked around, and ambled up to the bar and ordered a boilermaker. Tony eyed Ben for a while

48

before he made up his mind. "I think I'll go buy the good deputy a drink."

Ray and Victor sat drinking their beers and watched as Tony sat down beside Ben. Tony bought him another drink, and after a while, he and Ben walked outside. "Think we should go outside?" asked Victor.

"Naw. Tony would have signaled if he wanted that."

Outside, Ben and Tony stood off in the darkened area. "So, you said you got a business proposition?" Ben asked as he took a drink.

Tony's study of Ben never wavered, "Yeah. I'm willin' to pay good, Deputy Clark. But it might mean you changin' your loyalty."

Ben's shoulders stiffened, "What'd you mean?"

Tony surveyed Ben's every nuance, "Those Todd brothers."

"What makes you think I have an arrangement with them?"

"We're careful, Deputy. We have our ways."

Ben studied Tony and took another drink. "Okay, but it's goin' to cost you."

"What are you willin' to do?" Tony asked as he took a swig from his beer.

Ben turned up his glass and gulped down its contents. "I don't care as long as you pay me enough."

Tony eyed Ben, "Let me get this clear, Deputy. We can do anythin' we want?"

soon left. Familiar with the trauma Sean had endured, Jake knew he was in trouble.

Jake called Tanner who flew to Key West and found Sean. He was shocked to see Sean's condition. Tanner argued that Clint would never want this for him and that it was time for him to pull his life together. Sean eventually agreed to let him take him back to his parents' home in Bekbourg. Tanner called Sean's dad to prepare him. Sean cleaned up, but he had lost weight. His eyes were haunted and his face gaunt. Sean and Tanner flew into Columbus, Ohio, and Tanner drove them southward toward Bekbourg.

Chapter 10

Sean had not returned to Bekbourg since he joined the Marines. When his sister got married a few years back, the wedding was held in Cincinnati where she had attended law school. He had seen his parents then, but that was one of the few times during his twenty years in the military. He kept in touch by phone, calling on holidays and special occasions. His parents visited him twice when he was in the states and once while he was at the military hospital. The demands of the service and his responsibilities did not give him much time for leisure. Also during this time, he had completed his college degree in Criminal Justice.

He had mixed feelings about returning home, but he knew he needed help. He looked out the window watching the passing scenery. The landscape seemed lifeless yet supported life, much like Sean thought of himself. Weighty despair seeped deeper into Sean as he observed the coldness and dreariness the unrelenting winter had left behind.

As they approached town on the familiar Bekbourg Highway, he noticed off to the right some large new homes along with a new golf course. He realized that Bekbourg now had suburbs. The service station where Danny had worked was still there, but it had been enlarged and renamed "Chambers." There was a new strip mall with a large super market, a drug store, and other miscellaneous businesses. The one-story, ten-unit motel had been spruced up and repainted a fresh white with green trim. The County Fair grounds were still there as well as the large light-green water tower with, "Welcome to Bekbourg," painted on the side. Barns and animal feed silos still stood north of the old downtown. Some houses and businesses still displayed Christmas decorations.

The old downtown area was somewhat transformed. Some of the businesses had been fixed up, and some of the boarded-up businesses now had new life. Toward the end of the town, an old clothing store had been converted to an outdoorsman shop. The bank was still there. One of the old stores now had what looked to be an assortment of things, like greeting cards, gifts, stationery, and other what-nots. A woman's clothing store was close by. Across the street, the old boarding house had been converted into Bri's B&B. Next door was a new coffee bistro. An antiques store occupied the previous five-and-dime store. The old movie theater's exterior had been refurbished, and the marquee showed it hosted special events and offered live music on weekends. The courthouse looked about the same, and behind it on Court Street were the county services, county offices, and the police station and jail.

Near the courthouse stood the old hotel, which was quite elegant and grand for its time. Its days as a hotel had ceased many years ago, but an upscale restaurant, the GilHaus, had been serving patrons since the 1950's on the entry floor level. While some buildings remained in disrepair and some store-fronts had "for lease" signs and boarded-up window fronts, overall, the downtown was more vibrant.

The five-mile stretch of highway south of the old downtown was changed the most and now sported a Shopper's Pavilion box department store, another chain grocery store and drug store, as well as a number of fast food restaurants. Some smaller vinyl-siding homes and townhomes were scattered in a small development. There was also a movie theater complex featuring six screens and two newer motels. He saw a huge car dealership, Bekbourg Auto Mall.

Sean's parents lived in the house they had lived in for about forty years. It was a couple of miles southwest of the old downtown. Although newer homes had been built in his old neighborhood, several vacant lots remained. A two-story brick home had been built across from his parents where the Burkhart house had burned twenty years ago.

An American flag still hung off the front-porch post, which was no surprise, because his dad had flown "Old Glory" for as long as Sean could remember. Tanner pulled into the driveway and turned off the motor. Sean sat looking at his parents' house and thought about asking Tanner to drive away. He wasn't sure he was ready to face his parents, Bekbourg or the world for that matter. Anticipating Sean's arrival, his father swung the front door open and walked out. Jim walked toward the car, and Tanner said, "Sean, let's get out."

Taking a deep breath, Sean opened the door, and Tanner got out, "Mr. Neumann, I'm Tanner Bradford, Sir."

Jim greeted Tanner and then turned to Sean, "Welcome home, Son."

Tanner left, and Sean and Jim entered the house. Helen ran to Sean and flung her arms around him, "Sean, Sean! I am so happy you are back!"

Helen put her arm through his and nudged, "Let's go in the kitchen. I've cooked your favorite dinner and made a fresh apple pie."

Chapter 11

Tanner pulled some strings, and a counselor who specialized in PTSD drove to Bekbourg twice a week for the first four weeks to talk with Sean. Jim knew Sean's demons were more than he could help Sean with. He heard Sean yelling out in his sleep and saw the dark circles under his eyes that never left. He knew that Coach Jackson had helped Sean get back on track after the football injury shattered his dreams. Unknown to Sean, Jim went to see Coach Jackson. Sean was sitting on the front porch despite the temperature being in the low 50's when a car drove up. Sean didn't know who was in the car until his old coach stepped out. As he walked up to the porch, something told Sean the Calvary had arrived.

Sean started going to the high school gym and working out with Coach Jackson after the students left school for the day. He started running and eventually got back to his five-mile-a-day routine. He gained some weight—although he was still thin. One day, Coach Jackson asked Sean if Mike could come by. At first, Sean resisted, but he finally consented. Coach Jackson told Mike that Sean was recovering from a serious injury and that he was home to heal. At Coach Jackson's request,

Mike didn't tell anyone about Sean's return, not even Geri.

Mike and Sean embraced like long-lost brothers, both fighting back tears for their individual demons and for the uncertain future. Sean thought Mike must work out regularly, because he had the same physique that he had twenty years ago, only slightly heavier. Mike's hair had started to gray along the edge of his hairline. He was a good-looking man, but deep lines made him appear older than Sean. Heeding the Coach's words, Mike kept the conversation light.

"Matt is playing football for the University of Montana. Wide receiver, if you can believe that." They both laughed, since that was the position that Mike had played. "Miranda just started college at UCLA. She's got more brains than me and Geri together. I don't know where she got her smarts, but she got a scholarship to study some type of biochemistry. I don't understand it enough to talk about, but she seems to like the school."

"Wow, you and Geri must be proud of them both. That's impressive."

Sean and Mike also enjoyed reliving the glory days of their high school football team.

On one of his visits to the high school, Sean noticed Coach Jackson seemed preoccupied. It was a sunny, but cool day in March, and Sean asked the Coach to show him the improvements that he had been talking about.

"Okay, Sean. Let's go out to the stadium. We've added new bleachers and a big concession stand since you left. The Boosters even raised enough money for us to have an electronic scoreboard."

Sean admired the improvements. "Coach, all this wouldn't have happened if the people around here weren't so proud of what you've done with the football program. Mike told me how you coached three more championship wins since ours."

"I love it, Sean. They've tried a couple of times to get me to become a principal or assistant principal, but I don't want that. Coaching football and working with these boys is what I love. I plan to coach as long as the Good Lord has that plan for me."

"Coach, I know there is something weighing on your mind. You want to tell me about it?"

He looked at Sean for a good minute and then he told him that one of his best defensive linemen was jacked up on drugs and had gotten into a fight and was expelled.

"Something's got to be done around here about the drugs. These kids are getting hooked and even dying. It's bad, Sean. I tell the players how bad that stuff is and to stay away from it. Some of them don't listen."

"How much do you know about it?"

"Well, I don't know many details, but to have such a big drug problem, I think they are being processed around here."

"When did this start to be a problem?"

"Pot is bad enough, but about three or four years ago, the bad stuff started showing up. Crystal meth came on the scene and became the major problem. There have been some overdoses with the high school kids, and unfortunately, two died from meth overdoses. The kids are even taking their parents' and grandparents' painkillers. We've put drug education in all the schools around here, including the elementary schools. It's probably helping some, but not nearly enough."

Sean asked, "Any idea where it's coming from?"

"No, I don't know, and no one else seems to know. With Mike as sheriff, I thought he could clean it up, but I swear it's gotten worse."

Sean decided he would see what he could find out about the drug problem. The torment of Clint's death and his inability to remember what happened that night was never far away, but Sean was determined to survive. Looking into the drug problem around Bekbourg gave him a new mission.

One evening, Jim told Sean that he wanted to show him something in the barn. Sean saw his dad's '56 Plymouth Fury sitting there, but beside it was his grandpa's '63 Buick Riviera. "Your grandpa wanted you to have this Buick, Sean. It probably needs some work, but it's here whenever you want it."

His grandpa loved that car, and he remembered riding around with him. "Dad, I had no idea grandpa left it to me. I'm happy to get it. Thanks for keeping it all these years."

"Yeah, sure. I wanted to surprise you."

Sean told Jim about his discussion with the coach about the drug problem at the high school.

"Sean, even many adults are hooked. I have spoken at a few of the county commission meetings about the need to do something about the drug problem around here. The last time I spoke, it got pretty heated, because I basically accused them of not doing their jobs for the county. Jeff, in particular, was steamed and told me that they were working on it, but that it was more complicated to address than people, meaning me, understood. I told him I understood that it would never be solved if they sat on their backsides. He threatened to have me thrown out if I didn't 'sit down and shut up.'"

Sean could tell his dad had more to say. Finally, "You know that Mike is the sheriff."

"Yeah. I thought that seemed like a good thing. Why, is something going on with Mike?"

"I don't know. I know he was your best friend, and I always liked Mike and thought he had his head on straight. Not like those other two boys, Jeff and Gary. But, I swear. I don't see how a sheriff who is good at his job could let this drug thing get so out of control."

Sean was surprised that both his dad and Coach Jackson felt Mike wasn't doing all he could to combat the drug problem. During high school, Mike didn't party like either Gary or Jeff. He rarely drank more than two beers, and while Gary and Jeff occasionally smoked pot, neither Mike nor Sean ever touched drugs. Mike even made a point of telling Jeff and Gary not to bring "the shit" around.

Jim went on to tell Sean that Gary owned the large auto dealership that Sean had seen on his drive in, Bekbourg Auto Mall. "You remember

Burkhart—who was murdered that night across the street?"

"Yeah. I saw that someone has built a house there."

"Your mom knows the wife pretty well. They have two younger kids. I only know them to speak to. Anyway, Gary's dad ended up buying the car dealership from Burkhart's nephew, who inherited the business. Al got it for a song. After Al died a few years back, Gary expanded the business."

"I hope he doesn't have the same types of TV commercials as Burkhart," Sean said smiling.

His dad faked a cringe, "No, nothing like that."

"You said the milk business is going to close. So, what's supporting the growth around here? Gary must have someone to sell to for his business to grow the way it has."

"Well, the paper company was bought by a group of deep-pocket investors. They still make a small amount of paper products in the old part of the factory, but they did a major expansion that went on line in 1992. The new plant is producing polystyrene cups and plates for the fast food industry. They hired a bunch of people, and the company is growing each year. Also, soybean and corn production is way up, and most of the dairy farms have changed over to beef cattle. Tourism came out of nowhere and is now a big part of our economy. We're lucky here. Some of the other counties around here have not rebounded. Their economies are still depressed."

Bookends of Murder

As they walked toward the house, Jim thought to himself that Sean had improved since he returned, but he knew Sean still suffered. He heard him yell out some nights from nightmares and then leave the house to walk or sit on the porch to escape the demons tormenting him. Sean still incurred pain from the shrapnel in his body and the serious leg wound which caused an occasional limp. Sean was on the road to recovery and was strong, but he would suffer to some extent the rest of his life.

Chapter 12

During Gary's childhood years, his dad, Al Werner, worked at the Geisen Paper Company in the office doing payroll and bookkeeping. During Gary's freshman year in high school, his dad was concerned about the company going under and went to work part-time at the Burkhart car dealership. Sean knew that Gary was dependent on the football scholarship to go to college. Gary had two sisters and a brother. Even though Gary's dad had a good job, there wasn't a lot of extra money to go around. His mother had been a seamstress, which allowed her to bring in extra money while working from home. She had plenty of work, and the high school band members usually sought her help in altering or repairing the band uniforms. Gary had worked at the paper company loading and unloading boxes during summer months starting when he was fifteen.

Sean walked around the showroom floor looking at cars and the building. Gary came hurrying around the corner with a big smile saying, "Well, if it isn't the best quarterback Schriever High ever had."

Sean found himself in an affectionate bear hug. Gary stepped back and looked at Sean. "Man, you haven't changed at all. You look great. I bet you could walk on the football field tomorrow and never miss a beat."

Sean laughed. "Nothing like that. You look great yourself."

"How long are you here for?"

"I retired from the Marines, and I'm back here for a while."

Gary couldn't hide his surprise. Sean wasn't sure what to read into Gary's reaction, but he could have sworn he detected a faint grimace. Sean said, "That's why I'm here. I can't think of anywhere else I'd go to buy a car."

Gary was clearly happy that Sean was there to buy. "Well, you came to the right place. We've got a large selection, new and trade-ins. Tell me what you're looking for, and if we don't have it, I'll get it for you."

"Gary, you've done well for yourself. This is a big operation."

"Thank you, Sean. I'm happy with the success we have had since I took over from my dad. Dad seemed to have a knack for the car business. He turned it around and did a modernization at the downtown lot a couple of years after he bought it. He basically upgraded the facilities and expanded the service department and showroom. When I graduated, I joined him. We worked hard to build up the business, and then when a franchise became available, we grabbed it and never looked back. In 1993, when the manufacturer was redefining the modern dealership, we built this place with plenty of room to expand and moved out here in early '94. Unfortunately, I think the stress of everything was too much on Dad. Right after we moved here in 1994, Dad died unexpectedly—of a heart attack."

"I'm sorry about your dad, Gary, but it sounds like you and he worked well together and had a lot of success."

"Yeah. I miss him. He was the brains behind our success, but I'm glad I have been able to build on what he accomplished. In 1997, the opportunity of a lifetime came around, and I acquired a distributorship for trucks for the whole region. That's on the other side of the building. I wholesale to all dealers in this part of the country. My territory covers a three-state area, mostly rural, since big cities have their own. We get a lot of orders for pickups and cargo vans. And then two years ago, we got into leasing farm equipment, like combines and harvesters."

They walked through the new car section to the used car lot. Sean could also see where the garages were. He saw some cars sitting off to the side. "What are those cars over there?"

"Those are cars that we use for parts. They are either defective or sent to us by mistake."

"That red one looks brand new."

"Yeah, it's either defective or a mistake. There's a big company, Atvale Depot Company, that is used by many of the manufacturers to hold and distribute their excess inventory to dealerships. It's located in Michigan. I've visited their place. Cars, trucks and vans are parked for as far as you can see. Many of the cars are sent to us from Atvale. They sometimes make mistakes. That's the only complaint I have against them. They sometimes send us a vehicle that was supposed to go to another dealer. If that red one is one of those, it'll be shipped out soon to the right dealer. It's possible, though, that the red one is defective. Sometimes we get a car from the manufacturer that is defective. Whether we receive it directly from the manufacturer or Atvale, the manufacturer usually takes them back. Fortunately, there's not many of them, because it's always a pain to convince them that the car is a lemon."

As Gary and Sean were looking for a truck, it gave Sean a chance to observe Gary. His reddish-blond hair was thinning on top. He had not aged well. His face was splotched with red spots on his portly cheeks. During high school, Gary was solid muscle, but since then, he had put on weight and had a beer belly. But, he was still the outgoing, talkative person he had been in high school, and Sean could see why he had been successful in the car business. He knew his vehicles, and he was a natural salesman.

Sean decided on a used pickup truck that a farmer had traded in for a new model. He could tell it had been well maintained.

"Sean, you sure you want an eight-year-old truck? I'll give you a good deal on something newer. Just show me what you want."

"Thanks, but this is all I need."

Gary called over one of his salesmen and told him to get the paperwork prepared and to have the shop inspect the truck. If anything needed fixing, he was to let Gary know. "I want the truck running like a new one."

"Let's go have lunch. When we get back, everything should be ready, and you can check it out and sign the papers. I'll have it delivered to your parents' home."

During lunch, Gary asked, "Have you seen any of the others we used to hang around with?"

"Just Mike."

Gary brought Sean up to speed on Jeff and Danny. Sean wondered when Gary would get around to mentioning it. It happened toward the end of their meal. "Sean, as you probably know, Becky and I got married after we graduated. When she got to OU, we ran into each other and started talking. We were friends for a while, but then things started to change. I sometimes think that she waited to see if she ever heard from you, but after a while, she must have given up on that. Anyway, we have two daughters, Kinsey is 16, and Kara is 14. Kinsey is a sophomore at the high school, and Kara will be there next year."

"Yeah. Linda told me years ago you were married. Becky and I are ancient history, Gary. I'm glad you're both happy."

Gary looked relieved and changed the subject. "Say, they built a new golf course up north of here. I'm a member. Do you golf?"

"Yeah, but I haven't played much over the years. I can golf, but I'm not very good."

"Well that's okay, Sean. Maybe for once, I'll have a chance. It's just a friendly game anyway. Now, playing with Jeff is another matter. He never lost his touch from our high school days. He's sure good and plays to win."

"I guess some things haven't changed."

They both laughed.

"Do you live around here?" Sean asked.

"No, I live north of the old downtown, up where the new golf course is. We moved there a few years back."

The next morning, Sean drove to the police station. Built in the 1930's, it had that classic police station look. On the outside, it looked much like it did when he was growing up. He walked through the plate-glass doors into an open reception area. He was surprised at what he saw. Unlike many police stations he had been in, it was clean with a nice sitting area.

Sitting at a desk on the other side of a counter that divided the room in two was a heavy-set, middle-aged woman with short, grayish hair. By the conversation she was having on the phone, Sean figured she probably knew most everyone in the county and their business. She was assuring a cattle farmer that a deputy would be out that afternoon to check on some missing cattle. She then took a moment to ask how his mother was doing—who, Sean gathered, had been sick with the flu. He could tell from the one-sided conversation that she knew how to run the police department. She had been looking at him while she was talking on the phone. When she hung up, she asked in a friendly way, "What can I do for you?"

"Is Sheriff Adams in?"

"Want to give me your name, Sweetie?"

"Tell him Sean Neumann is here to see him."

A wide smile appeared as she stood, "He told me to make sure I got him if you came in. Hi. My name is Kim Connor," she said as she extended her hand. "I'll go tell him you're here. Would you like some police-house coffee?" she asked with a chuckle.

Sean laughed, "No thanks. I just finished some coffee, but maybe another time."

She walked down the hall and knocked on one of the doors. She stuck her head in, and she stepped aside to let Mike pass as he came to greet Sean.

With his arm around Sean's shoulder, Mike turned toward Kim, "This man here is the best quarterback to ever play around here."

Kim laughed, "You look just like the picture Mike has in his office of the two of you when the *Bekbourg Tribune* took your picture before that state championship game."

Mike indicated for Sean to walk ahead of him toward Mike's office. "Come on, Sean. Let's go on back to my office. Kim, hold my calls unless it's an emergency."

"Sure thing, boss."

As Kim walked away, Mike told Sean, "I couldn't run this place without Kim. You saw the reception area, didn't you?"

"Yeah, it was more like a doctor's office than a police station."

"Well, that is Kim's handiwork."

The picture of them in their football uniforms was on a bookcase along with a picture of Geri and their two children when they were younger and photographs of the two high school graduates. Sean picked up both graduation pictures. "Your son looks a lot like you, Mike, and your daughter is the spitting image of Geri."

"Thanks. They're good kids."

Sean set the pictures down and sat down in the chair in front of Mike's desk. Mike had moved to sit in his worn chair behind the desk. Sean said, "They both are a long way from home. You and Geri must really miss them."

"Yeah, we miss them a lot. Geri tries to talk to them on weekends, and she and I make it to a couple of Matt's games each year. Matt is studying forestry, and he has interned there the last two summers, so I expect he'll stay there after he graduates."

Sean didn't want to push the issue since he and Mike were getting reacquainted, but he felt there was more to the story about why Mike's kids were attending college so far away.

Just then, Mike's intercom buzzed. He said, "Just a minute" as he pressed the button and picked up the receiver. Mike heard, "Sorry to interrupt, but I thought you'd like to talk to Geri."

Mike smiled at Sean as he said into the phone, "Put her on."

He laid the receiver in the cradle, and said into the speaker phone, "Hi, Honey, guess who's sitting in my office?"

"Honey, I hope you didn't marry me because you thought I was clairvoyant," Geri said laughing.

Mike laughed and winked at Sean, "Here's a hint. He was the best quarterback to ever play at Schriever High."

For a brief second, she was silent, and then Geri squealed, "Oh, my gosh, I don't believe it! Sean, is that you?"

Sean laughed, "Yeah, Geri, it's me."

"Oh, this is wonderful! What are you doing for dinner tonight? Why don't you join Mike and me for dinner? I guess Mike's told you about the kids. We need some company."

Sean and Mike were both laughing at her exuberance. "I'd like that. What time should I be there?"

"Mike, do you think 5:30 would work?" she asked.

"That sounds fine, Honey. See you then."

"Sean, I can't wait to see you. Bye to you both."

Sean said, "I won't take up any more of your time, Mike."

Mike wrote down the address and handed it to Sean. They both stood, and Mike walked Sean out to his truck.

"Say, I need to find a place to stay. I'm looking to stay in Bekbourg, at least for a while. Do you know of any apartments or houses for rent?"

Mike seemed surprised but not displeased, "I'll ask Kim to make a list."

"Sounds great."

Mike watched his old buddy drive away. He suddenly had a feeling of hope, something he hadn't felt in years. He saw Sean's return as a way to turn things around. His quarterback had returned.

With time to kill before he went to Mike's, he decided to see Danny. The name on the sign was now "Chambers," and the station had been expanded to include four additional garage bays, and each had a mechanic working on a vehicle. Sean walked in the front door, and Danny was standing behind the counter looking through a parts catalogue. Sean recognized him right off. His movie-star looks were enhanced if that was possible with a two-week's beard growth. Sean didn't see a gray hair on his head or in his beard. Sean laughed to himself, because even though girls were always flirting with him, Danny, being super shy, didn't notice their attraction to him. He was always polite and never had a bad thing to say about anyone. Because of his good looks, Gary and Jeff called him a "pretty boy." Gary and Jeff could be mean-spirited in their kidding of Danny, and Sean sometimes had to tell them to back off. Danny either ignored, or was indifferent, to their pranks or jokes.

Danny looked up and stopped dead in his tracks. With disbelief in his voice, he asked, "Sean?"

Sean smiled, and said, "Yeah, Danny, it's me. How you been doin'?"

Danny didn't take his eyes off Sean as he rounded the counter. "I don't believe it! What are you doing here?" he asked as he warmly gave Sean a quick hug.

"Well, I retired, but I'm planning to find something to do and stay for a while."

"Sean, we have a coffee machine out in our waiting area. It's not the best coffee, but let's have some and get caught up."

Danny told Sean about how he and his dad had bought the gas station and that his dad still worked. He talked about Sally and his son, Drew, who was about to graduate with a degree in accounting from OU. Sally owned a beauty salon. Danny described how he also restored old cars in a warehouse he owned down off Jackson Road.

Sean asked Danny if Drew was planning to return to Bekbourg once he graduated. "I don't know, Sean. I think he probably would have a better chance to get a job in Athens or maybe Columbus. He's interviewing for jobs there. As much as Sally and I love him, we don't know if we want him to move back here."

"Why's that?"

Danny shook his head, "Things aren't like they used to be around here. When we grew up, kids mostly drank, and a few, like Gary and Jeff, smoked some weed. But the drugs around here now are bad news. Meth is the latest problem. Some high school kids have died. There have been fights and shootings all around the county. I don't want Drew around all this. I wish the police would stop it."

They talked for a few more minutes, and as Sean was leaving, Danny said, "Give me a holler when you want to see where I restore cars."

Sean was happy that Danny had done well. Danny's early life had seen its share of challenges. Danny didn't remember his mother. When he was about one year old, she started using drugs. Norm tried to support her and get her help, including getting the local minister to help her, but she rejected his efforts. When Danny was about three, she died of an overdose.

Sean knew that his mom had helped Norm a lot during Danny's early years. Norm worked long hours, so Danny often stayed with his family during the days until Norm got off from work. Sean liked playing with Danny. After Danny started to school, he didn't stay with them as much, because a neighbor was able to keep him until Norm got home. Even so, they remained good friends.

As Sean started to get out of the car, Mike opened the front door and walked out. Geri came running out with her apron on and nearly leaped into his arms. With tears in her eyes, "Sean, you're as sexy as you were in high school." Both he and Mike laughed.

He kissed her on her cheek. "Now don't go trying to make Mike jealous. It's great to see you. Mike showed me pictures of Matt and Miranda. You and Mike have two beautiful children."

She glowed with the compliment and took his hand and led him toward the house. "I sure think so. Let's go in. I hope you like my cooking."

Their house was a modest, three bedroom ranch. Geri had done a good job making their home comfortable and welcoming. Sean enjoyed being with them. It was like old times, almost. Geri was her bubbly self, but her eyes seemed sad. Mike, who had always been reserved, seemed withdrawn at times. Mike told Sean that his mother had passed away thirteen years ago, and his father was in a nursing home in the final stages suffering from cirrhosis of the liver. They weren't expecting him to last much longer. They asked about Sean's career and were interested in the places he had traveled. Realizing that Sean wasn't going to go there, Geri probed, "I don't see a ring on your finger. Are you married?"

Smiling, Mike said, "Geri, let's not ask Sean about his personal life on his first visit."

"Sean knows me. He's not surprised I'd ask."

Sean laughed, "You're right, Geri. You haven't changed a bit. No, I'm not married, and before you cross-examine me, I've never gotten married. Been too busy and never found the right one."

To get Sean off the hook, Mike changed the subject, "How's Linda doing?"

Geri affectionately swatted Mike's arm, showing she knew he deliberately changed the subject, but she let it drop.

After they had finished the dessert, Sean said, "Geri, that was a good dinner. I appreciate it. Mike, if I had pot roast, cornbread and chocolate pie every night, I'd have to double my running and workouts. I don't know how you do it."

Mike grinned, "Yeah, I'm lucky. Geri's a great cook. I do have to work at it to keep my slim figure."

They all laughed.

"Sean, let's go downstairs and get out of Geri's hair." Once they were settled in the den, Mike handed a piece of paper to him. "Oh, by the way, here's the list of rentals that Kim came up with. If you have any questions, let me know."

"How long have you been Sheriff?"

"About ten years ago, Sheriff Rhodes, he was the sheriff when you were here, had a major heart attack. I was his assistant and basically took over his duties. I ended up running for his position, because he wanted to retire. I won, and I've been sheriff since. He moved to Florida after I was elected, but I haven't stayed in touch."

"You like being the sheriff?"

"It's got its ups and downs. You aren't going to believe this, but Ben Clark and Kyle Ramsey still work for me."

"What? You mean the Ben Clark from high school that was always bullying kids and got kicked off the football team for extorting money from the freshman players?" Sean couldn't believe that. "That joker is still a police officer?"

"Yeah. You may not remember him, but Kyle was the officer with Ben that night when the house across from your parents burned down."

"Yeah, I vaguely remember someone with Ben, but I didn't get a good look at him. I can't believe that Ben is still there."

"I've had my suspicions about Ben over the years, but I've never had proof, so I couldn't fire him."

"What kind of suspicions?"

"Harassment of people, maybe even assault. I wouldn't put it past him to plant evidence, but no one has ever come forward with any complaints. Say, Sean, you mentioned that you are planning to be here for a while. I know you have all that law enforcement experience in the Marines. One of our deputies left for a job in Columbus late last year, and I never got around to filling it. I don't know if you would be interested, but if you are, I can look at the budget and check about filling that position."

"What do you have in mind?"

"Well, except for Ben and Kyle, and Mack Harris, the other guys out of this department are pretty inexperienced. Mack has been in the department longer than anyone, and he's my assistant. I was thinking that you could work more in the detective squad for the county and be another set of eyes on the reports as well as handle other things that come up. Actually, there is an investigation I have in mind for you to head-up. You may have heard about it the other day in the news. Someone was running his hunting dogs in a remote area, and they came across two bodies that were partially buried. Both men killed by gunshot. They didn't have any identification. We haven't ID'd the bodies, much less have any suspects. I know the things we deal with around here will seem small potatoes, but if you're interested, it'd give you something to do for a while and help the Department. It wouldn't pay much."

"Well, I appreciate this. Let me think about it."

"Yeah, let me know."

"You know, Mike, I suffered some injuries in the Marines. They have healed, but there's still some pain at times. It won't affect me doing the job. I don't know what Coach told you about what happened, but if you change your mind about wanting me, I understand."

"How bad was it, Sean?"

Sean paused, not sure he wanted to talk about it. "It was bad. We were a team. We were there on an investigation. I don't remember what happened the night I suffered the injuries. I was told there was an explosion, and my partner and close friend was killed. Beyond that, I don't want to talk about it. I really don't remember that night."

Mike focused on his friend, thinking about the suffering Sean must have endured. "Sean, you think about my offer, and I'll check with the Treasurer on filling the position."

One of the furnished rentals from Mike's list caught his attention. Sean decided while talking on the phone with Kye Davis that he was going to rent it. Moving in was easy since he only had clothes and a few personal things.

The duplex was in a quiet neighborhood about three blocks from the courthouse, which meant he could walk to the station if the deputy position came through. The area houses were pre-

Sherrie Rutherford

War, 1920's vintage, with two-bedrooms, one bath, and a single garage or carport. Some had been remodeled or enlarged. A few duplexes were interspersed among them. Sean suspected the residents consisted mostly of the elderly, but there were likely some singles or young couples.

An older model, green Buick was parked on one side, so Sean parked on the other side and walked up and rang the doorbell on the side where the Buick was parked. He heard a TV go silent, and soon a petite, white haired woman opened the door. She was nicely dressed in a pink flowered dress with a white sweater.

"Sean, I don't believe it. Come in."

"Hi, Mrs. Davis. It's great to see you."

"Come in and have a seat. I have some homemade cookies on the table over there. Do you have time for coffee?"

She had been the best English teacher in the school. He learned a lot about writing papers and classic literature his junior year and figured the B he got was an accomplishment.

"By the way, please call me Kye. It makes me feel old to be called Mrs. Davis."

Sean smiled. Sean told her about his time on the railroad after graduation, because he knew that her husband, who had been a locomotive engineer, had retired about the same time as his grandpa. He told her about his time in the military. She told him that her husband had suffered a stroke and was mostly bedridden for about a year before he died. Before he retired, they sold their home and bought the duplex. Cecil, her husband, thought it would be a good way to supplement their retirement income.

"What are you going to do? You said that you're retired, but you're too young to be completely retired."

Sean laughed. "Mike Adams offered me a job as a deputy. With my background in the Marines' criminal unit, he thinks I can do the job."

A serious look came to Kye's face. "Sean, did he tell you about the drug problem here in Bekbourg?"

"Some people have mentioned it. They say it's a real problem, especially with the high school kids and young adults."

"I am very concerned about what it's doing to the young people. I hope you can get to the bottom of it. I don't know why the kids have turned to drugs the way they have. If there weren't so many drugs available, I think the problem wouldn't be as bad as it is."

Chapter 13

Sean was troubled by how many people had mentioned the drug problem around Bekbourg. Lloyd Wiseman, the high school principal, explained to Sean how the school was trying to educate students, but felt they were fighting a losing battle. Drawing on his experience as a Marine investigative agent, Sean drove around the county looking for places that might be used to manufacture or store drugs. He looked for barns, warehouses, or old grain facilities. There were a couple of places that he noted to check out later.

He also walked around the downtown checking out the older and newer stores and eateries. The barber shop that his dad took him to as a boy was still in business. The old barber had retired, but his son now operated the business. Sean used these opportunities to renew acquaintances as well as to find out as much as he could. Sean was pleased to see more minorities and Hispanics around town. When he left Bekbourg, few minorities lived in Bekbourg, and he didn't remember any Hispanics. He also visited Knucklepin's, the favored beer joint, which was virtually unchanged. It was dimly lit, with most light coming from behind the bar, supplemented only by wall lamps over the few wall booths. Round bar stools bolted to the floor extended along the unadorned bar. Battered, curved, dark oak chairs surrounded matching round oak tables set with plastic salt and pepper shakers, paper napkins and single-sided laminated menus. Even the old plastic-faced wall clock with a beer logo was still the same.

Sean arranged to meet Danny at his warehouse to see his restoration business. Since Danny's warehouse was near the railroad tracks, Sean drove past the new paper plant, which was located on the rail line. Sean remembered how the train would stop outside the city and then bring cars into the plant yard to be loaded or unloaded. The empty cars would be taken by the engine back to the train. He was amazed at how large the plant now was. There was a fence around the back, but the tracks were still there for the rail cars to service the plant. The newer part of the plant had been added to the side of the old factory.

Sean then drove past the railroad yard. It was still operational, but it looked like its operations had declined dramatically. Some old grain storage facilities and warehouses had been converted into garages and small businesses, but long abandoned warehouses sported broken windows, peeling paint, overgrown weeds and were surrounded by broken and unlevel concrete. Sean was glad to see though that the milk plant had been maintained despite its dwindling business.

Sean whistled as he looked around, "Is this all yours?"

Danny smiled, "Come over here, Sean, and let me show you a beauty."

Danny explained, "This Alpha Romeo was owned by a woman up in Pennsylvania. Her husband bought it about two years before he died. For a while, she drove it once a week to the store and the beauty parlor but then got to where she couldn't drive. The car sat in the garage for twenty years, and the tires were completely rotted. Anyway, she recently died, and her son decided to restore the car, so he got in touch with me. I've heard about these cars but never seen one. I jumped at the chance to restore it."

"Wow, this is some car, Danny. How long will it take?"

"Depends. I'm going to try to restore it as close to the original as I can, so I'm going to have to try and locate parts. I have some contacts that I need to call once I have a list of everything I need."

"Danny, how did you get into this? How is it someone from Pennsylvania called you?"

Danny was still shy. A slight blush spread across his cheeks. "Well, there was an old lady, Mrs. Perkins, whose car I had taken care of since before I graduated from high school. Anytime she brought it in, I filled up the gas tank and checked everything out for her. She always asked for me to do the service. One day, she drove in and told me that her father left her a 1955 Thunderbird. It hadn't been driven in thirty years. She wanted to know if I could help her get it running again. She wanted to give it to her grandson when he graduated from college. She liked what I did to the car. She showed that car to a lot of people. People started calling me, and I started this as a side business. Somehow, my name has gotten around, and I've worked on cars from people in other parts of Ohio, some in Indiana and Kentucky, and now Pennsylvania."

Walking around the warehouse floor, Danny showed cars he had bought and restored to keep for himself. They were in mint condition, and Danny told Sean that every one of them was drivable. He would take them out for a spin every couple of months. Sean could tell that Danny took a lot of pride in what he did, but that had been the case at the service station as well.

Danny noticed a slight limp and an occasional grimace. Out of concern, he nodded toward Sean's leg, "You doin' okay, Sean?"

"Yeah, it's an old injury. It sometimes acts up, but I'm fine."

The night before, Sean had awakened from the same tormenting nightmare. The pain was more noticeable after having a nightmare.

Chapter 14

Mike called Sean one morning and asked if he could run by. Sean was doing spring cleaning around Kye's duplex while she kept him company, talking about the railroad and some of her previous students. Mike pulled up out front and walked up and put a bag on the front porch. He spoke to Sean and Kye, and they watched him walk back to his car. He came back carrying a chocolate Lab puppy, which was squirming and eyeing Sean and Kye as Mike got closer. Kye was smiling. Sean asked, "What have you got there, Mike?"

Mike handed the puppy to Sean, who took hold of the puppy and held him up, looking at him, and said, "Hey, Bud."

The puppy tried to lick Sean's face.

"I'm glad to see you two have already bonded."

Sean looked confused at Mike, "What do you mean?"

"I thought you needed a companion. Our neighbor's dog had a litter eight weeks ago. I spoke for him with you in mind." Nodding to Sean and the puppy, he added, "I'm glad to see I made a right decision."

"Wait a minute." Sean was now holding the puppy up against his chest. The puppy had calmed down, resting comfortably against Sean's chest. "I can't keep him. What am I going to do with him while I'm away? Also, Kye may not want a dog here."

Mike smiled, nodding toward Kye who had walked up to pet the puppy's head while Sean continued to hold him. "Kye and I have already talked about it. She is okay with the puppy being here, and she said she will be glad to keep him while you're gone. There's some food and a couple of bowls in the bag. I remember how Billyboy loved to chase balls, but I thought I'd leave it to you to get him a ball. He needs his next round of shots in four weeks."

Mike turned and walked toward his car, waiving to them.

Sean was stunned. Kye said, "He is such a cutie. I've always loved dogs. Cecil and I always had one, but when Rufus died, Cecil was sick, and we didn't get another one." Looking at the puppy's big eyes, "I'm going to love having him around. Let's call it a day on the yard work. You need to get him settled."

Sean set him down to let him do his business and started to put away the yard tools. The puppy frolicked at his heels, staying right with Sean. He said, "Kye, I guess I've got a dog. I need to get a leash and collar and I guess some other things."

Sean put the puppy in his truck and drove over to the Shopper's Pavilion. He bought a bed, chew toys, a container of tennis balls, a leash and collar. The puppy sat right over next to him all the way over and back from the Pavilion and whined when Sean left him in his truck while he was in the store.

While walking Buddy in his neighborhood later that afternoon, Sean saw an elderly man struggling to change a flat tire. Sean stopped and asked if he could help. The man seemed relieved and stepped back to allow Sean to remove the lug-nuts. As he worked, Sean told him that he was renting from Kye. Earl Pinkston said that he and his wife had met Kye and seen her around. Sean asked him if he had lived there long.

"Well, I was born and raised in Bekbourg, but not right here. I ended up with the family place where I was born in Possum Gap, about fifteen miles from here, and Ruth and I lived there until 1998. It got too much for us, and we wanted to be in town where things would be easier. So we sold it, 'bout a hundred acres, and moved here. I hated to sell it, but Ruth likes it better here, and it's okay for me. A lot less work, that's for darn sure."

"Sounds like things worked out well for you. Sometimes, it can be hard to sell acreage around here."

"Yep, but it worked out just fine. My brother lives over in Tapsaw County. Family being family, I asked if he wanted to buy it. As it turned out, my nephew and his wife decided to buy it. Tony and Ruby have two kids and were happy to buy the house and the acreage. I'm glad they bought it and the place stayed in the family."

Sean finished changing the tire and put it in the back of Earl's truck. They shook hands, Earl grateful that Sean had stopped to help.

What Earl Pinkston did not know was that his brother, Zeke, who lived in the next county over, Tapsaw County, operated a large marijuana growing enterprise. Tony Pinkston and his brother, Ray, saw the opportunity to purchase Earl's property as a means to expand the family's illegal drug business. They had additional plans to increase their profitability by setting up labs to make crystal meth. One of their labs was close behind the house that Tony and Ruby lived in with their two children. On down the main road about a half mile away, there was a gravel road, Shailer Road—that had not been used for many years. It was barely noticeable but ran parallel to the boundary of Tony's property.

Ray and their cousin, Victor Shultz, found an abandoned mobile home and moved it to the wooded area on that part of Tony's property to live in. They moved in a second trailer for a larger meth lab behind their trailer. In addition to the two meth labs, they grew a large amount of marijuana on the property. They could walk back and forth across the hollow to get to each other's place. By 2002, they had a profitable business, with their meth and marijuana distribution reaching throughout southeast Ohio and as far away as Columbus.

Chapter 15

Sean and Mike were already in the conference room when the others started filing in. Sean was dressed in a deputy's uniform. Ben Clark was the last one in, five minutes late. He abruptly stopped when he saw Sean sitting there. Sean pretended not to notice him. "Is this some kind of joke? What's he doing here?" demanded Ben.

"Glad you could make it, Ben. Come in and have a seat," Mike said.

For a moment, Ben seemed frozen to the floor. He never took his eyes off Sean as he pulled out a chair to sit. Sean thought that Ben had thickened around his waist. He still had that combative and arrogant attitude.

Mike began, "Some of you may already know Sean Neumann. Obviously, Ben does. Sean grew up around here, and he and I played football together. He is probably the best quarterback Schriever ever had. He's been gone from the area for twenty years. He recently retired from the Marines. He was in the military police and a special investigator. I've hired Sean to fill Lang's place. Ben, I've asked Sean to be the lead investigator on the case of the two males found shot. Since you were the responding officer, I thought you could work with Sean."

Causing everyone to turn their attention to him, Ben erupted, "I don't believe this!" He was staring hard at Mike.

"Believe it, Ben. Now, Sean, let me introduce the rest of the team."

Kyle Ramsey, who Sean had seen with Ben the night of the fire across from his parents' house, was one of the officers. Of course, there was Ben, who was staring daggers at both Mike and Sean, and there were four other officers. Two officers, Wade Frisch and Darrell Logan were coming off night duty. Mack Harris and Alex Ogle were the other two deputies.

Alex Ogle, a good-looking kid, looked like a high school student. He had reddish-colored hair and wore glasses. He was almost six feet tall and had a slender frame. Wade was a tall, wiry man in his mid 20's. Darrell was probably a couple of years older.

After the meeting adjourned, with the exception of Ben, who charged out right after the meeting's conclusion, the men came up and welcomed Sean.

The following day, Kim had already left for the evening, and Mike was about to call it a day. His telephone rang.

"Why didn't you run it by me first?" The man on the phone was in a rage. "Have you lost your mind? Neumann was in the military police. I bet he's just like that single-minded old man of his—'clean up this county.' I don't know how many times I've heard him say it. Now, you've hired his son, who is a legitimate law man. What were you thinking?"

Calmly, Mike said, "It's going to be okay. You will be fine." Before Mike could finish what he was going to say, the tirade erupted, "What do you mean, 'it'll be okay?' This is the stupidest thing I have ever seen, and you're supposed to be smarter than this."

"Take it easy and give me a chance to explain. I told him the job may be temporary because of the budget. He may not even stay here in Bekbourg for long. There was some accident in the Marines, and he was injured. His partner got killed. I think he's probably just here until he decides what he wants to do."

There was a long pause. Finally, "If he gets hurt, it'll be on your conscience." The phone line went dead. Mike sat there a long time thinking. He wasn't sure how he felt about that call. Mike was happy Sean was back, but he was also apprehensive.

Over the next couple of weeks, Sean worked overtime, learning everything he could about the Bekbourg County Sheriff's Department. He quickly got to know each deputy and their abilities. He was impressed at the quality of the young recruits but felt some were looking to move on to the State or with the large city departments. He worked at least one shift with each deputy with the exception of Ben, who refused to talk to him.

He learned many new things about the county: who abused their wives, who the petty criminals were, where to catch speeders, and where drunk drivers where most likely to be. He re-familiarized himself with all the back roads in the county and who lived there. At the end of this break-in period, Sean knew the department, the county and its deputies. The one thing he did not know, and it seemed the deputies did not know, was the source of the drugs in the county. Most of them felt they were coming from outside the county, but the sheriff's department didn't have the money or manpower to investigate the problem. They were waiting on the commissioners and the state to come through with the resources necessary to combat the problem.

On day one on the job, Sean began his investigation into the two men found shot to death. He reviewed the police and coroner's reports. He asked Ben about his findings, but Ben's only response was "Go screw yourself!" Sean examined the missing persons reports and saw where a woman who lived in Madison, Indiana, had called in a report about two missing men a couple of months before he returned to Bekbourg. He called the woman. She explained that her brothers, Jed and Brody Todd, had moved to Bekbourg almost three years ago, but that neither she nor her parents had heard from them for some time. She called the Sheriff's department, but the officer she talked to, Mack someone, didn't discover anything helpful. Sean followed up, and the coroner confirmed through dental records that the bodies were those of Jed and Brody Todd.

As he made his way to a table, Sean considered how it was like walking back in time. Very little had changed in Frau's from when he was a boy. The chairs and bar stools were still covered in a mixture of red, gray and yellow plastic on stainless steel frames dulled from age and wear. Fluorescent light fixtures cast a cool white light, and someone had dropped a coin in the jukebox to play an old favorite country song. A variety of framed black and white photographs of Bekbourg's rich history hung on the walls, including pictures of the old trains and depot, which brought back memories of his grandpa and his time on the railroad. Sean sat at a table where he could observe the people. He figured there was a mixture of railroad employees, laborers and construction workers along with friends and family members.

As he waited for his dinner, Sean saw an old friend from his railroad days walk in. Dusty Shaw was one of those characters that Sean and his grandpa used to talk about. At about the same time, Dusty looked over in Sean's direction. He looked hard and started walking toward Sean. A big smile came on his face. "I can't believe it. When did you get back in town?"

Sean stood and shook his hand, "A few weeks ago. Done my time with the Marines, but like everyone else, I decided to head home for a while. Why don't you sit down and join me?"

Dusty sat, and Anita, the waitress, came and took his order.

"So, are you now with the Sheriff's Department?" Dusty asked, noticing Sean's uniform.

"Yeah, I had some training while I was with the Marines, so the Sheriff recently hired me. Where's your ponytail?"

Dusty used to have a beard and wore his hair long, pulled back in a ponytail to keep it out of his face when he was working. He was now clean-shaven and his hair trimmed short and showing some gray. He was still about the same weight. He was dressed in typical railroad clothes, jeans, flannel shirt and heavy work boots. Sean recalled how many railroaders wore overalls year-round. During warm weather, several wore tee-shirts, but others opted for long-sleeve denim shirts. Ball caps protected against dirt and dust. A heavy jean coat and wool hat were standard attire on cold days, but heavy-duty leather gloves were a must year-round.

Noticing Sean's expression, Dusty laughed, "I cleaned up my act, Sean."

"Oh?"

"Sean, you wouldn't believe what's happened. About fifteen years ago, I hit bottom. I decided I was either going to end up in jail or dead, and I was certainly on the way to losing my job. I went into treatment, and I've been clean and sober since then."

"Congratulations, Dusty, that's good to hear."

Dusty was still full of nervous energy. His foot was shaking up and down, causing his upper body to vibrate as he talked. "The railroad's really changed a lot. The town has changed. You probably know that, 'cause it's changed everywhere."

"Tell me about it. What is going on with the railroad?"

"Well, first of all, they pretty much closed down the yard here in Bekbourg. It's a place to set off cars. We really don't do much switching here anymore. All we have here is the operator. Trains come right on through; they don't stop anymore. In fact, ever since we merged and became the OMVX, everything is running along the Ohio on the old MV&O line. All we get is local business, and not much of that. Just one train a day, one east and one west. The only reason I'm still around here, I work a local between here and Chillicothe and service the industries in both places. Even that business is drying up. Trucks will probably soon take care of all the business."

From the early days, the railroad had played a major role in Bekbourg's growth. To boost access to markets and suppliers for local businesses, the City of Bekbourg built in the 1840's a two-hundred-forty mile railroad from Cincinnati, Ohio, to Wheeling, West Virginia. Named the WVB&C Railroad in recognition of connecting West Virginia, Bekbourg and Cincinnati, the City also located a switching yard and depot in Bekbourg. Because of the rail service, in 1892, Harry J. Schriever started the Bekbourg Springs Milk Company—enabling farmers forty miles away to get their milk to Harry's dairy. In 1909, another major industry began when Gregory E. Geisen moved to Bekbourg and opened G. E. Geisen Paper

Products. He started manufacturing paper plates but soon expanded to manufacture paper cups, napkins, straws and other paper goods. The railroad provided the transportation means to distribute his paper products to distant markets.

In 1905, owners of the large MV&O rail system, which served regions in Ohio and Appalachia, wanted more rail lines and entered into a one-hundred year lease with the City of Bekbourg to operate the WVB&C line. Over time, most people forgot that Bekbourg owned the rail line, and people, including the railroad employees, identified the rail system as being part of the MV&O. Much later, the MV&O company merged with another railroad, forming the OMVX Railroad Company. This merger eventually led to less service on redundant lines and closure of some routes. People in Bekbourg were proud and loyal to the train, and Sean knew it pained everyone to see its business shrink.

Dusty asked, "You remember Chaw?"

"Sure."

"Well, he's getting up near retirement. He's the conductor on the run to Chillicothe. When he retires, I guess I'll become the conductor."

"What about Mule Head?"

"He's retired from the railroad on disability—got injured on the job. I see him around. Maybe we can catch up sometime."

"I'd like that."

Sean asked, "How's your love life, Dusty?"

"Me and the old lady broke up when I hit bottom. I still see my kids when I can, but she stayed in Cincinnati."

"I thought you lived in Cincinnati?"

"I did at first. I really liked it there, but I moved here, 'cause I was having to spend most nights at the boarding house since the deliveries at the plants were at night."

"Why didn't you move back to Cincinnati? You could work out of there."

"I got used to living here. This is a good job, and I feel this is my home. Plus, I met a new girl here, and I go to my meetings here at the church. I now run most of them. As much as I love this town, it's changed in ways that you would not believe."

"What do you mean, Dusty?"

"Meth. We drank, smoked weed and played around with some other drugs, but what they're using today is really frying their brains. There are kids around here destroying themselves—and doing it fast. Within a year, they can't recover. It's bad, Sean. Parents are scared to death."

"Where's it coming from?"

"I don't know."

About that time, a woman walked up. Dusty stood and Sean followed suit. Dusty said, "Hi, Hon." He turned to Sean, "This is Carla Huber, Sean."

Sean extended his hand to shake hands with Carla. She said, "Hi, Sean. I didn't mean to interrupt. I just left a school committee meeting, and I thought I'd stop by to see Dusty before he got on the job."

"It's nice to meet you, Carla. If you have time, please join us. Dusty and I used to work together on the railroad."

"She's a teacher up at the elementary school," Dusty explained. "Most of the time, she has to do her lesson plans and get ready for class. She sometimes drops by here before I catch my shift. Carla and I run a program at the church. Anyone can come. Some parents have approached us to start a program for teenagers, 'cause so many of them are getting involved in drugs. There's no way that's going to work. It's the parents asking us to start it, but the kids aren't interested. They are the ones that have to want it. The parents don't want to go public, but a program isn't going to work for these kids if they don't want to do it themselves."

Chapter 16

"Say, Mike. I found out who those two men were: Jed and Brody Todd. They moved here from Madison, Indiana, almost three years ago. Turns out, their sister had called in about two months before I came back to Bekbourg. I found the call in our reports. I drove up to where their place was. It looked like they left the place intending to return but never did. Rotten food remains, dirty clothes, food in the refrigerator. Even dirty dishes in the sink and trash were left inside. The house was in pretty bad shape with all that in there. What do you know about them?" Sean asked.

"Nothing. Why?'

"Well, there was a metal shed out back. The lock had been broken, and the door was standing open. Not much left inside, but I think it may have been a meth lab—even though most of the equipment seems to be missing."

"Meth lab? That's interesting. Never heard of them. Don't recall any calls to their place."

"Yeah, I checked our files," said Sean. "We don't have any reports on them. Probably won't do any good, but I thought we might want to have our forensics go through their place. See what they can find."

"Yeah. I'll call and have them check it out. Did these guys have a record?"

"Yes. I talked to the police in Madison. Jed had a breaking and entry and domestic violence assault. Both were charged for small amounts of marijuana possession. Jed served a year for the domestic violence conviction since he was on probation when he decided to rough up a girlfriend. No other arrests showed up anywhere else."

"Wonder why they moved here?"

"I asked their sister. She said they told her that they just wanted a clean start where they weren't known. Jed's probation period was completed, so they moved."

"Well, if your suspicions are right that they had a meth lab here, maybe they wanted to start fresh where they could cook their meth without someone looking over their shoulder."

"Well, they obviously were on the wrong side of someone to have been shot and buried in that remote area." Sean said.

"For sure. I'll let you know what I find out from the forensics."

Chapter 17

Sean was in a twilight sleep. He fought to wake up to avoid the nightmare, but he couldn't rouse himself awake. The nightmares, which now tortured him with a grotesque glimpse of Clint, were tenacious in refusing to release their grip until he was hurled to a terror-drenched consciousness.

Everything was dark. He and Clint, with guns drawn, were entering a dark building. Sean's senses were strung tight. He felt they were being watched; something wasn't right. His heart was pounding, and perspiration soaked his body. Evil was surrounding them, starting to suffocate them. They couldn't move, couldn't break free. He was screaming for them to run, but Clint didn't seem to hear him. Suddenly, Clint's head turned toward him, but bloody sinew was all that was there. "OH, GOD, NO!"

Sean lurched off the bed, nearly falling. He was trembling and dripping with sweat. Buddy ran over next to Sean, whining and rubbing up against Sean's legs. Sean slowly got his bearings and sat down, putting his head in his hands. Buddy jumped up on the bed and started pushing his head against Sean's hands, trying to get Sean to pet him. Sean took a hand and started rubbing Buddy's neck. He despaired that he couldn't remember and couldn't shake the debilitating nightmares.

Clint Neely had been Sean's partner for nine years. Together, they had traveled the world investigating crimes. Clint was not only Sean's partner, but they were best friends. Clint bragged about growing up in Dothan, Alabama, "playing baseball, attending church on Sundays and raising hell the rest of the time." As if his handsome face, perpetual five o'clock beard and blond hair wasn't enough, his deep southern baritone drawl and boundless personality were irresistible to women. Sean kidded him that women never noticed him when Clint was around. No matter the situation, Clint could flick on his charm, and "talk himself out of a steel drum," Sean was always saying. He turned truisms and spun stories as naturally as breathing. Sean admired Clint's instincts and uncanny ability to hone in on a suspect, and once within his sights, Clint was like a bulldog until the case was solved.

Talbert (Tally) Rawlings was the third member of Sean's special criminal team. All four of Tally's grandparents had been sharecroppers in Alabama. They moved to Huntsville, Alabama, to give their children better lives. Tally's father, Curtis, was working as a janitor at one of Alabama's universities when he met a beautiful young woman in her sophomore year pursuing a degree in education. They fell in love, but Winney refused to marry him until she graduated. A year after they married, Tally's oldest brother was born. At the urging of some family members who lived in Maryland, Tally's parents moved to Baltimore where Winney taught high school math and Curtis worked as a mechanic for a large trucking company. They raised three boys. Tally was the youngest. A daughter was born four years after Tally. All four children knew the destiny preordained by their parents, to graduate from college. The three boys joined an ROTC program to get their college degree, and once in the armed forces, they sent money back home, which along with scholarships, enabled their younger sister to become a doctor.

Tally joined Tanner's unit a few years earlier and was assigned to work with Sean and Clint. Despite being reserved, Tally had a good sense of humor. Where Clint was always talking, Tally spoke in the fewest words possible. Clint loved to rib Tally to try to get a rise out of him. Tally pretended he was ignoring Clint, but he was entertained by the chaos that was always circling Clint.

The three men knew each other well and had each other's backs. The trio was one of the best teams in the special criminal unit. It was their record and unblemished reputation that precipitated their assignment to Kuwait in October 1998.

One of the schemes uncovered by the United States intelligence agencies was that the president of Iraq was allowing heroin produced from opium grown in Afghanistan to be transported through Iraq and delivered to a criminal organization comprised of Afghanis, Kuwaitis and Americans, that had distribution outlets around the world. This enterprise served two purposes: it could weaken coalition military forces through the use of drugs, and there were immense financial gains to Iraq's president.

Sean, Clint and Tally were sent to Kuwait to investigate United States personnel rumored to be part of the heroin drug trafficking operation. Not only did U.S. authorities want to stop these criminal activities, there also was a growing concern about drug use among the coalition troops. They were assigned to the local criminal investigation command and appeared to be part of the normal personnel rotation. Their secret orders, however, gave them broad investigative powers to unmask the military personnel rumored to be participating in the heroin trafficking operation.

Chapter 18

Competing musty odors and tobacco smells permeated the interior of Ray Pinkston and Victor Shultz's mobile home. Laminate, mismatched end tables held ash trays overflowing with ashes and cigarette butts and tin containers for tobacco spit. Dark cheap paneling muted the light effect emitted from the single watt bulbs in the couple of lamps. Several discarded beer cans were strewn around, and each man was enjoying another can. "So, what'd that deputy have to say?" asked Ray.

Tony took a drink. "He said that the Todd boys have been identified, but the deputy that's investigatin' their deaths is chasin' his tail. There ain't no evidence. Told me that nothin's goin' to happen."

"That's good," said Ray.

"Yeah, that's good, but Clark don't like how we've grown our meth business." Tony took another drink from his beer can. "He's afraid we might get the feds' attention."

"What'd you say to him?"

"I told him that's what we pay him for, to watch out for them. He hasn't seen no sign that they're nosin' around here, so I told him to quit worryin'. He didn't like it. We kind of got in a pissin' match, but in the end, he saw it my way."

"You don't think we made a mistake with him?"

"Naw. He's done our biddin'. Helped us get rid of those Todd boys—an' a few other things."

For the first time Victor spoke up. "Yeah, and he never told no one."

"Did you ask him 'bout there bein' another competitor around here?" Ray inquired.

"Yeah, I asked. He wanted to know why I was askin'. He said, 'Have you seen any signs of other drugs?' I said, 'no.' He asked then why was I askin'? I told him, 'just curious.' He told me since I don't know any reason to be suspicious, to mind my own business."

"What are you thinkin'?"

"We keep our eyes and ears open, and don't completely trust that deputy," Tony said as he crushed his beer can and pulled the tab on another one.

Chapter 19

Sean had just finished his night shift when Danny called him about an abandoned cargo van he was about to tow. When Sean arrived, Danny was waiting with his tow truck, and the cargo van was sitting off to the side of the road.

"Sean, I got a call this morning from a customer who said there was this cargo van broken down. He thought it might need to be towed. I haven't touched anything. It's brand-new and doesn't have any tags. But the main reason I called you is that the back door was open, and there's something unusual."

Sean stuck his head in the open door, and there was a distinct smell. Sean recognized the odor of meth from work he had done for the military. Danny said, "I could smell something. I thought it should be looked into." Sean walked around looking at the van.

Sean asked, "Do you know what's wrong with the van?"

"I can't be sure, but I think it's very low on oil. The engine locked up."

Sean thought this might be the break he had been hoping for in learning something about the local drug problem. "Thanks, Danny, for calling me on this. I'd appreciate it if you kept this under your hat. I'll take care of this." Sean didn't want to leave the cargo van unattended in case someone came to burn or tow it. "But, if you don't mind, let's get it out of here. Can you tow it down to the old warehouse district for me?"

Sean had worked on several matters with a Drug Enforcement Agent official, Russ Bozeman, while he was in the special criminal unit. After Danny drove off, he used his private cell phone to call Boze. Boze was out of the country, but his assistant assured Sean that she would send a tow truck, inform Boze, and keep Sean posted on the inspection of the van. Sean stayed with the van until the DEA showed up and loaded it in a fully-enclosed tow truck.

Next day, Sean decided to pay Gary a visit. He left Buddy in his truck perched, looking out the rolled-down window—waiting for Sean's return. While Sean was waiting, he saw two men talking off to the side of the show room. One he figured worked for Gary, but the other was a well-dressed Hispanic man. After saying hello to Gary, Sean asked who the men were.

Gary looked, "Oh, the bald-headed man is manager for my truck operations, Joe Sommers. The other one is Dante Gomez. He's new since you left town. He moved in here in the early '90's and started a cleaning service business. They clean public buildings, warehouses and large businesses and factories, like our car dealership and the paper plant. There's even talk that they might start cleaning the schools. He also has branched out into landscaping and takes care of quite a few of the larger homes in the area as well as the new golf course. He's just beginning with the landscape business, so I don't know how that'll go. He's quite an entrepreneur. He buys his service vehicles from us. Hey, Sean, ready to trade that truck for a new one?"

Sean laughed. "No. I'm actually here on a different matter. Yesterday, I got a call about a brand-new cargo van that was found nearby on a rural road. It was towed by the authorities. They're checking it out, because it may have had some meth in it. They ran a trace on the van and didn't find any name associated with it. They checked with the manufacturer, but they couldn't find any record in their database. It's the brand you carry. Do you know anything about a new van disappearing from your lot?"

Gary was confused, "I've been busy. I'll have to check on that, but I haven't heard anything."

Sean looked puzzled, "Wouldn't you have been told if a new van was missing?"

"Well, it's not the first time it's happened if it's ours."

"Any thoughts on why meth might have been in it?"

"I don't know anything about meth. Probably it was stolen to transport meth. There's lot of meth around here."

"Any reason to think someone from your business might have taken it?"

"No, and I wouldn't keep someone if I thought they would. Were there any finger prints?"

"No, it was wiped down, which is what a thief would do. It's peculiar that the manufacturer didn't have a record of where it's supposed to be."

"Oh, well, that's typical of some manufacturers." Gary was put out at the thought. "It'll probably be an ordeal to get the van back, but we need to get it back here if it's our van. Say, Sean, would you like to play some golf?"

"Yeah, that sounds good as long as you're okay playing with someone who's not very good."

"I'm not that good myself. It'll be fun."

After Sean left, Gary located Joe Sommers in the service department. Seeing Gary, Joe started to walk away, but Gary yelled, "Hey, Joe."

Joe stopped and waited for Gary to catch up to him. Gary said, "Joe, let's walk outside."

When they got outside, showing irritation, "I got a visit from Sean Neumann."

Bored, Joe asked, "Who's that?"

"The new deputy. He was asking me about a missing cargo van. Said the authorities have the van. I guess that's the Feds. Drugs may have been in it. They think it must have been stolen from here. What is this all about, Joe?"

"Don't worry about it, Gary."

"Don't tell me to not worry about it! The Feds have the van. What happened?"

"Look, after the delivery, they were going to take it to the dealer in West Virginia, but it broke down. The idiots left it unattended, and that deputy somehow got there before we could get it. Anyway, there is no way they can trace anything back here. The computer records have been altered. There's no record it was delivered here. Instead, it should have been delivered to the dealer in West Virginia."

"Neumann thinks it was stolen from here."

"Well, let him think what he wants."

"Look, Joe. Sean's not like the other deputies. I've known him for years. Once he gets something on his mind, he won't let go."

"I'm not worried about another bozo cop. Just take care of your end, Gary," Joe said dismissively as he walked away.

Sean answered his phone. "When was I going to hear from you?"

Sean laughed, "Hey, Jeff. How's it going?"

"Better now that I'm talking to you. What about us getting together for lunch? Are you free tomorrow?"

"Sure. Sounds great. Where and what time?"

"Let's meet at the GilHaus around noon. You remember it?"

"Yep. I'll see you then."

"Looking forward to seeing you, Old Buddy."

Chapter 20

"Pappy, what do you have on your mind that you wanted to see me about?"

"You know that I never was too keen on you and the boys movin' over to Bekbourg County and gettin' mixed up in that other drug business." Zeke spat a wad of tobacco. "That's not our territory. Our business is pot. We know pot. We know how to work that. Not meth. I don't have a good feelin' 'bout that over there in Bekbourg. I've been hearin' that there's a big operation there. You know as well as I do that some competitors aren't the type to work things out. Are you boys watchin' your backs?"

"Yeah, Pappy, we've got that deputy that works for us. He's been some useful, but we ain't sure just how much we trust him. We heard rumors 'bout a big operation there, too. The deputy claims he don't know nothin' about it, but we're not sure how true that is."

"You know, Son, my experience tells me that a big operation has its protectors. Can't help but think that the Sheriff there is involved somehow. Sometimes, you have to shake a few trees to get a understandin' of what's goin' on in a place."

"You mean talk to the Sheriff somehow?"

"If the Sheriff is somehow involved, if somethin' happened to him, it might flush out who's runnin' the big business. Then, you can see if they want to split the territory or if you have to take care of them the way you did with those brothers."

"You mean kill the Sheriff?"

"It might come to that, Tony. Don't let this go too long. One more thing: keep an eye on that deputy. He might be playin' both sides."

"We are. We don't trust him. If we have to, we'll take care of him."

Chapter 21

The GilHaus was an elegant restaurant located in a hotel opened in 1912 across from the courthouse. It was like so many grand hotels built in the early 1900's. The first floor had a twenty-foot-high ceiling adorned with large crystal chandeliers and ornately-carved crown molding. Its walnut hardwood floors were partially covered by several richly-colored Oriental rugs, and beautiful Chippendale furniture filled the lobby and select seating areas. The imposing twenty feet wide hotel desk was an elegantly-carved walnut fixture that had a high back panel with the old fashion nooks for mail and keys along the back and an exquisite desktop of white marble.

The hotel had gone into decline during the Great Depression and closed in the late 1930's. In the 1950's, the main floor of the hotel was restored, and the restaurant that was located off to the right of the entranceway was opened by a grandson of Gregory Geisen, Gilbert Geisen. The GilHaus still offered the elegance of a bygone era with white tablecloths, crystal goblets and china. The food was reasonably good and not so expensive as to price itself out of the Bekbourg market—with the clientele primarily being local business people and professionals.

The hostess walked up to him. "Sir, are you here to meet Commissioner Thompson?"

"Yes. How did you know?"

She laughed. "He described you and said he hadn't seen you in over twenty years, so he hoped he was right."

Sean laughed.

"Right this way. The Commissioner always sits back here."

The hostess led Sean toward the far back corner. As Jeff saw him coming, he stood and gave Sean a hug. "See, Margo, my description was pretty darn close."

She smiled, "Please enjoy your lunch. Jan will be right over."

"Sean, you haven't changed a bit. It's great to see you, Pal."

"I've probably added a few gray hairs," Sean laughed. "It's great to see you."

The waitress, who Sean gathered waited on Jeff regularly, was a cute brunette with a bubbly personality. "Commissioner, can I refresh your drink? And what can I get your guest?" Jeff ordered another whiskey, and Sean ordered iced tea.

Sean said, "I understand you've been busy over the last twenty years. Gary told me you were the county prosecutor for a while and now a county commissioner."

"It's been a fun ride. After I got out of law school, I went with the prosecutor's office and did that for about five years. The prosecutor retired, and I decided to throw my hat in the ring and run for county prosecutor. Couldn't believe I won.

Anyhow, I did that for eight years, and decided to run for the county commission's seat that was opening up. I was branching out into some business arrangements and didn't have time to be the prosecutor. It was actually the seat that my dad was stepping down from. He was ready to retire to warm Florida, and I can't blame him for that. Anyway, couldn't believe the good folks in the county voted for me again."

"That's great, Jeff."

"I'm the head of the county political party here." Jeff laughed, "I hope that's not the reason I got voted in. What have you been up to the last twenty years?"

Sean told him about his time in the Marines. "I enjoyed it, but I put in my twenty years and decided to try something else. I came back here and got lucky. I guess Mike told you he hired me as a deputy?"

"Yes, he told me. It's great for Mike and for the town to have you back, Sean. Is there a Mrs. Neumann?"

Sean shook his head, "No woman would have me."

Jeff laughed, "Well, I guess you heard, but I finally settled down a little over two years ago. Her grandfather is Theodore Zimmstein, who ran the state house with an iron fist for thirty years. He got out and started a law firm, and Mary's father went to work there. It's a big practice in Columbus— does a lot in real estate and commercial law: Zimmstein & Zimmstein. They do work all over the state—and even in other states. They've got around fifty attorneys. Anyway, it's big money. I went to law school with Richard. He and Mary were married after he graduated, and he went to work for the Zimmstein firm. Richard and I kept up with each other. He became a state senator and was planning to run for governor. It's tragic what happened. He was on a plane with one of the governor's aides going to a Michigan and OSU game. There was some engine trouble, and the plane crashed. Both of them were killed.

"I went up to the funeral, of course, and talked briefly to Mary. I got up to Columbus about every two weeks or so and would go by and see her. I started to take her and her little girl—Rachel's her name—to different things. After about a year, we started to get more serious about each other. At first, she was hesitant to fly, but I finally convinced her to let me take her to Naples, Florida, where I have a place. She and Rachel met my parents, and I guess the rest is history."

"I'm happy for you, Jeff. How're your mom and dad?"

"Living the good life. Dad retired a few years back, and they moved to Florida. They're down there golfing and playing Bridge. When dad and mom decided to move to Florida, I moved into the old home place, and that's where Mary and I live. Before we were married, I told her to have it remodeled anyway she liked. You'll have to come see us. I'd like for you to meet Mary and Rachel.

"I'd like that."

"Hey, I got a better idea. Mary and I are going to have a welcome back party for you. It'll be like old times to get the old gang back together."

"You don't have to do that."

"It'll be fun. I'll get back to you on some dates. How are your folks and your sister, Linda, isn't it?"

"They're doing great, too. Dad's probably going to be retiring soon. Mom's still helping at the church. Linda is an attorney, and so is her husband. They live in Cincinnati with their two kids. Seem to be doing well."

Sean changed topics, "Bekbourg seems to have grown while I was gone."

"It has, Sean. I guess you saw all that new growth out the highway where Gary's dealership is. There's also been some new residential development because of the business growth. The old downtown is looking better, and some new shops have come in. Even the old movie theater has been restored, and it's doing well. The milk plant's not doing so well, but I guess your dad told you about that."

"Yeah, he mentioned that. It's a shame. That company has been here a long time."

"You're right. One other thing: I don't know if you know about this, and I don't want to sound like I'm bragging, but I was part of a group that worked to save the old paper plant. Well, not exactly save that company. It was on its last legs. Dad and I worked with a couple of other guys and invested a little money, and a company that makes polystyrene foam products took over. I'm part owner. I saw it as a chance to keep jobs here. We did a major expansion, and it's doing real well."

"That's great news, Jeff. The last time I saw inside the plant was when I worked the railroad. I'd like to see it sometime."

"Give me a call, and I'll be glad to give you a personal tour. I'm also invested in the local real estate market. A lot of property became available the last twenty years, and I invested in it. I'm also a partner in a couple of housing developments."

Sean said, "This is impressive. You've done well for yourself. You must keep pretty busy."

"Oh, no more than anyone else, I'm sure. Say, have you had time to see the high school? It's grown, too. Your old football coach is still there winning championships. He's a legend around here."

"Yeah, he is. I also saw Lloyd Wiseman. They both seemed concerned about the drugs that the kids are getting into around here."

"Yeah, that meth is bad stuff. Say, how 'bout you, me and Gary playing some golf? The new course is really nice."

As Sean got in his car, he thought about how much Jeff still looked like he did in high school, slender and still preppy in his dress. Even his hair looked the same. However, his aged face betrayed his otherwise youthful appearance. More significant was that something unfamiliar in Jeff's eyes had unsettled Sean. He wasn't sure what it was, but his friend had changed.

Jeff probably could have been class Valedictorian if he had applied himself. He played on the golf team all four years, leading the team to the state tournament in Columbus his senior year. Jeff met several businessmen during those years playing golf with all his dad's friends and acquaintances. Sean recalled Jeff being personable and easy-going, but he could also be a jerk. He liked to kid people, and he loved to flirt with the girls, who liked to hang around him, because he was from a rich family and drove a "hot" car. Jeff's parents' house was on several acres away from town, which Sean and his friends only visited a few times.

Sean's dad had once told him that Jeff's grandfather had made his money as the area's bootlegger during Prohibition and controlled the county's liquor supply. When liquor become legal in Ohio, he opened a red-neck bar off the main highway called "Koot's" and continued his hold on liquor sales in the county.

Jeff's dad, Randall, started working in the bar when he returned from the army in 1945. He was older than the other fathers by ten or twelve years. Randall also had connections to some Indian reservations and would buy tax-exempt cigarettes and liquor and sell them for hefty profits at Koot's. Randall became a County Commissioner, and the law never busted his bar. He used his position to control the county. His involvement with women was another hushed source of discussion. He was powerful, and people didn't want to cross him. He controlled the bookies, gambling, alcohol, drugs, and even the police in Bekbourg County. The county was far enough away from the big cities that it was pretty much left alone.

Joe Sommers figured he best call "the Boss" about the van. When he answered the phone, there was no greeting, because he knew it was Joe's number. "What is this I hear about a missing van, Mr. Sommers?" Being the point man in charge of the operations in Bekbourg, the Boss had his sources and always was informed.

"The van was delivered to the dealership with the supplies. We pulled it out like we always do and put it off to the side. The supplies were delivered, and it was being transferred to a dealer in West Virginia to be incorporated into its stock for resale, but it broke down. The men left it unattended, which was a mistake. It will not happen again, but before they could get back to it, that new cop got to it."

"Can it be traced to the operations?"

"No. The cop thinks it was stolen off our lot, which is fine. I have the computer trail showing it was never supposed to be delivered here, that it was supposed to go to West Virginia. Either way, nothing can be traced to us."

"We cannot afford mistakes or loose ends, Mr. Sommers."

"I agree. Also, I think we should keep our eye on that new deputy, Sean Neumann. I don't think he has any way of learning anything. He's probably just another cop chasing his tail, but I like to keep the bases covered."

"Yes. I agree. We need to keep our options open, Mr. Sommers. If he starts to be a problem, we will not hesitate to eliminate the problem."

Mike had reported back to Sean that the county forensics found traces of meth in the metal shed behind the Todds' house, but there was no evidence of any violent crime there. There wasn't any evidence that could be helpful in finding their killer. Sean visited people who lived near the Todd brothers and any others that might have known them, but even for those who knew or remembered them, they were surprised they were dead. They hadn't noticed not seeing them. None of the people Sean talked to knew, or admitted to knowing, the Todds were making meth. He had not turned up any suspects.

As Sean entered Frau's for dinner, he saw two familiar faces. About the same time, they looked up and saw him and motioned for him to come over. Sean immediately recognized the man sitting with Dusty. Mule Head's short stocky build had thickened some, his face had weathered, and he still had those bushy eyebrows.

Mule Head firmly shook his hand, "Hell's bells! Sean Neumann!"

Dusty said, "Sean, you remember Mule Head here, don't you?"

"Sure I do. How could I forget him?" he grinned.

"Here, sit down, Sean, and join us," Dusty said, motioning to a chair.

Mule Head said, "Well, I'm still stubborn, Sean, so my nickname's still the same."

Sean laughed, "I'm not surprised. If I remember, you two guys used to be at each other's throats all the time. What's happened?"

Mule Head said, "Things change, Sean. We're good friends. We worked together so much over time, we decided to become friends. Even though I'm on disability, we still get together a lot, especially here at Frau's."

The waitress brought their Monday Meatloaf special orders to the table. Sean wasn't that fond of meatloaf, but Frau's was the best he knew of.

Sean said, "I heard that you moved to Bekbourg."

"Yeah, you remember Barbara Stanton? She used to work here when you were on the railroad. I moved in with her. We got married, so now I'm living up here."

"Congratulations. I'm glad you found someone who could put up with you."

They all laughed.

"You got any kids?"

"No, Barbara can't have any kids, but considering all the problems around here, it's probably a good thing." Changing the subject, Mule Head said, "I guess you heard, I got hurt and ended up with a disability."

"Yes, I heard something about it."

"You remember Melvin O'Keefe?"

Sean smiled, "Oh, sure."

Mule Head said, "Well, one night we were setting off and picking up cars at a plant. I don't know if you remember this, but we always had to stop the train outside the city so we didn't block the road crossings.

"Usually, the train was longer, and we had to stop about two miles from the plant. Well that night, we had a short train, so it would fit closer to the factory. Instead of two miles out, we stopped in the section over a mile away between Vine Street and Route 16. It took a long time to switch out our cars that night because we had to wait on the shop foreman to release the cars and unlock the gate.

"By the time we were finished, Melvin must have forgotten where the train was. He never really wanted to talk about it, but he must have been thinking we stopped at the two mile marker instead of one. I was riding on the rear car with a bright flashing red light. We were moving about 30 mph. That was below the speed limit, but it was too fast. As we came around that last curve, I tried to get him on the radio to tell him to slow down and that we were getting close.

"It was very dark in that section of the track at 3:30 in the morning. When I realized he had lost track of where the train was, I knew we were going to have a collision. About two-hundred feet from the boxcar, I had to bail off or get killed. I've gotten off at pretty fast speeds, but this was the fastest I had ever tried. I lost my balance and went rolling in the ditch and hit a concrete signal block. I thought I had broken my back. I was afraid I wouldn't walk again, but after a while, I was able to get up. My arm was really hurting.

"It was a mess. I had five broken ribs, broken arm, a shattered shoulder, and a sprained ankle, which I thought was broken at the time. I also had a big bump on my head, but it's hard, so that was okay.

"But at least I was alive. Unfortunately, the train didn't fare so well. The six cars we picked up buckled and rolled over into the ditch and jumped on top of each other. Lucky I wasn't crushed. But the train itself had a load of some fragile cargo, electronics and furniture. The damage to that cargo was pretty severe. Melvin, himself, was banged up pretty bad: had a concussion and a couple of broken ribs. It was really something, but we survived.

"They cleaned it up. They took me to the hospital. In those days, they patched me up best they could, but my shoulder was a complete mess. Told me I would probably never work again. I was awarded a full disability and a settlement from the company for my injury, which set me up pretty good."

Sean had been listening with interest. Storytelling was second-nature to railroaders. "That's quite a story. How is your shoulder now?"

"It's pretty good. I heard there is an operation where they can replace a shoulder. It hurts all the time, and arthritis is setting in. They're doin' the surgery at Ohio State. I might look at it. Barbara told me about the surgery. She's a good woman. She quit Frau's and went to college. She got her nursing degree. That's how I got to know her, when I was in the hospital recovering."

"You've been through a lot, Mule Head. What are you doing now?" Mule Head had mellowed with age.

"Well, I make a few bucks up at the car dealership."

"What do you do there?"

"Mostly, I move cars around. When the cars come in, I don't take the cars off the truck. They have someone that does that. But once they're moved off the truck, I take the cars in and put them in the storage lot, and if they have problems, I put them in the defect lot. I also take cars out of the service bays when they're finished, and put them in the customer lots, so they can pick them up. That's mostly what I do. I have taken some to Chillicothe and Columbus."

"Well, Mule Head, I'm glad you seem to be getting along pretty good."

Mule Head, Dusty and Sean talked a few minutes more. Sean enjoyed hearing their stories. It reminded him of his grandpa and some of his tales.

Parents of Jamie Hayes, Hugh and Pat Hayes, had gone to Columbus for the day to visit some friends. When they returned home, they found their son and two friends, Jared Fellows and Ronny Mueller, unconscious. Sean handled the scene, but before he arrived at the hospital, he received a call that one of the boys, Ronny Mueller, had died.

The three boys' parents were in the hospital's waiting area along with a hospital chaplain. Because of the sorrow and pain among the adults, Sean's arrival went unnoticed. He gently pulled Hugh Hayes aside but got little from him other than the boys were close friends as were the parents.

Since the parents were in no shape to talk to him, he located the doctor. She told Sean that she suspected the drug, Methamphetamine, in the overdose. All three boys had high levels of alcohol in their systems, which made for a bad combination. She thought the Mueller boy had some type of undetected heart condition. Jamie and Jared were in stable condition.

When he could, Sean talked to the boys, but he couldn't get them to tell who got the drugs—much less where the drugs came from. They told Sean that it was the first time they had tried something like this. They had smoked a little pot and thought they would experiment with something different. They had no idea it could be as bad as it was.

Sean visited with Lloyd Wiseman, the high school principal, but he didn't have any information that helped in the investigation. "These were good kids, Sean. All three were good baseball players and popular. Ronny was the class vice president. I guess you know his dad owns his own architectural firm here in town and designed many of the renovations of the downtown buildings. He's also on our tourism board. This is such a tragedy."

"I ain't raised you and the other boys to do stupid things." Zeke Pinkston's irate voice boomed through the phone line. "What are you thinkin'? Is it that son of yours who sold them kids the dope?" Tony didn't have a chance to answer. "I'll tell you one damn thing. If he were my boy, he wouldn't be doin' somethin' stupid like that. I hear every cop around is sniffin' around Bekbourg. What is goin' on there?"

"Pappy, no one can track nothin' to us. I talked to Aaron. No one will tell his name. He'll make sure of that. You taught us well. No one will rat on us. They know better. We'd know if the cops know about us. They don't. We've got it all covered."

Zeke had taught Tony well, but he still didn't like not knowing more.

Tony continued, "This might work to help us. We'll keep our ears to the ground. We might be able to learn about the other drug business with so much goin' on. We're goin' to talk to that deputy. It might be time to do somethin' about the Sheriff."

"Yep, I think it's time to find out about the other business interest. Then, you can see if they're willin' to split up the territory. Just watch yourselves, Tony. I don't trust no one there."

The older model pickup truck sat idling off the side of the deserted road. A shotgun lay across the driver's lap. Ben pulled up beside the truck and glared at Tony Pinkston. "I warned you you were gettin' sloppy. That son of yours has shit for brains. Those kids that overdosed are from important families. It's a shitstorm."

"I talked to my boy. He won't be sellin' around the high school."

"What good does that do?"

"I'm beginnin' to think I made a mistake with you, Ben. I never took you for a coward, but I'm beginnin' to wonder."

"Look, Pinkston. I thought you were smart, but I'm beginnin' to think you might just be dumber than dirt. You should be worried about attractin' the attention of the feds. Gettin' people around here riled up is sure goin' to do that."

As Tony put his truck in gear, he warned Ben, "You just keep your nose where it belongs. I know what I'm doin'."

As he pulled away, Ben thought, *"No, asshole, you don't."*

As it so happened, Sean and his dad both had the same day off, so he suggested that Jim meet him for lunch at the GilHaus.

"This is a treat, Son. I take your mom here occasionally, but I rarely get here otherwise."

"Well, when Mom said you had the day off and she was getting her hair done, I thought it'd be something to do. How's the milk plant doing?"

During high school, Jim worked as a laborer loading box cars on the loading dock of the Bekbourg Springs Milk Company. After his return from the Marines, he rejoined the milk company and worked his way up to be the plant manager.

"Well, about the same: still running the one shift. I wouldn't be surprised if it closes sometime soon. When it does, I'm going to retire."

At the far end of the restaurant, there was a stairway that led up to the second floor, where private rooms hosted larger groups and special events. Sean looked around when he saw some men coming down the stairs. Two of the men were Jeff and Jeff's dad, Randall. Jim saw them about the same time as Sean. "There's Randall Thompson. We don't see him in Bekbourg very often."

About that time, Jeff saw Sean and Jim. He touched his dad's elbow, and they both walked over to the table. Sean and Jim stood and greeted them.

Sean said, "Mr. Thompson, it's been a long time since I saw you."

"Call me 'Randall.' Yes. I remember Jeff telling me you had joined the Marines. I guess you heard, Margaret and I moved to Florida. I get here occasionally to catch up on things. I've got an ownership interest in the planned community near the lake, and we were having a meeting about that."

Jeff said, "Jim, it's good to see you again. I know you must be glad that Sean is back."

"Yes, I am."

"Well," said Randall, "we better head on. It's good to see you both."

Sean and his dad sat down. After there were out of earshot, Jim said, "That was interesting. I guess Randall still gets up here. I probably shouldn't be surprised though, because it would make sense that he still has some business interests around here."

Sean agreed, "Yeah, I guess it does. What do you know about the four men they were with?"

Jim said, "Well, I've never met Harvey Bennett. All I really know about him is that he's that developer for that golf course and upscale homes up toward the lake area. Charles Martin is the bank president. I've met him a couple of times. The other two, Tyler Forquet and Nickolas Garrison, they're politicians. Forquet is the County

Prosecutor, and Garrison is a County Commissioner. Forquet was hand-picked by your friend Jeff to replace him in the prosecutor's office. Randall, as I recall, tapped Garrison to run for a commissioner's seat that was vacant when he was still on the Commission."

"What do you think of them?"

"Well, Bekbourg is pretty much a one-party county, so these guys both ran unopposed. I don't know if they would have won if they had competition in the race. I guess I don't have a real opinion one way or the other. But, what I can tell you is that the group of men, along with Jeff and your other friend, Gary, along with a couple of others, control the town. They make most of the decisions around the county. The Mayor here is basically Jeff's puppet best I can tell. Jeff has been influential for a long time around here, ever since he became prosecutor. He's the one who brought Harvey Bennett into town to start that development. The other commissioners pretty much rubber stamp whatever he wants. Folks around here refer to the group as 'The Committee' even though it's not really a formal committee. Within the group, from what I can tell, Jeff is the ringleader.

"I know one thing. With those three kids overdosing and Mueller's boy dying, the citizens here are fed up with no one doing anything about the drug problem. The Commissioners and Sheriff are sitting on their asses, but we're getting together a meeting, and if they want to come, fine, but we're not waiting on them any longer."

"I've heard some scuttlebutt about a meeting. What's happening?"

"Sean, I don't want to get you cross-ways with Mike, but after that happened to those kids, I went up to the high school and talked to Lloyd and Coach Jackson about getting some attention focused on this mess. They agreed, and Lloyd and I went to see Jeff and the other two county commissioners, who I don't have much use for. We wanted them to hold a town hall about the drug problems, to hear from the citizens and hear what the Commissioners and the Sheriff are planning to do. Those jerks blew us off. Said the problem was complex and it was premature to have the meeting. So, we went to Dusty Shaw who works with the addicts down at the church. We also talked to the woman who runs the B&B, Bri Sanderson, and her husband, Max, as well as Dusty's girlfriend, Carla, who works with kids. Anyway, with their help, we've arranged to have a town hall meeting. Bri and Max paid to run announcements in the *Bekbourg Tribune* and to print posters that businesses could put up around town about the meeting. I'm going to be interested to see if those jackass Commissioners show up."

"Dad, don't worry about causing any problems for me. I think this meeting is a good idea. Do you know if Mike is going?"

"I don't know, but I wish he would."

Chapter 22

Boze returned Sean's call. "Sean, I just got back in the country. What's the story on this van?"

Russ Bozeman, Boze as they called him, was one mean-looking man. He was of Italian heritage and was a legend. Before joining the DEA, he served four years in the Marines and then as a vice officer in New York City. He knew his stuff, and Sean trusted Boze's experience and instincts. The first time he was shot, he was somewhere in Mexico—a shoulder wound. More serious was the second time when he was shot three times. His team was in a remote area in Columbia when a gun battle ensued. Had it not been for one of the agents having medical training, Boze wouldn't have made it.

Sean told him about the pervasive meth problem, but how nothing seemed to have been done to address it in Bekbourg. "Boze, I don't know why, but the powers-that-be here don't seem to have any urgency. I'm beginning to wonder if something might be going on."

"Do you think the sheriff is in on it?"

"I don't know, Boze. I sure hope not, because he was my best childhood friend. He hired me knowing I had been in the special criminal unit. If he had something to hide, I don't think he would have hired me, but I don't know why he's not done more. What can you tell me about drugs in this area?"

"Sean, there's some things we should discuss. I can be in Cincinnati tomorrow. Would you be available to meet me?"

The next day, Sean learned from Boze that Bekbourg was suspected of being a hotbed for a cartel's national distribution operation. The problem was the DEA wasn't sure the scope of the operation or how the drugs were transported. The DEA needed someone undercover to investigate, and with Sean being a deputy and a hometown hero, they thought he was the perfect person to assist them in discovering the source of the drugs.

"Sean, if you're willing to help, I would be your primary contact: 24/7. We are laser focused on this operation. The FBI is tracing the money. We're talking about millions, and they have good reason to think some of it is being laundered and funneled into the Middle East to fund terrorist groups. The drug cartels in recent years have partnered with the terrorists, and we have seen a big uptick of money flowing there. It seems that there are four or five drug operations across the U.S. that are part of this organization, and Bekbourg, Ohio, is one of them."

Sean said he would work with them, but he had been looking for possible drug sources and had not found anything that looked suspicious.

Sean was surprised to learn that an informant from Bekbourg occasionally passed on information. They didn't know his name, and to protect Sean, the DEA was not planning to tell the informant about Sean's cooperation. The informant had heard rumors of suspicious activities at the large car dealership, something about vans being brought in but not sold and then disappearing. The DEA wasn't sure if this was a helpful lead—given how vague it was. The mention by the informant of a private airstrip was more titillating.

"Sean, the informant told us someone casually recounted to him hearing planes flying over at odd hours of the night. Apparently, it doesn't happen on a regular basis—but enough to catch someone's attention. It's a rural air strip. That's not surprising, since these exist all over. Private planes are flown in and out for a variety of reasons. They're for small planes, because this activity hasn't come under scrutiny from the FAA or other authorities, which are hypersensitive since 9/11. We don't know whether this information means anything, but it's worth checking out."

Boze also confirmed that traces of meth as well as microscopic evidence of cocaine had been found in the new cargo van that had been towed. They determined the manufacturer's origin, and paperwork indicated that the van had been delivered to the central distribution lot owned by a company called Atvale Depot Company where it was waiting to be transported to a dealership. The van was supposed to go to a dealership in southern West Virginia, but it got diverted. Boze told Sean that the manager at Atvale told an agent that they didn't know about the particular van, but every so often, a vehicle gets delivered somewhere else. This van simply vanished from their lot.

Chapter 23

The church's sanctuary was filled with people who wanted to participate in the discussion about the drug problem in Bekbourg. Seated at the front table were Lloyd Wiseman, Coach Clyde Jackson, Doc Emerson, Dusty Shaw, Carla Huber and Bri Sanderson. Lloyd was the moderator and had brought in a specialist from the state to speak about what the educational system was doing to fight the drug problem and how they had teamed up with law enforcement and other state agencies. Doc Emerson spoke about the physical effects of drugs, such as meth and cocaine, and Dusty and Bri talked about available addiction programs.

After the presentations, Lloyd opened the meeting to questions from the audience. After a few questions directed to the panelists, one woman stood and asked, "Why isn't the Sheriff here? Seems we need our local law enforcement to participate. I think the Sheriff needs to do more to find where these drugs are coming from."

Discontent started to swirl among those in attendance.

A man stood, "I think that's part of the problem here. I don't see any law enforcement or any County Commissioners. They don't care enough to even show up."

Rumblings in agreement from the audience grew louder. "Our kids are important to us. We need our leaders to care," voiced another woman.

Jim Neumann spoke up, "Folks, it seems to me that we need some new leadership here. This one-party county isn't working. We need people to run for office and not let the same old group decide who our elected officials are."

One man yelled, "Yeah, Lloyd, why don't you or some of your panelists run? They care, and they would do a lot better job than those yahoos."

Lloyd finally refocused the topics to the panelists. He urged people to contact the Commissioners and advocate for a formal town hall where they would attend.

The next day, the *Bekbourg Tribune* ran a front-page article summarizing the meeting and the vocal unrest. Particularly noted was the sentiment that the one-party system needed to go and that the Commissioners and the Sheriff weren't doing their jobs in combating the drug problems around Bekbourg.

After hearing about the town meeting, Jeff realized he had miscalculated the mood of the citizens. The town's leaders needed to get out front on the situation. Even Mary, his wife, had expressed concern. He was alarmed that she was considering sending Rachel to boarding school. That would not reflect positively on him in the community. There had been a few articles run in the *Bekbourg Tribune* in recent years and a splattering of calls and letters from the residents, but ever since those three boys had overdosed, residents had ramped up their contacts to his office as well as to the other two Commissioners. They needed an action plan that would quell the discord among the voters.

He reached out to Mike, "I've been thinking that we need to work up a plan that the Commission can show the people here that we're working on this drug problem. I want to talk to the *Tribune* so they can run something that gets the word out."

Mike was skeptical of Jeff's sincerity, but hoped that maybe the town's leaders would finally take the initiative to clamp down on the area's drug problem. "Jeff, I'm glad to hear this. It's something I've mentioned to you before."

"Well, why don't you find out what's available from the state for funding—something that we can do? I'll talk to some folks I know in Columbus and see what other towns are doing."

"Okay. What's your timing on this?"

"I'd like the *Tribune* to run my interview in a week or so."

"Señor Esteban was not happy with what was in your local newspaper. He is unhappy with you, Señor. You are not attending to matters as you should. I told you this Pinkston problem was getting out of hand. It has attracted too much attention. You are getting soft or careless, maybe both, and that is not acceptable. He is questioning whether you're up to the task."

The last sentence particularly rankled the second man, because he didn't appreciate being treated like an empty-headed errand boy. But, as always in dealing with the man on the phone, he kept his cool. After all, playing with the devil dictated one pursue a wise course of action. He was the Bekbourg partner and, in his way of thinking, success would not have been achieved without his efforts. On the other hand, he had to remain cognizant that everyone, except Señor Esteban, was dispensable in this organization.

"You can assure Señor Esteban that I have things under control here. It was a one-time thing. The people got things off their chest. They'll go back to work and do whatever keeps them busy. I know the people here. It's not something to be concerned about."

"That is not the way Señor Esteban sees things." His patience was running thin, "Our policy to not sell our products around Bekbourg was for that very reason: we don't want the State or Feds sniffing around here. I have raised with you the concern about drugs in the school and around the area. Time is now up. You say there is not going to be a problem. We know there's not going to be a problem, because you are going to fix it. What are your plans that I can relay to Señor Esteban?"

He had been thinking about how to deal with the Pinkstons, "I know where their labs are. We are going to burn them down. That way our local police and fire can handle everything. This will put them out of business, and there will be no need for the State or Feds to get involved. We can then assure everyone that the drug problem is gone from the area."

There was silence. He waited, hoping he had appeased the "Boss." Finally, "I will pass on your plan to Señor Esteban."

After the call ended, he wiped the sweat from his brow and poured a drink, thinking, *"What a mess."*

The *Tribune* ran a front-page interview with Commissioner Jeff Thompson. He assured people that the County Commission was working on the drug problem that had been plaguing their county for some time. He reassured the people that Sheriff Adams was also working with state officials on various funding opportunities to combat the problem. "I've talked to the principal at the high school, and we're going to put together a joint task force with the schools around here. This is going to be a full community effort that includes law enforcement, our educators and local and state experts on drug addiction programs. I want our great citizens of Bekbourg to know that this is a top priority for us, and we're going to announce the details of our comprehensive plan soon."

Chapter 24

It was near the end of his night shift when Sean returned to the precinct. He poured a cup of coffee and was preparing to start his paperwork when the dispatcher came out and said, "Sean, around 2:45 a.m., Mr. McClain called. He lives up in Possum Gap. He said his wife woke him up claiming she heard gun shots. He said he thought she was just hearing things, but she was pestering him, so to get her off his back so he could get some sleep, he called it in. Well, you had gone to check out the call at the Shopper's Pavilion, and Alex had gone to Knucklepin's to calm things down there, so I didn't call either of you. It didn't seem urgent. Mr. McClain said he didn't hear anything, and he didn't really think his wife heard anything. Well, he just called back. He's tried to tell her that people aren't out shooting guns in the middle of the night, but she's driving him crazy. She won't let it go. He said he's not been able to sleep since he called us the first time. She's fretting and walking around the house, driving him crazy."

Sean got the address and told Alex and the dispatcher he'd drive there and check things out. Sean hadn't been on the road more than twenty minutes when the dispatcher called and said, "Sean, I've just got another call about a shooting in

Possum Gap. You're probably almost there. It seems Mrs. McClain may have been right." He gave Sean the address. "Sean, the woman who called this in is hysterical. She said, 'They're all dead.' I'm sending back-up. It sounds like you'll need it."

Since Sean was in the vicinity, it didn't take him long to arrive at the address. The early light from the sun signaled that another day was approaching. As he drove up, he saw a woman sitting at the side of the road with a baby in her arms. Sean looked around, and scanning the surroundings, he walked over to her. She was distraught, and the baby was wailing. She had on a medium-blue uniform smock with jeans and dirty white tennis shoes. Two Dobermans were chained near the house on steel cables connected to two clothesline poles. The dogs were racing back and forth between the poles growling and barking non-stop. Sean hoped they didn't break loose.

Still keeping his eyes roaming the territory, he knelt down beside her. She didn't seem to notice that he was there.

"Ma'am, I'm Deputy Neumann. Can you give me your name?"

She was young. She was rocking back and forth, holding the baby. He could barely understand her between her sobs and the baby's crying, but finally got that her name was Suzy Pinkston.

"Do you know if there is anyone here or in the house?"

Suzy shook her head "no." She started moaning and rocking back and forth even harder.

"Ma'am, I need for you to calm down. I'm here to help, but I need for you to tell me what's happened here."

Suzy looked at Sean, her eyes red and dazed. Her hysteria began to wane, but quiet sobbing continued, "They're all dead. Oh, my God, they're all dead."

"Who's dead?"

"My mom and dad and Aaron," she answered—pointing toward the house, "Up there."

"Can you tell me why you and the baby are sitting here by the road?" Sean didn't know whether she was involved, and before he left her unattended, he wanted to hear what she had to say.

"I work at the hospital at night on the cleaning crew. We finished early, so I came home. That's when I found them." Mewling sounds were mixed with the sobs. "I grabbed Tootsie and ran out. Oh, God, oh, God, oh, God," she continued— her crying growing louder.

"I'm going to go have a look. You stay here. I'll be back, and we'll get you some help."

Suzy nodded, and Sean stood. He looked toward the house, and with caution, started walking up the drive. Straining against their chains, the dogs were snarling and lathered with drool. He spotted a body lying in the front yard with a gun lying close by. Sean approached and saw that the dead man had been shot. Sean had already noticed that the front door was standing open. He saw a second body lying on the porch with a rifle lying nearby. The second victim was also deceased.

Sean yelled into the house, but there was no response. With his gun at the ready, he walked in. He noticed the stale smell of cigarette smoke. The living room was cluttered with furniture. There was a large plasma TV in the corner next to the fireplace. The drapes were pulled closed, but the overhead light was on.

Off to the other side of the living room was the kitchen and dining area. Straight ahead was a hall. The first door opened to a bedroom that belonged to a male and had a strong stale cigarette smoke presence. The bed was unmade and clothes were piled on the floor. A female's bedroom was next. Next was a bathroom. At the end of the hall was a door. A light shone from within. A woman was laying half off the bed with a phone on the floor. He saw an empty crib off to the side of the room.

Sean left the house and headed back to Suzy and the baby. Although still crying, Suzy was more subdued and trying to soothe the baby.

Sean had seen a small, older model car parked in the driveway that he figured was what she had driven, "Ma'am, is there anything in the car for the baby?"

She looked at him, confused.

"The baby might need a bottle or something. Do you have a diaper bag or something in the car?"

She nodded, and Sean asked, "Are you okay if I get if for you?" She nodded again, and Sean went to the car and brought back the diaper bag. He set it down beside her. "Here you go, ma'am. Do you want me to hold the baby while you get out what you need?"

She looked at him and then hesitantly handed the baby to him. She opened the diaper bag and started fixing a bottle from some formula. Sean had searched the diaper bag when he retrieved it to make sure there was no weapon in it. Off in a distance, Sean heard the wailings of the emergency and police vehicles. The EMTs arrived first—followed by Darrell Logan, the first deputy to arrive.

Sean said to Darrell, "I'm going to try and reach Mike. He is out of town."

Sean called Mike's number but got no answer. He then told Darrell, "We need to get some action here. I can't reach Mike. We need the state police on this. The sooner they get here, the better."

"Yeah, that makes sense."

Sean called the state police and also requested their forensics team and coroner. Sean then called the dispatch and described the situation and wanted to make sure more cars were being sent. He also requested that they send someone to pick up the dogs. Barking and whining were coming from the dogs, but fortunately, not as loud and aggressive as when he first arrived.

Sean told Darrell that they needed to keep Suzy there for more questioning, but they needed to get some help with the baby. Sean walked back over to Suzy, who was feeding the baby. Suzy had quieted to sniffling. Sean knelt down beside her. "Ma'am, I've got a deputy here who can go pick up someone to come help with the baby. Is there someone we can call?"

"Yeah, my Ma Maw. Her name is Rose, Rose Waters. She lives down in Bekbourg." She gave Sean the phone number and address, and Sean asked Darrell to call Rose and pick her up.

As Darrell was driving away, Sean heard a second deputy car arrive. Ben Clark got out. Sean thought to himself, "*Just what I need.*"

Sean stepped away from Suzy. Ben came up to Sean. Right then, Wade Frisch and Alex Ogle pulled up. As they were walking toward Sean and Ben, Ben said, "What are you doing here Neumann? I thought you worked night shift?"

Wade and Alex had joined them. Sean ignored Ben as he typically did and spoke to the three deputies. He explained what he had found. Ben said, "I'm going to have a look."

Sean said, "I don't think that's a good idea. We don't want to contaminate the scene. The tech guys are on their way."

"Screw you. I know what I'm doing. Come on, Alex. Let's check it out for ourselves in case Mr. Football Stud missed something."

Alex looked at Sean like he didn't know what he was supposed to do. He finally turned and followed Ben. As Ben got closer, the dogs went wild barking and growling and trying to get to Ben. Alex commented, "Those dogs don't like you."

Ben mumbled, "I don't like dogs either."

Two State troopers' vehicles soon pulled up. They walked to where Sean and Wade were standing. Sean explained the scene. The older of the troopers, Harold Greene, said, "We need to secure the area." He turned to Wade and instructed him to set up road blocks to keep cars from driving by until they had a better handle on things. About that time, he saw Ben and Alex walking back down from the house.

Surprised, he asked, "What are those two guys doing up there?"

Sean shrugged his shoulders, and Wade was glad to be off to direct any traffic.

Ben saw the troopers and veered off trying to avoid them. Harold told the other trooper, "Go over there and get those two jackasses' names and find out what they were doing up there. Be sure and find out if they touched anything."

Harold happened to be nearby on his way to Columbus when the call came in, which was a good thing in Sean's mind since he commanded state police investigations for southeast Ohio. Sean was relieved that Suzy was calm enough to be coherent so he and Harold could question her. She told them her parents, Tony and Ruby Pinkston, lived in the house with her brother, Aaron. She lived here with her baby, Tootsie. When she arrived, the dogs were agitated. She went up on the porch to walk in, and that's when she saw her brother lying on the porch.

She panicked, thinking about her baby, and rushed into the house. She heard Tootsie squalling and turned on the light in the living room. Then she went back to the bedroom where Tootsie slept in the same room as her parents. The nightstand lamp was already on, and she saw her mother lying on the bed with blood all over her. She grabbed her baby out of the crib and ran outside, and that's when she saw her dad lying in the front yard. She found her cell phone and called the police. Sean made a note to call the supervisor to verify that she had been at work, but he didn't have any reason to question Suzy's alibi.

Sean told her that she would need to stay at the scene, because others would want to talk to her, but that when Rose got there, Darrell would drive Rose and the baby back to Rose's house. Sean helped Suzy into the back of his cruiser where she and the baby would be more comfortable and out of the early morning sun.

Harold had walked away to talk with the troopers who had arrived. About that time, Mack Harris, the assistant to Mike, arrived and walked up to Sean. Before Sean could update him, Ben walked up, and Sean could tell he was angry. Ben demanded, "Neumann, what did you say to that State man? He crawled all over me."

Sean responded, "I didn't tell him anything. I didn't have to. I told you it wasn't a good idea to walk up there. You know not to do something that could contaminate the scene."

Alex had walked up to overhear Sean.

Ben snarled, "Neumann, you better stay out of my way." He turned to Mack, "I'm going back to the station and see if I can help Kim get in touch with Mike." Looking at Sean, he said, "I'm glad you're here, Mack. We need someone who knows what they're doing." Turning toward Mack, "I'll be back after a while."

"Sean, I wish I had listened to you. That trooper ripped us a good one," Alex said.

"Alex, you're new. Still, the academy surely taught you better than that. Make sure you learn from this. Ben knows better. Trooper Greene wanted Wade to set up the road blocks. He needs some help."

Alex was glad to get out of the way. "I'll go help him."

Mack had been standing there listening. "That's just like Ben."

A short while later, Darrell came walking up with an elderly woman. He introduced Suzy's grandmother, Rose Waters. Sean took her over to the car where Suzy was sitting, still holding the baby. Suzy got out of the car and went to Rose. Rose put her arms around Suzy and the baby, who was now sleeping. Both Rose and Suzy were crying. Sean explained that Suzy had to stay for a while. Suzy tenderly handed Tootsie to Rose. Sean picked up the diaper bag out of the back seat and handed it to Darrell. He told Darrell to take Rose and Tootsie back to Rose's house. "If she needs something from the grocery store for the baby, stop on the way and pick it up." Sean handed Darrell a twenty-dollar bill.

The State forensics team and coroner were well into their work. Sean was standing close to his car where Suzy was still sitting. He had offered to have food delivered to her, but she didn't want anything. He had given her a bottle of water from a cooler he kept in the back of his patrol car.

Shortly after ten o'clock, a woman drove up to the road block and wanted to know what had happened. Alex, who was manning the road block, told her that there had been some trouble at the Pinkston home and that no one could get through. Darlene Hicks told him that she was a close friend of the family. Alex didn't want to do something again that he shouldn't do, so he asked her to wait in her car and he would check. Alex walked up to Sean and told him that a Darlene Hicks was in the car and that she said she was a close family friend. Suzy jumped out of the car and pleaded, "Please let her up here. She's like family." Sean told Alex to go ahead and bring her up.

Darlene was about ten years older than Suzy. She ran up to Suzy, "My God, what's happened here?" asked Darlene as Suzy ran into her arms.

Suzy cried, "It's so awful. Mom and Dad and Aaron are all dead."

"Oh, my God! What happened?"

"They were shot."

Darlene asked, "Oh, God! Oh, God! Do they know who did it?"

Suzy shook her head. "No."

"Have you seen Victor?"

Suzy said, "No, I haven't seen him or Ray."

Sean had been listening. He questioned, "Who are you talking about?"

"Victor, my boyfriend. He and Ray live right down there," Darlene said pointing at the woods behind the house.

Sean asked, "Who are they?"

151

"Ray is Tony's brother, the man who lives here. Victor is their cousin."

"Do they live together?"

"Yeah, they pulled a mobile home onto the lower end of Tony's property and are fixing it up. It's right down the road here. There is a gravel road on the right. It's hard to see. It's the old Shailer Road that farmers around here used a long time ago to get to their fields, but I don't think anyone uses it anymore other than Ray and Victor. You can also get to their place by crossing that hollar from Tony's place here," she said pointing toward the woods. "That's how they usually get here; they walk across the hollar."

Alex was still standing close, waiting to hear what Sean wanted him to do. Sean did not have a good feeling about things. Looking intently at Darlene, Sean said, "We didn't know about this place. Alex will stay here with you. We need to go check it out."

Sean went over to Harold and repeated what Darlene had relayed and asked if a couple of the troopers could go with him to check out the other place. Sean and the three troopers got in a police van and slowly drove down the road. They almost missed the turn. It was overgrown and didn't look like it was used much. If there ever was a street sign, it had been removed. They went down a hill and round a curve. They then saw a driveway with a mobile home sitting up on the hill. A pile of beer cans and a couple of big oil drums were off to the side. Two older model pickup trucks were sitting near the mobile home.

Sean said, "I guess we have to go up the hill. Let's park here."

All four officers pulled their guns. When they got out of the van, they stood, looking all around them. It was quiet, real quiet. Sean yelled, "Hello! Ray, Victor! Police! We need to talk to you!" No response came. Sean tried again. "Ray! Victor! There's a problem at Tony's place. We need to talk to you."

"This doesn't look good." Sean said to the driver, "Sound the siren for a few seconds." They waited, and nothing happened. When no answer came, one of the officers volunteered to stay back. The other three cautiously started up the drive. They saw that the front door was open. As they approached, Sean called out, "Ray, Victor, we're here to talk to you." They then saw two bodies. Sean said, "We need to call the lab guys. We've got another crime scene."

Cheryl Seton was a reporter for *The Cleveland Presenter*, a small but high-quality evening newspaper in Cleveland, Ohio. She loved working for *The Presenter*, which had a loyal following because of its heavy-duty investigative reporting that had garnered many awards. She interned for *The Presenter* between her junior and senior years of college, and Keith Jamison, her editor, hired her after graduation.

Keith, a nationally respected newspaper editor, was one of the hardest working people Cheryl had ever known. He was hard-nosed and gruff and demanded quality reporting from those on his staff. During his younger years, Keith had covered assignments in Vietnam during the war and covered tumultuous stories in the U.S., like the Kent State shootings and violent anti-war protests.

Keith had seen in Cheryl early on a reporter's instinct and an uncanny ability to reach beyond the surface and peel back the onion to expose angles that the average reporter might miss. She was a dedicated, hard-charging reporter who had written several noteworthy stories over her years of reporting and had a loyal following from the newspaper's readers.

Cheryl was in the process of putting the finishing touches on a story when something crossing the news wires caught her attention. A family of five had been brutally murdered in Bekbourg, Ohio. Little information was yet available about the murders, but mention was made of an alleged drug operation on their property. Cheryl all but ran to her editor's office, dashing into Keith's office with barely a knock on his open door. "Keith! A story broke in Bekbourg. I can be on the road in an hour."

Keith was sitting in his well-worn leather chair, with a cigarette hanging out of his mouth, and one smoking in an ash tray overflowing with butts. A large coffee mug—most assuredly not washed in the foreseeable past—was almost empty. Piles of disheveled papers were strewn on his desk and across a long table. A path around files stacked on the floor had to be carefully navigated. Fortunately, a chair in front of his desk was void of papers and files—allowing Cheryl a place to sit.

"Whoa. What's this all about? What's happened in Bekbourg, Ohio, and why would we be interested in a story there?"

"It just hit the wires. Five family members were murdered, and there's a rumored drug angle."

His keen eyes were sharply trained on Cheryl, and his reporter's intuition hit overdrive. "What makes this a story for our newspaper?"

"Drug use has been growing throughout Ohio and even the rest of the U.S. These murders have to be related to a drug operation. The local authorities haven't said that yet, but it has to be the case. This story could be a chance of a lifetime. We could look at the drug problem from not only the destructive forces it unleashes on people, but the drug operations themselves, and the culture that promotes it in a place like the Appalachian region of Ohio."

Keith looked hard at Cheryl. "Mmm. I can see the possibilities."

Before he could finish his thoughts, Cheryl was jumping up out of her chair.

"Hold on! Sit down!"

Cheryl sat on the edge of her seat, ready to bolt as soon as he finished.

"This is not a blank check, okay? Go down there and see what you can find out. Once we know more, I'll decide the next step, but you need to be careful there. It's not like Cleveland. That's a rural area, and they don't take kindly to strangers—especially newspaper reporters. I want you to report in to me every day if you don't send us an article to run. You have to promise me that you won't take any chances. If something doesn't feel right, get out. Now, do I have your commitment to these terms?"

Cheryl wrapped up the story she had been working on. She grabbed what she needed, stopped by her apartment and was on the road to Bekbourg.

When Harold saw Sean walking toward him, Harold said, "I've heard. You want to talk to the Forensics or do you want me to? We need to get them over there."

"I'll go talk to them. What's her name?" Sean asked, pointing to the woman he had been earlier told was head of the forensics team.

"Ronnie Vin," answered Harold. "She knows her stuff."

Sean walked up to the middle-aged woman with short dark hair. She was a petite woman who was talking to a couple of her team members. They saw Sean approaching, and he heard one tell her, "We'll check around the lab again," and they walked away.

She turned to face Sean. "Ms. Vin, I'm Sean Neumann. We've got another crime scene down the road. We think it may be part of this, because the two men that we found there are related to these people. One's a brother and the other a cousin of Tony Pinkston."

"Please call me Ronnie. What's the scene there?"

Sean explained what he had seen. "I understand that there is a path back there that leads to the second scene, but it'd probably be easier to take a vehicle. It's right down the road about a half a mile. The place to turn off the main road is hard to spot. One of Harold's men is standing at the turn."

"Okay, I'll send some techs there. One thing, the two techs I was talking to when you came up were telling me that there was a trip wire at the meth lab up behind the house. Since the older man was in the front yard, it could be that the trip wire had alerted him that someone was around the lab, or the dogs started barking."

"Interesting."

Ronnie said, "I thought so. We're going to see where the alarm is stationed. I'll keep you posted."

Sean walked over to Harold and told him about the trip wire. He also suggested that the path across the hollow be blocked off until Ronnie's people could check it out.

Sean and Harold drove over to the McClain's house. They were sitting on the front porch. An old dog was lying there beside them. It raised its head, and its tail lifted a little, and then it laid its head back down.

"Mr. and Mrs. McClain, I'm Deputy Neumann, and this is trooper Greene with the state police. We'd like to talk to you."

They were an older couple. He was sitting in a straight back chair smoking a cigarette and she in a rocking chair. Both had gray hair and deep wrinkles. Mrs. McCain wore a floral duster, and Mr. McClain had on an older pair of jeans and a flannel shirt.

"Come on up here and have a seat. We've been expecting someone to show up—given how I called last night."

"Mr. and Mrs. McClain, can you tell us what you heard last night?" Sean asked after sitting down.

"Well, I'm gonna let her tell you—seein' she's the one who heard the shots."

Mrs. McClain said, "I wake up a lot of times at night, and sometimes, I have a hard time goin' back to sleep. Last night, I woke up 'bout 2:00 and went to the bathroom and came back to bed. I was layin' there listenin' to his snorin', and I swear I heard some shootin'. I looked at the clock, and it was twenty after two. It wasn't just one shot, there was several. I don't know how many, I just know'd there was a lot. I started pushin' on him to wake him up, and I told him what I heard. He didn't believe me, but I know'd what I heard. I kept tellin' him we had to call the police.

"Finally, he did, but I heard what he said. I told him afterwards, that he didn't sound too convincin', that I should have talked on the phone. There was no way I could go back to sleep. I kept waitin' for the police to call or show up, but no one did. I told him he needed to call back. He finally listened and called back. After a while, we started hearin' all those sirens. I told him, 'See, I told you. I know'd there was gun shots.'

"Well, after a while, a neighbor 'round here called and asked if we know'd what happened. We didn't know just what, and I told her that. She told me that somethin' happened up at the Pinkston place. Some people had been shot."

Mr. McClain spoke with the cigarette hanging from the side of his mouth, "That's 'bout it."

Sean asked, "Was it just the one round of gun shots or were there more?"

"Nope, just that one time. I didn't hear a second round of shootin'."

Sean and Harold figured that she only heard shooting from where Ray and Victor had been found, because that was closer to where the McClains lived.

Milton Grant was an institution at the newspaper and around Cleveland for that matter with his extensive network of sources and contacts. He had been with *The Cleveland Presenter* for almost forty years. He had taken Cheryl under his wing and taught her the ropes for being a newspaper reporter. After suffering a heart attack five years ago, he replaced chain-smoking with incessant gum-chewing. Tucking in his shirts and combing his irreverent white hair were not routinely part of his daily rituals. Since his heart attack, he mostly helped around the newsroom and was a resource for information and such.

As she was dashing out of the newsroom, Cheryl told Milton about the story she was heading to Bekbourg to cover and asked for a favor. She wanted to hit the ground running when she arrived.

He was waiting for her call. Milton said, "I haven't heard of a press conference or official news release, so you probably want to go to the crime location to see what you can learn, even though it's getting late in the day." Milton gave her the address. "I've learned a couple of things, unofficially of course. The property where the murder happened is owned by Tony Pinkston and his wife, Ruby. There are five fatalities, all shot to death and all related. My sources tell me that there's some meth labs on the property."

Cheryl was writing as fast as she could to capture the information.

"Another thing: apparently, a baby was found alive at the scene. That's about all I know now."

"Thanks, Milton. I really owe you. I better get going. I'll keep you and Keith posted."

"Oh, yeah. One more thing—there's one lead that might be valuable. The baby's great grandmother lives in the town there. Her name is Rose Waters." Milton gave Cheryl Rose's address. "Let me know if you need anything else. I'll keep checking my sources."

When she arrived, Cheryl found a beehive of law enforcement. Harold Greene had called in the DEA. Crime techs were crawling over both crime locations. Inventories were being collected, pictures taken, and evidence bagged. Troopers were posted around the meth labs, and the acreage was being walked for possible other evidence and drug operations. The dwellings, structures and vehicles were all secured. The State morgue had finally left with the bodies.

Very few bystanders were milling around. For the most part, the neighbors and those in the community didn't congregate, because they didn't want to be questioned by the press, didn't want to draw attention to themselves, and they knew the grapevine worked well.

While bystanders were sparse, the same could not be said for the media. Several newspapers from both inside and outside the state had reporters at the location. TV news crews from Columbus and Cincinnati were there along with some national media outlets. The state police had cordoned off an area for the media. An onslaught of questions was yelled at anyone coming within hearing distance.

Late that evening, the local authorities decided that they needed to make a statement to the press. Being Mike's assistant, Mack was tasked with reading a brief statement, and no questions were entertained.

Chapter 25

Sean was beat. Shortly after the press briefing, he left.

Buddy was excited to see him. They went for a walk, and Sean threw his ball for a while at the nearby park. After he ate a frozen dinner, he called Boze and told him that he didn't think the murders were a professional hit. He didn't understand why the labs were not destroyed unless it was to throw the investigation off regarding the motive, or if it was a revenge murder. He told about the Todds' meth operation, but didn't see a connection. Neither man thought the Pinkston operation was of the scale the DEA was searching for, but it was possible this was a supply feeder. There was no indication that any of the Pinkstons had pilot licenses.

Boze said, "Yeah, our agents on the ground there today had about the same report. The lab at the second location looked newer and had a larger capacity. Seems their old man in Tapsaw County is into marijuana production, but we haven't found any proof that he is behind meth operations or any connection with his sons' operation. We're following up and will keep you posted."

Miranda, Geri, and Mike had flown into Missoula to spend the weekend together celebrating Matt's graduation from the University of Montana.

Because Matt was a football player, his graduation festivities began with an early morning breakfast and ended with a boat ride on one of the nearby lakes followed by a cook-out and live music. Mike had turned off his cell phone the night before during the dinner and reception for the graduating athletes. With all the excitement and the post-graduation festivities and dinner, it had slipped his mind to turn on his cell phone. It was around 9:30 p.m. when Mike and Geri made it back to their hotel. He turned it on to find numerous messages. He knew that something was up and called Sean.

"Mike, how did the graduation go?"

"It was great. It's hard to believe he's graduated from college."

"Great. That's good to hear. I don't mean to ruin your day, but early this morning, five members of the Pinkston family were found dead on their property. Marijuana was found growing at different locations on their property, but what's made this such a big case is that two meth labs were found. I was the first to arrive at the scene. I called you to let you know and to tell you what I thought, but when I couldn't reach you, I called in the State authorities. This is too big for us to handle alone, and we needed their expertise to secure the crime scene."

Mike sat silently, in shock, thinking of the implications. "Have they any idea who did this?"

"At this time, there isn't any evidence pointing anywhere. One more thing: there is a throng of media—even from national outlets."

"Thanks, Sean, for handling this," Mike said wearily. "I'll fly out there tomorrow."

Chapter 26

Cheryl was glad in her search for lodging to find a boarding house had been converted into a B&B. The owners of the B&B had restored it to its intended grandness, but with flare. The exterior siding was painted a medium shade of baby blue, and the shutters and trim were white. The large walnut and leaded glass front door had been refurbished to its original beauty. White rocking chairs along with white wicker tables on the front porch made for a nice seating area for the guests. Colorful petunias and hanging pots of fern accented the porch.

Inside, the oak floors and rich woodwork on the staircase, baseboard and the eight-inch crown molding along the top of the ten-foot ceiling reminded Cheryl of stately historical residences she had seen in Columbus and Cleveland. The walls were painted a warm light yellow, and the upholstery and accents were beiges and warm blues and greens. Everything was tastefully done with a welcoming and comfortable feeling.

She instantly took a liking to the owner, Brianna (Bri) Sanderson. Bri was laid back and personable. Her appearance reminded Cheryl of an earth mother, with long wavy hair and a little on the ample side. She was dressed in a floral oversized smock with jeans. She was a pretty woman. Her face had a healthy glow to it, and she appeared to be somewhere in her 40's. As she was showing Cheryl to her room, she explained the layout of the B&B and told her that she and her husband, Max, also owned the coffee bistro next door. She offered to send up some food, but Cheryl had stopped at a fast food place.

Getting a story to *The Cleveland Presenter* was her first priority. In the article, she described the setting and the deputy's brief public statement. Cheryl spent the remainder of the evening researching on her laptop computer as much as she could find out about the Pinkstons, the local officials, and meth. Milton had learned the name of Victor Shultz's girlfriend, Darlene Hicks, and Cheryl made a note of her address. Cheryl decided to wait until after the family members' funerals to contact Rose. She wanted Rose's cooperation, and to get that, she needed to be empathetic about her feelings. She also planned to try to find some acquaintances of the deceased.

The next morning after Sean got off duty, he drove to the Pinkston murder site. Harold and other troopers were already there. Harold said, "Hi, Sean. We were just talking about you. Do you know Lucky Brennan?"

"Sure. He and I worked on some cases together when I was with the military criminal unit."

"That's what he said. He and I talked last night. He asked if we needed the FBI's help on this case. He and I go way back. I told him what we knew, and when I mentioned your name and that you were a deputy, he couldn't believe it. I told him that I didn't think you had been with the sheriff's office very long."

"No, I got my twenty years and decided to come back home for a while. I guess Mike Adams thought I had enough potential to give me a try."

"Well, according to Lucky, you're one of the best investigators he worked with. He'd like to talk to you about joining the FBI if you're interested."

Sean laughed, "Well, when you talk to him again, give him my regards. I'll give him a call sometime to talk old times."

Harold laughed, "Any idea how he got that nickname, 'Lucky'?"

Sean laughed, "If you ever hear, I'd like to be let in on the secret."

Harold smiled. "Anyway, you got here just in time. Ronnie wanted to talk to us about what she found."

Ronnie concluded that the alarm had recently been installed by amateurs, certainly not professional electricians. Ronnie speculated that the meth lab behind the mobile home was newer and capable of manufacturing about double the quantity coming from the lab behind the house. She noted that they had not found any casings.

"The Pinkstons knew what they were doing. They had the right type of ventilation, and things were organized. You might talk to the DEA agent that was here yesterday, but they probably were able to supply this whole region."

Harold said to Sean, "I talked to DD earlier this morning, and he said that he would be ready to talk to us around noon today with the preliminary autopsy results. He put a rush on things for us. I talked to your sheriff this morning, and he'll be back in town around 2:00. We're probably going to have to have a news conference later today. Would you like to ride up to talk to the medical examiner?"

Sean said, "Yeah, I'd appreciate tagging along."

"You know," Harold said on the drive to Columbus, "we don't get down here that much. Your sheriff never calls us in. He seems to want to handle things himself. There have been several times I thought he'd call us down here, but he never did. I guess he doesn't need our help, and of course, we've got other things to do around the state, but most counties like us to help out. It saves them some money."

Sean remained silent.

"Not surprising finding those meth labs and pot fields," Harold continued. "This area is pretty remote, being rural and all."

Sean said, "Yeah, it's something of an ideal location."

"Like I said, your sheriff doesn't call us in much, but if you ever need me, call. Lucky sure gave you a 'thumbs up.'"

"I appreciate that, Harold."

Harold and Sean went on discussing the investigation. Harold told Sean that they had talked to Rose Waters, but she was too shaken to really be of assistance. They had sent a team over to the nearby county to talk to Tony's family who were closed mouth about things. Tony and Ruby moved from there in 1998, when they bought the one-hundred acres from Tony's uncle and his wife. The state police also interviewed Earl and Ruth, but other than confirming the sale of the property, they didn't appear to know anything and had not stayed in touch with Tony or Ruby.

"Another person we interviewed is Pete Vance. He is the ex-boyfriend of Suzy and the father of the baby that was found in the house. According to Vance, he and Suzy had been dating almost a year when she found out she was pregnant. He wanted them to get married so she could move away from her family. Pete said he didn't know anything about the Pinkstons being in drugs, but he suspected something. He said he never asked, because he didn't want to know. He was afraid they might kill him.

"He wanted him and Suzy to live in Bekbourg, but again, according to Pete, she wouldn't leave her family. After the baby was born, he tried once more to get Suzy to take the baby and move in with him. He went up there, and Tony, that's Suzy's father, came outside and approached Pete before he could get very far up the driveway. He had a shotgun and threatened to kill Pete if he ever came there again. Vance claims that's the last time he ever saw any of them."

Sean asked, "What do you think? Do you believe him?"

"He has a motive, but I don't think he could have done this by himself. Also, why would he have killed the other two? They lived down the road."

"Does he have an alibi?"

"He works at the Shopper's Pavilion in the loading area: Day shift. That's where the detectives found him. They say he seemed surprised when they told him why they were there. He claims he was home from around 9:00 pm. Said his dad spent the night with his woman friend, so his dad can't vouch for him."

"Does he have a gun?" Sean asked.

"Yeah. It's a shotgun. He rode with us to his house and gave it to us to test. We don't have the results back. He was afraid he might lose his job at Pavilion's."

Sean said, "Do you mind if I talk to him?"

"Not at all."

Sean asked, "Has anyone talked to the principal at the high school about the boy?"

"Not yet, but that needs to be done soon. One other thing: the woman, Ruby Pinkston, it appears she was trying to call Ray Pinkston when she was shot."

When they arrived at the State morgue, Sean was introduced to Dennis Douglass, frequently called by his nickname, "DD." DD detailed the gunshot wounds to the five casualties. There were no preliminary signs that any of the victims were meth users. All four of the male fatalities were cigarette smokers. Ray Pinkston and Victor Shultz were intoxicated, well above the legal limit. Tony Pinkston had a low level of alcohol, but no alcohol was found in the woman's or boy's systems. At Harold's request, DD agreed to attend the press conference in Bekbourg.

When Harold and Sean returned to the Pinkston place, they walked over to where Mike was standing with Ben and Mack.

Mike and Harold nodded up to each other, "Chief, what do you have for me? Sean, how are you doing?"

Harold told Mike what they had learned from the coroner in Columbus. "It's preliminary, but they rushed the report for us."

Mike said, "That sounds good. I'll be looking forward to the report. It looks from our perspective that the meth production in our county is now gone."

This surprised Harold. "It's a little early to be making that conclusion."

"Chief, you don't know this county," said Ben.

Harold ignored Ben.

Mike said, "The press conference is going to be at the elementary school near here. I'll be there and so will Mack, the officer who was in charge of the crime scene from the beginning." Mike asked Harold, "Will there be any one from the coroner?"

"Yes, and Ronnie Vin, heading up this forensics team, will be here, too. Sean will be there as well."

Mike said, "I don't think that's necessary. Our chain of command has Mack in charge of the first responders, and we really don't want to have too many people answering questions at the press conference. It's confusing enough as it is. We don't have a lot to tell them anyway."

Harold looked at him, "Sheriff, with no disrespect to Mack, Sean was the first to arrive at the scene, and he was much more involved at the early stages of discovery, and I really feel he should be at the press conference."

It was obvious that Mike didn't like being told what to do, but said, "Okay, Chief. We'll include Sean, but we got to be sure we keep it simple and not say too much. We don't want to jeopardize our investigation."

The Chief pointedly looked at him, "Mike, I know how to conduct a press conference."

As they were breaking up, Mike said, "Sean, I want to talk to you."

"Sure, Mike, after the Chief clears out, we'll talk."

Harold said, "I'm finished for now. I'll see you down there. I'm going to talk to some of my people to get ready for the press conference."

Mike told Mack, "The press conference isn't starting for a while. You don't need to hang around here, but be there by 4:45 in case we need to go over anything." Sean knew that Mike wasn't planning on Mack speaking. Mike was out of sorts, but Sean figured by the sheepish look on Mack's face he knew Sean had done the right thing. Ben sneered at Sean as he walked away, but Sean could have cared less what Ben thought.

After Mack and Ben were out of range, Sean said, "I know what you're going to say, Mike, and before you say it, I want to tell you something. This is much bigger than this county and your department. I followed proper procedure to call this in. We did not have the man power or the expertise to deal with this properly, so don't screw this up with some turf war. Frankly, I don't even know why it would be an issue."

Mike looked at his old quarterback and knew Sean had made the right call, but he was angry about the entire situation, "Why couldn't we have at least tried to evaluate the scene first?"

"With the people we had, we would have contaminated the crime scene beyond recognition. With me telling them not to, Ben and Alex walked back over the grounds around the house. Alex told me that the state police dressed them down for doing so. I did what I thought was right. I've been in this business for a long time."

Mike looked at Sean for a long time and knew he was right, "*but he sure didn't need this trouble,*" he thought to himself.

As they started to walk back toward their cars, Mike asked Sean what he saw when he first got to the scene. Sean summarized the basic facts and then said, "I filled out a complete report describing everything that happened. Also, you'll get a thorough report later tonight about our meeting with the state coroner in Columbus."

Mike realized that he didn't have any report from Mack. As much as he hated to admit it, he was grateful that Sean was part of the investigation. He brought a level of professionalism to his department that was sorely needed. Things were beginning to unravel around the county. What was behind these murders? Why did he have such a strong feeling of dread?

Taking the stage were Jeff, Mike, Harold, Ronnie Vin, DD from the state coroner's office, Mack and Sean.

Being a County Commissioner, Jeff spoke on behalf of the county and expressed condolences to the Pinkston family and friends; introduced the people standing with him on the stage and told the reporters they would take questions after the initial remarks. Jeff continued, "Yesterday, a tragedy hit our community. Five people were brutally murdered. We've been aware for quite some time of the growing meth problem in our area. You'll hear from law enforcement that there were two labs on the property that were used to make methamphetamine. We think that the source of these drugs in our county is now gone. Even though this crime will result in these meth labs being shut down, Sheriff Adams and his deputies will continue to work diligently to keep drugs out of our area. Anyone involved in the production or sale of drugs around here will be prosecuted to the fullest extent of the law. Now, I'd like to ask Sheriff Adams to step to the podium."

Mike identified the victims. He stated that the 911 call reporting the crime came in just after six o'clock a.m. "We appreciate the hard work that we have received from the state police on this matter. They have brought to this investigation the man power needed to coordinate this type of crime. We also appreciate the state forensics team and coroner that have worked long hours to process the evidence and conduct the investigation this far."

Mike then introduced Harold, who described the two crime scenes. DD addressed the approximate time and cause of death for the five victims.

Jeff then opened the press conference to questions.

The first question was whether there were any suspects. Mike answered, "Not at this time."

There were a few questions about the deaths, which DD addressed.

One of the reporters asked about a rumored marijuana operation on the property. Harold stated that they had found marijuana, but they were not going to address the specifics.

Someone asked about how much meth could be manufactured by the two labs. Harold again declined to get into those specifics.

Another reporter asked if there was any truth to a Columbian drug cartel being behind the murders. Harold denied that they had any evidence to that effect.

Another question posed was whether the murders were in response to a vendetta. Harold responded that it was too early to say.

"Was a rival drug gang responsible for the murders?" Again, Harold reiterated that it was too early to say.

"Commissioner Thompson, there's rumors going around that this might be a case of hillbilly justice. Is there any evidence to that rumor?"

Jeff walked to the podium, "We can't rule anything out."

"Commissioner Thompson, do you think this could be the work of a serial killer?"

"We don't have any evidence to support that. Right now, all our evidence points to this as being limited to something to do with this family. Our investigation is in the early stages, so we're not ruling anything out, but there's nothing to suggest there is a serial killer around here."

"How many shooters are we talking about, Chief?"

Harold looked at Ronnie and then responded, "We're not going to discuss the specifics at this time."

Someone yelled out, "Was there a baby in one of the houses at the time of the murders?"

Harold said, "Deputy Neumann was the first law enforcement to arrive at the scene. He is the best to address this."

Sean moved to the mic and said, "Yes, there was baby. She is unharmed. She is the grandchild of Tony and Ruby Pinkston. When their daughter arrived at the scene, she panicked and ran into the house and found the baby in its crib, crying. She took the baby and left the house and called 911."

"Where was the crib?" yelled a reporter.

"It was in the same room where Mrs. Pinkston was found."

"How old is the child?"

Sean said, "I believe she's seven months old."

A reporter yelled out, "Sheriff Adams, do you agree with Commissioner Thompson that the meth problem in the area is being cleaned up?"

Mike stepped back to the podium, "As you know, there's been a meth problem in this area in recent years. Based on the size of the labs, we think this is the source of meth plaguing our county. We are not aware of any other sources, and we've been looking. These appear to be fairly new labs, which seems to coincide with when the meth problems started here. We are going to find whoever was responsible for these murders and bring them to justice. In the meantime, we're not going to rule anything out."

A young woman reporter asked, "Do you have any evidence to support your claim that this is the major source of drugs in your county?"

Sean looked at the woman reporter. She had hit the nail on the head. He couldn't figure out why Jeff and Mike were so eager to jump to this conclusion. Certainly, Harold Greene was not ready to accept it.

Mike looked at her and replied, "Like I said, we're not ruling anything out."

She said, "But Commissioner Thompson suggested that theory, and you seem to support it. I'm asking if you actually have any evidence."

Mike dismissed the inquiry, "We're not at liberty to discuss our evidential findings at this time."

The woman reporter had a confused look on her face, and justifiably so thought Sean. *How could they state so unequivocally that no other drug production was in the area? Certainly, the DEA didn't agree with that conclusion.*

Another reporter asked Mike if citizens should take extra precaution until the killers were caught?

Mike responded, "We don't have any reason to suspect that others are at risk in our county because of this incident. Of course, it is always a good idea to exercise caution by keeping your doors locked, but we don't think there is anything for our citizens to be afraid of."

"Is there any reason to believe other members of the family are in danger?"

"We don't have any reason to think that they are in danger."

"Sheriff, I want to know who is actually in charge of this investigation—the state police or your department?"

"We are working closely with the state police to solve this crime, and we really appreciate all the help they have given us. We have always worked hard to keep the people in our county safe, and we will continue to do this."

Other questions were asked, many of them the same basic question only reworded. Jeff finally thanked everyone for coming. He reminded people if they had anything at all that might help with the investigation to call the Sheriff's office, and told them that they would be kept apprised as new information became available.

Sean was walking out the side door when the woman reporter ran up to him. She was the one questioning whether there was evidence to support that the meth sources in the county were now eliminated. She was confident and, from his calculation, a seasoned reporter with an elegant and professional flair. When he had noticed her from the stage, he found her attractive, but he now saw that she was stunning. She had shoulder length dark hair and alert, sparkling brown eyes. She was about five feet, ten inches tall and slender. She was professionally dressed with a suit coat and scarf. "Deputy Neumann, can I ask you a question?"

Sean kept walking, "I don't talk to reporters."

"Please, just one—off the record."

Sean stopped and looked at her. "I don't believe an answer is ever 'off the record.'"

"If I say it's 'off the record,' it will be."

Sean continued to look at her. For some reason he believed her.

"What's your question?"

"Is there any reason at this time to believe that this was the only meth source in the county?"

"Off the record?"

"Yes," she replied.

"No."

Sean turned to walk away.

She tried to keep up with him, "One more question."

Sean kept walking. "We agreed to one."

Cheryl found Deputy Neumann to be an intense man. The look in his eyes would give seasoned criminals a feeling of unease. He had answered her question and sincerely so she felt. Now, she was more confident in her instincts that something was amiss here, similar to the penetrating unjustness she had experienced in the courtroom that day twenty years ago when her grandfather pled guilty to the Burkhart murders.

After talking to the principal at the high school where Aaron Pinkston was a student, Sean stopped at Frau's for breakfast. He had suffered another nightmare, and his thigh was throbbing. The night terrors were becoming more vivid, more in focus, like they were consuming him one nightmare at a time. Sean wasn't sure if he could handle the truth, but he also was beginning to wonder if he could survive not knowing.

While he was sitting at the counter drinking coffee and poking at his mostly uneaten breakfast, he looked up at the man who sat down beside him and saw a face from his past. Sean turned around on his bar stool and said, "You old son of a gun. If it isn't old Chaw?" Like with most railroaders, his nickname had carried over into his personal life.

Chaw looked funny at first, not recognizing Sean. All a sudden, it hit him. "Well, if it ain't Sean Neumann. I heard you were back."

Sean said, "Let me buy you breakfast."

"Just a minute, I got to put my choppers in," said Chaw reaching for his shirt pocket.

"When did you start doing that?"

"After I had all my teeth pulled. All that tobacco chewing rotted them out."

"I heard you are working with Dusty out of Bekbourg."

"Yeah, I'm looking forward to retiring. I don't have too much longer 'til I retire."

"Yeah, Dusty told me."

"Yeah, the good old days are gone, but I remember a lot of good times, especially with your grandpa. He was a conductor when I started. I would catch a job off the extra board with him in the early years. We worked the division between Cincinnati and Wheeling. He was quite a character, and he loved his cigars."

The mention of Sean's grandpa's cigars brought back fond memories.

Chaw continued, "This was back in the days when we were the MV&O. Nearly every MV&O passenger coach had a little of your grandpa on it."

"What do you mean, Chaw?"

"Well, like I said, your grandpa liked his cigars, and couldn't smoke where the passengers were. He had only a few minutes when walking between cars. He stood between the cars and would light up, get a few puffs. He'd knock the fire out and put the cigar on the ledge right where you walked into the passenger car. You couldn't see it, but every car had one of his cigars. Some of those things were probably a year old."

Sean laughed, "I never heard that story. Was he smoking those two-for-a-nickel Rasola's?"

"Yep, those are the ones," Chaw was laughing. "Well, it's one of many stories about your grandpa. If I had time, I'd tell you some more. So, how are you doing, Sean?"

"Well as you know, I was in the Marines. I retired after twenty years. I was in the military police, so I was offered this job and kind of like it. I get around the county and meet people."

"There are bad things going on."

"Yeah, I know, Chaw. Something I've been looking into, but seems no one wants to talk."

They finished eating breakfast while talking.

Chaw said, "I'm pretty tired. I've been working all night. The old lady will get worried if I don't get home. Good seeing you, Sean."

"Good seeing you. We'll have to get together again and talk about the railroad and my grandpa. I'd like to hear some more stories."

Chapter 27

Cheryl had lingered to drink her coffee. The other two guests had left shortly after breakfast, and Cheryl thought if Bri had time, she could ask her some questions about the area. Cheryl told Bri that she was here to cover the murders.

"Oh, I am close to a woman, Rose Waters, who used to work here. I am heartbroken for her. It was her daughter, Ruby, that was killed. I need to call her. I guess her granddaughter and great granddaughter are staying with her. They must be frightened, because their entire family was killed."

Cheryl said she had been born in Bekbourg but had been gone for many years. She told Bri that her grandfather used to bring her here for lunch.

Bri said, "Oh my goodness. Did you know Rose Waters, the cook here?"

"Yes, I remember her. I especially loved her grilled cheese sandwiches. I want to talk to her for my story, but I'll wait until after the funerals. I wouldn't feel right trying to talk to her right now. Tell me how you and Max came to Bekbourg."

Bri described growing up in Nashville, Tennessee. Her sister, who was four years older, struggled with a drug addiction and died of an overdose when she was nineteen. She and Max met during college. Bri graduated with a degree in elementary education and a minor in art. Max graduated with a dual degree in business and culinary arts. They moved to Cincinnati, close to where Max had grown up, where they both worked, but over the years, they got restless and started looking for opportunities to support themselves doing what they loved. They heard how some of the smaller Midwest towns were rejuvenating their downtowns. An acquaintance told them that Bekbourg was beginning to promote tourism for outdoor activities in the surrounding national forest, state park, rivers and lakes. They visited the town about ten years ago and fell in love with it and the area.

Bri smiled, "I kept my maiden name, so don't get confused if you hear two different last names. Well, that was probably more than you wanted to know, but I like to talk. I guess you know that by now."

Cheryl laughed. "I enjoyed it and wish I had more time to spend, but I better get going. Thank you for the delicious breakfast and coffee. Please don't worry about keeping food for me for dinner. I don't know what time I'll return, and I don't want to inconvenience you."

"Look, it's no inconvenience at all. If you're not here for dinner, I'll put a plate of leftovers in the refrigerator. If you're hungry when you get here, help yourself, but if you get something before you get back, I'll feed it to Brutus tomorrow." They both laughed. Cheryl had met Brutus, Bri's Golden Retriever, who wagged his tail at everyone entering the B&B.

Chapter 28

The local partner was trying to mask his anxiety. "You can assure Señor Esteban that everything is under control here."

"Please do not try to make me laugh. I can assure you that Señor Esteban is not laughing. How can you tell me everything is under control when law enforcement is crawling all over Bekbourg County, including the DEA? You were supposed to destroy the meth labs because they were bringing too much scrutiny to the area. Had you done that, the Pinkstons would have been out of business, but the whole world would not know about the drugs."

"People think the drugs are now out of the county," assured the local partner. "That's all they care about. There's no reason for the DEA to hang around, because the Pinkston's labs and pot fields are gone. The state police are focused on the murders, and the murders are a local matter, so the State will be out of the case soon enough."

"Why did you kill them?"

"That wasn't the plan. The plan was to ignite a small bomb at both labs and burn them down. My man went up there a couple of weeks ago at night to scope out the situation. I don't know why, but when we went there to burn them down, someone had put in a trip wire. The alarm must have been in the house. We had no choice. They can't trace us. There's no harm to Señor Esteban. We have the situation under control."

"For your sake, you should hope so. We are almost out of patience."

Chapter 29

The next morning, Bri and Cheryl were talking about the murders and the drug culture.

Bri said, "It's such a complex situation. Seeing my sister go through her drug addiction was so difficult for my parents and me. That's one of the reasons Max and I try to help at-risk women. We try to give them jobs when we can. I have a woman that cleans our rooms. She has been clean for a while now, thank goodness. Max hired her daughter to wait on tables part time. She is only sixteen, but Lilly and her mother really need the extra money.

"Sometimes, we are successful. We've helped women get on their feet and then move on to better jobs. You know, I don't know if you would have an interest, but Max and I work with a couple here in Bekbourg. They are dedicated to helping addicts. If you want, I will be glad to arrange a meeting with them for you."

"That would be great, Bri. I would appreciate that very much."

Sean walked into Bekbourg Auto Mall accompanied by Harold. Sean had told the state police about the missing van that had traces of meth and cocaine. Sean and Harold agreed that Gary should be interviewed.

When Gary walked out, Sean introduced him to Harold and told him they were there on official business. He asked if there was a place they could talk.

Once they were seated in Gary's office, Sean said, "We want to ask you some questions about the night of the Pinkston murders."

"What's this all about, Sean?"

"The van that was missing from here had evidence of meth and cocaine in it. We need to know where you were that night."

Gary was confused and angry. "Where else would I be? I was at home in bed with my wife, Becky, asleep like I am every night."

"Is there any time that your wife can't account for you that night?"

"No, Sean. I was there all night."

"Did you know Tony or Ruby or Ray Pinkston or Victor Shultz?"

"No. That's not the circle we travel in."

"Well, I guess you know we'll have to talk to Becky."

"Go ahead."

"You know, we have to verify things."

"How did it go?" Gary asked.

Becky was irked. "It went fine, because I had nothing to tell them. I told them you were here all night. How did I get pulled into this anyway? What are you into, Gary? Why are the police asking us about a murder? Why are they asking me where you were that night?"

He tried to calm her down. "It's normal police procedure to question people. We had a van disappear recently, and it was found abandoned on the road. I guess they think maybe the Pinkstons had something to do with it."

"But why did they want to know where you were?"

"Beck, I don't know why they want to know. It has nothing to do with me."

"Why didn't you tell me about the van disappearing? I had no idea something like that happened?"

"Now, Becky, I don't tell you everything that happens in the business."

Becky was growing more agitated. "Well, it's embarrassing to have people know the police are questioning us about those murders. I couldn't believe that I had to answer questions to Sean."

Now Gary started to get steamed. The mere mention of Sean raised his ire. At Jeff's "Welcome Back" party for Sean, Becky couldn't keep her eyes off him. He'd seen her flirt with Sean. Gary started yelling, "So that's what's got you fuming. And what does this have to do with Sean asking the questions? What difference does it make who asked the questions? Ever since he got back, I've seen you throwing yourself at him. That's really what this is about. You've never gotten over him."

Yelling back, "How dare you talk to me about Sean? You were never Sean! But, just so you know, Sean and I were done before he left for the Marines!"

Gary had been rethinking an earlier decision to take a family vacation to Europe to celebrate Kinsey's sixteenth birthday, but he now lashed out at Becky, "By the way, we're not going to Europe this summer. Too much is going on at the business."

Becky was incredulous. "What do you mean?"

"We'll think about doing it next year."

"We are going, Gary!"

"No we're not!"

"It's all planned, and the girls are excited about it. I'm not going to allow you to disappoint them. I'll take the girls without you."

"No you won't!"

"Yes, Gary, I will!"

Becky stormed out. Feeling that things might be starting to unravel, Gary grabbed a bottle of scotch and poured a tall glass.

Chapter 30

Cheryl parked in front of the Parrs' home. Little had changed to the nice brick home since she had last been there. Memories came flooding back of the times she had spent playing with Annalee here. In the early years, they had loved playing games and dressing their dolls and baking cookies. They had sleepovers here as they got a little older, watching movies late into the night, making popcorn, polishing each other's nails—all the things young girls enjoyed doing. Sitting there looking at the home, she remembered the solace she found in those last horrific weeks after her world came crashing down. While other kids stared or made cruel remarks and even some adults looked askance at her, Annalee and her parents never wavered in their devotion and love to her and her mother.

When the door opened, Ann Parr looked at Cheryl with a question in her eyes, and then with complete surprise, "Oh, my Gosh! Cheryl, is that you?"

With tears in her eyes, Cheryl said, "Yes, Mrs. Parr, it's me."

They hugged each other, and Mrs. Parr said, "Oh, Honey, come in. Let me look at you. You are so beautiful. I don't believe it's you. What are you doing here? Oh dear, where are my manners, have a seat. Can I get you anything?"

They both started laughing. "No thank you, I'm fine. I am a reporter for *The Cleveland Presenter*. I'm here to cover the Pinkston murders. I'm trying to renew acquaintances and learn about the drug problems here in Bekbourg while I also investigate the murders. I hate to admit to you that I am not here purely on a social call. How are you and Mr. Carr? How is Annalee?"

"Please, call us Lyle and Ann. Annalee got married a few years ago and has a three-year-old little girl named Kali. She goes to a pre-school in the mornings, and I keep her in the afternoon. You will love her. She looks like Annalee did at that age. Annalee is a guidance counselor at the high school. She will be so excited to see you. Lyle is still teaching at the high school, but I retired when Kali was born so I could help out. I was ready to retire anyway. That gave me the final push I needed. Dear, how is your mother?"

Ann must have detected the unavoidable sadness slicing through Cheryl. She reached over and touched Cheryl's hands with hers, "Oh, dear, I hope I haven't asked something I shouldn't have."

"No, not at all. She passed away a little over two months ago. She had been ill for two years, so it wasn't unexpected, but I hated to lose her."

Ann gave her a hug. "I am so sorry, Cheryl, that you lost your mother. And I know we could never replace her, but I would love for you to think of us as family."

"I will be honored. I always thought of you as family anyway."

191

"If you don't mind, please tell me what happened after you and your mother left here. I saw a realtor's sign in the front yard right after you and she left town, but I never knew where you went or what you did."

Cheryl told her about moving to Cleveland and her mother getting a receptionist job. She told her that her mother never married. She talked about going to OSU and then getting a job with the Cleveland newspaper. Cheryl said, "Ann, do you think Annalee would mind if I went to the high school to see her?"

"Not at all, Dear. I'll call and tell her you're coming."

"That would be wonderful. It has been great seeing you. I look forward to coming back and seeing Kali and Lyle."

"Of course, you must come back soon."

When Cheryl pulled into the visitor's lot at the high school, Annalee was sitting on a bench waiting for her. They ran into each other's arms. "Mom told me everything you told her. I am so happy for you, Cheryl, and you are even more beautiful than when we were in school."

"So are you, and to think you're a mother. I can't wait to see Kali. Your mom says she looks like you."

They talked for a few minutes, and Cheryl said, "I guess your mom told you what brought me here. I'm investigating the murders and the drug culture around here and the impacts. One of the victims was only seventeen. He must have been a student here?"

"He was a junior, Cheryl. Aaron didn't seem to have any close friends, but we had no reason to suspect that he was taking or selling drugs. It's so hard to lose a student like that. We've had grief counselors on call for any of the students who might need them. Even if they don't know him personally, it has its effects. Also, the police have been here. Our principal, Lloyd Wiseman, talked to the deputy investigating the murder. In fact, you probably remember him. He was the quarterback that you were so dreamy-eyed about."

Annalee was nodding and smiling.

Cheryl started laughing. "I know. I recognized him."

They both laughed. "I need to get back to the school, but can we have dinner either tonight or tomorrow night? We can talk some more about the drug situation and catch up."

"Yes, tonight works. What about your husband and Kali? By the way, what's his name?" They both laughed.

"His name is Boone. He is an attorney and is in Chicago for a couple of nights on business. Mom and Dad would love the extra time with Kali. Where are you staying?"

"Bri's B&B."

"Oh, my gosh, that's perfect. My favorite restaurant is next door. Max's coffee bistro. It's Bri's husband who owns it. What about 6:00?"

"Perfect! I'll meet you there.

Annalee was waiting at Max's when Cheryl arrived. Annalee was talking to a man in his 40's who was medium height and slender. He had a beard and wore his hair in a ponytail. "Max Brandt, this is Cheryl. She's staying at the B&B. We were best friends until she moved away in eighth grade."

"Any friend of Annalee's is a friend of Bri and me. Welcome."

"Thank you. You and Bri have worked a miracle on the B&B, and Annalee tells me your bistro is her favorite."

He smiled, "Let me seat you before you starve. Annalee, do you want Lilly's table?"

"Yes. Thank you."

Cheryl was admiring the bistro and getting settled when their waitress walked up.

Annalee said, "Hi, Lilly, how are you this evening?"

"Just fine Mrs. Carter. Here are our specials for tonight." She looked at Cheryl and said, "This is our regular menu also. Can I get you both something to drink?"

They gave her their drink orders. As she walked away, Cheryl thought how pretty she was. Lilly was slender, with straight dark hair, about 5'6".

Annalee whispered to Cheryl, "Lilly is one of the most talented students we have. She is going to be a junior and is a wonderful writer. She won a state competition in a freshman writing category. Her mother, Elena, works next door cleaning rooms for Bri. She was a drug addict but is trying to keep clean. Lilly works to help provide. We're all cheering for them. Mom and Dad have been her foster parents when Elena faced difficulties in the past.

"Cheryl, I wanted to follow up on our conversation at school today. We have had a terrible meth problem at the high school. We all have been concerned about it. We had two students die a while back of overdoses. Then, a few weeks ago, three of our students got hold of some meth. They had no idea what it was. They thought they were dealing with something like marijuana. Unfortunately, one of them died from the overdose.

"As serious as the overdoses are, though, what is equally disturbing is what it's doing to our student body. We have seen an outbreak of declining grades, absenteeism, petty theft, and a wide range of chronic health problems. In addition, there has been an increase in student fights. It is really impacting our ability to educate these young people."

Cheryl and Annalee continued to talk about what the schools were trying to do to educate students and parents about the problem and what could be done to combat the problem. They also talked about what Annalee thought could be done to identify kids at risk.

When Lilly brought the check, Annalee said, "Lilly, this is Cheryl. She and I went all through school together until she moved in the eighth grade. Cheryl is now a newspaper reporter for a newspaper in Cleveland, Ohio. It's called *The Presenter*."

Lilly's eyes lit up.

Annalee said to Cheryl, "Lilly is a wonderful writer, too."

"It's nice to meet you, Lilly. We appreciate you taking such good care of us this evening. I am staying next door, so hopefully, I'll see you again soon."

As they were leaving, Annalee told Cheryl how an Ohio university had given grant money to Schriever High School for a video production class where students would learn the technical points of filming and editing video as well as the "in front of camera" experience. Annalee had arranged for Lilly to work a few hours each day during the summer with the teacher to assist in developing the syllabus for the class. "Lilly is earning a stipend and learning about the field."

Chapter 31

"We have some complications. We must make adjustments."

"What complications? What adjustments do you mean?" the local partner asked.

"Señor Esteban has decided to take a couple of our larger production facilities off-line. They may have drawn the Feds' attention. It is a most inconvenient time because we have a very large order that must be filled soon. We are going to use our facility here to meet that order. We will increase our incoming supplies as well as the outbound shipments."

"How do you know the Feds aren't looking around here if they've found your other facilities?"

"We picked up noise around those facilities. There is no such noise around here."

"This increased activity that Señor Esteban plans, should I not be concerned that this will bring unwanted attention here?"

"That is why I am giving you this courtesy call. It is your responsibility to make sure that there is no problem."

There was a pause. "Is there anything else?"

"Señor Esteban does not want to jeopardize the exceptional operations we have here. After this special order is met, we plan to go dark with this operation for a few months to ensure that the Feds don't come sniffing around."

"Mr. Sommers, there's been a change in our plans."

"Tell me what you need." Joe always followed to the letter the Boss' orders.

"Two of our other production facilities are off line. We have a major shipment due soon, so we are going to use our Bekbourg operation to fill the order. More supplies will be delivered for our manufacturing operations, because we are going to have to increase our shipments to meet the schedule. More vans will be arriving that need to be unloaded, and we will use them to deliver our product like we've been doing."

Joe Sommers knew better than to voice his reservations, but he thought to himself, *"This is going to attract a lot of attention to have all these vans arrive and disappear."* He guessed if he had to, he could blame the mix-ups with the vans on a computer system at their distributor.

Joe said, "Let me know when and what to expect. Also, if they can be delivered in the late evening or at night, it would make things easier. Workers aren't here then."

"Our local partner has been informed, but you will handle matters."

Chapter 32

The next morning, Bri was waiting. "Hi, Cheryl, do you have a couple of minutes? I may have some good news for you."

"What's that?"

"I went over to Rose's house yesterday to express Max's and my sympathies and to see how she was doing. I hope I didn't do anything wrong, but I mentioned to her that you were here to investigate the murders and wanted to meet with her at the appropriate time. I told her how you loved her grilled cheese sandwiches. She said she remembered a special little girl named Cheryl and knew it had to be you. She started crying. She wants to see you. She told me to tell you to call her. I have the number here. She's not answering her phone, so this is her granddaughter's."

"Oh, my gosh, Bri, I don't know how to thank you."

"Cheryl, we're all on the same side trying to fight the drugs. I am hoping that the story you're working on can help in some way."

Chapter 33

Kelly Willis grew up in Bekbourg. She moved in with her boyfriend when she was nineteen years old. Cheryl was born two years later. Despite talk of getting married, it never happened, and when Cheryl was two, her father left, and Kelly and Cheryl never saw him again. They moved in with Kelly's parents. Kelly worked, and Cheryl's grandmother took care of Cheryl during the day.

She loved her grandmother, who showed her how to bake cookies and knit and sew. When Cheryl was about eight, her grandmother suffered a stroke. She spent a lot of time lying on the sofa or in bed. Cheryl began cooking and cleaning the house, because her mother was tired when she came home from work.

Cheryl's grandfather, Henry, had unsteady employment during her youth. Because he had a police record, it was hard for him to find work. He had spent some time in jail for passing bad checks and petty crimes. He worked part time for the car dealership owned by Roger Burkhart doing odd jobs like washing cars and cleaning the place. He also occasionally did landscape work and painted buildings for other businesses around town.

Cheryl adored her grandfather. He was a kind person. She thought her grandfather was so handsome, and he typically had a few days' growth of beard that he would rub against her face with her squealing with delight. Henry was a likeable person who enjoyed being around people. He was a tall, lanky man, and when she was a little girl, he would carry her around on his back pretending to gallop like a horse. Her love of gardening came from Henry, who showed her how to plant and tend tomatoes, corn and green beans. He taught her how to fish and play checkers, and would take her places, like the high school football games on Friday nights and to the park where he would push her on the swings. Every holiday season, she and Henry would go Christmas tree hunting in rural fields, where he let her choose a young pine tree. He would drag it back home, where she would help her mother and grandmother decorate the tree.

Henry had an imagination, and he used that gift to tell Cheryl stories, especially about nature. She loved to sit on his lap at night listening to him tell her stories about a bear family in the woods, trees that would talk to each other about visitors who came to their woods, and other made-up stories. Cheryl had always excelled in school in writing assignments, and she attributed her writing abilities to listening to the wonderful, colorful stories spun by her grandfather all those years.

When Cheryl was eleven, her grandmother passed away, and from that time on, it was only her grandfather, her mother and herself. Cheryl took on the role of the homemaker. Her mother worked long hours, so each night, Cheryl would plan and prepare the dinners and keep the house clean. After dinner, her mother and she would talk while they cleaned the kitchen. Many times after dinner, her grandfather went to the local bar to talk to the locals. Kelly never went out with friends; when she wasn't working, she was with her family.

Their world turned upside down when Cheryl was fourteen. Cheryl had heard about the killings of the Burkhart family and their house burning down. It was big news among her friends for a couple of days. A few weeks later though, Cheryl's mother started acting differently; she was quiet and often crying. Her mother and grandfather would whisper among themselves, and if she walked in, they stopped their conversation.

A few days later when Cheryl got home from school orientation, her mother was home waiting for her. She had been crying. She said, "Honey, I need to talk to you."

Cheryl was scared. She was afraid that her grandfather or mother was sick. After all, her grandmother had died.

Her mother guided her to the sofa, where she put her arm around her and pulled her under her shoulder. She couldn't see her mother's face, only hear her quivering voice, "Honey, something has happened. You remember what happened to the Burkhart family?"

Cheryl was frightened. She whispered, "yes, Momma."

"Your grandfather said he did it."

Cheryl sprang up off the sofa and stood looking at her mother, "No!" she yelled. "I don't believe it!" Cheryl was sobbing and shaking uncontrollably.

Kelly leaped up and pulled Cheryl into her arms. At first, Cheryl tried to resist, but her mom held her tight. Both of them were crying. Finally, when Cheryl somewhat calmed, Kelly brought them back to sit on the sofa. "Listen to me, Honey. Hear what I have to say. This is extremely important. You have to promise me that you will keep this as our secret." She was looking at Cheryl to make sure the importance of what she was getting ready to tell her was understood. Cheryl promised to keep the secret. "Your grandfather has a lot of pride. He doesn't want anyone to know, so you can't tell anyone."

If her grandfather didn't want his secret known, Cheryl was going to honor that.

"It's important, Baby, that you don't tell anyone, not your best friend or anyone."

"I promise, Mom. I won't tell."

"Your grandpa has had a full life, and he loves you and me very, very much."

Tears were now streaming down both their faces.

"He is sick. He has cancer. He wants us to go on with our lives. He is going to plead guilty to the Burkhart murders. This is what he wants to do. He wants you and me to be strong. We love him, and I think we should help him and do what he wants us to do."

They talked and held each other tight. They slept in the same bed that night. They went through the next few weeks like they were in a daze. She hated to start back to school, but her mother insisted that they both had to be strong; that's what her grandfather wanted.

The last time she saw her beloved grandfather was that day in the courtroom when he pled guilty. That day's events were seared in her mind. Two days later her mother sold the car and rented a small van. They loaded their things in one afternoon and left Bekbourg for good.

They moved to Cleveland where they first lived in an apartment. Kelly wanted them to start their new lives with a clean slate, so she changed their last name to Seton, her mother's maiden name. Cheryl started school, and her mother found a job as a receptionist for a large insurance company. After a couple of years, her mother bought a small home in a cul-de-sac. They fell into a routine, and her mother never wanted to talk about the past.

When she asked her mother about the incident a couple of times over the years, Kelly started trembling and pleaded for her to never raise the subject again. Cheryl and her mother were close, and she could not bear to cause her mother the distress she witnessed on those two occasions. However, Cheryl always intended to one day return to Bekbourg and find out why her grandfather had confessed. She knew he was physically and morally incapable of such an act. Her resolve hardened when Cheryl found a large sum of money in her mother's bank account after her passing. With Kelly gone, Cheryl went to the Cleveland public library and found a few articles from the Cincinnati and Columbus newspapers about the Burkhart murders and articles about her grandfather's arrest. Shorter news reports spoke of his guilty plea and his sentencing. His death was never reported. Cheryl was on the verge of telling Keith that she needed to take some personal time to return to Bekbourg when the Pinkston murders occurred.

Before she left that day to cover the Pinkston murders, she told Keith about her grandfather and that she intended to look into his case. He had been intrigued about the story but wasn't sure how much Cheryl could learn—given that it happened twenty years ago. He also knew that Cheryl was a lot like him, once something starts gnawing, there's only one fix: investigate the story. He cautioned, "Cheryl, if your suspicions about your grandfather's guilty plea are correct and others are somehow involved, they are likely still alive. For your grandfather to plead guilty to something he didn't do, you are talking about some powerful and ruthless people. They are not going to sit calmly by when they learn you are snooping around."

Cheryl now had a few hours before the afternoon press conference, so she stopped by the Bekbourg County library to see what she could learn about the murders and her grandfather's plea. Since it was a local matter, there were more reports about the victims, and in particular, about Roger Burkhart and his business interests in the car dealership, the fireworks stand and the pawn shop. She couldn't find anything about what eventually happened to the fireworks or pawn shop businesses, but she saw an article written a couple years later about a grand opening of the Burkhart dealership under new ownership. Al Werner was the new owner.

All three county commissioners were present for the press conference along with Lloyd Wiseman; Sheriff Mike Adams; Tyler Forquet, the County Prosecutor; and a couple of local ministers. Jeff Thompson conducted the press conference and laid out the plan that he had earlier foreshadowed in his interview with the *Bekbourg Tribune.*

"As I promised, we have been working with our community leaders to develop a comprehensive plan for addressing the drug problems in Bekbourg. While the loss of lives was unfortunate, we are convinced that the major sources of meth in our area were dealt a major blow with the discovery and ultimate destruction of the labs found on the Pinkston property. The DEA told us that the amount of meth capable of being produced in those operations could supply this area and even be sold in neighboring counties.

"While that major source of meth is out of our backyard, we're not going to stop there. We can't let other operations back here. Also, we've got to do a better job of educating our young people about drugs. We've got to increase funding to better staff and equip programs here to treat addictions. Today, we're going to lay out how we plan to move forward. While we believe that we will start to see results with what we announce today, this is the first step, and we will continue to look for ways we can fight the drug menace in our community.

"Sheriff Adams here has already started the paperwork to seek state funds for hiring two more deputies who will be specifically trained in drug enforcement. We will work with a joint task force with other state and county law enforcement officials on training."

Jeff further described how the County had set up an Action Committee comprised of local ministers; health care officials; Sheriff Adams; Lloyd Wiseman and a guidance counselor, Annalee Carter, from the high school. He offered, "The arrival of the Pinkston meth labs roughly coincided with the spike in drug use in the County. With the meth production stopped, it is a great opportunity for the community to deal with the drug problem around here."

Annalee called. "Cheryl, Mom called me. You know your grandpa and mine were pretty close friends. Mom called Grandpa and told him about seeing you. She thinks you should see him, Cheryl. There's something he wants to tell you. If you're available, I can go with you. You can meet me after school tomorrow, and I'll drive us over there."

"Sure, that sounds great. Do you know what it is he wants to tell me?"

"No, and he didn't tell Mom."

"Okay. Oh, by the way. I'm glad you called. You know, I've been thinking about Lilly. There are some college scholarships that are available for students who are interested in majoring in communications and journalism. They are available through professional media associations. Also, *The*

Presenter sponsors a scholarship. I was thinking about talking to Lilly about them, if you think that's okay."

"Cheryl, that's a wonderful idea. She is so talented and smart. I'll also talk to her about that, but hearing it from a real reporter might give her some confidence."

Rose was worried about who might be watching her house and wanted Cheryl to take precautions. Cheryl felt she was in a movie as she made her way across the back yard and walked to the back door of Rose's house.

When Suzy led Cheryl into the small living room, Cheryl recognized Rose right away. Rose was rocking a baby. She stood up and handed the baby to Suzy, "Lordy, Lordy. Cheryl, Baby, it's so wonderful to see you."

She and Cheryl gave each other a heartfelt hug. "This is my granddaughter, Suzy, and that's her baby, Tootsie. Have a seat, Honey."

"Thank you. Mrs. Waters and Suzy, I want you to know how sorry I am for your loss. I cannot imagine what you are going through."

"It's been hard, Cheryl. We can't believe what happened. It's bad enough with our family dying, but the police and the reporters won't leave us alone. The coroner hasn't released the bodies, so I don't know when the burial will be. Suzy here works nights at the hospital, but she's not gone back yet. She's afraid. She thinks someone might want to kill the rest of the family. Thank the Lord they didn't kill little Tootsie."

Suzy looked anxious, but not Rose. Cheryl remembered her as a feisty woman who loved to talk. Every time Cheryl and her grandpa went into the boarding house to eat lunch, she always came out of the kitchen to talk to them.

"Another thing: Pete is Suzy's boyfriend."

"Now, Grandma, we're not back together yet."

"Well, I'm hoping now that you and he are talking again, that might change. Suzy always loved Pete. She broke up with him because she was afraid what her daddy might do to Pete. Anyway, Pete is a good boy. He's Tootsie's daddy. He's been concerned about Suzy and Tootsie—calls here all the time checking on them. That boy didn't kill nobody."

"Well, I hope you don't mind talking to me. Did Bri tell you that I'm a reporter from *The Presenter* in Cleveland?"

"Yes, she told me all that."

"So, you're okay if I print what you say to me and use your name as my source?"

Rose looked at Suzy and then back at Cheryl, "I'll tell you if I don't want you to. You're the only reporter we've talked to."

"Okay, can you tell me when you last talked to your family?"

"I talked to Ruby almost every day. I had talked to her that evening. She usually called me after they finished dinner and she got the kitchen cleaned up. She sounded fine. We talked about little Tootsie. She loved that baby."

Cheryl heard a sob from Suzy.

"She was talking about what she had planted in the garden that day. She was a good person, Cheryl. She loved her kids and took good care of her family."

"How did she meet Tony? Wasn't he from another county?"

"Yeah. He was from Tapsaw County. There was a big July Fourth jig up at the State Park. Something young people like to go to. She and some friends drove up there. She met Tony, and they instantly hit it off. We had a small wedding here at the church, and she moved over there to live. His daddy bought them a new mobile home, and they put it on the property where they had some privacy."

Rose explained how Tony and Ruby came to relocate in Bekbourg. "I was thrilled, 'cause Ruby and Suzy and Aaron would be closer to me."

"What about you, Suzy? When did you last see your family?"

"Right before I left to go to work. Aaron had not gone anywhere, so he and Daddy were watching TV. I had given Tootsie a bath, and Mom was going to put her to bed."

Rose then talked about how Suzy had come home and what she had found and how panicked she was when she thought something might have happened to Tootsie.

"Do either of you have any ideas about who did this?"

Both of them said "no."

Rose said, "Cheryl, there is something that is a puzzle to us. We don't trust people 'round here, not the powers-that-be or the police. There's something that we want to tell you. We don't mind if you print it, but we sure don't want our names used or where it came from. I want my daughter's and grandson's killers caught. I don't want nothing swept under the rug or someone falsely accused."

Cheryl assured Rose and Suzy that she would maintain the confidence of her sources.

Rose looked at Suzy, "Suzy's scared, especially with the baby and all, but I'm not. I want justice for Ruby and Aaron and the others. Go ahead, Honey. You can trust Cheryl."

Suzy said, "One evening, Ray was there at the house talking to Daddy. I didn't mean to be listening. They were on the porch, and I was playing with Tootsie on the floor in the living room. Daddy told Ray that he thought there was a much bigger operation in the area. He believed their set-up was small potatoes, and that they had nothing to worry about from the authorities. There was a much larger fish in the pond, and the law would go after them. Ray didn't need to be concerned."

"When did this happen?"

"Well, I guess Tootsie was about three months old, so probably around four or so months ago."

Rose said, "That's what got us confused, when the leaders here and the police are saying the closing of the labs that Tony and his kin were running is the main source of the problem in the area."

Cheryl said, "Yes, I see your point."

Rose said, "Cheryl, I told Darlene, Victor's girlfriend, that we were going to talk to you. I told her I trusted you. She's not talked to any reporters, doesn't trust them. But she said she will talk to you. Suzy wrote her phone number on this piece of paper. If you want, I will call her and tell her that you'll call her."

"Sure. Thank you."

"Okay, that's put to bed. I should have asked when you got here. Honey, how's your momma?"

"Rose, she died almost three months ago. She had suffered for about two years from an illness."

"Oh, Honey. I'm so sorry to hear that. I'm so glad to be able to talk to you. After all that happened with your grandpa, you and your momma moved, and I never got to talk to you or her. I want you to know that I never believed Henry did that. He came in for lunch shortly after it happened, and he and I were talking about how we wondered who could have done it. Your grandpa was a gentle man. When I read he had confessed to the murders, I couldn't believe it. A lot of people didn't believe it. I always thought there was more to the story, but he had confessed. After he was sentenced and went to prison, people didn't talk about it no more. It was very sad. I wanted you to know my feelings on that."

"Thank you, Mrs. Waters. That means so much to me."

"Well, before you leave town, I hope you can come back by and see me. I'd like to talk about the old times, but you have to call me Rose."

Cheryl laughed. "I'd love to."

Darlene looked tired. She told Cheryl that she couldn't afford not to work, but she was having trouble sleeping. "This has been so hard to believe. God, as bad as it was, I am so grateful that those monsters didn't kill the baby." Darlene told Cheryl that she was concerned for her safety, because she knew them. "I really haven't known them long at all, and only met the rest of Victor's family twice, so I don't know hardly anything about them. I'm afraid someone might think I know more than I do and try to kill me, too."

Darlene told Cheryl that she and Victor had been dating about four months. She described him as a fun guy to do things with. He was between jobs and liked to fish and hunt. He didn't have a steady job but would sometimes pick up side jobs. She didn't know about the meth labs. She said that she only saw Tony and his family a couple of times when Ruby had invited her and Victor to dinner. She had only been to Victor's place once, and that was because he had to run there and pick up something, and she waited in the truck. There wasn't much said at all about any work they did, but once or twice, they referred to their farming business, and she didn't know where their farm was.

"They never seemed concerned about anything. I never heard them talk about any enemies or disputes or anything like that. Victor told me that someone had tried to get into Tony's workshop a few days ago, and he had helped Tony install a trip wire, but that didn't seem to be a worry to Victor."

Cheryl asked, "Did Victor tell you how Tony knew someone tried to get in there?"

"Well, he said Tony thought someone was probably trying to steal some of his tools or something. I asked him how Tony knew about it, and he said Tony told him the dogs started barking. He got his gun and went outside, but he thought it was okay, just an animal getting the dogs riled up. The next morning, he saw that someone had tried to cut the chain to the door. That's when he decided to put up the trip wire."

Cheryl told her that it might work to her advantage if Cheryl reported that she had only known the family a short time and did not know about the meth labs or any other drug business. Cheryl also reassured her that she would not disclose her source. Darlene agreed. She wanted to go about her daily life and not be concerned that people thought she knew more than she did.

Chapter 34

Martin Jackups was sitting on the front porch when Annalee and Cheryl pulled up. On the drive over, Annalee told Cheryl that, despite his age, her grandpa still lived by himself. He still drove and did small chores around the house.

When they walked up to the porch, Annalee said, "Hi, Grandpa," and Cheryl said, "Hi, Mr. Jackups."

He smiled and said, "Come have a seat, girls. I'm going to make the men in the neighborhood jealous having such pretty girls sitting on my porch."

Cheryl and Annalee laughed, "Now, Grandpa. I think they're already jealous since you're the most handsome man around here."

He smiled at that, "Cheryl, it's good to see you. Ann says you're a newspaper reporter now."

"Yes sir. I work for the Cleveland paper, *The Presenter*."

"So, that's where you and your momma moved when you left here?"

"Yes."

"Ann told me about your momma. I'm sorry 'bout that."

"Thank you, Mr. Jackups."

"Henry would be proud of you. I wish he could be here with us now shooting the breeze like he used to do."

"I do, too."

"Cheryl, when Ann told me that you were in town, I told her I wanted to see you. It's been eating at me all these years, and I thank the good Lord that I have the chance to make right something I should have done a long time ago.

"You know that me and Henry were good friends. We didn't see each other a lot, because we each had family matters to attend to and other things, but when we got together at the bar, we had a fine time telling stories. I know your grandpa had done some things, but nothing bad, and who hasn't done things. But, he was a good man, and I was glad he and I were friends.

"I don't know what that business was all about with the Burkhart killings, but I know your grandpa couldn't have done it. The night that it happened, he and I were at the bar together. We didn't like to go to Knucklepin's, because it was always crowded. The Bar's gone, torn down when they started expanding in that area where the Shopper's Pavilion was built. When we left, he was in no condition to do what he confessed to. He and I had both drunk our fair share that night. We left about 10:00 or 10:30 pm, and he couldn't have been sober enough to do all that."

Martin looked at Cheryl for a moment and then said, "There was something else. I think Henry was sick. The last couple of times I had seen him, he wasn't himself. I know he died of cancer about six months after he went to prison, but I think he had that before the killings.

"I never understood why he confessed, and I sure don't understand why the sheriff believed him. Even the prosecuting attorney and judge should have known better. How can a sixty something year old man kill five people? One thing's double damn sure, ain't no way Henry Willis would ever kill a kid.

"I've thought a lot about it over the years. I don't know why Burkhart was killed, but I have my suspicions. He was a loud mouth to start with. Those TV commercials used to drive me crazy. If I'd had a remote control then, I'd have silenced it or switched off every time one started. Then, he had loudly bragged about those gold and silver coins. It shouldn't be a reason, but I think someone thought he was getting too big for his britches. They were afraid he was attracting some unwanted scrutiny from the State and maybe the Feds. Not too long before the killings, his fireworks business was blown up. People around here won't hardly talk, afraid to, but there were rumors when that happened that it was a warning to him about something.

"Anyhow, I went to the jail to see your grandpa shortly after the paper reported that he had confessed. He told me at the beginning when he saw me to not ask him any questions about it. He knew what he was doing. He then changed the subject, and we talked about other things. He shook my hand when I left, and I had a feeling that I might not see him again.

"I heard that you and your momma moved. I kept hoping that Ann or Annalee would hear from you, where you were. Especially after I heard Henry died, I wanted to tell you what I knew."

"Mr. Jackups, thank you for what you've told me. I never believed my grandfather did it, not even back then, but I didn't know what was going on and why he confessed. My mother told me that he wanted to confess and didn't want me to ever talk to anyone about it. Grandpa did have cancer. I promised my mom I wouldn't tell anyone, because she said Grandpa didn't want anyone to know. Mom changed our last name after we moved to Cleveland. She said she didn't want us haunted by the past, but I wonder if that was the only reason.

"This is between us, but while I'm here reporting on the Pinkston murders, I'm going to look into what happened. I'm an investigative reporter, so I know how to look for things."

Martin was uneasy with Cheryl's plan, "You need to be careful, Cheryl. Even though it's been twenty years, whoever was behind that could still be around."

"Thank you. I'll be cautions, but I owe it to Grandpa, my mother and myself to learn the truth."

"So, you're stubborn like Henry could be?"

"Yes, sir."

Martin sat there for a minute, and Cheryl knew he had something else on his mind.

"Mr. Jackups, if there is something else, please tell me."

"I don't know whether I should tell you or not. If I tell you and something happens to you, God knows I will never forgive myself, but I know how you feel about wanting to make it right for Henry and you and your momma."

"Mr. Jackups, I'm going to investigate my grandfather's situation even if you don't tell me. It seems I'd be better off armed with whatever you want to tell me rather than somehow falling into it."

"Yeah, I guess that's right. Okay. You know the Bekbourg dealership down on the main highway?"

"Yes sir."

"Well, that was Burkhart's dealership. It was a small dealership near the old downtown. Al Werner worked for the paper company. That business started having some problems, and Al went to work part time for Burkhart at the car place. I never knew how it happened, but he wound up owning the business. Werner somehow got the money. I don't know how, since I never heard he had that much. Even after he got it, not too much time later, he even put more money in it. I don't know if this means anything, and I sure don't want to send you on a wild goose chase, or put you in any danger, but if you're going to investigate it anyhow, it's something you might want to know.

"If you need me, you let me know. You have to promise me you won't do anything foolish and that you'll be careful."

"I promise," assured Cheryl. "I am grateful for what you've told me. Hopefully, I can get to the bottom of this and set the record straight for Grandpa."

Chapter 35

It was Sean's day off, and he had just finished potting flowers for Kye when Danny drove up. They were going to Sean's parents to see what might be done with the '55 Plymouth Fury and '63 Buick Riviera parked in his dad's garage. Kye was thrilled to see Danny, and while they were talking, she told him about an old car her husband had stored that he might look at some time.

After Sean, Danny, and Buddy got on the road, teasing Danny, Sean said, "Danny, I didn't know you had Mrs. Davis. You sure made an impression on her."

Danny laughed, "Well, I don't know what it was, because it sure wasn't my grades."

They both laughed. "She spent a lot of extra time helping me in her class. You know, Sean, I wasn't a good student. She told me once that she had taught my mother, and that she had been one of her best students. I guess that's why she helped me."

"You ought to take her up on checking out that car. There's no telling what she's got. Her husband was a retired railroad engineer, and those old railroad guys sure liked cars."

"I will. Maybe sometime you and I can go check it out together. Another thing if you're ever

220

interested. This will probably come as a shock to you, but I am a much better shot than I was back in high school. I couldn't hit the side of a barn then. I've gotten a lot better, nowhere as good as you are, but if you ever want to go to the shooting range, I'm game."

"Sounds good, Danny."

Just then, Sean's phone rang. It was Hugh Hayes, the father of Jamie, the boy who had recently overdosed. Hugh asked Sean if he could stop by after dinner tonight. "There's something that we think you should know."

After Sean hung up, Danny said, "I couldn't help hearing. I'm glad you're back, Sean. These drugs need to be cleaned up around here. Sometimes, I hear things at the service station. People don't like to talk. They're afraid they might say something to the wrong person. One thing I've heard is there's an air strip. Sometimes during the night, people hear a plane landing or taking off."

"Have you ever been there?"

"Just a couple of times. Once was to tow a car that was parked there that wouldn't start, and one time, one of my customers took me for a plane ride. I guess he liked the way I rebuilt his engine. Some people around here, like farmers and local business men, have their own small planes there. Jeff keeps a plane there. There are some metal buildings where some store their planes. There isn't a tower that I could tell, so they probably take off and land by sight. I don't know if the milk company still has a plane there. They used to, but the paper company has a small plane it keeps in one of the hangers. I saw it that day I was there to tow the car."

When Sean arrived home, Kye stepped out and asked Sean if she could talk to him for a minute. They sat down on the front porch with Buddy plopping down between them. Sean could see that Kye was not herself. "Kye is something wrong? Are you okay?"

Kye said, "Sean, I've been thinking all afternoon. There's something I need to say, to get off my chest." She had turned to look Sean in the eye.

Sean said, "Okay."

"I trust you, Sean. I know that you will know what to do with what I'm about to tell you. It might be a secret that should go to the grave. I know Danny has always looked up to you, and I know you would never hurt Danny."

Kye turned to look out over the front yard but didn't seem to be focused on anything in particular.

"You're right, Kye. I would never hurt Danny."

"Danny's mother was a beautiful girl. She was so sweet and sensitive. Her parents were poor and not very educated. She was smart though, and she loved learning. She would come to my classroom after school sometimes, and we'd talk about the great writers and the possible hidden meanings in their works.

"During her junior year, she was working at the GilHaus but still made a point of stopping by to see me. Then something happened. She started to seem withdrawn. I knew something was wrong. Then one afternoon, she came into my classroom and started crying. She told me she was pregnant. I wanted her to see a doctor for her health and that of the baby. She wasn't interested in that or really any help. She never confided in me as to who got her pregnant. She dropped out of school soon after that. I never saw her again.

"After her death, I went to see Norm, the man she married. He talked to me. Apparently, Emily had told him how close we had become. Norm was a year older and had secretly loved her in their early years of high school. He thought she was the most beautiful girl he had ever seen, and she was so sweet to everyone. He didn't dare approach her, because he was a 'nobody.' The grease on his hands from being a car mechanic could never be completely removed, and he didn't have much money.

"One day, she drove the family car into the gas station for gas. Norm was kind to her in helping her with the car. After that, she found reasons to stop by the gas station. Norm was madly in love with her. They soon got married, and Danny was born. I don't know if Danny ever found out about Norm not being his real father.

"Norm told me he couldn't figure out who supplied the drugs. Emily would never tell him. Norm was heartbroken, but he saw in Danny the love he had for his wife. Sean, this is between you and me, but I think I know who Danny's real father is. I probably shouldn't tell, but I'm an old lady, and if I die, there's probably no one who would know."

Kye paused for a minute, looking down at her hands that were crossed in her lap. A tear ran down her cheek, and she pulled a tissue from a dress pocket. "God forgive me if what I tell you is wrong, but I think it was Jeff Thompson's father. He was always hanging out at the GilHaus even though he was married. His wife was never in there with him. I saw him flirt with the young waitresses. I always thought Gill Geisen should have stopped that, but I guess he didn't want to get on the bad side of Randall Thompson. One time when Cecil and I were in there, I saw him put his hand on Emily's hand as she started to take away his plate. It didn't look right to me, even though he quickly pulled it away, it was not inadvertent. Emily blushed and hurried off to get the check. I watched, and another waitress brought his check. He asked where Emily was, and the waitress said that it was time for her break."

Sean said, "Kye, I don't know if Danny knows or not. He's never said anything about it to me. He and Norm still run the gas station together, and they're close. I don't want you to be upset. This is not good for you. I don't plan to tell anyone, Kye. It will work out the way it should."

Sean was deep in thought as he drove to the Hayes' that evening. Something was suspicious about Gary's business; something about Jeff seemed off; and now this about Danny. Even Mike was acting strange. Sean couldn't put his finger on it, but something was amiss with his friends.

Jamie was sitting in the den waiting when Hugh brought Sean into the room. "Have a seat, Sean. We appreciate you coming over. There's something that Jamie told me last night, and I thought you should know."

Jamie looked at his dad, who nodded, "Go ahead, Jamie. Tell Deputy Neumann what you told me."

Twisting a baseball in his hand, Jamie murmured, "Well, it was me that bought the meth, Deputy Neumann. You know the stuff that we took that night when we overdosed? Don't worry, I'm so grounded, I won't have money to buy anything for a long time. I didn't know what I was buying was meth. I really didn't know what it was. I thought it was something like pot. We had just tried pot a few times. I know now we shouldn't have, but I guess we wanted to act cool." Jamie paused and looked at his dad, who nodded for him to continue. "The person I bought the meth from was that kid who got murdered the other day—the one whose whole family was killed."

"Aaron Pinkston?" Sean asked.

Jamie nodded. "Yeah, Aaron."

"How did you know to buy the drugs from him?"

"Umm, the kids around the school who wanted drugs, we knew Aaron had things. That's where I got the pot from."

"Did he have other drugs?"

"I don't know. All I know is the pot and the meth. When I asked him what else he had beside pot, all he pulled out of his jacket pocket was the meth."

"Was this at school?"

"No. I think he was afraid of being seen at school by a teacher or something. I'd meet him at the gas station down the road from where the high school is."

"Why didn't you tell me earlier about Aaron?"

Jamie glanced at his dad and turned back to Sean. Tears filled his eyes. "I should have. My dad told me I should have. I was scared. I knew it wouldn't bring back Ronny. After I got back to school after it all happened, Aaron came up to me and asked if I had mentioned him to anyone. I told him 'no.' He told me if I knew what was good for me, I'd better not ever tell anyone. He even threatened to do something to Mom and Dad and my younger sister. Aaron was mean, Deputy Neumann. He was tough. I know I should have said something, but I was too afraid."

"Okay, Jamie. You and your dad did the right thing by calling me. If you think of anything else, let me know."

As Hugh and Sean were walking out to the car, Sean asked Hugh where he was the night of the Pinkston murders. Hugh didn't seem surprised by the question. "You can ask Pat if you like, but we were both here all night that night. Since that happened with Jamie, we've been staying around home most evenings with Jamie and Hillary."

"Okay, Hugh. I had to ask. If anything comes up, I may need to talk to you again."

The next day, Sean followed-up, and the alibis checked out for the parents of Ronny Mueller and Jared Fellows.

Cheryl stopped by Frau's on her way back. When she walked in, she took in the furnishings and atmosphere that seemed unchanged from the few times she had come here as a child with her grandparents and mother.

She sat at a table by herself eating her dinner and watching the patrons and staff. She didn't recognize anyone from the press briefings or anyone she felt might have some information about the Pinkston murders. As she started to walk to her car, a deputy walked up to her. Something about the man set off alarm bells. She tightened her grip around the key chain which had an alarm. Cheryl noted that his badge said, "Deputy Clark." Cheryl's eyes scanned the parking lot, but she didn't see anyone.

The Deputy leered at Cheryl's body, "I've seen you around. You're that reporter from up north of here, aren't you?"

"Yes. I'm a reporter from *The Cleveland Presenter*. Is there something about the case you would like to discuss?"

Ben barked a contemptuous laugh and spit some tobacco off to the side. "There's no news for you 'round here. We'll find who did it, and we don't need no reporters tryin' to stir up trouble. So, you'd best get back up there, unless you're lookin' for something more than a story."

Cheryl fought to quell the apprehension that sought its grasp or show intimidation. She breathed a sigh of relief when a car pulled into park near them. He pointedly raked his eyes across her body and smirked as he slowly turned to walk away. Cheryl thought, *"What a repulsive and vile man."* Driving back to the B&B, Cheryl watched to make sure she was not being followed.

Chapter 36

Cheryl went to the County Clerk's office and asked to see police reports and court documents covering 1980 through 1982, because she did not want to tip her hand about the matter she was investigating. Over the next couple of days, she was referred from one office to another, but to no avail. There were no documents pertaining to the Burkhart murders. She didn't know if they were inept at record-keeping back then or if there was a more sinister reason why she was unable to find police reports and court documents. She was going to have to find another way to locate the pertinent information.

Sean was working closely with the state police and keeping Mike updated on the investigation. Mike was meeting with the County Commission and business leaders to keep them informed on the progress of the investigation. However, Mike was letting Sean handle the details of the case.

Sean stopped to visit Rose Waters again. When he arrived, she seemed hesitant at first to talk, but when she realized he was only there to check on her well-being, she seemed to relax. He told her that he was still working the case, but they didn't have a lot to go on. Rose said, "Well, that must explain why the Jackass was trying to squeeze poor Pete at his job. Deputy Neumann, ever since the murder, Pete has been over here spending time with Suzy and the baby. He is a good boy. I keep hoping that he and Suzy get hitched, and they might, but if Pete loses his job at Pavilion's, that's going to be hard on him and Suzy."

"What are you talking about, Rose? What deputy? Who's leaning on Pete?"

"Pete came over here real worried last night when he got off work. That Jackass Ben Clark showed up there accusing him of killing them. Seems he really made a show of it. The boss asked Pete after he left what it was all about, and Pete tried to tell him he didn't know, but Pete's afraid he is going to get fired."

Sean drove over to the Shopper's Pavilion and asked to speak to the supervisor. The supervisor was not happy to see Sean. Sean said, "I understand that a deputy visited Mr. Vance yesterday here."

"Yeah, that's right. First, the state police right after the murder, then that deputy a couple of times, now you. Pete's been a good worker, but this is a distraction to everyone here. I could get sideways with the higher-ups with all this going on."

"Mr. Vance is not under suspicion."

The supervisor interrupted, "Well, the deputy yesterday sure didn't make it sound that way."

"He's not. I came by here today to assure you and Pete of that. I'm sorry if we've caused a problem here. It happens he knows the people who were killed. We're trying to find out what he knows about the people. Hopefully, we won't have to bother him again."

The supervisor called Pete up to his office, because he didn't want the employees to see the police visiting Pete again. When Pete walked in, he saw Sean and got nervous. Sean reassured him, "Pete, I'm here to apologize to you and your supervisor. I told him, and I'm telling you, that you are not under suspicion. Deputy Clark is not going to come here bothering you again."

Sean asked the supervisor if he might speak privately with Pete, that he wouldn't take much of his time. The supervisor was relieved that Sean seemed to be taking charge of things and that Pete was not under investigation. "Sure, that's fine. Pete, I'll walk back and punch you out for a break."

After the supervisor walked out, Sean asked, "What happened yesterday when he was here?"

"That cop yesterday, he was accusing me of killing them because of Suzy. He said I killed them, because they wouldn't let her marry me or see Tootsie. I told him I didn't do it, and he kept trying to get me to confess. I told him that I don't know nothing and to stop trying to pin it on me. I told him that he was going to cause me to lose my job. He didn't care. He told me I hadn't seen the last of him, that he knew I was guilty. To tell the truth, I was glad I was at work. I don't know what he would have done. He was downright nasty and accusing me of killing them. I didn't do it."

Sean said, "I'm sorry about that. I'll make sure Ben doesn't come to your job and get you in trouble."

Sean walked into the precinct to see Mike. "I gotta talk to you about something. I was over at Pavilion's today, because Ben caused a commotion with a young man named Pete Vance. He is the ex-boyfriend of Suzy Pinkston and the father of Suzy's baby. He is not under suspicion, but Ben went there and read the riot act to him. Accused him of committing the crime and even made the young man feel threatened. In other words, he made a complete ass out of this department and, in particular, this case. I don't think he should be involved in this anymore."

"Sean, we have reason to believe this young man was involved. Sometimes, if you come on really strong, this kind of suspect breaks."

Sean was flabbergasted, "You knew about all this and you approved?"

"Well, I didn't know all the details, but Ben told me he was going over there and lean on him a little bit."

"I wouldn't call it leaning. It's more like lying right on top of him and trying to suffocate him. We don't have any evidence linking him to this crime. Forensics ruled his gun out. All we can hope to get from him are insights on who this family was and if someone might have had something against them. He's been cooperative, Mike. Vance was afraid he might get fired. Ben needs to be taken off this case."

Mike was defensive and uncomfortable, "I was afraid this was going to happen. I think the only one I should take off this case is you. From the beginning, you have been working at cross-purposes with the rest of the department."

Sean looked hard at Mike, "The only one I'm working at cross purposes is Ben and maybe you. I've been working closely with the state police, their crime scene squad and the medical examiner. The Chief and I have been communicating every day, and one other thing, Mike. You seem to be so worried about your turf. I can assure you if you pull me off this case, you will have the state police down here, and they will take this case away from you. The only reason they haven't done so is because I have been working so closely with them."

Mike glared at Sean. "I'll call the manager at Pavilion's and talk to him."

Sean glared back and nodded his head. As he was leaving, he said, "Be sure to tell Ben he's off the case."

After having spent a restless night, Mike walked into the precinct and told Kim that he needed to talk to Ben. Mike was still upset about his run-in with Sean the previous day. He knew Sean was right, but he knew there was going to be trouble.

"Yeah Sheriff, what do you want to talk to me about?"

"Have a seat, Ben." Mike stared at Ben for a few seconds, "Ben, you really messed up this time."

"What do you mean?"

"Just what I said. You went out to the Shopper's Pavilion and harassed Pete Vance. There's no reason to think he had anything to do with the murders. The supervisor there is upset."

"I told you I was goin'. He's the ex-boyfriend of that daughter of Pinkston. He could have been pissed at them for some reason and killed them. Those state police pansies just go in there and ask a few questions. That's not goin' to get nowhere. You've gotta shake the trees to get the fruit."

Mike was angry, "We're not playing games here, Ben. First, I didn't know you were going to embarrass this department. Second, you didn't even report this to me. Sean told me all about it. It sounds like you were being a loose cannon—throwing your weight around. I can't have this type of behavior. I've got to take you off the case."

"Neumann? What's that SOB got to do with this?"

"He had to smooth things over at Pavilion's with Vance and the supervisor there."

"You can't do this, Mike. It's my case."

"First of all, it's not your case, and it never has been your case. Technically, it was Mack's case, but I'm pulling both of you off the case and turning it over to Sean. He had a lot of experience when he was in the Marines with a lot of things like this. He has a good relationship with the state police, and frankly, your track record on things like this is not that good. Anyway, the state police are still sniffing around. We don't want to get cross-ways with them. I hope they'll be pulling out soon."

"He's not your quarterback no more," Ben angrily retorted. "He's only been here a short time, and now he's taken over. You're the sheriff."

"Yes, I am, and I'm telling you you're off the case."

Ben was seething, "You'll regret this."

"Ben, why don't you take a few days' leave? Tell you what, take four or five days. I'll tell Kim to mark you off the schedule."

Ben stormed out—slamming the door. Mike hoped Ben calmed down before returning to work.

Most of the day shift had cleared out for the day. Mike was working on a report when his phone rang. "What do you think you're doing taking Clark off the Pinkston case?"

"I had no choice. Ben got himself cross-wise with some people while he supposedly was investigating it. Listen, I'm trying to keep the State out of this best I can. Any more shenanigans like this, and the State's going to start to wonder if something's going on down here. Ben is a loose cannon. I can't risk what he might do."

There was a silence from the person on the other end. Mike was hoping he was getting ready to hang up. Finally, he said to Mike, "Say, what's Neumann's alibi for the night of the murders?"

A tightening churned in Mike's stomach, "What are you talking 'bout? You think Sean had something to do with this?"

"Well."

"There's no way Sean had anything to do with this."

"Check out his alibi. See where he was. I want to know if there is any time he was unaccounted for that night. Let me know what you find out. Like yesterday!"

The phone line went dead. A sweat had formed on Mike's forehead. He hoped to God Sean had an air-tight alibi. Mike opened up his computer to check the reports Sean filed for that night.

Chapter 37

Sean had not slept well. After waking from another nightmare, he had not been able to get back to sleep. Finally, he took Buddy for a long walk. His leg had really bothered him today. As Sean got out of his truck at Frau's, he was deep in thought about his investigation. Even though he had bits and pieces of information, a pattern was not emerging. The breakup of the Pinkston meth production made local people believe that the drug problem was solved. The DEA didn't believe that. The information they had still pointed to a major drug operation somewhere around Bekbourg. Staking out the landing strip several times had not been fruitful. He had observed Gary's business, but he didn't see anything that jumped out at him. He was beginning to think he was spinning his wheels.

In walked Dusty and Mule Head. Sean waived at them, and they came over to join him for dinner.

"How you doing, Sean?" asked Dusty.

"Doin' fine. How 'bout you two?"

They glanced at each other and then looked at Sean. Sean knew something was up. Mule Head said, "You know, you're working for the sheriff now, aren't you?"

Sean laughed, "Yeah, you can tell by my uniform."

Sean was trying to ignore the pulsing pain in his leg.

Mule Head looked at Dusty, who gave him a little nod.

Mule Head said, "We were hoping you'd be here. You know there's something odd going on at this car dealership where I work. And it seems to be happening more often. A load of cargo vans will come in, and for whatever reason, one of them won't have the right paperwork. One of the guys, seems like the same one every time, unloads them off the trucks. He takes it himself to the defect lot. He never takes any others to the defect lot. I take care of the other ones. I happened to notice this over time, and it's happening more often. What makes it really odd, is the next day, it's gone. Vehicles that go to the defect lot usually sit there for weeks until someone from the manufacturer comes to fix it or haul it away. But this van is gone the next day. I don't think anyone is stealing the vans. No one ever says anything. I asked once, and they told me to mind my own business."

Dusty looked inquiringly at Sean.

Sean had a serious look, "Don't ask anything, Mule Head. I don't want you to get in trouble or lose your job."

"Well it's none of my business, but it's an odd situation, and once I get something in my head, well that's why they call me Mule Head."

"I've got a long night ahead of me. I'm glad you told me. Here's a card with my number. If you see anything else, let me know."

"Boze, I learned something that might be useful."

After Sean told Boze what Mule Head had told him, Boze said, "Good work, Sean. I'm going to put a surveillance team on the car dealership. We're still working the distributor where the cargo van went missing. We've got someone under surveillance who seems to have something to do with some other missing vehicles."

Sean mentioned, "It might be helpful to see what we can find out about this dealership. It's certainly grown over the last twenty years, when many of these rural dealerships went under. Many of these dealerships couldn't compete with the foreign cars."

"Good point, Sean. I'll get someone looking into this. Smuggling drugs using vans like this could be bigger than Bekbourg. This could be a way drugs are making it to the big cities. We'll stay in touch."

Sean had periodically gone by the landing strip at night to watch for any aircraft activity. He was still skeptical about the DEA's thinking that Bekbourg was the distribution hub for a major drug operation. There had been the cargo van that was found abandoned by the side of the road, and the mysterious activity at the car dealership needed to be investigated, but no hard evidence. Nothing was really turning up on either this or the murder investigation. He had worked investigations enough to know that as more time goes by solving the case becomes more difficult and often turns into an unsolved mystery, especially in murder cases. However, he still hoped for a break in both cases.

He was sitting here tonight, because Boze had told him that a shipment would be coming in this week and for him to watch the local air strip. He parked in his usual spot behind some trees and had been waiting for about two hours. He had seen some headlights go by about a half-hour before. Now, some headlights were coming back from the other direction. The vehicle passed and pulled in and stopped in front of Sean's car. Sean checked his gun, not knowing what this meant.

He got out of his cruiser, stepped back in the shadows and waited to see what was going to happen. The headlights were still on, and finally, an old man got out of the truck and walked up to the cruiser and looked in. Sean spoke, "What can I do for you?"

The old man jumped back startled, because he had not seen Sean in the shadows. "I thought I would stop and see what was going on. I've seen your cruiser here quite a bit over the last month or so. I live near here and was curious. Maybe I should introduce myself. I'm Herbert Ward. I live up the road about half a mile."

Sean introduced himself and checked the man for weapons and checked his truck to ensure no one else was there. He told the man that he was there checking out the airport to see if there is any activity at night.

The old man said, "Well, I live around here. There are never any planes that come in here at night except on rare occasions, but if you're looking for night flights, you might check down the road from here at the old Steinsen place. It's 'bout five miles from here. It's really isolated. No one's lived there for years. I'm getting old, but every so often in the middle of the night, I hear what sounds like a plane coming in for a landing. I know it's not here, because it's coming in from the wrong direction. It flies over my place kind of low, like it's getting ready to land, and then a little while later, it flies out. I haven't given it much thought. I mind my own business, but it's been happening for several years. Lately, though, it's been happening a lot. In fact, that's why I stopped. Because I thought you might be interested in that."

"Well, have you ever gone up there and looked around?"

"No. They've got new barbwire fence all around the place and a new gate. It's none of my business, but I do know that farm from years ago. A field on top of a hill in the middle of the farm would be a perfect place for a landing strip."

"Well, that's interesting, Mr. Ward, and could be quite helpful. I'm glad you stopped."

"Oh. There's another thing. It seemed like I'd hear some trucks go by, especially when I hear the planes, but I might have been sleeping. It seems though that it's been more regular lately."

The next day, Sean went to the old Steinsen place and climbed onto the property. About five-hundred yards up the hill behind the old home place he saw what he knew was a flat, recently-mowed surface used as an airstrip. He saw the tracts left by the planes as well as vehicles. He also saw where long strips of lights were rolled up. He gathered that they were unrolled at night to light the outer edges of the runway, power generated by a nearby generator. Off to the side was a large windowless steel building, large enough to house a plane. A large generator sat outside. The garage doors as well as a side door were locked, so Sean was not able to see inside.

Sean called Boze and told him that he may have found the runway used in the local operation.

Two nights after Sean inspected the secret air strip, he was hiding in underbrush overlooking the landing strip. Around three o'clock a.m., he saw a cargo van pull up to the side of the air strip. He could make out people rolling out lighting strips along both sides of the landing strip. He heard an engine's buzz growing louder, and the plane simply materialized out of the darkness to land—then rolled to the end of the runway and took a sharp turn in position for takeoff. The men rushed the plane and unloaded boxes into the truck while the lighting strips were removed. Almost as quickly as it landed, the plane took off, and the truck drove away. Sean sprinted to his truck, but by the time he got there and pulled out on the road, the van was gone.

Chapter 38

Cheryl had put calls in asking to interview the Sheriff and Commissioner Thompson. The Sheriff's office told her that he didn't comment on ongoing investigations beyond public statements. There had been no word yet from Commissioner's Thompson's office.

She met with a couple of different neighbors of the Pinkstons. First, they wanted to make sure that they would not be identified in any of her articles. They both had basically the same thing to say. They had no idea about the meth labs, but they weren't too surprised about the marijuana. They didn't really know these Pinkstons that well, because they had only lived in the area for a few years. They knew Earl and Ruth Pinkston much better. Earl and Ruth were nice people, and they couldn't imagine them ever growing or selling drugs. The neighbors were scared a little but had guns to protect themselves if there was a killer on the loose. However, they thought it more likely was the acts of a rival drug group, but they had no idea who that might be—they didn't know anyone involved in drugs. It could be a Columbian cartel, but they never heard of a cartel in the area.

Earl and Ruth Pinkston talked to her. Earl told her that he and Ruth had both been born in

243

Bekbourg County. He had a brother, Zeke, who left when he was about nineteen-years-old and moved over to Tapsaw County. Earl's parents had been dead for many years. He and his brother weren't estranged, but they just weren't in contact much. However, "Family is family," Earl said, so when he and Ruth decided that it was too much to live so far away from town, he called his brother to see if he wanted to buy the property. Zeke wasn't interested, but Tony wanted the place.

Earl and Ruth said that they never had any contact with Tony after he bought the property. At first, Ruth would call Ruby to ask about how they were doing and how they liked living there, but, while Ruby was polite, Ruth didn't think she really was interested in communicating with her. Eventually, there was no more communication between them. Earl did not know when Ray and Victor moved onto the property, and he had no idea they were growing marijuana or making meth.

That evening, Cheryl went to dinner at Max's. He greeted her with a big smile, "Hi, Cheryl. Ever since you talked to Lilly about scholarship opportunities, she has had a smile on her face."

"That's wonderful to hear. If you don't mind, I'd like to talk to her for a few minutes this evening about what a newspaper reporter does."

"Be my guest. Right this way, and I'll tell Lilly you're here."

After dinner, Cheryl returned to her room and drafted her article. She told Earl and Ruby's story and, without disclosing her sources, reported the information the neighbors had told her. Cheryl also wrote that Tony was overheard saying that his drug operations were "small potatoes," and that there was a "much bigger operation" in the area. Another point she made in her article was: *Tony Pinkston reportedly was heard telling someone that there had been an intruder near the meth lab behind his home about two weeks before the murders. Victor Shultz, one of the victims and cousin to Tony, allegedly assisted Tony in installing a trip wire to alert him of any trespassers at the meth lab.*

Sean read Cheryl's article and wondered how she had discovered these facts and what other things she might have learned. Usually, he tried to avoid talking to reporters, but he remembered her. She was quick to ask the probing question about why Jeff had jumped to the conclusion that the area's meth source had been shut down. Her energy and looks actually made him look forward to talking to her. He wanted to see what she might divulge about her report. Probably nothing, but it was worth a try.

He briefed Boze about seeing the plane and the truck at the air strip. Sean told Boze that he had learned that the property had sold at a tax sale, "pennies on the dollar."

Boze planned to set up surveillance to monitor the landing field. "I have a gut instinct about things, and I think you are closer than you think. I don't have to tell you, Sean, that these guys don't play nice."

Dusty called, "Sean, there's something really important me and Chaw need to talk to you about, but I don't want to do it in public."

"Sure, Dusty. What do you have in mind?"

"I'd like to meet at the old depot before we go to work tonight. We sure don't want that snooty engineer, Jules Leroux, to see us. Come by a little after nine o'clock. That way, he'll already be on the engine. We need to talk in private. Be sure to park where he won't see you."

That night at the depot, Dusty said, "Sean, we don't know if this means anything or not. You told us to keep our eyes open. This is what I saw, and Chaw can back me up on this. Last night when we got to work, something really strange was going on at that paper factory.

"Usually, we switch our cars and spot them at the paper plant and finish around midnight before we go to Chillicothe. Last night, the Wheeling train that had the load for the paper plant was late coming. We thought that we'd do it when we got back from Chillicothe. So anyway, we spotted the few cars in the milk plant. It was a light night, and we got finished a lot sooner than we thought.

"We got back to Bekbourg about four o'clock a.m. We went up to the factory and opened the gates. When we were getting ready to pull the empties out, a couple of guys came out of the shadows—yelling at us to get out. They said that we weren't supposed to be there then and there was going to be big trouble if we didn't leave. It was awfully dark around the factory. We weren't sure what to do, so we called the dispatcher. These guys were getting madder by the minute. I told them 'I don't work for you, I work for the railroad,' and he said, 'you're supposed to switch at midnight. It's four o'clock, so get out.'

"The dispatcher told us not to cause trouble, and that we should leave. The dispatcher said, 'Tomorrow, if they don't have anything to do because they wouldn't let you switch, it's not our problem.' As we were leaving, there were four or five dark vans up near the loading dock. We went ahead and put the engine back in the yard and left. I didn't think much at the time, but since then, it's something that rankles me."

Chaw, during the whole discussion, was nodding his agreement with what Dusty was telling Sean. Chaw then said, "But there was something that I saw. I was at the main line at the switch waiting for Dusty to pull the empties out. I noticed at the loading dock and the road leading to the factory, there were four or five dark vans and there were men loading them with something. At the time, I believed it was cups. Maybe they were stealing things. About the time Dusty was being kicked out, all these men hurried back into the factory. It was almost like they had been warned. After we were leaving, I didn't notice anything around those cargo vans. With Dusty's experience and what I saw, there's something going on at the paper factory."

Sean asked them, "Did you say anything about this to anyone?"

Dusty responded, "Well, I told the dispatcher that we got kicked out, but I didn't tell anyone 'bout the vans. We got out of there. I don't know what's going on. I really don't know what those vans were doing there, but they sure didn't want us around."

"Thanks for telling me," Sean said. "It's probably wise not to tell anyone else about this right now. It may not be anything, but if they were really angry about something, they might be concerned that you saw something."

"Yeah, you could be right, but I haven't noticed anything like that before. Only seen the cleaning guys," Dusty said. "There is a large cleaning crew that goes in there. We can see them get off an old school bus. There are quite a few of them. Most of them are Hispanics."

"Boze, I now know you're clairvoyant."

"How so, Sean?"

"You thought things might start to shake a little."

"Yeah?"

"I've heard something tonight you ought to know." Sean conveyed what he had heard from Dusty and Chaw.

"Sean, this is certainly suspicious."

"I'm going to go by the County permit and code department and see what I can find out about the plant. I'm also going to visit the paper plant and have a look around."

"Good idea. We still have the car dealership on our radar as well. Take care."

"We had some trouble last night with those blasted railroaders. For some reason, they did another run before coming here. They didn't get here until around four o'clock a.m. We had the vans being loaded, but I don't know if they saw anything or what they might say."

"Your people need to be more careful. They should have paid attention to know the train had not come earlier. We can't have mistakes."

Chapter 39

Cheryl had received a call from a woman named Stella Long. She explained that she knew that Cheryl was investigating the drug situation around Bekbourg. "I've got something that might be useful to you, Ms. Seton, but I don't want my named used. I don't even want anyone to know that I am talking to you." Cheryl suggested that they meet at Bri's.

When Stella arrived, Cheryl noticed she was apprehensive. "Stella, I can tell that this isn't easy for you. I won't name you as a source."

"I've never talked to a reporter before, Ms. Seton. I'm a little nervous, but it's also emotional to me because this is about someone who I was very close to. Missy Collins was my best friend."

"Okay, go at your own pace, and please call me Cheryl." Cheryl poured them both a glass of lemonade.

"Thank you. Well, Missy moved here and started work at the plant, and we hit it off right away. I never understood why she worked at the factory, because she didn't fit in there. She looked like a model," Stella laughed. "Not one of those razor thin models. She had the body like those 1950's movie stars—if you know what I mean. She was so beautiful inside, too. Someone like that could be a snob or catty, but she wasn't like that at all. Her smile would light up the room. She was so much fun. I asked her once why she came to work at the factory. She laughed and said that she needed a job after moving to Bekbourg, and they were willing to hire her."

"Where did she move here from?"

"She never said exactly. Somewhere in Ohio I think, but I don't know. That's the one thing about her. She was the life of the party, but she had secrets."

"What do you mean?"

"She didn't work too long at the plant before she quit. She had moved into a mobile home, a nice one. Had it fixed real cute. I don't know for sure where she got her money. She had a boyfriend who I think must have given her the place to live and the money she spent. That's the thing. I know she had a boyfriend, but she never told who he was. She would talk about her 'Honey,' how rich he was, but she never told who he was."

"Do you know why she didn't tell?"

"No, but for some reason, he must not have wanted people to know. I don't know why, because she was so beautiful. Maybe he was married. I don't know."

"What has this got to do with drugs in Bekbourg?" Cheryl was confused.

Stella's demeanor changed to more somber. "Well, that's the thing about Missy. She had a drug problem. I tried to talk to her about getting help, but she told me it wouldn't work. I think she may have died of a drug overdose."

"Oh, dear," said Cheryl. "I am sorry."

"Me, too. What is odd is that it was like puff, she was gone. I never knew if she had any family. There was nothing in the local paper or news. She and I called each other a lot even if we didn't have time to get together, but she stopped answering her phone, so I drove over to where she lived. No one was there, so I went to a neighbor. She told me that Missy had died, but she didn't know the details. That's the last I ever heard about her—happened about five years ago."

"Any idea what she was taking?"

"Missy was a party girl. She drank for sure. As far as drugs, it was harder stuff than pot. She once mentioned something about trying meth, but I don't know what else."

"Where did she get the drugs from? She had to have money to buy them."

"Oh, I don't think she bought them. I think the man she was seeing was supplying them. I don't think it was like he was pushing them on her. Missy could be very persuasive if she wanted something. Anyway, the reason I called you is that, like I said, one day, it was like she never existed. I know you're looking into the drug situation here in Bekbourg. I think she was one of the causalities. For my piece of mind, I wish you would check into what happened to Missy."

"Where did Missy live?"

"Acorn Knoll trailer park."

It was odd that Stella thought Missy might have been taking meth, particularly since that was before the Pinkstons moved to Bekbourg. *Where would meth have come from?* She didn't know if there was much she could learn about Missy, but she told Stella she would try. Cheryl researched the title of the Acorn Knoll Mobile Home Park. During the Depression, Jeff's grandfather bought thirty acres of rural property. He willed the property to Randall, Jeff's father, and another son, Edward Thompson. Cheryl couldn't find anything about Edward. In the 1960's, Randall developed the infrastructure and pulled mobile homes onto the land. Cheryl assumed he started the mobile home park to house people who came to the area to work for his various enterprises. Randall, in the early 90's, then purchased an additional seventy acres on the other side of the hill but adjacent to his thirty acres and expanded the Acorn Knoll development.

The next morning, Sean went by the County Recorder's office to check the property records for the paper plant. The clerk finally located the file pertaining to the paper company. It had information from the plant's origin and the minor renovations that the factory underwent during the early years. He came to the file dealing with the major expansion that was completed in 1992 under the new ownership. Sean found the permits, but no plans or blueprints, which were supposed to be there. Everything had been signed off on by the county engineer.

He asked the clerk if there was another file, because something was missing. She went back and checked and told him that the file was complete.

Sean asked, "Is there a possibility that part of the files could have been archived?"

She looked at the file, "No, because there would be a stamp on it, and there isn't one. It's complete. Lots of our old files are like this."

Sean said, "But there are no plans or blueprints here."

"Well, someone must have checked them out."

"Isn't there a record of that?"

"We require that today, but back then, things were more lax, so if someone in the building wanted to see it, they would get it."

Sean called Jeff to take him up on his offer to show him the paper plant.

Jeff greeted Sean in the plant's reception area and introduced him to Stan Andrews, the foreman. As they headed into the plant, Jeff said, "This is the new part of the factory. It was added about ten years ago. When the plant was bought out, it was only making paper products. I don't think it would still be in business if it had not been sold. You'd appreciate this. It's location on the train system was viewed as an asset to a group of investors who were eyeing the company for a potential takeover. Me and the other investors bought out G. E. Geisen and expanded it. In 1992, we began manufacturing polystyrene cups and plates. We renamed the company Geisen Products, Inc. Our diversification into polystyrene foam products turned out to be more successful than we thought, because of the growing demand from the fast food industry. The plant is now three times as big as the original plant. We still produce paper products in the old plant facility, but it's a small part of the operation. I'll let Stan take you around. When you're done, he'll bring you to my office for us to talk."

Stan explained that he started when the new plant came on-line. "There was a lot of empty space in here then. Just one production line was in service. We weren't sure whether the business would grow, but the demand grew each year, so we added two more production lines. That's in addition to the old part of the plant—where we have the regular paper product operations. We actually shut down one of those production lines since the demand for paper products has dwindled. We may eventually switch over to just the foam products."

Sean said, "This is a lot bigger than it looks from outside."

"Yeah, it's a pretty big plant, about 200,000 square feet of factory. For a little town like this, it's quite a big operation. As you can see in the new part, a lot is automated, but the old part is a lot more labor intensive. That's another reason that we might phase it out. The equipment in the old part dates back to the 1950's, but the old building was built in the early 1900's. We get our paper for the paper production from Chillicothe. It used to come in by rail, but now, it's mostly by truck. The raw materials for the polystyrene foam products, we still get by rail, though, since that's the cheapest way to get those materials. I know you used to work for the railroad when we were using the paper. You may know this, but for the pellets used in the foam products, the train has large grain-like railcars that transport them. A huge vacuum sucks the pellets out of the large railroad containers into a massive holding tank located inside the plant."

"No. I didn't know that. I'd like to see that before I leave."

"Sure."

The old part looked a lot like it did in the old days when he spotted the rail cars, but he was amazed by how big the new part was. Sean looked above at the huge ducts and commented they were big enough for a steel mill.

"Well, we have to keep the place clean. The state inspectors would not like a dirty factory. We have a state-of-the-art ventilation system here in the factory that includes large scrubbers. We've kind of over-engineered it to keep the place clean."

"I'm really impressed with the operation here and appreciate your time showing me around."

"I was glad to do it," Stan said. "There's the elevator that will take you to the top floor."

Sean noticed unusually wide doors, much larger than used on a normal elevator. The heavy doors separated, and a cavernous interior greeted Sean. He was surprised to see how big it was, because it was more like a freight elevator than a regular office elevator. When he got off, he stepped onto a plush gray carpet into a large open area. An attractive woman with a black suit coat and colorful scarf was watching him. Her desk had some open folders and a computer. She could have easily fit in at a big city office. The name plate said, "Christy Finnigan."

"I'm Sean."

"Yes, sir. He's on a phone call but should be off soon. Can I get you something to drink?"

"No, thank you. I'll wait over here."

Sean saw a hall with several doors and a large conference room. He asked her what that area was used for.

"That's the Board room where the Board meets. It's also used for meetings with our customers, suppliers and machinery reps. Those offices are for the Board members. They're really a courtesy for them. If they want to drop by, or during Board meetings, they have their own office space to use. Mr. Werner is the only one who uses his, and he comes fairly often. I guess he sometimes likes to work here where it's quiet."

Sean remembered what Gary had said at Jeff's welcome back party. Gary had bought a place in Hilton Head and a boat with money he received as a Board Member for the paper plant. Interestingly, Jeff had seemed out of sorts with Gary for discussing that in front of everyone that night.

Jeff walked out. "Sorry, Sean, I see you've met our office manager, Christy Finnigan. We couldn't make it around here without her. Come on in. I hope that was okay. I was expecting a couple of calls. I'm sorry I couldn't walk around with you. I'm only here a couple of times a week and needed to take these calls. Sit down and let's have a drink."

After a short visit with Jeff, who had a lunch meeting, Sean rode the elevator back to the main floor. He noticed that off to the left was the loading dock. Cups and other products came down the line

257

on a conveyor belt. At the end, the employees would bag them and load them in boxes. The boxes were then sealed, and the finished products were loaded onto the massive racks by two forklift trucks making their way between five or six long rows. From there, they were ready to be loaded into tractor trailers for shipment. He thought how things had changed from the paper plant he remembered.

Chapter 40

Jeff stood to shake Cheryl's hand. About that time, Jan, the waitress, came up. "Hi, Jan. I've already eaten lunch, but if Ms. Seton wants something, bring her whatever she wants. I want my regular drink."

"Thank you, Commissioner Thompson, but I've already had lunch as well." Turning to Jan, she ordered a cup of coffee.

"So Ms. Seton, I understand you are all the way down here from Cleveland. Why does a Cleveland newspaper have an interest in Bekbourg?"

"I appreciate you taking the time out of your busy schedule to meet with me, Commissioner Thompson. Drugs are a growing problem throughout our state, and the U.S. for that matter. When drugs are a factor in the murder of five people in the same family, it's definitely news. Reporters from Cincinnati and Columbus as well as the national media are covering the story."

Jeff said, "Yeah, you're right. It's like a media circus here. What we don't need are reporters coming here who don't know anything about our town and scaring our citizens and exaggerating things."

"What do you mean?"

Jeff took a drink, all the time never taking his eyes off Cheryl.

"I've read your articles. Don't you think printing things that make people think there is a much larger drug problem here than the meth labs found on the Pinkston property scares people? This stuff about people putting up trip wires, that sounds like something out of a movie. We don't need out-of-towners spreading rumors that causes anxiety in our people."

"Are you denying that a trip wire was found on the Pinkston property near one of the meth labs?"

"I'm not going to comment on the investigation. I don't want people around here to get the wrong impressions."

"What impressions are those?" Cheryl asked.

"That there are drug rings all over the county."

"What's that supposed to mean?"

"There's no evidence that there are any more drug operations around here. We think these two meth labs were the source of our drug problem. Now they're shut down. We don't need people like you spreading rumors to the contrary."

"How can you be so sure? Law enforcement didn't seem to know about these two meth labs before the murders."

"Well, the Pinkstons were new to the area. They brought the drug operations with them. We didn't have a problem before that. Our sheriff's department knows the territory around here and its people. If there was a drug operation, they would know it."

"You think there was no meth in the area before the Pinkstons arrived?" Cheryl was thinking that Missy had died of a meth overdose five years ago, a year before the Pinkstons moved to Bekbourg.

"Well, there may have been some pot. All these areas around here have a little weed. Now that these two meth labs are gone, there's no proof that we have any other drug dealers."

Cheryl was skeptical at what the Commissioner was saying. How could he be so sure, and why was he so adamant that he was correct?

"So, Ms. Seton, maybe your talents would be better served if you go back to Cleveland. It's a much bigger city with a lot more drug problems than we have here."

"Mr. Thompson, this isn't exclusively about drugs. Five members of one family were murdered. That's significant—no matter what city you're talking about."

Jeff said, "I have a meeting that I'm late for. Ms. Seton, our law enforcement will solve this murder."

As Cheryl walked out of the GilHaus, she realized that the Commissioner had no intention of answering her questions, but instead, seemed to be sizing her up as if she was some adversary of his. Also, she hadn't heard of any breaks in the Pinkston case. She hoped he was right that the crime would be solved.

Sean called Boze and told him about not finding any plans or blueprints of the paper plant at the County office, which he thought was irregular. He also described the paper plant and told him what he learned. "Nothing seemed out of line there. The elevator seemed oversized. Another thing was the extensive ventilation system which had large scrubbers, but I can't say these were unusual."

"Well, I'm not ready to remove the plant from our list, Sean."

"I agree. I'll keep looking."

They talked about the Bekbourg dealership and other possibilities.

Cheryl had been giving consideration to what Annalee's grandfather had told her and decided to visit the dealership.

After asking to speak with Mr. Werner, Cheryl was approached by a large man. "I understand that you are a reporter down from Cleveland to cover the murders. I'm not sure why you want to talk to me, but what can I do for you?" he asked in an engaging but guarded tone.

Cheryl said, "Mr. Werner, I'm here to cover the murders, but also, drugs are a big problem across Ohio. Since the murders here were horrendous and were obviously drug related, I am looking at the broader issue of how communities and people are being affected by drugs. Is there someplace we might talk?"

Gary said, "Sure, let's go over to that table."

Once they were seated, Gary said, "I still don't know why you want to talk to me."

"You obviously are a successful businessman here in Bekbourg." Cheryl noticed that Gary sat up a little. "How does the drug problem affect your business? How does it affect your employees and their families?"

"Oh, I see. Well, fortunately, we've not really had a problem with employees using drugs. There may have been a couple of people over the years who took drugs, but as long as they did their jobs and worked their schedule, it didn't impact our productivity. I have a manager that deals with employees, so if someone lost their job because of that, you would need to talk to him."

"What about the community in general and the schools?"

"Well, we have had some problems with people getting hooked on drugs and even some overdoses. There were a couple of kids, unfortunately, who died from overdoses. I've got a couple of kids, so I don't want that stuff around. I'm glad that those meth operations are gone. I hate that those people were killed, and I hope they find their killers, but I'm glad that the drug problem in the area is now gone."

"You think that those two meth labs were the main source of drugs in the area?"

"Well, there might be a little weed being grown around here, but yeah, I think it's gone. That's what the sheriff said, and he would know."

"Thank you for taking the time to talk to me. I appreciate it. I couldn't help but be impressed with your dealership here. This is as big, if not bigger, than the ones we have in Cleveland."

Cheryl noticed Gary's interest level rose. "Yeah, we've got a good size operation here. I guess you noticed we handle a wide selection of manufacturers and large farm equipment. We actually have a distributorship for three states in the rural areas."

"I understand it's been hard for rural dealerships over the years. Have you always been this big?"

Gary laughed. "Oh, no. You're right about rural dealerships having a hard time. My father actually started this. About twenty years ago, he bought a small dealership that was on the verge of going bankrupt. He managed to keep it afloat and gradually started turning a profit. When I got out of college, I started helping him. We made some good decisions, and one thing led to another. Unfortunately, I lost my father a few years ago. We moved from the old location to here, and well, here we are today. I'm proud of what we've done, and I think it's good for the area to have successful businesses like this one."

"Yes. Well, I won't take any more of your time. I appreciate you talking with me."

Cheryl researched the property records relating to the car dealership. Roger Burkhart owned the dealership for twenty-four years. The dealership was founded by Roger's grandfather, and Roger inherited it because his father died prematurely. Roger didn't have a will, and the closest relative was a nephew who inherited the dealership. The nephew's name was Joshua L. Burkhart, and his place of residence was Oakland, California. Two years after Roger's death, the estate matters were settled, and soon after that, Albert J. Werner acquired the dealership for fifty-thousand dollars.

Further review showed that Al Werner took out a loan for fifty-thousand dollars from First Guaranty Bank of Bekbourg. As Cheryl dug deeper, she found that the collateral given for the loan was the residence of Al Werner and his wife, Cindy Werner, but the appraisal value was only eighteen-thousand dollars, well below the loan amount. The only name she recognized on the Board of Directors was Jeff's father, Randall Thompson.

There were five people named Joshua Burkhart in the phone listings for Oakland, California.

Jeff wanted to be proactive so people wouldn't stew over Cheryl's article. He penned an Opinion letter that was published in the *Bekbourg Tribune*.

> *A couple of days ago, a reporter from a Cleveland newspaper ran an article that has unnecessarily caused anxiety in many of our citizens. While a reporter from a northern newspaper does not have responsibility for the well-being of the residents of*

Bekbourg County, the local elected officials do. Our obligation is to protect our citizens and promote their safety, health and welfare. That obligation includes being honest with the people and setting straight misleading stories.

Our elected officials never condone lawlessness and murder, and our Sheriff's department is diligently working to bring justice to anyone responsibility for the deaths of the Pinkston family. They will find those responsible. Make no mistake about that.

While we send our deepest sympathies to members of the Pinkston family, it cannot be disputed that two labs capable of producing enough methamphetamine to supply Bekbourg and surrounding counties were being operated by them. The Pinkstons moved to Bekbourg in 1998, and soon after their arrival, meth started appearing around Bekbourg. This fact is substantiated by police records. When law enforcement authorities seized those meth labs at the time of the Pinkston deaths, the operation responsible for the local meth problem ceased. Doctors at the local and area hospitals have reported a spike in treatment for people suffering from withdrawals from meth addiction. Lloyd Wiseman has also reported an increase in the number of students treated for meth withdrawal. If meth was still being produced in the area, the hospitals and high school would not have seen an increase in treatments for meth withdrawals.

The facts are clear. When the Pinkston meth labs were shut down, the source for the local meth problem dried up. Our commitment to you is that we are working diligently to ensure that meth does not get its ugly grip on our County again. We have recently rolled out a number of initiatives that have been reported on—programs that detail our undertakings to stop drug production and distribution as well as increasing funding and services for both drug treatment and education for our citizens. As you go about your daily lives, you have one less worry: meth production in Bekbourg County is no longer.

Chapter 41

Sean walked into Frau's and saw Mule Head at the bar talking to someone. As Sean walked up, Mule Head said, "Hey, Sean. How's it going?"

"Pretty well—how 'bout you, Mule Head?"

"Fine, Sean. Say, this is Rollie. Rollie, Sean used to work for the railroad."

"Nice to meet you, Sean."

"Good to meet you. I wanted to come over and say hi, Mule Head. I saw you sitting here."

Standing, Rollie said, "Don't leave because of me. I need to shove off anyway. See you both later."

"Sean, I've got time to talk if you want to order something to eat. Let's move to that table."

After they got settled, Mule Head said, "I'm only there part time at the car dealership and not ever really around the manager, and I'm sure glad. That manager is a jerk. Rollie works there. People need their job, so they kowtow to him, but it's not easy. He thinks he owns the place."

Sean asked, "You talking about the owner or the manager?"

"That manager acts like he can tell the owner what to do. The other day, I saw those two in a heated argument."

"What does the manager do?" Sean asked.

"He runs the place, I guess. I try to stay out of his way, but some of the others have to put up with him."

Mule Head changed the subject, and they went on talking about Mule Head's shoulder and some other things.

Sean stopped by the Auto Mall the following day. He didn't see Gary right off, so he asked to see the manager. A tall, wiry man, who Sean had seen before, walked over. He looked to be in his late 40's—even though he was bald. Sean introduced himself, and the manager said his name was Joe Sommers.

Sean said, "I bought my truck here, and the steering seems to be off. Could someone check it for me?"

"Sure, Sean. I'll have someone come pull it around and take a look."

"I appreciate it. You must stay pretty busy here. This is a large dealership."

"Yeah. Let me get going on this, so we can get your truck back. You must have things to do."

"Sounds good."

About that time, Gary came walking up. "Hi, Sean. I didn't know you were here."

Joe had already walked away. "The steering seemed a little noisy on the truck, so I thought I'd stop in and have it checked out. He's checking it." Sean nodded toward Joe. "How long has he worked here?"

It was obvious that Gary didn't want to talk about Joe. "Why? Did he not help you?"

"No, nothing like that. Just curious."

"Well, that's good. I want my customers to be treated right. Come on. Let's go get a cup of coffee. It shouldn't take long."

While they were drinking their coffee, Sean said, "Gary, if you need to talk to me about anything, you should do it."

Gary looked surprised at Sean, "What are you talking about, Sean? I told you I didn't have anything to do with those murders."

"Whatever it is going on, Gary, I'll figure it out. I'm giving you a chance to tell me about it before things start to cave in."

Gary looked uncomfortable, and sweat had broken out on his forehead. "Sean, I don't know what you're talking about. I'm not sure you even do. We've been friends a long time, but we're not going to stay friends if you keep trying to pin me with something. I'm goin' to go check on your truck."

Gary never returned, but soon, a serviceman came and told Sean that his truck was ready.

Sean asked Boze to check out Joe Sommers. When Boze finally had an answer a couple of days later, he reported back, "Sean, I thought you'd be interested in what we found out about Joe Sommers. Actually, it's probably more accurate to say what we didn't find out."

Sean dryly replied, "Sounds intriguing."

"Yeah, it actually is. If I didn't know you had met the man, I'd think he didn't exist."

"One of those, huh?"

"There is no record of him—nothing."

"Wonder if he has anything to do with the vans that come in, are put in the defect lot and then disappear?"

"We'll keep digging. I'll let you know if we find anything. Say, how's your investigation going into the murder case?"

"Well, I'm running into a brick wall. I've been working with the state police. We can't find anyone from around Bekbourg or from where the Pinkston family lives in Tapsaw County who look suspicious. As we've talked, Pinkston was running a meth operation, but he thought there was a much larger drug operation than his. I think the murders are related to the drugs. I guess it's possible that a family member of someone who died from the Pinkston drugs took their own justice, but I haven't found any evidence there. Nothing points toward a vigilante killing, and can't find a personal reason. I keep thinking that if Pinkston was right, that someone is running a big drug deal around here, they maybe didn't like the competition, so they killed them. If that is the case, whoever is running that could also be responsible for the murders. So, if we solve your investigation into a drug operation in the area, we would solve the Pinkston murder case."

Chapter 42

During her call with Keith and Milton, Cheryl said, "Since the last press conference, the authorities haven't released any more information. I sent you a copy of Commissioner Thompson's Opinion letter in the local newspaper."

"Yeah, we read it. You should back down until you get more evidence, but keep looking and digging. If your instincts are correct, you'll find it. You don't want to get in a back-and-forth with the local authorities."

"I agree. It's odd how the leaders here are persistent in their theory that there are no more drug operations in the county, except for a small amount of marijuana which they say has been around forever. Yet, something still doesn't feel right."

"I read your email about Missy Collins. So, you think she died of an overdose of meth?" Keith asked.

"Well, that's what her friend, Stella, believes. I checked the records at the County offices, and they are sealed. Why would her file be sealed?"

"That's a good question," replied Keith. "Your email said that she died before the Pinkstons moved to Bekbourg. She couldn't have gotten the meth from them. Wonder where she got it?"

"Stella seems to think she got it from her boyfriend, but where would he have gotten it since the Pinkstons weren't in Bekbourg?"

"All good questions," Keith said—changing the topic, "Cheryl, what are you learning about your grandfather?"

Cheryl told them what she learned and how she had not been able to locate any records in the county offices. She told them what Rose Waters and Annalee's grandpa had said to her. She told them about her research on the Bekbourg car dealership. "It's been twenty years, but I'm going to keep digging."

"You could end up being disappointed, because it might be a dead end. Like you said, it's been twenty years." Keith warned, "Don't forget five people were killed, and if what Mr. Jackups said is true, someone or some people wanted it swept under the rug. If you step on the wrong toes, Cheryl, you could be putting yourself in danger."

Around 12:30 that afternoon, Cheryl's phone rang. When she answered, she heard, "Ms. Seton. This is Deputy Neumann. I was wondering if we might meet somewhere. There is something I would like to discuss with you."

Cheryl's heart did a flutter when she heard it was Sean.

"Uh, yes. When did you want to meet?" she asked.

"Are you available this afternoon?"

"Yes. I'm staying at the B&B in the old downtown. There's a coffee shop next door."

"I know the place."

"What time were you thinking?"

"How about 2:30?"

"I'll see you then."

Cheryl smiled to herself. She still had that school girl crush. She remembered sitting in the stands when she was eleven and twelve watching Sean Neumann lead the team down the field. Her grandpa would be cheering him on, and every time Schriever scored, Henry would say, "Best quarterback around." Cheryl thought she'd better bury those feelings because no way did she want Deputy Neumann to detect her attraction to him.

Cheryl came out of the B&B about five minutes early heading next door to Max's. As she stepped on the sidewalk, she almost ran into Sean, who was walking toward Max's.

"Oh, I'm sorry. I didn't see you."

"It's quite alright," said Sean. "Are you enjoying your stay at the B&B?"

"Yes, it's great."

As they came to the entrance to Max's, Mary Thompson, Jeff's wife, was walking from the opposite direction. Sean had met Mary when she and Jeff had hosted a "Welcome Back" party for him at their home. Sean and Mary spotted each other at the same time. "Hi, Mary, are you going in for a cup of coffee?"

"Actually, a Cappuccino," she nodded.

Mary was a small, attractive woman. She wore a tailored sun dress and short summer coat and stylist, strap sandals. Cheryl noticed her designer handbag.

"Mary, this is Cheryl Seton, a reporter for *The Presenter*, down here from Cleveland covering the Pinkston murders. We were going to get a cup of coffee. Would you like to join us?" Sean felt obligated to ask her to join them because he didn't want to be rude to Mary.

Mary replied in a smooth, cultured voice, "I'd love to, but I barely have time for one cup."

It was obvious that Mary and Sean knew each other and that their meeting was happenstance. She understood that Sean would not want to be rude, but Cheryl was glad to hear that Mary was in a hurry.

Between lunch and dinner hours, patrons placed orders at the counter. They found a table, and Sean went to place their order. Mary said to Cheryl, "I've read your articles. I am most impressed with your research and reporting."

"Thank you, Mary. I really hope to make a difference on this."

When Sean returned with the coffees, he asked Mary how she had been.

"I'm okay, Sean. I'm running errands today trying to pull together last-minute things. Rachel and I are leaving in two days for Spain. I'm looking forward to getting away for a while. The murders were horrific, and I think the stress of finding the perpetrators is taking a toll on Jeff. He tells me that people in the area are worried that there could be a serial killer running around. You know how rumors can be. Anyway, I hope by the time we return, the criminals will be behind bars."

"I hope so, too, Mary. We are all working hard to solve the crime. I know people are anxious."

Cheryl liked Mary. She was classy and elegant. Cheryl asked, "Where in Spain are you going?"

"My family has a villa in the hills overlooking Marbella. Rachel, my nine-year-old daughter, and I go there every summer for several weeks."

"That sounds fabulous."

"It's something I look forward to. I cherish my time with Rachel."

"Thank you for the cappuccino, Sean. Cheryl, it was nice to meet you. I appreciate the quality job you are doing on the reporting. I must go. I have one more stop before I return home."

Sean and Cheryl stood to say goodbye and wished her a safe, fun summer with Rachel. After she had left, they sat to finish their coffee. "Such a lovely woman," Cheryl said. "For some reason, I feel sorry for her. She seems lonely or sad."

"I agree. I'm not sure she's ever adjusted to living in Bekbourg. She apparently visits Columbus a lot, and then she is gone for several weeks during the summer."

"I gather that she hasn't lived in Bekbourg very long?" Cheryl asked.

"No—about two and a half years or so."

"Who is her husband?"

"Jeff Thompson."

Cheryl's eyes narrowed. "You mean the county commissioner?"

Sean couldn't help it; a smile twitched on his lips, "That's the one."

Cheryl's look had shifted to full suspicion. "From what I gathered, you've been friends with the commissioner for a while."

The twitch on his lips grew slightly bigger. "Since first grade—I take it you've met Jeff?"

Despite the scowl that now consumed Cheryl's face, Sean couldn't help but smile.

She arched her left eyebrow with a look that Sean knew booked a note she was making in that lovely head of hers.

"Deputy Neumann, you wanted to talk to me about something?"

It took every ounce of will Sean had not to laugh. Obviously, she did not have a favorable impression of Jeff, which was understandable. Given that she now knew he was friends with Jeff, he was already in the hole in getting her cooperation.

"I agree with what Mary said that you've done a good job on your reporting about the murders and related matters. You've been busy. You know, it's not easy to get people around here to open up to anyone, but it's darn near impossible for them to talk to an outsider. I'm impressed that you've been able to breach that divide with the locals."

Cheryl was still looking at him with that raised eyebrow. *So much for flattery*, Sean thought. Cheryl felt he was fighting hard to prevent a smile from breaking out on his handsome face. Cheryl took the opportunity to observe his face weathered with maturity. He was ruggedly handsome with the square jaw and piercing brown eyes. His sandy colored hair was peppered with gray.

"Ms. Seton. In our investigation, we also heard the same thing about Tony recently installing the trip wire because he thought someone had been up at the lab. Sometimes witnesses think of things later, so we don't always get the full picture in our first interview or another witness may know some additional details. Do you mind sharing the details that your source told you about the trip wire?"

Cheryl considered his point. She didn't see any harm in what she had learned on this. Also, if she was cooperative with Sean, maybe he would be with her when the time arose.

"Okay. My source said that late one night the dogs started barking, so Tony went out to look around. He didn't see anything, but the next day, when he was up at the lab, he saw that someone had tried to cut the chain where the lock was holding the door shut."

"I know better than to ask your source."

Cheryl nodded in the affirmative.

"I thought so. So, your source believed that Tony felt that someone was trying to get into the lab?"

"That was my impression."

"Well, off the record, okay?" Cheryl nodded that what he was getting ready to tell her was off the record. "The forensics said that there were marks on the chain on the lab's door. Someone had probably tried to cut the chain. You asked me that day of the first news conference if I thought there was another drug source in the area. I told you that I did. You obviously had your suspicions and reported that Pinkston believed there was a larger player in the area. You mind giving me your thoughts on this?"

Cheryl looked at him. Over the years, she had trusted her instincts, and so far so good on that. From the local authorities' statements, and what he had told her the day of the first press conference, he was swimming alone on his view that there were other drug sources in the area. Something told her she could trust him on this. She didn't, of course, disclose her sources, but she told him that Tony had told someone that he thought that his operation was "small potatoes" compared to some other area's operations and, because of this, he believed law enforcement wouldn't bother looking at his meth labs. They would be looking for a much larger player. "My impression from my source is that Tony felt pretty confident that there was a much larger player in the area."

"Did your source mention when Tony's conversation took place?"

"My source said it was about four months ago."

"Well, that rules the Todd brothers out," Sean said.

"The Todd brothers?" Cheryl hadn't heard about them. "Who are they?"

"We need to keep this off the record, too, but my first murder investigation here was looking into who murdered Jed and Brody Todd. Their bodies had just been found in a wooded area. They had been dead for over a year. There was evidence that they manufactured meth, but even if they were still alive four months ago, I don't believe their size of operation would amount to what Pinkston termed a large operation."

"How long had they been producing meth?"

"Actually, they hadn't been in Bekbourg more than a year or so before they were killed. I don't have any suspects in their murders. Case is still open, but I'm not too optimistic about solving it."

"That's not the situation my source described," Cheryl said.

"You've obviously talked to several people around here. Someone even confided to you about the trip wire. I want your thoughts. Do you think there are other drug operations in the area?"

It pleased Cheryl that Sean asked her opinion.

"Yes, I believe that there is something more going on in the county as far as drug operations are concerned, and I'm not talking about marijuana."

"Is this a feeling or do you have proof?"

Sean now had an intense look on his handsome face.

Cheryl looked him straight in the eye. "I'm working on something. I'm not prepared to say anything else right now."

"Ms. Seton. We're rowing in the same direction on this."

"I have a question for you, Deputy Neumann."

"What's that?"

"Are you working to solve the murders or to solve a bigger drug problem?"

Sean kept his face expressionless even though he was impressed by her perceptive question. Sean asked, "Is this off the record?"

"Yes, I promise it will be off the record."

"Both."

"Meaning?"

"I think if one of those parts is solved, the other is solved."

When Cheryl returned to the B&B, she reflected on her conversation with Sean. He had been honest with her, and unlike Commissioner Thompson and the Sheriff and even Gary Werner, Sean did not believe the county's drug problem had been solved.

Sean walked into Knucklepin's that evening and saw Stan Andrews sitting at the bar. Sean walked up and sat down beside Stan. Stan looked up and saw Sean at the same time that Sean spoke, "Hey, Stan. How're you doin'?"

"Fine, Sean, how's it goin' for you?"

"Very busy."

The bartender walked up, and Sean ordered a beer and a hamburger.

Sean then asked Stan, "How are things at the paper plant?"

"Busy. I'm glad to see it."

Sean said, "Yeah. Good thing the plant did the expansion into the poly products a few years back. It's sure helped folks around here."

Sean's order arrived. He took a bite and asked, "You're not from around here, are you?"

Stan took a drink from his beer and said, "Nah, I've moved around a lot over the years."

"Where are you from?"

"I spent a while up in the northeast and in Michigan—even spent a couple of years in Florida."

Sean asked, "How do you like it here?"

"I like working at the plant. It's a good business to be in. Like any place, it has its drawbacks, but I'd say it's been fine."

Stan motioned for the bartender to bring his check.

Sean said, "Yeah, if you're used to a bigger city, it probably is a change."

Stan stood, "Well, I'd better shove off. Got some paperwork I need to do this evening."

"Okay, Stan. I'll see you around."

"Yeah, see you."

Sean finished his meal thinking about his conversation with Stan. It'd been the first time he had seen him since the tour of the paper plant. He'd been knowledgeable and informative, but tonight, he seemed evasive and even uncomfortable with Sean questioning him. Sean had learned long ago to pay attention to the details. It might not be anything, but he was going to ask Boze to see what he could find on Stan Andrews.

Chapter 43

After multiple attempts and phone calls, Cheryl finally tracked down Josh Burkhart.

"Ms. Seton. I don't know how I can help you."

"Please call me Cheryl. I have a few questions if you don't mind answering them."

"Okay, I'll try."

"I understand that you inherited your uncle, Roger Burkhart's, estate?"

"That's correct. I was his only living heir. There wasn't a will, so everything had to go through the court. I was only twenty-five at the time living all the way out here in California with my wife and baby daughter who was fifteen months old, and we had just learned that we were having another baby. From what I could gather, the car dealership was not doing so great. I didn't have time to fool with it. The fireworks business had burned down before that. There was some cash, but not a lot.

"I flew there to check on things and met with the judge who was handling the case. The guy managing the dealership when Roger died had left, so I asked a man named Werner to run it. He called me one day and said that he was interested in buying it. To make a long story short, I didn't have time to fool with it, and the dealership was heading toward bankruptcy best I could tell. After the probate proceeding concluded, I sold it to him for fifty-thousand dollars. I was glad to be done with the worry. I eventually sold everything, the properties where the fireworks business and house had been and the cars, boat, all of it. I hired someone to inventory everything in the pawn shop and sold all of it. When all was said and done, I came out with a little money from the inheritance, which helped having two young children, but it wasn't a large sum."

"There was some mention in the court proceeding of some coins that supposedly were in Roger's home. They were the reason for the attempted burglary that led to the murders. Did you ever find those coins or know what happened to them?"

"No, but you're right. There was the claim that Roger had received those coins, but the authorities didn't find them in the house rubble, and there wasn't anything like that in the pawn shop."

"Do you know how Al Werner came up with the money to purchase the dealership?"

"No, I don't. I wanted a straight cash sale. I didn't have time to deal with anything else. When the time came, he had the cash."

Chapter 44

"Hi, Milton. Sorry I missed your call."

"I've been reading your daily briefings, Cheryl. Sounds like the police don't have much to go on yet for a suspect."

"Yes, that's right."

"Well, hopefully something will shake loose soon. Say, I looked into the financing of the car dealership that Werner bought from Burkhart's nephew. You're right that the collateral for the bank loan for Werner to buy the dealership didn't come close to the $50,000 loan, although from everything I could find, Werner paid the loan off. It gets a little more interesting. About two years later, Werner got a larger loan for $250,000 from First Guaranty Bank of Bekbourg. It was used for a renovation. What really makes it odd is that it was a signature loan."

"What does that mean?" Cheryl asked.

"That he didn't put up any collateral. Risky for the bank, but the loan was repaid. One more thing, the loan was co-signed by someone named Samuel Walters. Have you run across that name anywhere?"

"No."

"I haven't either. I'll keep digging."

Cheryl told him about her conversation with Burkhart's nephew. "It seems pretty straightforward regarding the nephew. I don't really see a reason to look in his direction."

Boze called Sean. "Sean, you've stumbled into a new club there. I'd call it the 'No Past Club.'"

"What are you talking about, Boze?"

"This is the second time you've asked me to check out someone's background that doesn't seem to exist. Joe Sommers, the manager at the dealership—remember we couldn't find anything on him? Well, same with Stan Andrews. They have no records of any kind. No social security numbers, no work history, no birth certificates, no tax records, no nothing to speak of. What are the chances that we'd find two people like that in a small town like Bekbourg?"

Sean considered the significance of what Boze had told him.

"Have you seen them together?"

"No. The only place I've seen Sommers is at the dealership. I've only seen Andrews twice—once at the paper plant and that one time at the local bar."

Boze responded, "I'm going to put some people on the plant, too. I'll let you know if we find anything."

"One more thing," Sean added. "A while back, I was at the dealership and saw Sommers talking to a well-dressed Hispanic man. Gary Werner, the owner, told me that he ran the cleaning crew operations around town, including for the dealership and paper plant. His name is Dante Gomez."

"It sounds like we need to check him out. However, I won't be surprised if that's an alias as well."

Sean quipped, "Part of the 'No Past Club?'"

"Yep. Seems like it's a popular place."

Cheryl had just hung up with Milton, when her phone rang. "Hey, Cheryl, how's your day going?"

"Well, it's going fine, Bri. I had a really informative discussion earlier with the principal at Schriever High School. I was getting ready to head toward Frau's to meet you."

"Well, that's why I'm calling. The air conditioner unit has quit cooling, and I've got to stay here to meet the repairman. I called Dusty, and he and Carla are planning to be there. I told him what you looked like, and he'll be looking for you. You're going to like meeting them. Dusty's a colorful character, just so you know, but he and Carla are good people and really dedicated to their program there at the church."

"I totally understand. I look forward to meeting Dusty and Carla, and I appreciate you arranging the meeting. I hope things go well with the repairman. I'll catch up with you tonight or tomorrow."

Cheryl walked into Frau's, and a man came up to her, "Are you Cheryl Seton?"

Cheryl extended her hand, "Hi, I take it you're Dusty?"

"Yes. It's nice to meet you. Carla is sitting right over here."

Cheryl followed him to the table, where a woman stood to greet her, "Hi, I'm Carla Huber."

They sat, and Dusty motioned to the menu, "They've got the best fried chicken in town, and so is their chicken-'n-dumplings special, but if you want something else, it's all good."

"Thanks, Dusty. I think the chicken-'n-dumplings sound perfect."

It didn't take Cheryl long to realize what Bri meant by Dusty being a colorful character. He told her about working on the railroad, and Carla told her that she was an elementary school teacher. They talked about the program they ran for drug addicts, and Dusty shared his personal story. They talked about the drug problems around Bekbourg and how they had gotten much worse, especially in the last three or four years. Dusty told her about how some parents wanted him and Carla to work with their teenagers in their program, but Dusty told the parents that it had to be something the kids wanted to do, not the parents, or it wouldn't be successful.

Cheryl nodded, "I agree. I met with the principal of the high school today, and he basically said the same thing. They are really trying to educate the students about the drugs, but not all kids are receptive."

Carla asked, "What did you think about the high school?"

"It's changed so much since I was here," answered Cheryl.

This surprised Dusty and Carla. "You're from here?" asked Dusty. "I thought you were a reporter from Cleveland."

"I was born here and lived here until I was fourteen. We moved to Cleveland then. This is the first time I've been back since we moved."

"Well, I'll be. Things have changed a lot since you were here."

Cheryl laughed, "Yes, Dusty, they really have."

They talked on for a while, when suddenly Dusty stopped in mid-sentence. Cheryl's back was to the front entrance. Dusty had seen someone he recognized. "Hey, Sean!" Dusty yelled, waving.

Cheryl said to herself, "*Oh no.*" The thought of Sean Neumann sent warm tingles through her body. It had taken her a long while to calm down after she had met him for coffee the other day.

Sean walked up. Dusty said, "Hey, Sean, this is Cheryl Seton." The shocked look on Sean's face was priceless. Cheryl could barely hide a smile.

Sean said, "Yes, we met the other day. Hi, Ms. Seton."

Cheryl was warm all over. She hoped the blush she felt didn't show. "Nice to see you again, Deputy Neumann."

Sean said, "Hi, Carla. How have you been?"

"Just fine, Sean."

"Sean," Dusty offered, "why don't you have a seat? Carla and I need to leave in a couple of minutes, but we'd like to talk to you."

"Okay, Dusty."

Sean was still looking at Cheryl with suspicion.

Dusty said, "Yeah, Sean, I guess you didn't think you'd see me and Carla talking to a reporter from Cleveland when you walked in?"

"I learn something every day, Dusty."

Cheryl picked up her coffee cup to take a sip to hide her amusement.

Carla said, "Sean, it's really bad what happened to the Pinkston family."

Dusty added, "You know, Sean, the commissioner seems to think finding those two meth labs will take care of the drugs here, but I'm not so sure I agree with him."

For the first time since he sat down, Sean turned his attention away from Cheryl, "I know. We are still investigating. Hopefully, we'll get to the bottom of this."

Dusty said, "Carla and I hope so, too." Dusty turned to Cheryl and said, "Sean here has been gone twenty years doing police-like work in the Marines, and returned to take a deputy job, and just a couple of months on the job, he's working on the biggest murder case here in twenty years."

Cheryl's eyes blink. Sean wondered what that was about.

"Well, we need to get going." Dusty continued, "Cheryl, anytime you want to talk, give us a call. Also, like Carla said, if you want to attend our meetings, not as a reporter, but to see what they're about, you are welcome."

"Thank you both so much. I really appreciate you talking to me. I will plan to come to one of your meetings soon."

Dusty and Carla each said goodbye to Sean.

Sean once again turned his focus to Cheryl. "You sure get around, Ms. Seton. I never thought I'd see you here when I walked in, number one, and having dinner with Dusty and Carla, number two."

When Dusty mentioned that Sean had been gone for twenty years and just recently returned, Cheryl thought that if there was anyone in law enforcement around here she could trust, he would be the person. She hoped her gamble was correct. Looking around, she exclaimed, "Well, I'm glad to see that Frau's hasn't changed over the years."

For the second time that evening, Sean looked surprised.

"What do you mean?"

"I lived here until I was fourteen. In fact, my grandpa used to take me to watch you play football when I was eleven and twelve. I watched you play your senior year when the high school won the state championship."

Sean thought to himself, *"This can't be."* He asked, "So, you went to school here?"

"Yes."

"Who were your parents? Where did you live?"

"My mother was a single parent. Her name was Kelly. We lived with my grandparents. My grandmother died, so it was me and my mom and Grandpa."

Cheryl took a sip of coffee. Sean was intently watching her. He could tell that she was hesitating. Finally, when he wasn't sure if she was going to complete the picture, he asked, "Who was your grandfather?"

Cheryl girded herself, thinking, *"Here goes,"* before she responded, "Henry Willis."

Cheryl watched. He tried to think about if he knew a man named Henry Willis. She saw when it dawned on him who Henry Willis was. Sean was momentarily stunned. He sat staring at Cheryl. She was suddenly nervous and picked up her cup to drink more coffee, but her cup was empty. Sean noticed and motioned for Anita to bring Cheryl another cup as well as one for himself.

He said, "Well, I've now learned two things since sitting down here, and I suspect the tally's going to rise before the evening is out. Now, Ms. Seton, you mind telling me what you're really doing in Bekbourg?"

One of her grandpa's sayings was, "In for a penny, in for a pound."

Cheryl told Sean that she came here to cover the story about the murders and the drug problem in Bekbourg and to investigate about her grandfather. She told him of her discussion with Annalee's grandfather. She then found herself telling Sean everything. She told him about what happened to her family after the Burkhart murders, about how her mother had moved them to Cleveland and changed their last name, and how her mother had died almost three months ago. She even told Sean about talking with Gary Werner and what she had learned about his father buying the Burkhart car dealership and her conversation with Burkhart's nephew who had inherited the estate. She told him about the second big loan that Al Werner got to invest in the car dealership, but that she had so far run into a dead end in finding any records in the County office.

Cheryl said, "When Mom knew her time was near, she told me where her will was. After her death, I found the will, but also a bank account book that had both her name and my name on the account. It had a little over $280,000. My mother was a receptionist her whole working life. There is no way she could have saved that much money. We lived a modest lifestyle, lived in a modest home. My mom only bought two new cars after we moved to Cleveland, and the first one she drove for ten years, before she traded it in on the one she had when she died—both small economy cars. We traveled some, but never did we stay in expensive hotels or resorts, and she paid for all my college. I never had to take out student loans.

"And, something that no one knew but Grandpa, Mom and me—and I assume Grandpa's doctor—was that he had cancer when the murders happened. Grandpa was a proud man, and Mom made me promise not to tell anyone that he was sick. Annalee's grandfather, Martin Jackups, when he was talking to me the other day, told me he thought Grandpa was sick when this all happened. Grandpa died six months after he went to prison."

Sean had absorbed every word. "What are your plans on this? You know, if what you're thinking is right, it's possible that whoever killed the Burkharts is still around. If they think you are digging this up, you could be in danger."

Sean was definitely thinking about Gary. If his father was somehow involved in the Burkhart murders to get the dealership or whatever, and if Gary is involved in some drug ring, big or small, Cheryl could be in peril.

"That's what Keith, my editor, and Milton, my mentor at the newspaper, said."

"Well, they're right. But you're still here, so I take it you're disregarding that logical and sensible advice?"

When Cheryl smiled, Sean knew he was in trouble. Actually, he had been since she ran up to him after that first press conference. Every time he had been around her, he felt a strong attraction, something only taking her to his bed would solve, and then he would probably never be free from the pull he felt toward her.

"So, you must have a game plan for what your next step is?"

"Actually, I do. It seems that the Pinkston investigation has hit a wall, at least for the time being. I've been able to talk to several people here about the drug situation. I'm thinking about driving to Cleveland for a day or two and going through my mother's house to see if I can find anything that might shed some light on why Grandpa would have confessed to a crime he most certainly did not commit. My mother and I were very close. It's been too painful to go through her things, but being here and learning what I have, I feel I need to do so."

"When are you thinking about going?"

"I might leave tomorrow or the next day."

"Cheryl, if what you're thinking is correct, that murder case needs to be reopened. It falls under this department's jurisdiction. How would you feel about me going with you to help look?"

Cheryl liked that he had used her first name. She looked at Sean for a minute and said, "If you have the time, I would appreciate your help on this."

Sean thought they were through and started to push back his chair. Cheryl said, "Do you have time to talk about something else?"

Sean's head was already spinning. *How could one woman stir so many pots?*

"Sure." He pulled the chair back up and motioned for Anita to bring more coffee.

"What else do you have?"

Cheryl explained what she knew about Missy. "Missy's friend seemed to think Missy had taken meth. If so, that was before the Pinkstons moved here. The file on her death was sealed, which seems bizarre."

Sean was dumbfounded that she had discovered so much in such a short time. "Tell you what. I'll see what I can find in our files tomorrow about Missy. If you can leave late tomorrow evening, we can drive to Cleveland tomorrow night. I have a day off the next day. We'll drive back that night. On the drive up, I'll tell you what I've found."

"That sounds good. I can drive if you like," offered Cheryl.

"That'll work."

The next morning, Sean pulled the file for Missy Collins. He was surprised to see that it simply contained an incident report. She was found unconscious and died at the hospital. Sean found it interesting that Ben was the investigating officer, but given the brevity of the report, he shouldn't be surprised. Cheryl had been told that the file had been sealed, but when he checked with the Clerk of Court, there wasn't a file to be found. Since she was taken to the hospital, he assumed that the County coroner would have a file, but he ran into a dead end there. No one in the coroner's office knew anything about the file and why they couldn't locate one.

After finishing up with that file, he figured that something had to be in the archived files pertaining to Henry Willis and the Burkhart murders. "You're in luck, Sean," Fred said, "We're not too sophisticated here, so all our evidence boxes are stored here. We have a large store room below this building. I'm glad you've got the year it happened. You said it's a rush. I'll pull it when Pinky gets here. Come back in a couple of hours. I should have it by then for you."

A couple of hours later, Fred had set the box in a small windowless room with a built-in desk top. As he was walking Sean to the room, Fred said, "Sean, you don't know this about me, but I played linebacker in the championship game when you whipped our butts."

Sean was surprised. "What?"

"Yeah, between your passes and Mike's catches, I didn't know my butt from page two."

Sean laughed. "Well, you all gave us a good fight."

Fred said, "It's a shame what happened to your arm. I had you pegged to be an NFL quarterback that I could brag about having played against in a state championship game."

Sean laughed again, "How did you end up in Bekbourg?"

"Well, after I graduated, I went into the army. I followed my older brother's steps. I stayed ten years, and when I came back, I went to the police academy. My younger sister had roomed at OU with a girl from Bekbourg. She was up visiting, and I met her, and when we got married, we moved here. I got injured when someone ran into the side of my cruiser, so I've worked the evidence room since then. I've lived in Bekbourg about seven years now."

"We'll have to get together and talk football sometime. Thanks, Fred, for pulling this for me."

Fred opened the door and nodded to the box, "When you finish, leave it here. I'll take it back."

"I appreciate it, Fred."

Sean closed the door and sat down and opened the box. He stared at what he saw. It was virtually empty. There was a manila folder with a report taken by the responding deputies, and two folders below that. He picked up the second folder, and it contained the fire marshal's report. The other item was an accordion folder that had the coroner's report. When he reached in to pull out the report, he noticed something in the bottom corner of the file. There was a small plastic envelope from the hospital marked "Carol Burkhart: Chest Cavity" with a bullet in it. It had been pushed down to the bottom of the accordion file folder under a file containing some paperwork and the county coroner's report. It looked to Sean that the bullet had gotten lodged underneath the folder. There were no other bullets; there was no other evidence in the box. Someone had tampered with the file. Carol was the only victim who had been taken to the hospital; this bullet had been separated from the bullets taken from the other victims. The bullet must have been over-looked, because it was pushed deep under the coroner's report.

Sean rang the bell for Fred. When Fred walked up, Sean said, "Fred, I found something here I need to check out. What do I need to do to check out evidence?"

"You've got to fill out a report. I'll sign off on it, and then you can take it. Where are you taking it?"

"I'm taking it to Columbus to have it checked out by the state forensics."

"Isn't there a report on it in the file?"

"No. There's not much of a report on any of this. Lots of odd things about this evidence file."

Fred started looking through the box. "Yeah, this doesn't look right. This happened before I got here. Just fill out the report, and you can take the bullet. This is quite unusual. I would have remembered this. There's no record of any anyone checking this file out since it was put in here."

"Well, I'm going to take this and have it checked."

Sean called Ronnie Vin, who was working the forensics for the Pinkston case. He said he was working another case. "Ronnie, I need a bullet looked at by the State. I'm working on something that, right now, I need on the QT."

Ronnie asked, "Is this related to the Pinkston case?"

"No, it actually dates back to another murder case here that happened twenty years ago."

"I see. I'll need to look at it in Columbus. Do you have it with you?"

"Yeah. I'm planning to drive back through Columbus tomorrow afternoon. I'll drop it off then if that works for you."

"Sounds good. I plan to be here."

As he was leaving the building, he considered how so many files were incomplete. *It's odd, to say the least.*

Chapter 45

As Cheryl and Sean were driving to Cleveland, they discussed finding the bullet, and the possible implications that the evidence box from the Burkhart murders wasn't complete. The drive also gave them a chance to get to know each other better. She talked about her grandfather and her mother and what her life had been like. He told her about working on the railroad and his career in the Marines. She loved hearing about Buddy, laughing at Sean's "Buddy" stories. Cheryl was observant and had noticed Sean rubbing his thigh at Frau's the preceding evening and during their drive to Cleveland. "Is your leg bothering you?"

Sean stopped massaging his thigh. He didn't answer for a while and then said, "Yeah. It happened on my last assignment. That's why I retired. I couldn't continue with my criminal unit, and I didn't want a desk job."

Although Cheryl thought there was more to the story, she didn't pursue the topic. She figured that if Sean wanted to tell her, he would.

The drive time evaporated. Sean and Cheryl enjoyed each other's company. Cheryl was electrified by Sean. He was so sexy, of course, but there was a lot more to Sean Neumann. He was quick-witted and intuitive. He preferred listening to talking, but he was an interesting conversationalist.

Except for a rare grin, he didn't seem inclined to display emotions. A couple of times a laugh had escaped, which made her laugh. She had no doubt he would be a formidable foe and figured numerous criminals had learned that first-hand.

Cheryl was one of the most intriguing women Sean had ever met. She was determined and dedicated. Not many people would bide their time for twenty years to pursue something like she had done regarding her grandfather. She was intelligent, engaging, caring and a professional. Her high energy level was contagious. She had a way with people that made them feel comfortable like she had done with Dusty, and she had clearly made people feel safe to confide in her about the Pinkston murders and the drug problems. He couldn't deny that he was captivated by her.

The sunlight was beginning to fade when they pulled into the home that Cheryl and her mother had lived in. Sean saw a neat home, modestly furnished. There were three small bedrooms, the smallest of which was used as a miscellaneous room with an ironing board, a book case, small desk, and chair. Boxes were stacked in the closet along with a few hanging coats.

Sean could tell right off which room belonged to Cheryl. It had a bookcase with some soccer trophies, yearbooks, and framed articles from the high school newspaper that Cheryl had authored. A colorful blue and white comforter on the double-sized bed matched the window coverings. A director's chair sat in one corner. A mirror adorned with beads hung on the wall above a small oak dresser.

Everything was orderly. "My mom was a receptionist. She loved meeting the people and coordinating things. Her colleagues, the few times I met them, talked about her organizational skills. That was the way she was here. She wasn't a fanatic, because with school projects, soccer games and practices, things could get piled up, but you'll see that her filing in the extra bedroom is organized."

"This is a nice home, Cheryl. When did you move into your own place?"

"It was soon after I graduated from college. I thought it was time. She understood I needed to have my own space. She was even talking about moving into a condo or an apartment, but then she got sick, and the idea of her moving got pushed to the back burner."

"Well, we should get started. I know you want to get this done so that you have time to stop by the newspaper tomorrow before we head back. How do you want to do this?"

"I'll start in my mother's room. That's personal to me. There are some things stored under the bed and in the closet. There might even be things in her dresser. Do you mind starting in the extra bedroom? There's the closet and also the desk."

"What about the garage and attic and basement?"

"The only things Mom kept in the garage were yard tools and other tools and our Christmas decorations. You can have a look if you want to, or I can, but I don't think there's anything out there. The only way to get to the attic is in the garage with a pull ladder. To my knowledge, I don't believe anyone ever went up there except maybe a repairman. The basement is unfinished. When I moved out, Mom and I cleaned it out. Almost everything there was mine, like toys, art projects and old costumes and some clothes. Unless Mom put something there after I moved, there shouldn't be anything."

"I'll take a quick look so we can check those off the list, and then I'll start in the other room."

Sean made short order of the garage, attic and basement, because they were as Cheryl had described. He started with the desk in the small room. The files were all labeled and papers neatly filed. There were files relating to Kelly's illness and copies of doctor and hospital invoices. There were files of the most recent records for bank statements, utility invoices, insurance statements, tax filings, and other general items.

Sean then started on the boxes, which were more of the same for earlier years. He also came across records for air-conditioning and heating service calls, owner's manuals for the washer and dryer and the small appliances. One box contained several years' worth of tax filings. Another box contained records when Kelly had purchased this house. She had paid cash—which peaked his interest. There were some boxes of things pertaining to Cheryl's activities during school and school pictures. Two boxes of photo albums were in the closet.

He and Cheryl had been working for a couple of hours when Sean came to a box that captured his attention. It had files with copies of Cheryl's and her mom's birth certificates, Kelly's mother's death certificate, Henry's death certificate, and the sale of Henry's house in Bekbourg. He almost missed it, because he was looking for file folders which everything else had been filed in. Between two file folders tucked toward the bottom of the box was a letter-sized envelope paper clipped to another folded document. "Cheryl, come in here. I may have found something."

When she walked in, she saw that boxes had been pulled from the closet and stacked against a wall. He had cleared off the small desk and had a box sitting on top of it. He was holding the envelope and the other folded document. "Look. Your mom's first name is written on the outside of the envelope."

"That looks like Grandpa's writing. He always printed in all capital letters. What's inside?"

"That's just it, there isn't anything inside, but there was at one time. From the impression on the envelope, it looks like there could have been cash. This other document is more interesting. It's a life insurance policy from Bekbourg Farm and Community Insurance. Your mother is the beneficiary, and the person whose life was insured was Henry Willis. The policy was taken out August 4, 1980, a short time before your grandpa confessed to killing the Burkharts."

Surprised, Cheryl said, "This is crazy. How much was it for?"

"$500,000."

Cheryl gasped, "So, does this mean that when Grandpa died, the money came to Mom?"

"Yep. It's interesting. The insurance company is Bekbourg Farm and Community Insurance. I remember it being there when I was growing up, but I don't remember seeing it since I've been back."

"You know, Sean. I don't understand this. Does it say how much it cost to take out the policy?"

"No."

"Well, there is no way my grandpa had enough money to take it out, no matter how much it cost. I'd be surprised if he had fifty dollars to his name when he confessed to those murders. He always kept some money to buy a few things or go to the bar, but practically everything he made, he gave to Mom for the expenses. She was good at managing the money. There is something that doesn't add up here."

Sean said, "Well, it adds up if this was a pay-off to confess to those murders. You said your grandpa knew he was dying. This may have been a way to make sure you and your mom were taken care of. If no one knew he was sick, which is what your mom said, whoever paid for this policy probably convinced the insurance company that they had some time before a pay-out would occur. It raises some interesting questions. Also, maybe whoever did this gave your grandfather some money as an initial payoff, plus the insurance policy, and he gave the cash to your mom."

"This would explain a lot. We lived in an apartment here at first, but she bought a car. When Grandpa died, Mom must have gotten the money. She used it to buy the house, and then only used it as necessary if her job couldn't cover all the expenses, like my college education. She probably had some medical bills, too, that her medical insurance didn't completely cover. Wow." Cheryl was silent for a minute and then looked at Sean with tears in her eyes, "Grandpa did this for us. It was his gift knowing that he didn't have much time to live. That's why Mom was so distraught at the time. She knew. It wasn't that he was confessing to the murders, it was because she knew he was dying and he was doing this for us."

Cheryl couldn't hold her emotions any longer. She put her hands over her face and started sobbing. Sean put his arms around her and pulled her tight against him and held her. He felt her softness against him. The entire drive to Cleveland had been torture. There had never been another woman who he had been drawn to the way he was with her. It was almost from the first time he had seen her. He didn't want this, but he couldn't help it.

She finally quieted and wiped her face with her hands and looked up at him. She was so beautiful. He slowly lowered his head and, with a feather's touch, kissed her. She melted into his embrace and his kiss. The dam broke. The enormous chemistry they had felt toward each other exploded. Not allowing any distance between their bodies, they made it to Cheryl's old bedroom where their needs were finally quenched in the early morning hours.

Their night-vision goggles did nothing to erase the blackness bearing weight on them. He and Clint, with guns drawn, were on alert as they entered a dark building. Sean was tense. Something was not right; things were not as they should be. Evil began to surround them, starting to suffocate them. It was as if they were sinking in quick sand. They couldn't move; they couldn't break free. He was screaming for them to run, but Clint didn't seem to hear him. His screams grew more desperate. Sean saw himself hurled backward, slamming against the wall. Something warm was flowing on his body and down the side of his head. Though stunned and not comprehending his condition, he tried to focus to see where his best friend was. He knew his eyes were deceiving him before he lost consciousness, because something was wrong. A human leg was lying near him. He felt horror sweep over him. He had to find Clint. Clint had to be okay. He was trying to hold his head up to locate Clint. He was trying to call out to him, but his mouth wouldn't work. He finally got his head to stay up long enough. God no! Clint's body wasn't in one piece. Clint's head turned toward him, but his face was missing.

Cheryl felt Sean writhing beside her and reliving something horrific. She sat up on the bed, not sure what she should do, whether to wake him or not. She knew he was in the throes of a night-mare. *If she woke him, would he know where he was or even recognize her? Would it startle him more to wake him? Oh, God. What should she do?* Sean suddenly screamed out, forcibly nearly throwing himself out of bed.

"*NNNNOOOOO!!!!!*"

She urgently turned on the lamp. Except for gasping for air, Sean sat frozen, staring ahead but seeing nothing. Cheryl sat for a couple of minutes giving him time and then she slowly put her hand on his back and began softly rubbing it. His body was soaked. Once she felt he would not be startled by her, that he was back to the present, she wrapped her arms around him and held him.

After a while, Sean murmured, "They're getting more graphic. My God. Oh, my God. His body was torn apart." Sean put his hands to each side of his head and rubbed it in an agitated way. "It's awful. I see some of the aftermath of whatever happened, but I can't see what happened."

"Honey, can I get you a glass of water?"

He reached and put his hand on her arm to hold it in place. "No," he hoarsely whispered.

After a while, he laid back and tucked her under his arm against him. Sean started talking, telling her about Clint and Tally, that they were on assignment in Kuwait. He told her that the last thing he could remember was walking with Clint toward the warehouse at night, and then he woke up at the hospital in Germany. He explained that the counselor thought his dreams would eventually help him to remember the missing parts. He described the recurring dream. "But this nightmare went further than the previous nightmares. I saw myself being thrown against a wall. Blood was dripping down my face. Oh God. I saw a leg lying near me." He shuddered. "Oh, God, I hope it wasn't Clint's," he whispered. She waited for him to continue. "Then, the way the dream always ends, Clint's face turns toward me, but his face is no longer recognizable." Sean's voice was hoarse as if he was transfixed by what the nightmare might be trying to tell him.

Cheryl rose up on her elbow and began to rub his chest with her fingertips. She leaned forward and tenderly kissed his lips. Sean's eyes met Cheryl's. He needed her. He pulled her under him. Their desire, need and emotion filled their consummation.

They woke embraced in each other's arms. "Good morning, Beautiful," Sean murmured into the top of her head as she lay with her head against his chest.

"Mmmm. And good morning to you. This is a wonderful way to start the day."

"Yes, it is. I wish we could spend all day like this; but unfortunately, we've got a lot to do."

"Mmmmm, I know. I'll check, but I believe there is some coffee. If you want, you can shower while I get it going, and then, I'll follow you."

She started to get up, but he pulled her back to him. The kiss was deep, wanting and sensual. The start of the day was delayed a while longer.

While Cheryl was showering, Sean finished looking through the last three boxes. Sean stacked all the boxes back in the closet, and after Cheryl was dressed, she tidied up her mother's room, back to the way it was before she had started her search. She knew that soon, she would start the process of cleaning out the house and putting it on the market.

They were drinking coffee. "About last night, I guess it's a good thing you saw what can happen. Look, Cheryl. I don't have any control over these tormenting nightmares, and I can't remember what happened. It's a lot to lay on someone, so if you —"

Before Sean could finish, Cheryl put her hand on his, "Don't say it, Sean. I can make my own decisions. Please don't push me away. I am strong. Look what I've been through. I don't want to scare you away, but since we're being honest, I think I am in love with you. I had a crush on you when I used to watch you play football twenty years ago. These feelings I'm having started that day at Max's coffee shop. I can handle this, Sean, and I am here to help you in any way that I can."

Sean was happy to hear that Cheryl had feelings about him because he was attracted to her, but he wasn't sure about his feelings or even if he was prepared for a serious relationship. He owed Cheryl honesty. Cheryl picked up on some internal debate within Sean and continued, "I don't expect you to feel the same, Sean. You don't have to reciprocate. I know how I feel, and I want you to know that and that I am here for you. "

Sean smiled, "I'm really attracted to you and really like you, Cheryl, but I've got a lot of mess in my head. You saw that last night. Let's take things a day at a time. Okay?"

Cheryl smiled, picked up her cup for a sip and nodded "yes."

Sean's smile widened. "You had a crush on me twenty years ago?"

Cheryl giggled and again nodded "yes."

"Well, I've got a confession to make. I felt a pull toward you that day at Frau's when you arched your eyebrow at me."

Cheryl started laughing.

"If we weren't expected at the newspaper, I'd carry you back to the bedroom where we'd stay all day."

Cheryl's laugh was happy. "Well, as much as I would love that, we better leave before one of us changes our mind."

They both were laughing as they leaned toward each other to kiss one more time before washing the coffee pot and cups and locking up the house.

Cheryl and Sean arrived at *The Cleveland Presenter* and headed to Keith's office. Milton saw them and followed them in. Cheryl introduced Sean to Keith and Milton. Sean said, "I'd like to be candid here with you all, so can we state that this meeting is off the record?"

Keith said, "Yes, we're good with that as long as everything Cheryl finds on her own—or jointly with you—outside this meeting is good to go."

"Understood," Sean said.

Keith asked, "So what have you got?"

Sean and Cheryl took turns telling about the life insurance policy they had found last night at Cheryl's mom's home. Sean also told them that as of now there weren't any suspects in the Pinkston case. He told them that he didn't buy the local representatives' views that the meth was now gone from the area.

"What about this life insurance policy on your grandfather? The key is finding out who paid for it." Keith said.

Sean said, "That's right. I called my dad this morning and asked him about the company, Bekbourg Farm and Community Insurance. He said they closed down about fifteen years ago. He doesn't know much about the company, and he didn't know why they closed. I have a friend who's FBI in Columbus. I've already called him. Cheryl and I are going to stop on our way back to Bekbourg, and I'm hoping he can help us get to the bottom of that."

Milton said, "That's good. Something like that, you probably need the FBI's help. By the way, I've made progress on the way the car dealership raised its capital. I've got some friends at the manufacturer who I'm also talking to who know Werner. Here's what I know. Werner added the other lines. Until 1993, Al Werner owned 100 percent of the dealership. Around 1993, he sold 49 percent of his ownership when he converted it to a corporation. Some of the investors were from out of the country, but some locals bought shares like Randall Thompson and Jeff Thompson and other businessmen. Werner used those funds to build the large dealership. Apparently, he put in a large lot on one side in anticipation of bringing in additional lines at some point. His largest manufacturer also put up some money in the form of low-interest loans for inventory. Al died of a sudden heart attack in 1994, soon after the new dealership opened.

"In 1997, Gary Werner got the big franchise arrangement that covered trucks and vans. He applied for it, and best I can tell, the powers-that-be were impressed with his operations and awarded the franchise. The way the deal was structured, Gary didn't have to come up with much of a cash outlay for the franchise. The trucks' products were put on the side of the dealership which had been left vacant for future expansion. In 2000, he started leasing farm equipment."

Sean and Cheryl walked into Lucky Brennan's office. "Sean, it's great to see you. I couldn't believe when I heard from Harold that you were out of the Marines. You should have told me. I'd have made a place here for you."

Shaking Lucky's hand, Sean said, "It's great to see you, Lucky. This is Cheryl Seton, a reporter for *The Cleveland Presenter*. She's covering the Pinkston murder case and another drug overdose case in Bekbourg, but we need some help on a third case."

"It's nice to meet you, Ms. Seton. You all have a seat and tell me what you need."

"'Cheryl,' please." Cheryl looked at Sean, and he nodded to her to start. She walked Lucky through everything that they knew about her grandfather, including the life insurance policy.

Sean said, "Here is a copy of the policy that we found. We think if we can find who paid for it, we might be able to determine who actually killed the Burkharts. We're hoping you can unravel the facts about this company and see if there is any way to ascertain who bought this policy."

"I'll get started on this and keep you apprised. Sean, it sounds like you might be sitting on a powder keg down there. Watch yourself. If you need anything else, let me know."

Sean and Cheryl's last stop before returning to Bekbourg was to see Ronnie Vin. Sean introduced Cheryl and told Ronnie about the bullet. She took it and told them that she would get back as soon as she had the results. While talking to Ronnie, Sean also asked her if it was unusual for the County coroner to not have a file on someone who was found unconscious and died at the hospital.

"Yes, that would be unusual, Sean. What's this about?"

Sean explained everything that he and Cheryl knew about the situation.

"Mmmm. I don't know why the County wouldn't have some type of record about Ms. Collins' death," said Ronnie. "The County should have sent us something. Let me check our files and see if we have anything."

Chapter 46

Mike had met Zeke Pinkston when he came to Bekbourg to claim the bodies to take them back to Tapsaw County for burial. Since then, Zeke had call Mike several times checking on the status of the investigation. Sitting across his desk, Mike looked into the face of a determined man.

"Sheriff, seems us talkin' over the phone hasn't impressed on you how important it is that you find who killed my boys and grandson. I thought I'd best meet you in person."

Mike knew his type. Zeke was business-like and wasn't the kind to throw his weight around or show anger. There was no need for that. If things didn't get handled the way he believed they should, he simply took matters into his own hands. "Mr. Pinkston, like I told you over the phone, this is an ongoing investigation, and we are following every lead we have to find the perpetrators of this crime. As you know, the state police are also involved in this investigation, and then there is the question of the meth labs that has brought in the DEA. So as you can see, in such a complicated crime scene, we have to carefully evaluate all the evidence."

"Well, Sheriff, you already told me all this over the phone, but I wanted to come over here and tell you personally that I won't be satisfied 'til you have captured the people who done this."

Mike looked Pinkston squarely in the eyes, "I think you are about to overstep your prerogative as a parent, Mr. Pinkston. We are doing everything we can to solve this murder, but I will not tolerate anyone coming in here and threatening us or this investigation with their own personal vendetta. Whether you like to admit it or not, your sons were engaged in an illegal activity, which it appears resulted in their deaths. We will get to the bottom of it, and I will keep you informed, but don't come back here and threaten me or my department again."

"Sheriff, get off your high horse. I haven't threatened you, and if I did, you would know it. I don't want you to put this on the back burner just 'cause my boys were playin' around with meth. They are dead, and someone's got to pay. I want you to fully understand what I mean."

As Pinkston stood to leave, Mike said with steel in his voice he seldom used, "Pinkston, if you interfere or try to take things in your hands, you will be dealt with by the full extent of the law. Stay out of this. I will keep you informed, and we will solve this."

As Pinkston started his truck, he thought to himself, *"Ain't no sheriff goin' to blow me off. If that Sheriff thinks I'm goin' to sit on my ass while he sits on his and does nothin' to find the killers, he's got another think comin'."*

Chapter 47

"Sean, I've got some information on that insurance company. It's not much. I'll keep digging, but here's what I've found so far." *If anyone could hit pay dirt blitzing through a quagmire of records, it was Lucky,* thought Sean.

"The company was started in 1952 as Bekbourg Farm and Community Insurance primarily covering farm equipment, but it grew to cover house and auto insurance policies. Eventually, they added life insurance policies, but from what I can tell, it only had a small number of life insurance policies. When it went out of business fifteen years ago, it sold all the policies. The Chairman and CEO was Randall Thompson. Al Werner was on the Board of Directors. There are some files in the state's archives where the annual filings were made. I'm working to get a hold of those. I'll keep you posted."

"Lucky, I appreciate this. There's something that I found that seems odd. I went to the records department and pulled the evidence box on this. You'd think that a murder case where five people were killed would have more in the file than I found. Looks like the file had been sanitized."

"Sean, I'll get back to you as soon as I know something. Whoever had the ability to clean a file had to be an 'insider.' Watch your back."

Sean and Cheryl were waiting for a table for dinner at the GilHaus when Mike and Geri walked in. Geri was intrigued when she saw Cheryl. Sean said, "Mike and Geri Adams, this is Cheryl Seton."

Geri said, "Are you waiting on someone else? If not, would you like to join Mike and me? We would love the company." Geri was not aware of the tension between Mike and Sean, but Mike was not going to put a damper on Geri's invitation.

"Sean, we would like for you and Cheryl to join us."

Cheryl turned to Sean, "It's fine with me if you're okay."

"Sure," Sean said.

Margo walked up about that time, and Sean asked for a table. She seated them at a table next to a window.

Once they were seated, Mike and Sean were quiet. Geri had a way of filling a conversational void. To Cheryl, she said, "Mike and Sean probably already know. I sometimes find myself in the dark, but have you known Sean for a while?"

Cheryl already liked Geri. She was a genuinely warm and vivacious person.

Mike, for the first time, spoke up, "Geri, maybe we should look at the menu."

Cheryl laughed. "It's okay, Mike. I don't mind. Geri, your husband may know this, but I am a reporter from *The Cleveland Presenter*. I came down to cover the Pinkston murders and also a broader story about drugs in the area. I recently met Sean. I suspect he invited me to dinner to learn my sources and leads."

They all laughed.

Cheryl said to Mike, "I love Buddy. He's a great dog. Sean told me that you gave Buddy to him as a puppy."

Mike and Sean looked at each other and chuckled. "I'm glad to hear you like him." They all laughed.

Geri said, "Wow, Cleveland. Well, welcome to Bekbourg. I'm sorry it's to cover murder and drugs. We're actually a nice town."

Cheryl said, "Oh, yes. I have met some fantastic people here."

Geri said, "Cheryl, Mike was a wide receiver, and Sean was the quarterback for Schriever High School and won the state championship game their senior year."

"I know. I remember watching them play football. I was six years younger, and my friend and I would go to the games. My grandpa, Henry Willis, would take me."

Mike and Geri both looked surprised. Geri asked, "You lived here?"

"Yes, I was born here, but we moved away when I was fourteen."

"So, you aren't new to Bekbourg?" asked Geri.

"No, but a lot has changed."

Sean had been gauging Mike as Cheryl and Geri talked. He saw when realization hit Mike who

Cheryl's grandfather was. Mike turned to stare at Sean. Sean stared back and then returned his attention to the conversation.

It turned out to be a nice evening. Cheryl and Geri did most of the talking, but Sean and Mike seemed to enjoy listening. Sean could tell that Mike was still processing the fact that it was Cheryl's grandfather who had pled guilty to the Burkhart murders.

On the drive home, Mike was considering what it might mean that Cheryl had returned to Bekbourg after all this time. He had a feeling that things were going to get more complicated. However, his concern was tempered as he had observed Sean during dinner. Mike knew his best friend had been ensnared in the torment of whatever happened when he was injured. But the weariness had begun to wane, and shades of the man he knew were emerging. The tightness in his facial features was eroding, and Sean seemed more at ease. Mike was relieved that Sean had battled back, but he couldn't help but also think about how they all had been affected by life's tugs.

His thoughts were interrupted when Geri said, "I didn't know that Sean was seeing anyone. I'm glad. He seems really happy."

"Yeah. He's been through a lot. Cheryl seems good for him."

Geri thought back to when Sean and Becky were dating. Geri and Becky had been best friends since elementary school. At the Thompson's welcome back party for Sean, Geri could tell that Becky was upset. She couldn't take her eyes off

Sean, but Sean was paying her no mind. Years ago, Becky had misjudged Sean. She had wanted them to get married, and Sean either wasn't interested or wasn't ready. Becky believed that if she tried to break up with Sean, he would agree to get married. She never imagined he'd sign up for the Marines and leave Bekbourg.

Becky ran into Gary during her orientation at Ohio University. He showed her around the campus, giving her a personal tour. After that, Gary started asking Becky out. She finally agreed, and they started dating. After all, prestige went with dating a starting football player. They dated through the rest of college, and after graduation, they married and had two daughters. Geri didn't think that Becky ever really loved Gary, but she was a good wife, taking care of their home and the girls.

Geri wasn't sure about Gary's feelings. He had married the captain of the cheerleading squad from Schriever High School. Becky was beautiful, smart, and a people person with an outgoing personality. She was an asset to him on OU's campus and as his wife as he grew his business around town. But, Geri was convinced that the biggest reason of all for him to marry Becky was that she had been Sean Neumann's girlfriend.

They made love and drifted into a deep sleep. Sean, still sleeping, could feel himself being dragged into a familiar pit. He struggled to avoid the trap, but it was no use.

Everything was dark. He and Clint, with guns drawn, were entering a dark building. Sean's senses were strung tight. He felt they were being watched. Things weren't going as planned; things were not as they should be. Evil was surrounding them, starting to smother them. It was as if they were sinking in quick sand. They couldn't move; they couldn't break free. He was screaming for them to run, but Clint didn't seem to hear him. Then, suddenly, Clint turned toward Sean, looking at him, and yelled, "Bomb!" Everything was recast in slow motion. Sean saw Clint's intention. He screamed to stop him and started to lunge forward, but with steel determination, Clint spun and threw himself on top of the device.

Cheryl woke, feeling Sean's body going tense and hearing his groans. Buddy had walked over and laid his head on the bed, whimpering. Without warning, Sean bolted straight up in the bed, screaming and gulping for air. She waited, knowing he needed to come back to reality. She gently massaged his shoulders, and Buddy jumped up on the bed and lay down beside him and started nudging Sean with his nose. When Sean started to rub his neck, Buddy laid beside Sean with his head on Sean's lap.

Sean sat there for a long time. He finally whispered, "I remember it all. I know what happened."

He turned to look at her. "I remember. Oh, God. I finally remember."

Sean then was able to unburden his soul.

He, Clint and Tally had made substantial progress while in Kuwait in ascertaining facts for a court martial against some lower-level military personnel. They also had determined many of the workings of the trafficking routes, arrangements and foreign participants. They had recently discovered that the head of the trafficking ring from the military's standpoint was a colonel, but they did not have enough evidence to bring charges against him.

Through their contacts and investigations, an anonymous Kuwaiti informer, Jyot Al-Nashi, emerged. At first, they were unable to learn his identity. When they did learn who he was, they never let him know that they knew him. He was the traffic manager for the Kuwaiti government. Jyot first reached out to them by a written correspondence, and after a while, he began to call them. The tips were small tips, but they were determined to be credible. They didn't hear from the informant often, but when they did, each tip led one step closer to cracking the case.

Jyot had passed along to Sean a couple of recent tips that heroin had been delivered to a particular site and was waiting pick-up. When Sean, Clint and Tally arrived, however, they discovered that the heroin had already been moved. They felt they were getting close, but were frustrated they could not get any closer to the main players.

One night around two o'clock a.m., Jyot called Sean and told him that a shipment of heroin was in a warehouse in an abandoned part of town, but a pickup was due in about three hours. Upon hearing the tip, Clint was ready to roll. Even though this informant had never failed them, Sean never completely trusted an informant. According to Jyot, time was of the essence in getting to the warehouse before the pickup.

Sean said, "I don't know about this, Clint. I think we need to take a deep breath and think this through."

"Sean, this is the break we have been waiting for. He's proven to be reliable. He's not going to roll on us. He wants us to stop this as much as we do. Let's boogie, Pal."

Sean drove and got there early and parked where their jeep could not be seen from the road. They used scopes to closely observe the surroundings. Nothing seemed unusual or suspicious.

Clint urged Sean to set up an ambush inside the warehouse for when they came for the drugs.

Sean said, "Hold on, Clint. We don't even know if there are any drugs in there. We have to check it out first. Also, we want to take these guys alive so we can interrogate them."

Sean decided that it did make sense for two of them to go inside, check for the drugs, and wait for the traffickers to arrive. Sean told Tally to call for reinforcements and to watch the outside. He asked him to notify him if anything suspicious happened and let him know when the traffickers arrived.

Tally asked, "Why do I have to stay outside?"

"I'm in charge of this case, so I'm going in, and you know there's no way to keep him," Sean said, pointing to Clint who was standing outside their jeep, "away from that warehouse."

"You guys have all the fun."

Sean and Clint worked their way to the warehouse on alert, watching their surroundings. Tally had called for backup and sat looking for any movement or change. Sean and Clint finally made it to the building, and using special equipment, they opened a side door. The warehouse was one story, long and narrow. No one appeared to be inside. As they entered, their flashlight beams fell on five plastic containers sitting off in the back left corner.

After clearing the offices and closet and toilet at the front of the building, they stood motionless, surveying the situation. Finally, they slowly started to make their way to the center of the room. Sitting off to the right was a table and some crates. Sean slowly moved to the crates, but determined they were empty. He turned to move back to where Clint had been standing, but Clint had moved closer to the containers. Sean's flashlight beam was shining in the direction of the containers when suddenly, Clint froze and a faint beeping could be heard. Sean jerked his flashlight beam to Clint's face. He threw himself on top of the device, trying to shield Sean from the bomb's impact.

Tally heard and saw the explosion and ran to the warehouse, frantically screaming into his radio for assistance. Tally burst into the smoky warehouse, urgently shining his flashlight trying to find Sean and Clint. Then, he heard what he thought was a faint moan off to the side. There, he found Sean leaning up against the wall covered in blood. While he focused all his efforts on saving him, he ignored the severed leg lying nearby. He figured Clint was gone. Sean never knew that Tally had arrived.

Sean was sweating profusely. Cheryl eased out of bed and got a towel and tenderly dried his body.

"I love you, Sean. You've got me, Honey. I'm here. Don't ever forget that."

She kissed him, and he pulled her back on the bed. Buddy jumped off the bed and lay down on his bed. Their lovemaking reinforced the love they shared for each other.

Ever since Sean and Mike had the argument about Ben, they hadn't talked much. Sean didn't know exactly what Mike had said to Ben, but he knew he was no longer on the Pinkston case. Sean learned from Kim that Ben had taken a few days off.

If Mike thought giving Ben some time off would diffuse the situation, he was sorely mistaken. Ben had mostly stayed drunk and dwelled on his nemesis. *"I hate that ass. Ever since he got back, he's caused trouble. He stuck his nose into the murder investigation by sucking up to that state police chief. Now, that panty-waist sheriff is letting him run the department. He's got no right pushing me off the investigation."*

It was later in the afternoon when most of the people in the precinct had gone home. Ben was watching for Sean. He knew he would be pulling into the parking lot. Ben's hostility toward Sean had reached a boiling point, and it didn't help that Ben had had a few drinks.

Sean pulled into the lot and got out of his car. Ben jumped out and yelled to Sean, "Come here, Football Stud. I want to talk to you."

Sean stood there, forcing Ben to walk over to him. Sean knew there was going to be trouble.

"How dare you tell Mike to pull me off the case? This was my case. You holier than thou SOB, you come in here after all these years and act like you own this place. You're goin' to be sorry you messed with me."

Sean didn't want to escalate the scene. In a reasonable voice, Sean said, "Ben, calm down. This case is bigger than both of us. The state's involved, and the Feds are involved. I'm sorry, but you were getting in the way. In fact, I think I did you a favor to get you off the case, because you were out of your element on this. Let's calm down. I've got to go in the office and do my reports."

"You don't know what you're gettin' into. You'll pay for this."

"Ben, I'm not going to take any threats from you. Just move on."

As Sean walked away, Ben glared.

An unexpected call came in from Stella who wanted to talk to Cheryl about something that had happened in the paper plant, but she didn't want anyone to know that they were meeting. "Can I come over this evening to Bri's?"

As they sat on Bri's back porch, Stella said, "You know, there's something that's been bothering me for a while. I haven't told anyone, because I'm not sure that it's anything, but if it is, then it's making me uneasy. Also, I didn't know who I would talk to, because I didn't know who I could trust. After I talked to you about Missy, I thought you are someone that's easy to talk to, and I also trust you. I may have a wild imagination, but there's something that doesn't seem right at the paper company.

"I'm responsible for the boxes that are ready for shipment. The boxes have been packed and sealed when they get to me. I then put the labels on them and indicate where the forklift driver needs to load them on the racks. I keep an inventory of the boxes for each delivery shipment, so that we load the right number of boxes into the right truck. I know my boxes. I always check them once they're on the racks and oversee them when it's time to load them.

"Well, every so often, when I come back the next morning, I can tell that the boxes that were put on a certain rack aren't stacked exactly the way they were when I left. What's interesting is that the labels are printed slightly different. I keep my mouth shut and act like I don't know anything, but I have known for a long time this has been going on. I don't know how or why it's happening, but I know it is."

"Stella, do you ever see anyone around the boxes after you're finished with them or before the boxes are ready to be loaded on the trucks?"

"No, that's just it. I never see anyone around those boxes, so I can't figure out how things are happening. The only people that would be there at night are the cleaning people, but they wouldn't have any reason to touch the boxes. Those are on the racks."

"So, does everyone leave at the same time?"

"Yes, as far as I know. Mr. Andrews, our foreman, may stay a little later sometimes, but that's the only person I know. But I don't think he would be doing anything, because there are a lot of boxes on these particular racks that I'm talking about—hundreds of them.

"There's one other thing, but I don't know if this is important. One night, I got home and realized that I had left my cell phone in my locker at the plant. I had it out on my lunch break and laid it on the shelf in my locker rather than putting it in my purse. I drove back to the plant and drove around back to where the employee parking lot is. I thought there might be a security guard who would let me in. I had parked and was deciding what to do when a dark school bus came driving up. It must have been packed. All these Hispanics got off and went in. It seemed like a lot of people for a cleaning crew."

"What did you do?"

"I got an uncomfortable feeling. I waited until they were all inside and I didn't think anyone was around to see me, and I drove quietly without my lights on out of the parking area and waited until I was on the street to turn my car lights back on. I was scared, Cheryl. I don't know if I should have been, but I was."

"Did you ever tell anyone about what you saw that night?"

"No one. Like I said, I try to mind my own business and keep my head down."

"Stella, I don't know if any of what you said means anything, but I think you did the right thing to not say anything to anyone. I think it's important that you not mention this. Do you trust me?"

"Yeah, that's why I told you, Cheryl."

"There is someone that I trust. I'm going to tell him, but I won't use your name for now. I don't know what he'll think, but if he needs to know more, I'll let you know. For now though, be careful and do your job like you have been. And, Stella, thanks for trusting me."

"I'm glad I finally could tell someone. If you trust him, that's good enough for me, so if you need to use my name, I'm okay with that."

Chapter 48

Erlene Avery lived in a duplex in an older residential development out near the main highway. Lisa Rimes lived next door in the duplex.

Erlene was Ben Clark's girlfriend. Ben lived in a mobile home out in the rural area, so she didn't see him every night. Actually, it was an on-again, off-again relationship, because Ben came and went when he wanted to. Ben hadn't called Erlene to say that he was stopping by tonight. When she opened the door, she knew it was not going to be a good night. Ben was drunk. He pushed in past Erlene and slumped on the sofa. "Get me a beer."

"Okay, Hon." Erlene brought Ben a can of beer. She could tell he was steamed about something. "Hon, have you eaten? Can I fix you something?"

Ben sat staring ahead drinking his beer. Erlene wanted to be as far away as she could get. She walked into the kitchen to act like she was busy on something in the kitchen. After a few minutes, she heard the beer can crashing against the wall. "Where are you? Get me another beer."

"Hon, I'm sorry. That was the only beer in the refrigerator. I'll run to the store to get you some more. I'll be right back." She grabbed her purse off the kitchen cabinet and started to open the back door. Ben was there before she could get out the door. He roughly grabbed her arm and slapped her hard across her face. "What did I tell you about keeping beer here?"

Trembling, "I'll go get you some. It won't take long. You know that store is right down the street."

Erlene could see the coldness in Ben's eyes. He started dragging her away from the back door. She started crying and screaming, "No, Ben! Please!" The beating started. She was screaming as she felt the savage punches to her face and stomach and to her ribs. The phone started ringing. Ben must have thought it was a neighbor, because he stopped and slammed her down on the ground and kicked her in the ribs before storming out.

Lisa came running in the back door. She knew Ben's temper. Many times, she had heard arguing and screaming from Erlene's duplex and then seen bruises and black eyes. "Oh, my God! You poor thing."

Erlene was curled up on the floor whimpering. There was blood on her mouth and a large cut on the side of her face, and both eyes were swollen.

"Baby, we've got to get you to the hospital."

"Noooo," she moaned.

Despite Erlene's protest, Lisa finally convinced her to go to the hospital. Given the viciousness of the beating, Lisa was afraid there may be internal bleeding. As they pulled up to the emergency room, Erlene hoarsely urged, "Don't say anything about Ben. Promise me."

Lisa didn't want to make that promise. She parked and ran in to get help. The doctor put stitches in the gash on the side of her head and did x-rays and examined her. As he was working on Erlene, he asked her what had happened. She told him she fell down the steps at home. She was carrying some groceries and missed the step and lost her balance. The doctor knew better. He said, "Ms. Avery, I'm going to step out and check on another patient, but the nurse is going to stay with you. If you need anything, let her know. I'll be back in to check on you, but I want you to try relaxing." He nodded for the nurse to stay in the room.

The doctor walked into the waiting room and saw Lisa sitting there. He asked her what had happened. "I saw him leaving, so I ran in through the back door and found Erlene on the floor." She explained that she finally convinced Erlene to let her take her to the hospital. The doctor said, "I'm glad you did."

The doctor then called the police station. Sean was working late, trying to catch up on his paperwork. When Sean answered the phone, the doctor told him that he had a woman who had been badly beaten and the police should investigate. Sean decided to go to the hospital and not bother the other two deputies on night duty. He might as well take Kyle along—as he was just sitting at his desk not doing much.

When they got there, the doctor met them and explained the situation. The doctor then introduced them to Lisa.

Lisa demanded. "What are you going to do for her? She didn't want me to bring her in. I've probably made things worse for her. You'll protect your own."

The doctor looked with suspicion at Sean, who in turn looked with confusion at Lisa.

"Ms. Rimes, I don't know who did this, but if you're telling me that it was a deputy, you can be sure that we will treat him like anyone else. You have my solemn promise on this."

She studied Sean. Something about the sincerity in Sean's voice made her believe him. "The doctor told me what you said occurred. I need to talk to Ms. Avery, but it would be helpful if you could give me the name of the person who did this."

She looked at Sean, Kyle and the doctor. "Erlene didn't want me to tell anyone his name, but something needs to be done. This is the worse I've seen. I'm afraid that if he isn't stopped, one day he may hurt her so bad she can't recover or even kill her. Erlene may be mad at me, but he's a deputy. His name is Ben Clark."

Sean was livid that Ben had taken his rage out on Erlene.

The doctor said, "Deputy Neumann, it's probably best if only one deputy talks to her. Would you like to talk with Ms. Avery?"

"Yes, and Ms. Rimes—thank you. You did the right thing. I'm not going to let this go. Kyle, why don't you wait here?"

"Sure, Sean."

The hospital bed was elevated, so Erlene was sitting up when Sean entered. Fear instantly shot to her eyes. Sean wanted to make her feel more at ease.

"Ms. Avery. I'm Deputy Neumann. The nurse here is going to stay with you while we talk. Is that okay with you?"

Tears started rolling down her cheeks.

"Ms. Avery, will you tell me what happened?"

"I fell down the steps. I was carrying some grocery bags and lost my balance and fell down."

"I want to help you, Ms. Avery. The doctor told me theses injuries are not consistent with falling down steps. Will you tell me what happened?"

"I can't, Deputy Neumann."

"The doctor is going to keep you here tonight for observation. Get some rest, Ms. Avery."

Finally, much later, Sean returned her call, "Hi, Babe. I just left the hospital on a matter that I was handling there."

"Sean, I need to talk to you about something that may be important. Is it too late for you to drop by the B&B?"

"I'll be there soon."

Bri was sitting in the parlor when Sean arrived. "Hi, Sean, I'm Bri. It's nice to meet you."

"It's nice to meet you, too, Bri. Cheryl has told me a lot about you."

"Sean, would you like something to eat? I've got leftover fried chicken and vegetables."

"That's nice for you to offer. I don't want to put you out, but frankly, I've had a busy night and haven't had dinner."

"Say no more, Sean. Cheryl, if you and Sean want some privacy, there's the little nook where Max and I eat off the kitchen. I'll bring Sean's dinner in there when it's warm."

"That's wonderful. Thank you."

Once Sean had eaten the dinner, Cheryl told Sean everything that Stella had told her. He said, "That's interesting. I don't know what to think about all that. I was in the factory, both the new part and the old part, and I didn't see anything unusual. I saw where the boxes are kept. That's especially interesting about the large cleaning crew. It's a large area, but I can't imagine they need that many people to clean it."

Cheryl and Sean talked a little more about the paper plant, and then Sean said, "Do you think Bri would have a problem if I stayed tonight?"

Cheryl laughed, "No, not at all. I mentioned to her about our trip to Cleveland. I think she would be happy if you stayed the night."

Sean walked into Mike's office the following morning and closed the door.

"What's up, Sean?"

"We need to talk. When I got back to the station yesterday evening, Ben was waiting for me. He was really angry at me for being pulled off the Pinkston case. I tried to calm him down. I think he took it out on his girlfriend, Erlene Avery." Sean told Mike about Lisa Rimes taking her to the hospital, the doctor calling him and what happened once he got to the hospital. "I'm going to stay away from this, Mike. You talk to her and see what you can find out. The whole town will know about this, probably already talking about Ben."

When Sean walked out of Mike's office, Mike thought, *"Can it get any worse? This is all I need, news getting around that Ben has assaulted his girlfriend, and according to what Lisa Rimes said, it had happened several times."* He picked up the phone and dialed a number. When she answered, Mike said, "Bri, sorry to bother you, but I need your help. There's a woman in the hospital who is the victim of domestic violence. She's not willing to cooperate with us. You might be able to help her.—Great, I'll pick you up in about fifteen minutes. Oh, one other thing, it's one of my deputies that did it. I'll be there soon."

Mike and Bri walked into Erlene's hospital room, and Mike introduced Bri.

Mike said, "Erlene, we're here to help you. Tell us what happened."

"I can't, Mike, I can't."

"Look, we have ways to take care of you, but you have to tell us what happened."

"I lost my balance and fell down the steps."

"We know you didn't fall down the steps, but the only way we can help you is if you tell us."

Bri gently interrupted, "Mike, why don't you step over there. I want to talk to her."

Mike walked over to the corner and could see them talking, but he couldn't hear their conversation.

Finally, Bri asked Mike to join them. "Honey, tell Mike what you told me."

"Umm, it's not Ben's fault. He didn't mean to. He was really angry about something. I don't blame him. I told him it would be okay. I should have known better. I provoked him. Don't do anything to him. He's a good man. He just knocked me down and slapped me a couple of times."

Bri said, "I'm going to stay awhile with Erlene. I can get home. You go ahead, Sheriff."

Mike told them both "goodbye" and left the hospital. He was angry to his core.

When Mike returned to the office, he asked Kim where Ben was. She told him that Ben had taken the day off. Mike asked if she could try to find him. Mike went to his office and closed the door. Mike didn't have a good feeling about things. Kim buzzed him and said, "Sheriff, I called his house, but he doesn't answer. Sometimes he goes to Knucklepin's if you want to check there."

Mike pulled up to Knucklepin's and saw Ben's pickup truck.

It being mid-afternoon, it was early for the regulars. There was only one person sitting at the bar. The bartender looked up and saw Mike and disappeared into the back. Sitting on the bar in front of Ben was a boilermaker. Mike walked up to Ben and stood off to his side, "Ben, you've gone too far this time. I need your badge and gun."

"What shit is this?" Ben turned to glare at Mike. "What are you sayin'?"

"I know what you did to Erlene, Ben."

"I don't know what you heard, but it's a damn lie." He turned back to his drink.

"Ben, give me your badge and gun."

"You're not gettin' either one," slurred Ben, looking straight ahead of him holding the glass in his hand. "You don't do that to me."

"It's already done, Ben."

"I've got people a lot higher than you lookin' out for me."

"We'll see about that, but right now, you're suspended from the sheriff's department, and I don't want you coming anywhere near the precinct. If you do, I'll have to put you in a cell."

Ben glared at Mike. "You've gone too far."

Ben slapped his gun and badge up on the bar and said, "I'll have that back before you know what happened. We'll have this out."

"Ben, what you did to that woman is a crime. You'll be lucky if you don't end up in jail."

Ben downed his shot. "We'll see."

Mike walked out shaking his head, knowing he'd really stirred the hornet's nest this time, but he was determined to see this through.

Chapter 49

Sean called Boze and told him about the information Stella had shared with Cheryl. "Boze, this is the second time someone has raised suspicious activities at the paper plant. This might be a wild goose chase, but that place is certainly big enough for warehousing drugs. And with trucks coming and going, we might be on to something."

Boze said, "My people are still looking at the plant's ownership. It's a private corporation, and it's more complicated than I thought. Seems there's some complex corporate structures involved. We've learned that Randall and Jeff Thompson are two of the investors. Some locals are also investors. The others are from out of the country. We're still trying to track that information down. The Board of Directors is comprised of some local people. Particularly of note are Jeff Thompson and Gary Werner. Blake Olson, an attorney out of Tampa, Florida, is the Chairman. He appears to leave the day-to-day operations to the local people, but he votes the shares of the other investors who live outside the country. He doesn't travel to Bekbourg often, basically for Board meetings.

"Also, this probably doesn't come as a surprise, but so far, we haven't found any information on a Dante Gomez in the area."

Chapter 50

Kyle stopped by Knucklepin's to get a drink. He sat down at the bar and ordered a whiskey. It had been weighing on his mind how upset Lisa Rimes had been at the hospital about what Ben had done to Erlene. Kyle had stayed in the waiting room while Sean went back to see Erlene, and Lisa had given him an ear full about Ben and seemed to indict the entire department—even Kyle. Kyle had seen Ben rough up people he was arresting, so he knew Ben had a violent streak, but he didn't know it went beyond the "lowlifes" he was arresting. Kyle wasn't even sure Ben should have done that, but he didn't interfere with him and usually followed Ben's instructions on investigations. Hearing about Erlene though had bothered Kyle.

As Kyle was deep in thought, Ben plopped down beside him. Kyle could tell that Ben had drunk a few, but he had seen him that way before. Ben ordered his usual beer and shot of whiskey and continued to look ahead, not acknowledging Kyle. Finally, Kyle said, "Hey, Ben."

Ben mumbled something. Kyle sensed that he was seething. Kyle was thinking about leaving, because he didn't want to be around Ben when he was like this. Ben suddenly said, "Just so you know, it's your fault and that asshole's I got suspended."

Kyle was unaware Ben had been suspended. Surprised, he asked, "What'd you mean?"

"I know'd you went to the hospital with Sean the other night."

Kyle said, "You talkin' about when Erlene was there?"

"That's exactly what I'm talkin' about, shit brains."

Kyle didn't say anything for a minute and then, trying not to get Ben more riled, said, "Well, we were at the station when the call came in. We didn't know what it was about 'til we got there."

Sipping his drink, Ben finally muttered, "Yeah, well, it wasn't you that talked to that dumbass sheriff. He said it was Sean. I hope he is happy—'cause he's goin' to get what's comin' to him. He's screwed with me for the last time."

"Ben, you best go home and get some sleep. It's not good for you to be thinkin' like this. Sean's just doin' his job, and from what I heard, you beat Erlene pretty bad."

"Kyle, I don't want to hear your shit. Like always, you don't know what the hell you're talkin' about. I've got powerful people on my side. They might be glad if I take care of Neumann."

"Ben, I seen you do things before, but this is different, what you did to Erlene. I don't think whoever they are can help you. Sean's a good man. Don't make things worse for yourself."

Kyle put some money on the bar and left. Ben's mood further blackened. In the past, he could always count on Kyle, but now even he had turned against him. He ordered another boilermaker.

Chapter 51

"Sean, this is Ronnie Vin."

"Hi, Ronnie. How are things going?"

"Pretty busy, Sean. You are the main source for my lack of boredom."

Sean laughed. "Well, sleepy Bekbourg does seem to have its share of things going on right now."

"Sean, I've found something interesting on the bullet that you brought to me from the Burkhart evidence bin. It came from a 357 Magnum. I double checked, even triple checked the results. The bullet from the Burkhart case matches the bullets from one of the guns used at the Pinkston murder scene."

Sean was silent, stunned in fact.

Ronnie continued, "In other words, the same gun used in the Pinkston murders was used twenty years earlier in another murder."

"Ronnie, we're looking for someone who had access to a gun that has been around twenty years and connects two mass shootings?" Sean's silence, Ronnie figured, was Sean thinking through the ramifications. Finally, "Ronnie, I appreciate this. I need to talk to Harold Greene, but I'd like to keep this information in a small circle."

"I understand, Sean. Say, on that matter you asked me to look into concerning Missy Collins, we do have a record that the Bekbourg County coroner sent us shortly after her death. Here is what it shows. She died of a mixture of meth, heroin and crack cocaine as well as having high levels of alcohol in her system. The coroner's report didn't show any signs of recent physical abuse. Ms. Collins had sexual relations within twelve hours of her death. The report also stated that traces of styrene were found on her clothing and body. You probably know this, but that is a chemical used in the manufacturer of polystyrene cups and plates."

After he hung up, Sean thought, *"The mysteries in Bekbourg abound. What and who do these two murders have in common? And, according to what Stella told Cheryl, Missy hadn't worked at the plant for a couple of years before she died. I wonder if whoever had sex with her worked or spent time at the plant."* Even though Ben was the responding officer, he knew that Ben would be of no help. It was time to ask Mike what he knew.

The information that Ronnie gave him about the guns, however, was more troubling and altered the direction of the murder investigation. He called Harold Greene and updated him. Harold agreed that it was best to keep this recent finding between himself and Sean and Ronnie.

Sitting in Gary's office, Sean said, "Gary, something I have to talk to you about."
"What is it?"

"I've been hearing some disturbing things around town. I've been trying to get to the bottom of the drug problems around here and the Burkhart murders."

"The Burkhart murders?" Gary was puzzled. "You mean the ones twenty years ago?"

"Yeah."

"What's that got to do with me? Didn't someone confess to those? Sean, I don't know what this is all about. You keep harassing me about things. Does this have something to do with that reporter? She came around here not long ago asking questions about how my dad got started in the business. Why's she trying to dredge things up?"

"That someone who confessed was her grandfather."

Shock hit Gary like a ton of bricks. "What?"

"Yeah, Henry Willis was her grandfather, and Gary, she doesn't believe that he committed those murders."

"Well, I sure don't know why you're talking to me about this." Flustered, Gary continued, "Sean, if I didn't know better, I would wonder if your attitude toward me has something to do with Becky marrying me."

"There's no indication that you're involved in anything, Gary, but there are some questions about some of the people who work at your dealership. Also, some recent developments raise new questions on how your father got this dealership from Burkhart. I'm investigating these. I'm telling you right now, if there's anything you need to talk to me about, you need to do so. I don't believe you're naïve. If you know anything or if something happens, you'll go down, too."

Sweat had broken out on Gary's forehead. He managed to respond, "I don't know what you're talking about, Sean."

Sean walked into Mike's office, "You wanted to talk to me, Mike?"

"Yeah, have a seat. Gary called me about you stopping by and asking him about his car dealership and his father buying it after Roger Burkhart's murder. Do you really think there's a connection? Sean, you knew Gary's dad and Gary. Gary was upset. What's going on? Cheryl's granddad confessed. The case is closed."

"Mike, Cheryl is convinced that her sixty-six-year old grandfather who was dying of cancer at the time, who was intoxicated that night, could not have, and would not have, killed those people. Frankly, I think she's right. I was asking Gary some basic questions. His dad benefitted from Burkhart's death in that he got the dealership for almost nothing. I'm not saying he had anything to do with it. I wanted to ask some questions. I don't know why Gary would get bent out of shape on this."

"Look, Sean. We don't have time to be running after twenty-year old cases where someone confessed. You're in charge of the Pinkston case, which hasn't been solved. That's the priority."

"Mike, if what Cheryl believes is true, then whoever was behind the Burkhart murders could still be in town. It seems you'd want to know the truth about that—even though it happened twenty years ago."

"I'm not saying that it shouldn't be looked into at some point if there is enough evidence to raise a doubt, but I don't see that is the situation now. I need to make some calls."

"One more thing I need to ask you about."

"What's that?"

"What do you know about the death of Missy Collins?"

"Who?"

"She lived in the Acorn Knoll trailer park. She died about five years ago. There are some people who think she died of a drug overdose. What's curious is that all that's in the police files is an incident report that says very little. Ben was the responding officer. There's no file at the County coroner or at the Clerk of Court. Do you know why all these files are missing?"

Sean thought he saw a hint of recollection in Mike's eyes before Mike impatiently replied, "What's this about all these old cases, Sean? We, you specifically, have full plates. I need for you to solve the cases you've got, not go digging up stuff that has no relevance to anything. The Todd murders haven't been solved either. Now, I've got some things I've got to take care of."

Sean got up to leave and didn't say anything. Mike hadn't specifically said not to help Cheryl. Also, Mike knew more than he was saying about Missy Collins. Sean would have to follow up another time with him about that.

Chapter 52

About two hours later, Mike received a call while he was doing some paperwork. Kim knew something had happened when Mike walked out. "Kim, I just got a call that Dad died. I'm going to meet Geri at the nursing home. Tell Mack to handle things. If you need to reach me, you know how to contact me." With that, Mike walked out of the station.

Later that afternoon, Sean knocked on the door to Mike's and Geri's home. Geri opened the door and went into Sean's arms. She was crying. After a minute, she said, "I'm sorry, Sean. Come in. Please, have a seat. Oh, God, it's so hard. We knew this was coming, but it still hurts. I think what hurts the most is seeing Mike in such pain."

"Is he here?"

"No." She wiped her eyes with a tissue. "You know the football field where you all played Youth Football? Mike's dad used to take him down there and pass the football to him. Mike once told me they went almost every weekend, even when it wasn't football season. Eventually, they quit going when Mike got in high school. That's where I think he is, Sean."

Sean looked over on the bookshelf where Mike always kept it—the football that he and all the Schriever players received when they won the state championship. The football was engraved, "Schriever High School State Champions 1977."

"Mind if I take that with me?" Sean asked pointing to the football.

Geri was now softly weeping, "Go ahead."

Sean drove over to the football field and saw Mike sitting on a bench with his back to Sean. Sean walked up from behind and put his hand on his shoulder and squeezed. After a minute, Sean asked, "You okay, Buddy?"

Mike sat there and then dropped his head forward. Sean moved around and sat beside him and started pitching the football back and forth between his hands. Mike saw that, and the corners of his mouth gave a hint of amusement.

Mike said, "He was a good man. Mom once told me that he changed after Mandy died, that he never got over it. I have an empty feeling now that he is gone. Some of the best years of my life were when we used to do things together. Back when things were simple. I'm having a hard time with this, Sean, but I know he's not suffering anymore. That's some consolation."

Sean said, "You know how I felt about your dad. I share your grief, but it's something we all have to face. As they say, time heals all."

"Yeah, that's what they say."

Sean touched Mike on the shoulder and said, "Get up, Buddy. Go long."

Mike looked at Sean with a small grin and took off in a trot. He turned, and Sean threw a perfect spiral right into his hands. Mike caught the ball and turned and trotted to the goal line.

After Sean left, Mike closed his eyes. Now that his dad was gone, Mike was through. He also knew that he might have to face his past, but he was getting out. His children were far away. He had seen to that. Fortunately, Geri had not objected when he suggested colleges out west. He didn't know why Geri was still with him. After he sold his soul, he became aloof. He had been faithful, but not an attentive husband. Geri had been a good wife, never turning away. She had tried to talk to him a few times, but finally let it drop. He had seen the worry in her eyes over the years. Tonight, he was going to tell her what he had done.

Also, he was worried for Sean. What had he gotten Sean into? Maybe it had been selfish to hire Sean. Part of Mike thought it would be great having his quarterback with him, but part of him also felt that if anyone could clean up the mess in town, Sean could. Already, Sean had proved a worthy opponent. Sean was smart. They would be gunning for Sean. They had already checked to see what Sean's alibi was the night of the Pinkston murders. Thank God, there was no daylight in Sean's alibi that night.

Late that evening, Geri was sitting propped up in bed. Mike sat down on a chair off to the side of the bed. He looked at her and said, "Geri, I have something to tell you, and I hope someday you can forgive me." He then told her the story. Moisture was in his eyes as he choked out the last thing he had to say, "You are a strong person. I love you, Geri. I always have, and I will until my last breath."

Geri had tears in her eyes. She got out of bed and walked over to Mike and knelt down in front of him. She gently lifted her arms around his head and kissed him. "Mike, I love you. It's going to be fine. Whatever it is, we will survive it."

They made love as if their lives depended on it. Mike and Geri held each other all night long.

Geri invited the old group of friends back together at their house. She felt Mike needed the distraction and that it would be good for him. Matt and Miranda were seeing friends tonight while they were in town, so it seemed like a good idea. Cheryl brought a delicious cobbler that Bri had baked and some sour dough rolls, and Sally brought a lasagna and salad.

Gary said, "Too bad Jeff had a conflict and couldn't be here."

"He told me he had a meeting that he couldn't get out of," Geri said. "He said that things were hectic with Mary and Rachel being in Europe. But, I guess you know about that with Becky and the girls in London. I know you hated to miss that trip. It's hard to believe that Kinsey is sixteen."

"Yeah, it's almost too quiet around the house." They laughed.

Sean, Gary and Danny came to lift Mike's spirits. They reminisced about their high school days. Sean said, "Time goes by fast. All our parents are getting up in years. Seems like yesterday when we were in high school together. Mark used to come to our games. All our dads came to the games. Those were good times, but time goes on."

Gary said, "There were a lot of funny things while we were going through school. Do you remember Tex Nierman, the history teacher?"

"Oh yeah, he was a character," said Sean.

"Sure was. He wore that cowboy hat to make him look taller." They laughed. "Remember," Gary continued, "he had that hearing aid."

"Sure do," Sean said.

Gary laughed, "Well, he still had trouble hearing. He'd be talking, and Lee Simpson would make a screeching noise. That'd distract Tex. He'd stop talking and start looking around."

They were laughing. Even Mike smiled.

Sean said, "Yeah, some guys were unmerciful to Tex, but you'd learn your history. He knew his stuff.

Gary said, "You remember Squeaky Unger?"

"You mean the Science teacher?" asked Sean. "Why'd they call him 'Squeaky'?"

"You mean you don't remember?" asked Gary.

"I might," Sean said, "but what was the reason?"

"Because of his shoes," replied Gary. "He'd walk up and down the aisles between the desks and around the lab, and his shoes would squeak, squeak, squeak. You'd hear him coming up and down the rows—had time to put the cheat sheet away."

Sean smiled, "Now that you mention it, I do remember."

Mike said, "Yeah, I remember him. You know, we sure had some good times at the barn."

"Oh, heck yes," agreed Gary. "We'd drink beer and talk like we're doing here. I can't believe some of the things we did."

Mike said, "Yeah, I'd been worried sick if I thought Matt was target practicing after he'd been drinking."

Gary laughed, "Danny had that smelly old blanket. God, that thing stunk. Danny, whatever happened to that thing?"

Danny smiled, "I guess it's still there—probably rotten by now."

Sean said, "We really thought we were grown up."

Mike now more somber, "Yeah, we had no idea. Our dads didn't know anything about it."

"I think they probably knew more than we realized," Sean said.

Sean stayed the night with Cheryl at the B&B but got up before dawn and left. He needed time to get home and change clothes before getting to the precinct. He hadn't brought any personal belongings with him.

Kye was an early riser, so some mornings Sean would see her taking a short walk in the neighborhood. This morning, she was returning from her early morning walk with Buddy when he walked out his front door.

Buddy squirmed and whimpered, his tail wagging with vigor, when he saw Sean. Kye released his leash so he could bound over to Sean. Sean bent down to pet him, "Hey, Buddy."

"Good morning, Sean. I heard about Mike's dad. I know how close you and Mike were. I'm sorry."

"Thank you, Kye. He had been in a nursing home for a while, but that doesn't make it easier for Mike."

"You and your group of friends were close during high school."

"Yes, we were. We used to hang out when we had time doing things I guess high school boys usually do, at least what they used to. We'd talk cars, fish, shoot hoops, and even target practice."

"Sean, you don't have to clean it up for me. I also know young men. They talk about girls, look at magazines and maybe drink a little beer."

Sean laughed.

"Also, Sean, I've heard rumors that you and that pretty young reporter are dating. You know, I'm not prying, but I'm not a prude. I won't mind if you have overnight guests," she said with a smile.

Sean laughed out loud. "Okay, Kye. I'll keep that in mind. You have a good day."

"You, too, Sean. And I'll take good care of Buddy while you're gone."

Sean was laughing to himself as he turned to walk to the station. Kye always knew things about kids in school. She had not lost her touch in keeping up with things.

While walking, he replayed in his head the conversation the evening before at Mike's. Sean's stop was so sudden that if someone had been following, they would have walked into him. He stood perfectly still, staring ahead as his mind raced. *"This is crazy. It can't be,"* he thought.

He kept telling himself that the notion was preposterous, but by the time he walked into the precinct, he had decided he needed to check it out. Otherwise, it would keep gnawing at him. He found a metal detector and drove out to where he and his friends used to hang out at the old barn. It was still there, but one side had collapsed. Behind the barn was an embankment—where they used to set up a target and shoot at it. Sean started digging through the side of the embankment where the metal detector had pinged. He found a few bullets and put them in a plastic bag. He called Ronnie. "Ronnie, I've got a couple more bullets that came from an old location that I need to have checked."

"Sure, Sean."

"If I leave now, I can be there in about an hour and a half."

"I'll see you soon."

Sean called Kim and said that he had to drive to Columbus and would be back after lunch.

As he was driving to Columbus, he called Cheryl and told her he was heading to Columbus.

"It's probably a wild goose chase, but I need to close this loop since it slapped me in the face."

"I know that feeling."

"By the way, the woman who I rent the one side of the duplex from was my high school English teacher. Her name is Kye."

"Yeah?" Cheryl asked.

"She said she knew about us and that she was okay with me having overnight guests."

Cheryl laughed. "I look forward to meeting her. I like her already."

Sean laughed and disconnected.

Chapter 53

Scott Talbot was an old friend of Danny's who used to live in Bekbourg. He was a construction worker, and a few years ago, he moved to Cincinnati where construction workers were more in demand. He had called Danny a couple of weeks ago and asked if he might visit Danny about restoring a 1957 Chevrolet that he had bought from a friend.

Danny showed Scott around the warehouse where he kept the remodeled cars, and they talked about the options for remodeling Scott's car.

"Danny, this is some operation you have here. I need to decide how much I want to spend and get back with you. I can get a buddy of mine to haul it over here. It runs, but I wouldn't want to try to drive it this far. Besides, I'd need a way to get back."

Danny said, "Sounds good, and if you think of any other questions, you have my number."

As they walked toward the entrance, Scott said, "I see the old paper factory seems to be booming. I helped build that addition. You know, there's a whole basement under that place. We didn't finish it, didn't even put a floor in it. I don't know why we didn't. Never figured out why they would build that basement and never use it. Guess it's one of those mysteries that you never figure out. I don't even know if there is a way to get to it."

Danny said, "I didn't know that."

"Oh, yeah, it's got about a twelve-foot ceiling. It was big. We put the big steel beams across to build the floor. The elevator shaft could have been used, I guess—the one that goes to the second floor. I don't know if they ever finished it for the elevator to go to the basement. Two pickup trucks could easily fit in that elevator."

Danny said, "Yeah, I remember all that, but I assumed it was filled in."

"Nooo, we didn't fill it in. I was proud of the work we did on that plant. One of the best projects I ever worked on. I'm glad to see it doing well."

Boze received a call that afternoon on his special phone. "Yeah, what can I do for you?"

"Yeah, I'm your man in Bekbourg. I don't know if this is anything or whether it's helpful, but I've got something I wanted to pass on."

"I'm listening."

After Boze listened, he said, "Thanks. You've been a big help through all this, and we appreciate it. Don't go investigating anything. That's not necessary. We don't want you to get hurt. Keep your eyes and ears open though, and if anything else comes up, give me a call."

"Will do."

"Mind if I ask you a question?"

"What?"

"Why have you helped us?"

"That's simple. My mom died of a drug overdose when I was a child. I don't want drugs around here. I thought you were going to ask me my name."

"Well, I figured if you wanted us to know, you'd tell us."

"Danny Chambers." With that, Danny hung up.

Sean made it back in time for the "receiving of friends" for Mike's dad. A large number of people showed up to pay their respects and support the family. Mike seemed distracted, but Sean guessed that's how he was dealing with his grief.

The next morning, only a few people attended the private funeral service. Mike was planning to return to the office the following day. His children were staying a couple extra days, which made him and Geri happy.

Toward the end of the service, Sean slipped out to take a call from Boze.

"Sean, I had an interesting call from our informant in Bekbourg. Seems there was a basement built under the paper plant. According to our man there, it had twelve-foot ceilings, and he said that the person he talked to, who was involved in the construction of the expansion, didn't understand why it wasn't finished out as part of the original construction."

"Interesting. As I told you earlier, no drawings or blueprints were in the County's files.

It's as if someone didn't want it known that there is a large basement area there."

"It's suspicious, Sean. We've got people pulling back the curtain on that plant, trying to find out more about the ownership and the financing and whatever else we can find. We'll be in touch. Oh, and by the way, we have a name now for the informant. He's Danny Chambers."

Sean was floored, "Danny?"

"I take it you know him."

"Yes, we grew up together. He's been a close friend."

"So, it's someone you trust?"

"Yes, absolutely."

"His tips put us onto Bekbourg, and this latest information may be what we've been looking for."

Something had been nagging Sean about the paper factory. It finally dawned on him that the county property tax assessor's office might have something since the taxes were based on both the land and the improvements.

There weren't any plans or blueprints, but he found the assessment basis. The property assessment was based on the land and the building and its useable square feet. The square footage figure in the assessment was large. It was about double the square feet of the floor space that he had seen. There had to be a basement under the main floor to account for that much additional square footage.

Sean drove to see Gene, the neighbor who had lived close to his parents since before the Burkhart murders. He thought he might know something about a basement.

"Gene, you retired from the paper plant. Do you know if there is a basement underneath the building?" asked Sean.

"Well, yeah. There was one under the original plant, but I can't say about the new part. I retired about the time it was sold."

"Was there a way to get into the basement from the outside?"

"Yeah. On the far side of the old building, there was a cinder block wall built at basement level with a concrete floor. The steps went from the ground level down beside that holding wall. That's where the door was that led into the basement. I don't know if it's still used. There was one like that at the old high school, and they put a grate over top of it so the kids wouldn't fall down the steps."

Chapter 54

The following morning, Mike got up to go to work. Geri, as she always did, had coffee with him and kissed him goodbye. As Mike was driving on the rural road he always took to get to the office, a vehicle pulled up behind him, and a shot came through the car's back window, barely missing him. Mike swore and pulled off the road and yanked open his car door with his gun pulled. The car sped by before Mike had time to react. Several bullets were fired at Mike, and Mike went down. Before Mike lost consciousness, his last thoughts were of Geri, Matt and Miranda.

Minutes later, dispatch received the 911 call from a passing motorist. Sean was the first deputy to arrive at the scene.

"Oh, God, please no! Not Mike!" Sean's brain screamed. Mike was unconscious. Sean saw other wounds, but the chest wound caused him panic. He pressed his shirt into Mike's wound to stem the bleeding and kept desperately urging, "Hold on, Buddy. You're going to be okay. Hang with me, Mike. We've got more football to play." All this while Sean fought back against the hellish image bursts of Clint's disfigured face that threatened to break him. Sweat was pouring off his face, and his body was drenched from his

perspiration. He was taking deep breaths to remain calm to save Mike.

The EMTs stabilized Mike the best they could before they loaded him in the ambulance. As they were tending to Mike, Sean called Harold and explained the situation, "Harold, I need to get to Geri, his wife, but I'm not leaving this scene until your troopers get here. I want you to take charge of the scene. It looks like an ambush."

Harold said, "We'll dispatch every trooper in the area. Someone should be getting there in a few minutes."

Sean had just hung up and was leaning up against his cruiser when an EMT rushed up in alarm, "Deputy, are you okay? Buddy, let me check you out. You may have been shot."

Sean thought, "*No! I'm not okay,*" but he managed to say, "I'm okay." The trauma of seeing Mike possibly dying in his arms coupled with the flashing images of Clint and that nightmare had felt like a thunderbolt strike. He was shaken and drained. The EMT's concerned scrutiny of Sean was shifting between Mike's smeared blood, his ghost-like pallor, and his trembling hand holding the phone. Sean managed to push away from the car and stand straight. He said, "It's not my blood. I'll be fine." The EMT didn't look convinced, but his attention was diverted as Mack and Darrell and Alex's cruisers came racing up.

Sean knew he had to pull himself together, because it was going to be a long, challenging day. Sean told Mack to cordon off the area and told Alex and Darrell to manage the traffic. Even though

Mack was technically second-in-command, he didn't mind Sean taking lead and did as Sean directed. The state police began arriving five minutes later, and Sean briefed them and left to go do one of the hardest things he had ever had to do— tell Geri and the kids.

Sean called Cheryl from the hospital and told her the situation, and she came to the hospital to support Sean, Geri and the children. Sean heard from Harold that Ronnie was at the scene and had put a rush on the bullets. Forensics was going over the location with a fine-tooth comb. Harold told Sean, "There is a place off the road where there are fresh tire prints. Ronnie's taking impressions of those. Right now, we can't be sure, but I think someone had pulled back in there and watched for Mike's car to drive by. I've got troopers going to people who live along here to see if they know anything. I'll keep you posted. We need to talk to his wife at some point."

Sean said, "I know. She is distraught. I did manage to ask her if she had any idea why or who might have done this, and she told me she had no idea. You might send someone over later to talk to her, but right now is not a good time."

Mike had been in surgery for several hours when the doctor finally came to the waiting room. "Mrs. Adams. Your husband's health is good, so he has that going for him. He suffered three gunshot wounds: one to the shoulder, one in the side, and one that barely missed his heart. He lost a lot of blood. The fact that someone was there and applied pressure to stop the bleeding probably saved his life. It's the wound near the heart that is our major concern. Your husband is in critical condition. We've got him stabilized for now. We have considered flying him to Columbus. I've talked to a surgeon there, who is on call if that's our decision. The next forty-eight hours are going to be the most critical. Of course, we have to watch for infection after that. He's going to be in ICU. Only one person can see him at a time, and right now, we're going to restrict visitors to seeing him every six hours for fifteen minutes at a time. I'll let you go back in a couple of hours. Do you have any questions?"

Geri was pale and dazed. She shook her head, "No." He looked at the children and Sean, but no one had any questions. The doctor said, "Okay, I'm going to be here along with another doctor monitoring him. If you need anything or have any questions, let one of the nurses know." The doctor reached over and squeezed Geri's hand and left.

Sean said to Mike's family, "Is there anything I can get you?" They all shook their heads. Sean started to get up, and Geri put her hand on his arm to stop him. Her voice faint, "Sean, I'd like to talk to you for a minute in private."

Cheryl said, "Sean, I'll ask the nurse where you and Geri can talk in private."

Cheryl soon reappeared with a nurse who showed Geri and Sean to a nearby vacant office. "Sean, the night that Mike's father died, he told me that he had something he had to tell me. I don't know if this is related, but I feel you need to know. Mike was planning to resign soon. Here's what he told me. Many years ago, Mike got a call that there had been an accident. When he arrived, the Sheriff, Jack Rhodes, and Ben Clark were there. It was then that Mike saw it. He told me that he has relived this every day since. His dad was passed out behind the wheel of his car. Mark had run over someone. Mike could tell he was dead before the Sheriff checked his pulse. Mike was so stunned. He said he was having a hard time thinking. Mike told the Sheriff they needed to call the EMTs. The Sheriff said that it would be hard on Mike's dad and mom if this ever got out. Mike told me that he remembered telling the Sheriff that they'd have to handle it, but the Sheriff said that no one would ever have to know. Sheriff Rhodes told Mike that he and Ben would take care of the situation and for Mike to take Mark home.

"Mike said he knew it was wrong, but he kept thinking what this would do to his dad and mom. How could his dad live knowing he had killed someone? Mike said that his dad's car wasn't damaged. He put his dad in Mike's car and drove him to his house. He and the Sheriff never discussed it again. Mike told me that, as he was driving his dad home that night, he had to pull to the side of the road he was so violently sick.

"Mike never told his dad what happened. Mike's mom of course knew nothing other than Mike had brought Mark home. The next day she told Mark that Mike brought him home that night. Mark never had any recollection of even leaving the bar. Mike said he guessed his dad was embarrassed and knew that if he kept doing something like that it could reflect badly on Mike, so he stopped going to the bars after that, but for Mike, the damage was done.

"Sean, he told me that it has been eating away at him. I knew something was wrong, but he would never tell me. He was a great father. He was a great husband, but he had become distant, and he told me that he did so, because that was his way of coping. That is what Mike told me, but I think there's more. I don't know what, and it scares me to think what it might be. Mike needs help, Sean."

Sean said, "Geri, I'm sorry that so much weight has been put on your shoulders, but I know that you are strong enough to handle this. I'm going to see what I can find out. I think Sheriff Rhodes is the starting point. I heard that he retired to Sebring, Florida, so I'll start there. You take care of yourself, and let Cheryl or me know if you need anything."

"Thank you, Sean. I will. Also, I wanted to tell you that I like Cheryl."

He put his arm around her shoulders and walked her back to her family.

He asked Cheryl to walk to the hospital cafe with him. He told Cheryl that he had to leave to go to Sebring to talk to the retired sheriff. "I think he might have some missing pieces, Cheryl. Everything that's been going on, I have a hunch that it started several years ago, even before your grandfather's death. I'm going to catch a flight out as soon as I can. If you can, I told Geri that you or I would help her."

"Of course."

Sean kissed her and left the hospital.

Sean called Harold and repeated what Geri had said. "I'm heading down to meet with Jack Rhodes. I fly out tonight. I've already talked to Rhodes, and he's agreed to meet with me in the morning. I'll keep you posted."

Chapter 55

Jack Rhodes lived in a cinder block house typical of old Florida that backed up to Lake Jackson. There was a small rickety dock out back where he had spent countless hours fishing before his health had started to fail. The small fishing boat that used to be docked there was long gone. Now, all he could do was sit on the small concrete pad off the back of his house and look at the lake. His wife had divorced him years ago, and he hadn't seen his son since then. He figured he didn't have much time left, and he carried a lot of burdens on his soul. Now, Mike Adams was fighting for his life. Sean Neumann, who he remembered from the glory days of Schriever football, was on his way down. *Funny*, thought Jack, *Mike being the sheriff and Sean the deputy. Never would have seen that coming.* In his mind, Sean would always be the quarterback.

Jack heard the knock on the front door and muttered to himself, "*Showtime.*"

Sean stood on the step looking at the houses similar to Jack's. He suspected most people had returned north for the summer, because blinds were pulled and no vehicles were visible in the driveways. Finally, he heard the door knob turn and the front door opened. Sean's surprise at seeing Jack must have been evident, because Jack laughed,

"Come on in, Sean. It's been a long time since I saw you throwing those touchdowns." Jack turned his wheel chair and started though the small living room that led to the back where the patio was. There was a TV in the corner and a couple of mismatched, worn, upholstered chairs sitting along the wall. An end table sat in the middle of the room beside where Sean suspected Jack sat in his wheel chair watching TV. The small kitchen had a 1950's look to it, only in a bad way. All the lower cabinet doors had been removed, and the laminate counter top had scorched marks. There was a small laminate table with a chair pushed back against the wall. The plastic trash can was filled with carry-out wrappers. A coffee mug was sitting beside the empty coffee maker.

Jack continued as he rolled to the patio. "Sean, if you want some water or beer, there's some in the fridge. There's a chair out here for you. Sometimes, one of my fishing buddies comes by and we'll sit out here. Most of them are gone back north now. They say it gets too hot for them down here in the summer. It don't bother me, though. I suppose hell will be a lot hotter."

Sean sat down. He remembered Jack Rhodes as a robust man. He had played football at Schriever and was about six feet tall and a barrel of a man. He ruled the county with an iron fist. There wasn't much crime, because people didn't want to run up against Sheriff Rhodes. Jim, Sean's dad, never cared for Jack. He thought he crossed the line in how he dealt with some criminals, but Sean never heard his dad talk about Jack being corrupt or anything like that. Now, sitting in front of him was a shriveled up old man. He had a blanket across his lap—even though it was in the high 80's compounded by stifling humidity.

"Thanks, Jack, for seeing me."

"You said Mike's been shot, that he's in critical condition?"

"Yeah, it's really touch-and-go. His kids are in from out-of-town. They actually were already in town because Mike's father had been buried the day before this happened. Geri won't leave the hospital. It's bad."

"I hate to hear that. Mike's a good man. He doesn't deserve this. Do you know who did it?"

"No, not yet, but I'm not going to stop until I find out."

"So, you think the answer is here with me?" Jack asked matter-of-fact.

Sean said, "You want to tell me about it, about Mike's dad?"

"Just out of curiosity, how did you find out?"

"His wife told me in the hospital. Before he was shot, Mike told Geri. She didn't know everything that happened, but she thought you might know the entire story."

"I do, Sean. Indeed, I do. I'm not making excuses, and that don't make it right. What I did to Mike was similar to how they got control over me. I was drugged and put in a compromising position with a woman. Pictures were taken, and Randall threatened to show my wife if I didn't help out. No one ever asked me to kill or steal, but I had to run interference with outside law enforcement to keep them out, and look the other way at times. They knew Mike wasn't corrupt and not corruptible. He was a by-the-book deputy.

"I guess they wanted someone like that who the people trusted, only they wanted to control him. Everyone knew Mark Adams's ritual. He left work, went to Knucklepin's and went home. One night, someone slipped a drug in his drink, and before he was completely out, they helped him to his car, making it look like he was intoxicated. They put him in the passenger seat and drove him to the curve in the road. They already had a man lying in the road and ran Mark's car over the man. They moved Mark's body to the driver's side and left him there. I didn't know about any of this ahead of time. I got a call telling me to go to the scene and to clean up the matter. They didn't want anyone to know about Mike's dad running over anyone, and they didn't want Mike or anyone to report it. They said that the man was dead and to get rid of the body.

"When I got there, Ben was already there, and Mike then pulled up. Mike said that someone had called him and reported an accident. He then saw it was his father's car and saw his dad still passed out behind the wheel. I felt the man's pulse and knew he was dead. I told Mike to take his dad home and not to ever mention to his dad what happened. I told him Ben and I would take care of things. Mike wanted to do the right thing and follow the right procedures, but I persuaded him that it could hurt his dad's reputation and be hurtful to his mother. Mike was reluctant, but he did what I said.

Mike pulled his dad's car to the side of the road so he could come pick it up later. There was no damage done to the front of Mark's car.

"Ben offered to take the body and bury it, but I told him I'd take care of it. Ben had wrapped it in a large plastic bag, and we put it in the back of my cruiser. I buried it where I could find it if I ever needed to. I never told anyone until now. It's buried in the old cemetery next to my dad's grave on the left side. It's a family plot on top of the hill behind the old house I used to live in. People rarely go there, and I didn't think it would be noticed.

"One more thing about it—I was suspicious when Ben kept on wanting to take the body. I opened the plastic. It wasn't anyone local. I guess it was a hitchhiker, because I knew pretty much everyone in the county, and I didn't recognize him. He was a young guy with long hair and a beard. There wasn't any ID on him.

"The big thing here, Sean, is that Mike's dad didn't kill that man. He didn't run over him. The man had a bullet in his head. I had moved the body. I had tampered with evidence in attempting to cover up a crime. I knew the dead man was not from around there, so no one would be asking questions. I let it go. One thing I did do is tell Ben I knew he had killed that man and if he ever talked about that night, I would have him charged with murder.

"The stress of everything I had done, I guess, finally got to me. I had the heart attack, and that gave me the chance to retire. My wife had already divorced me. He neutered me when he set me up to blackmail me with that picture. I became a shell of a man. My wife couldn't take it and left with our son. I don't blame her. I know my mistakes. Maybe, I'll have a little peace before I pass on."

Sean was stunned. "Jack, who did this to you?"

"Randall Thompson. He ran the whole county. What people didn't know was how corrupt he was. His dad started things like that. He was the Boot for the county. Randall took what his dad started and expanded it. But, by becoming county commissioner, he really expanded his power."

"What happened to Mike after that night? I mean, did they start blackmailing him?"

"I don't think so, not then. I watched to see, but I never saw any indications of that, but then they didn't need to, because I was still running interference for them. Once I retired, I moved to Florida. I wanted to get out of that place. Mike was elected sheriff. I guessed they might do to him what they did to me, but I wasn't there, so I didn't know."

Sean said, "Jack, there's something else. Do you remember Henry Willis?"

Jack paused to think about the name. "You mean the man who confessed to the Burkhart murders?"

"Yeah. What can you tell me about those murders?"

"Well, I guess you've seen the evidence file, so you know the details."

"What I saw in the evidence box were just a couple of small folders. Is that what you mean?"

Jack looked surprised. "No. Someone must have taken some things, because that box was over half full of stuff. Do you know generally about what happened?"

"Yeah, that much was in the box. Do you think Henry killed them?"

"Not at all. I was as surprised as anyone when he came into the precinct and said he wanted to confess. He had a story about overhearing Burkhart bragging about getting those coins. That they were going to be delivered to Burkhart's home. Said he didn't think anyone would be there except Burkhart since his wife and kid were supposed to be out of town. Anyway, he claimed he broke in thinking he wouldn't wake up Burkhart, thought he'd be drunk, just go to his office and find them and take them. Burkhart got up to come downstairs, and Willis claimed he panicked and started shooting. Then, the others got up, so he had to kill them, too."

"Why would Willis confess?"

"That's what I wanted to know. He said his conscience was getting the best of him, particularly knowing a kid had died, but if he didn't do it, I guess they wanted a scapegoat to make it go away."

"Did he say he got the coins?"

"No, he said he didn't have time to look. Once they were all dead, he said he just wanted to burn the place to cover up any evidence."

"Did the coins ever show up?"

"Not that I know of. Anyway, with him confessing, it shut our investigation down cold. There wasn't much left for us to do."

375

"If Henry didn't kill them, do you have any ideas who might have killed them or why they were killed?"

"I don't know anything for sure. But if I had to guess, Burkhart had a big-mouth, and I don't mean on those silly TV commercials. He was always bragging about this and that. He had that pawn shop, and it seemed to be growing. There were a lot of people that came in there from out of the county. Probably was a fence. Then, he started bragging about getting into some type of gold and silver trade. That's what those coins were supposed to be. Thompson once asked me if the State or Feds had been in town looking at Burkhart's business. I told him that I didn't know about that if they had.

"A few days before the killings, Burkhart's fireworks business burned to the ground. That fire was suspicious. The state fire marshal came down and investigated, and they found an accelerant, but there was no insurance on the place, and Burkhart wasn't making any claims, so that was that. I think Thompson was concerned that Burkhart's activities might start to get the attention from outside law enforcement. The fireworks business being torched was likely a warning to Burkhart, but if what I'm assuming is right, Burkhart must not have heeded that warning, so he was murdered along with his family members.

"I don't believe Burkhart's family was the intended target. His wife and kid were supposed to be at the beach, but his brother and sister-in-law unexpectedly stopped by to spend the night, so she and the kid delayed their trip until the guests left."

Sean said, "Jack, I appreciate this. It clears up a lot of things." Sean stood to leave.

Jack said, "I hope so, Sean. Take care of yourself."

Sean called Harold and told him what Jack had said. "Harold, we need to get someone to exhume that body and see if the coroner can determine the cause of death."

"I'll get someone right on it. I'll call DD. We need to move fast on this. Things are getting deeper and deeper. I'll call you once the wheels are in motion."

On his drive from the Columbus airport to Bekbourg, Sean checked in with Harold. Harold said, "We've got a judge ready to rule on our request to exhume the body. Once we have the go-ahead, DD is standing ready. By the way, any change in Mike?"

"I'm going to stop by the hospital this evening. Last I heard, there's been no change."

"Okay. We'll be in touch."

Sean and Cheryl went by the hospital. Sean's parents were there. Matt and Miranda had gone home to get some sleep, but Geri had not been home since Mike had been admitted. Helen had her arm around Geri.

"Mike's still in critical condition, but the doctor says he's stabilized. Sean, I don't know what's going to happen."

"Geri, Mike's a strong man. I've seen Mike fight off two and three defenders to make a touchdown. He's a fighter. He's back there giving it everything he's got."

Geri nodded, "I know you're right, Sean."

Sean said, "Dad, want to take a walk?"

After Sean and Jim got outside, Sean told Jim the entire story about Mike and what Jack Rhodes had said to him. Jim shook his head. "You know, Sean, this doesn't come as a surprise. I never had much use for Randall Thompson. I can't say I heard of him doing anything illegal, but there were rumors about Thompson and women, and it wasn't honorable things. Of course, both he and now Jeff rule the Committee. I believed when he retired that his son might be different. I thought Randall was out of the picture until you and I saw him at the GilHaus."

"Dad, what about Sheriff Rhodes? What did you know about him?"

"Not much. He didn't ever seem to do much. I mean, his deputies arrested people for drunk driving, disorderly conduct, and burglaries. But, like with the Burkhart murders, I don't think most people believed Willis did that all by himself, and people who knew him didn't think he was guilty at all. Once he confessed, though, the Sheriff seemed to take the easy way out and dropped the investigation. He never seemed to bother to check whether the confession was legitimate. No one around town talked about it. They didn't want to draw attention to themselves, and anyway, he'd confessed. But now, with what you have told me about the way he was blackmailed, I can see a similar pattern with Mike. I never understood why Mike didn't do more on drugs. Maybe these guys are into drugs, Sean."

"Well, I'm going to get to the bottom of whatever is going on."

"Do you think someone was afraid Mike would stop cooperating now that his dad is dead?"

"I don't know, Dad."

Jim was quiet as he watched a passing car. Sean could tell his dad had something on his mind. Jim turned to look at Sean. "I don't know if this is relevant, Sean, but as crazy as all this is, it might be. You know your mother helped out a lot with Danny when his mother died. One day when Norm came to pick up Danny after he got off work, he told me something he wanted me to know if anything ever happened. He wanted Helen and me to raise Danny. He knew we would be good to him and that Danny thought the world of you. Anyway, he confided that Randall Thompson was Danny's father. He took advantage of Emily and got her pregnant and dumped her. He threatened her not to tell anyone. Helen and I never told anyone, but I thought you ought to know—given what's happened."

"Dad, do you know if Danny knows?"

"Norm told me that he was going to tell Danny when the time was right, but I don't know if he ever did."

Chapter 56

Sean was teasing Cheryl the next morning about bringing Bri's scones home. Cheryl laughed. "She practically forced me to take them, said she'd be surprised if you had anything at your place for breakfast."

Laughing, Sean said, "I'm glad she gave you these scones. Otherwise, we'd only have coffee this morning. Be sure to tell her, 'Thanks.'"

"Well, that's Bri, always thinking of others."

Sean's phone rang. Cheryl heard him say, "That's no problem. I will leave now."

"That's Ronnie Vin, forensics out of Columbus. There's something she needs to show me. I'm going to get on the road. I'm supposed to meet Danny at two o'clock at his gas station. He called me and said it's important, so I'll see you sometime after that." Sean wasn't sure, but Danny might be planning to tell him about the basement in the paper plant.

"Okay, Sweetie. Be safe, and I'll talk to you later."

"You, too. No rush on leaving. Kye will come over and check on Buddy. She usually takes him to her place. Just lock the door and pull it to. You don't need a key to lock it."

Sean gave Cheryl a passionate kiss. "I look forward to more of those tonight," she murmured.

"That—and a lot more." They both smiled.

Cheryl straightened up the kitchen and gave Buddy a big hug and was walking out to leave to return to Bri's when she saw an older woman walking up the walk. "Well, you must be Cheryl. I'm Kye Davis. I live next door here."

"Hi, Mrs. Davis, it's nice to meet you."

"Has Sean already left?"

"Yes, he had to run to Columbus, and I'm going back to the B&B to work on the story."

"Would you like to bring Buddy over here and join me for a cup of coffee before you leave? I'm so sorry about Mike. I went by the hospital yesterday and talked with his wife. I know he means a lot to Sean. Anyway, we won't dwell on that. I can tell you about your Sean, what he was like in high school."

"I'd love that."

Cheryl found Kye delightful and also intelligent. Buddy laid on the rug with his ears perked, acting like he understood what they were saying. They enjoyed talking about English, journalism, and Kye told about Sean and some of his friends when they were in high school.

Chapter 57

Gary was busy that morning. His secretary buzzed him, and he didn't pick up. She then knocked on his door. He swore to himself, and yelled for her to open the door. "Sorry to bother you, Mr. Werner, but a Mr. Dean Fairway is on the phone. He is with our largest cargo van manufacturer, and he is insisting on talking to you."

Gary wondered what that was all about. "Tell him I'll call him back."

"He says it won't take long, but he insists on talking to you."

Gary breathed a heavy sigh, "Okay, I'll take it."

Gary picked up and said, "Hi, Dean, what can I do for you?"

"Hi, Gary, I thought I'd give you a heads up before coming down to your dealership. We have been having some unusual activity with our cargo vans."

Cold sweat began to form on Gary's forehead.

Dean continued, "We're not quite sure what is going on, but we've decided to audit all of our distributors to get to the bottom of this."

"What are you talking about?"

"Well, we recently got a call from the Feds. Seems a brand new cargo van was found that had traces of cocaine and meth in the cargo area. It was found in your territory. They wanted to know where this van came from.

"At first, we couldn't find a record of it anywhere in our system. As it turns out with a little digging, it was at the Atvale Depot Company that we use in Michigan to hold and distribute our excess inventory. It was supposed to be delivered to a small dealership in West Virginia, but they never received it. Since you're the distributor for that region, we checked a written report, and the van was supposed to go through you to him, but there was no confirmation that you received it. However, the computer records at Atvale were inconsistent with the written paperwork we had. For some reason, they didn't show you were supposed to receive it. So, we've decided that we have to do a complete audit for all shipping and inventory records in Ohio, Western Pennsylvania, and West Virginia.

"We've got a team coming down tomorrow. It won't take us long. But since the Feds are involved, we have to get to the bottom of this."

Gary thought to himself, "*Damnit! They are going to find out about the other vans.*" He wanted to buy some time, so he said, "This is not a good time for me. I was planning to join my family in Europe. Do you think you guys can push this back a couple of weeks?"

"Oh, you don't have to be there. This won't take us long. We're going to move around the region tracing these vans. It appears the van was stolen, but we've got to get to the bottom of this. We do ask you to not mention this to anyone, especially any of your employees, because it could be an inside job. You've been with us a long time, so we thought we'd give you this courtesy call."

They hung up, and Gary sat there shaken, muttering a long list of obscenities.

After sitting for a few minutes, Gary started to get angry. He asked his secretary to locate Joe Sommers and to tell him to meet him in the shop.

"*I hate that pompous ass,*" Gary hissed to himself.

"Hi, Sean. Sorry to ask you to drive up, but it's sometimes easier to talk in person. I don't know what's been going on in Bekbourg over the years, but I guess that's what you're trying to find out. Come over here, I want to show you what we've got.

"Let's take the bullets that we found at the Pinkston murders. They came from two different guns: a 357 Magnum and a Glock 17. Some of each type were found in all the victims, except for Ruby Pinkston. The three bullets found in her were the ones from the Magnum. I ran a test on the bullets that Mike was shot with. It's a positive match with the gun at the Pinkston murders that came from the Glock. This is confusing. Are you with me so far?"

"Yeah, in other words, Mike was shot by one of the guns also used in the Pinkston murder."

"Yes, the Glock. Okay, now look at this. As I told you the other day, the bullet that you gave to me, the one from the Burkhart shooting twenty years ago, was from the 357 Magnum. It came from the same gun, and it matches the bullets from the 357 Magnum used in the Pinkston murders—even though they occurred twenty years apart. From the written reports, we know there were two different guns used in the Burkhart murders. One of those guns, the 357 Magnum, matches the Pinkston case."

Sean said, "There were two guns used at both places, probably because there were two gunmen. Assuming the guns weren't sold or stolen later or used by someone else, one of the gunmen was at both the Burkhart and the Pinkston murders, twenty years apart."

"Yeah, that's right. But there's another puzzle piece. Now, let's look at this. You gave me three bullets that you said you got from an embankment that had been shot for target practice over twenty years ago. I put a rush on this like you asked. I checked all three bullets, and they all came from the same gun. But what's interesting is that those bullets are a perfect match. They also were shot from the same 357 Magnum."

Sean stood perfectly still. Ronnie knew he was rapidly coming to the realization that there was a three-way match for the Magnum—the target practice, the Burkhart murders and the Pinkston murders. "Now," she said, "you need to know who the 357 Magnum belongs to."

Sean was rattled, "I know who it belongs to. Only one boy had a gun. We all used it for target practice."

"So," said Ronnie, "here's what you've got. Assuming the same persons had exclusive control of the two guns, there were two gunmen at the Pinkston murders. One of those gunmen also shot Mike. The other gunman from the Pinkston shootings was involved in the Burkhart murders and the target practice. You see why I thought it best for you to make a trip to Columbus."

"Yeah, Ronnie, I owe you."

"Anytime, Sean. Sounds like you're up to your ears in alligators. Good luck, and let me know if you need anything else."

Sean was sad that things had turned out the way they had. He now had a good idea of one person who was involved in the Pinkston and Burkhart killings, and if that person would talk, he'd also know who helped in the Pinkston murders as well as who shot Mike.

Even though his secretary got the message to Joe, he was nowhere to be seen in the shop area. Gary walked around talking to the mechanics as he liked to do. Joe finally walked out of the parts department and over to Gary, "What do you want?"

Gary said through clenched teeth, "Where have you been the last twenty minutes?"

Dismissively, Joe said, "I've been busy."

Gary's anger was at a boiling point, but he kept it in check. "Let's walk over to the defect lot."

Joe reluctantly followed as they walked out of earshot of everyone. Gary turned around to face Joe, "Remember that discussion we had recently about those cargo vans?"

"Yeah, what about it?"

"Well, I warned you we were overdoing it, that this was going to blow up in our face."

For the first time, Joe showed a slight interest, "Yeah, I remember, what about it? I told you to stay out of it."

"The shit's hit the fan, Joe. Do you remember the van a few weeks ago that disappeared? Well, the Feds have that van and found traces of drugs in the back, and now they've got the top brass at our biggest cargo van supplier involved, and they're coming down here to do a complete audit of the inventory, shipping records and deliveries." Gary's voice notched louder, "You know what that means?"

"Yeah, I know what it means, Gary. You're in the bull's eye."

Gary's sweating forehead betrayed his low whisper meant to strike fear in Joe, "How dare you. You're involved much deeper than me. I don't know what you and your partners are doing. This is your damn operation."

Not taking the bait, Joe smiled, "My name is not on anything, Gary."

Gary was so angry that if he'd had a gun, he would have shot Joe.

Although he hated Gary and had resented his arrogance over the years, Joe knew he needed a couple more days to get the shipment out. "Just go back to your office, Gary, and I will take care of this."

Gary didn't know the particulars and couldn't have fixed anything. He started to turn to go back to his office and muttered, "You son of a bitch. I told you this would happen, and I don't think that there is anything you can do to cover this up."

Gary went back to his office and told his secretary he was leaving for the day. Gary was fuming to himself, "*I told that SOB that this was going to happen. Everything I worked for all these years is getting ready to go down.*"

Kye and Cheryl were talking when Cheryl's phone rang. Bri said, "Cheryl, Elena called. She and Lilly are going to run by. I had told her that you wanted to ask her some questions." Cheryl had told Bri about Missy, and Bri thought since Elena and Lilly lived in the same trailer park where Missy had lived, that she might have known her.

Cheryl replied, "I won't be long."

She turned to Kye, "I'm sorry Kye, but something important has come up. I need to walk over to Bri's, but I have enjoyed talking with you."

"My dear, it has been all my pleasure. I look forward to seeing you again real soon."

Cheryl arrived at the B&B ahead of Elena and Lilly. She and Bri were waiting when Cheryl's phone rang. It was Lucky Brennan. "Cheryl, I'm sorry to bother you, but I couldn't reach Sean. Is he by chance somewhere around?"

"No, he went to Columbus this morning, but he should be back around two o'clock, because he has a meeting here in Bekbourg then. I tried to reach him myself, but he's either on his phone or out of range. Is there something I can help you with?"

"Well, I'll try to reach him again, but since you and he were working on this together, I'll tell you what I found about the insurance company that issued the life insurance policy for your grandfather. This took some digging, and quite frankly, we got lucky. I'd say 'no pun intended,' but you're probably on to that one." Cheryl laughed.

"For whatever reason, one of the clerks at the insurance company didn't know how they were supposed to do things, but anyway, as part of the yearly required filings with the state, someone sent copies of records of the new polices that the company signed up during that year. This was more information than was required. For that particular year, 1980, we found the records on the life insurance policy on Henry Willis, and the beneficiary was his daughter. It showed that a Samuel Walters paid for it.

"There was no Samuel Walters that we could find until we came to a bank account at First Guaranty Bank of Bekbourg. Turns out, Samuel Walters is an alias for another person who had an account there."

Cheryl remembered that Milton found that a Samuel Walters had co-signed the second loan that Al Werner took out to remodel the dealership. "Who was that?" Cheryl asked.

Cheryl took a deep breath when she heard the name.

"The records also reveal that the policy paid off for face value for $500,000 to your mother after

Henry died about six months later. One other thing: Sean asked me if I could find out who paid for the life insurance policy and if I could check the bank records to see if that same person had withdrawn any money around August 4, 1980. Turns out, he did. He withdrew $10,000.00 cash."

Cheryl's mind was reeling. "*My God,*" she thought. "*He paid my grandfather to take the blame for murders that he knew my grandfather didn't commit.*"

Lucky brought Cheryl's attention back to their conversation, "I'm sorry it took so long, but you can see it took a lot of digging for files that were twenty years old. We were fortunate that someone filed more information than they needed to. Anything else you need?"

"No, Lucky. Thank you for your assistance."

"Well, if there is anything else you or Sean need, you know where to reach me."

Cheryl walked into the kitchen. Bri took one look at Cheryl and knew something was wrong—she was tense. "Cheryl, what's the matter? Sit down and tell me what's got you so upset."

Cheryl was distracted, "I just got off the phone with Lucky Brennan from the FBI. He was trying to find out who paid for the life insurance policy in my grandfather's name, the one that paid out when he died." She told Bri his name.

Standing, Cheryl said, "I tried to reach Sean again, but I still can't get through. I can't sit around here any longer."

Alarmed, Bri asked, "What do you mean? What are you going to do?"

I called his office, and they said he is working from home today. I'm going out there."

"Oh God, Cheryl. Shouldn't you wait? Also, Elena and Lilly will be here any minute."

Cheryl already had her purse and keys in her hands. "Give Elena my apologies. If you don't mind, see what you can find out about Missy. If I need to, I'll follow up with her. If Sean calls, tell him where I am."

As Cheryl was walking to her car, another place popped in her mind where she might reach Sean. She called Danny. "Danny, it's Cheryl Seton. I met you the other day at Mike and Geri's."

"Sure, Cheryl. I remember you. I'm glad that you and Sean are together."

"Me too, Danny. Look, I need your help. I've been trying to reach Sean about something important, but I can't get through on his phone. I know that he is planning to meet you around 2:00. He wouldn't happen to be there, would he?"

"No, he's not here yet."

"Some things have come up." She told Danny whose house she was going to. "When you talk to Sean, will you tell him that I couldn't wait? He'll understand."

"Cheryl, maybe you ought to wait for Sean. I don't think he would want you to do something like this without talking to him first."

"Thanks, Danny. I need to talk to him. I called his office, and they said he is working from home today. If you'll tell Sean, I'd appreciate it."

"I don't have a good feeling about this, Cheryl, but I will certainly tell Sean."

Ever since Danny had found out about the large basement area under the paper company, he figured that's what the DEA was looking for. Although Boze had not told him, Danny suspected that Sean was working with the DEA. But now, Danny was concerned about Cheryl. She had obviously found something out about the man, and Danny was already suspicious of him.

Soon after Cheryl left, Lilly and Elena arrived. As Bri was pouring them some freshly squeezed lemonade, she explained that Cheryl had left after receiving an unexpected phone call.

"Oh, I'm sorry we missed her," Elena said.

"That's okay. She wanted to know if you knew a woman named Missy Collins. She lived in Acorn Knoll, but she died about five years ago."

Elena said, "Oh yes, I knew her. She lived down from us. I hated it when she died. She was such a nice person. She even kept Lilly for me sometimes—like when I ran to the grocery store. You remember her, Lilly?"

"Yes. She was so nice to me and also Mom. She was pretty."

"Lilly's right. She was beautiful. She had long blond hair that always was rolled. I thought she looked like a movie star."

"Do you remember when she died?"

"What I remember is that I was up late and heard some dogs barking. I opened my front door and saw some cars in front of her place. There was a police car and an ambulance. The next day, I talked to a neighbor, and she said that a friend of hers that worked at the hospital said that a woman matching Missy's description was brought in. She had overdosed on drugs. The doctors weren't able to save her. That's the last I knew. There was a van that came to her place, and I guessed they took her things away. A few months later, someone else moved into the trailer."

"I heard that she had an addiction problem."

Elena glanced at Lilly and looked back at Bri. "Yes, she and I talked about it sometimes. She knew I had a problem. I was clean then, but she wasn't, and I don't think she ever tried to quit."

"What was she taking?"

"Hard stuff, but I really don't know."

"Do you know where she got it?"

"Well, she had a boyfriend. I don't know if he gave it to her, but she didn't work, so I don't know how she bought it."

"Do you know who her boyfriend was?"

Elena looked uncomfortable but decided to answer Bri. "Yeah. They kept it secret, because he was a powerful man here. They met when he was on a business trip. She moved down here. He took good care of her. She drove a new car and had beautiful clothes. She called him her 'Honey' when she talked about him."

"Elena, will you tell me his name?"

"I guess it doesn't matter now since it's been so long." When Elena told her, Bri felt a shiver roll up her spine. Cheryl was on her way to his house.

Cheryl tried again calling Sean but couldn't get through.

She had pulled into his driveway and was sitting in her car, ready to get out when her phone rang. It was Bri, who told her what Elena had told her. Trepidation swept over Cheryl.

Bri asked, "Cheryl, where are you?"

"I'm sitting in his driveway."

Alarmed, Bri said, "Oh, God! Leave now. You should get back here and wait for Sean. I'm afraid for you. He might do something to you."

About that time, he walked up and pecked on her car window. Cheryl told Bri she had to go and hung up and rolled down her window. "I saw you pull in a few minutes ago, Ms. Seton. Do you have something you want to talk to me about or do you just like sitting in people's driveways?"

Cheryl was torn. She had come here to ask him about the insurance policy, which he may not know anything about, but she was now uneasy having heard from Bri about Missy. Missy had died with meth in her system, and it was before the Pinkstons were in Bekbourg. Where did he get the meth if he was the supplier? If she started to feel threatened, she could leave, or tell him others knew where she was, so she didn't feel as concerned about her safety as Bri had. She made a split decision that she would stay. She was already here, after all. She didn't want him to pick up on her uneasiness.

"I'm sorry. Just as I pulled in, I got a phone call. Can I have a few minutes of your time? I have some additional questions that I would like to ask you."

Chapter 58

Sean had been on the phone almost the entire time on his drive back from Columbus. First, he called Boze and explained the situation. "Boze, I need to move fast on this end. I'm calling the state police after I get off the phone with you to have them issue warrants for his house and offices for the gun and any other evidence related to the murders. Based on what we know about the square footage, I think the plant is where the drugs are being processed and stored. I've always thought the persons responsible for the Pinkston murders are somehow related to the drug operations around here. We won't do anything to raise suspicion that we're onto the drug operation at the plant or try to go into the basement area. I'll leave that all to you to decide how to handle, but I needed to let you know what's going down."

Boze said, "Sean, based on the things you've told us, we've been working things from our end. We've actually got enough evidence to move on the paper plant, but the timing is up in the air. We followed a van that left the plant last night. We don't want to tip our hand before we raid the paper plant, but it's under surveillance. It's currently sitting inside a warehouse outside of St. Louis. We've had the air strip and dealership under surveillance. Also, we've got some helpful information out of Atvale Depot Company. Seems one of Atvale's employees has been working for Joe Sommers and coordinating things for him. He would divert a cargo van out of the distribution lot. It was then taken to a place where drugs were loaded. It was then loaded on an eighteen-wheeler with other vans. Sommers knew the one that contained the drugs. After the drugs were off-loaded, the van was either returned to Atvale's facility or delivered to the dealership where it was supposed to have been delivered. Do what you need to do on your end. You'll know when we move on our end."

That was a relief to Sean, because he was somewhat concerned that Boze would want him to hold up until the DEA was ready to move. Now, he could call Harold.

Sean explained Ronnie's findings. "Harold, he may still have the gun. He's had it for more than twenty years. I want this handled out of your office at the state level. I don't trust who might talk to whom if we work at the county level. I also think we need to move fast on this for several reasons. Can you get the warrant to search his home and places of business?"

"Consider it done."

"One more thing, Harold: I don't know how he's going to respond, but I would bring backup."

Sean saw that Cheryl had tried to call, but her phone went to voice mail. Lucky had tried to call him, so Sean returned his call. "I'm glad you called back. I've got the information on the person who took out the life insurance policy on Henry Willis." Lucky told Sean everything he had told Cheryl.

Sean said, "This is a big help, Lucky. It might actually complete the puzzle for us." Sean described the fact pattern that had been unraveled.

"You're right, Sean. Like I told Cheryl, I got lucky, no pun intended. I'm glad I could help."

Sean didn't expect that, "So Cheryl knows?"

"Yeah, when I couldn't reach you, I called her. I hope that was okay." Lucky had noticed the catch in Sean's voice. "You and she were here together working on this."

Uneasiness punched Sean, because Cheryl was not answering her phone. "You are right, Lucky. We are working together. I owe you big time on this. I'll let you know how everything turns out. Thanks, again."

Sean immediately called Cheryl's number again, but there was no answer. If Cheryl knew who was behind this, hopefully, she wouldn't confront him. Sean tried one more time to reach Cheryl, and when there was no answer, he called Bri.

Bri said, "Thank God you called, Sean. I am so worried about Cheryl."

"Why? What's going on?"

"When Cheryl heard what the FBI friend of yours had to say, I couldn't stop her, Sean. She was heading to his house. She tried to call his office, and they told her he was working from his home today. But Sean, there's something else. After she left here, Lilly and Elena came here, and what they told me is also disturbing." Bri repeated what she knew before she concluded, "Cheryl was in his driveway talking to me about this, and then suddenly, she had to go."

His heart pounded. Fighting to remain calm, "Bri, if you hear from her, tell her to get back to your place. Let me know right away if she calls. I'm not too far away. I'm heading there right now."

"*Oh, God,*" thought Sean as he raced there, "*Cheryl has no idea the danger she might be in if she confronts him about her grandfather. Be smart, Honey, be safe. I love you.*"

Sean alerted Harold, "Everything has changed, Harold. Cheryl is at his house now. She doesn't know he may be a murderer, and I'm concerned that she might confront him about her grandfather's situation."

"We're on our way, Sean. Going in without backup could put you and Cheryl in danger. If at all possible, wait until we get there."

"Of course," Jeff responded. "Let's go in."

They walked back through the foyer that opened into a large open entertainment room with a high cathedral ceiling. Along the entire back wall were tall windows and French doors, which made the outdoor space feel incorporated into the interior entertainment area. A large stone fireplace was on the wall opposite the windows. At one end was a large bar area, complete with a TV, and a remodeled kitchen was at the other end of the room. The room was obviously designed for entertaining. "You have a lovely home. I love all these windows and the beautiful view. It's a nice day to have them all opened."

"Thank you, but I can't take the credit for it. It's my wife's remodeling inspiration and decorating genius that made it happen. I like the feel of the fresh air, so I leave the doors and windows open when the weather permits. Please have a seat. Would you like something to drink?"

"Thank you. No, I'm fine."

"I hope we're not going to cover the same territory we covered before."

Cheryl pulled out her recorder, notepad and pen. "You mind if I record our conversation? I'm here to ask you some questions about a story I'm working on."

"By all means, Ms. Seton, I'm totally at your service."

"Commissioner Thompson. Thank you for agreeing to talk to me. Do you know who my grandfather was?"

Jeff looked perplexed. "No, I don't believe so. I don't know too many people from Cleveland."

"I'm not originally from Cleveland. I was born here."

Jeff sat there thinking about the question, "What are you saying?"

"My grandfather was Henry Willis. When I was fourteen, I watched my grandfather plead guilty to five murders, the Burkhart murders that occurred on July 4, 1980. He was sixty-six years old at the time and was dying of cancer. He died in prison six months later. Commissioner Thompson, my grandfather did not commit those murders. There's no way he was physically able to kill five people like that."

"What's that got to do with me? I don't understand why you'd be talking to me about a murder that occurred over twenty-years ago. Your grandfather confessed."

"Well, he knew at the time he confessed he was dying. I came here to report on the Pinkston murders and to find out about what happened to my grandfather. After I got here, someone who knew who I was told me that he had been drinking with Grandpa late into the evening on the night of the murders. He told me that Grandpa was in no condition to have committed those murders."

"How does he know that? Your grandfather confessed."

"He told me that he never spoke up, because when he went to see Grandpa after he confessed, Grandpa told him not to say anything."

"Well, I don't mean to be rude, Ms. Seton, but I've got some things I've got to do. This is all an interesting theory, and that's all it is. He confessed. Now, I'll walk you to the door."

Jeff started to get up, but Cheryl said, "I've found proof."

Jeff looked annoyed and sat back down. "What fairytale are you going to tell me now? You've got two minutes. Then I'm going to have to insist that you leave."

"You see, there is proof that your father, Randall Thompson, bought a life insurance policy in Henry Willis' name on August 4, 1980. The policy was taken out at the Bekbourg Farm and

Community Insurance Company where your father was Chairman and CEO at the time. The beneficiary was my mother, and the face value of the policy was $500,000. The policy paid out to my mother six months later when Henry died."

Jeff was confused about what he was hearing. Cheryl could tell that he was unnerved, but he was trying to maintain his composure. "This is the first I've ever heard of any of this. It sounds like someone's imagination is working overtime."

"Is that the quote I should put in my story that I'm getting ready to publish?"

"Be careful what you print, Ms. Seton. I wouldn't want to see you and your newspaper regretting irresponsible action."

"One more thing, did you know Missy Collins? She died of an overdose."

Jeff's surprised expression was interrupted by the doorbell.

To Ben's mind, Sean had ruined his life, starting in high school. Sean thought he was so much better than everyone, the Big Man. Ben had been disappointed that he had left for the military before he could extract his revenge for what Sean did to him in high school.

Since Sean had returned, he had made Ben's life a living hell. He had wormed his way back in with his old football bud, Mike, and lied to Mike to cause him to push Ben off the Pinkston case. On top of all that, he had Mike suspend him for nothing more than a little smack to Erlene, who deserved it.

Well, Ben was not going to take any more from Sean, Mr. Football Stud. First, his plan was to make him suffer. Ben knew that Mike was his best friend—Mike, that weak-ass, who was kowtowing to Mr. Big Shot Sean. It's too bad that Mike didn't die right away. But maybe, Sean was suffering more, waiting for him to die. Ben had been following Sean, and luck was with Ben when he saw that reporter woman leave Sean's place this morning. Of course, she had chosen Sean. Didn't all the women? Well, too bad for her. Since Sean had enough feelings to screw her, Ben planned to kill her, too, so that Sean would suffer even more. Then, Ben would kill Sean, but not before making sure Sean knew why Mike and that woman had died first. Sean was going to pay for ruining his life, and pay big time.

Ben had followed Cheryl to Jeff's house. He was curious about why she was there. He parked his truck off the main road where it was hidden and walked around to the far side entrance off the kitchen.

On his drive home, Gary grew more and more despondent. He walked into his house, stripped down to his underwear, grabbed a large bottle of his favorite scotch and trudged to a chair by the pool. His phone started ringing on the drive home. It was ringing again. "Screw it," he mumbled as he flung the phone into the pool. His anger, self-pity and resentment all bore down on him. He hated his father for having allowed Jeff's dad to start using the dealership for some of his activities. Yeah, sure, he'd made it possible for Gary's dad to buy the dealership and expand, but his dad should have found a way to kick Thompson out. When Gary took over, Jeff and that bullying manager had him in a vice, and so he looked the other way, not wanting to know what they were doing. And, to make matters worse, Sean had to come back into the picture. Becky had seemed even more distant to him since Sean's return. Although he didn't believe Sean had any interest in her, Gary knew she had the hots for him.

By the time he had gotten half way through the bottle, his anger had turned more into self-pity. *"Why haven't I been stronger? I should have kicked Jeff out a long time ago. I knew this was going to happen."* As he continued to drink, his frame of mind continued to get more morose, thinking he would lose Becky and his kids and everything he had worked so hard for. *"How could I have been so stupid? I should have stood up to them."*

He finished his bottle of scotch and thought it tasted good. *"I probably should stop, but another few sips won't hurt anything, then I'll figure out what to do."*

He staggered over to the bar, grabbed another bottle, and wobbled back toward the chair.

Ben slipped into the kitchen in time to hear Cheryl talking about having proof that Jeff's father had somehow been involved in the Burkhart murders. He was listening to what she was saying to Jeff when the doorbell rang.

Hearing the doorbell ring, Jeff said, "Ms. Seton, if you will excuse me, it seems I'm a popular person today."

Ben heard some talking and then realized that Sean had arrived. He smiled, thinking he had hit pay dirt. Jeff might not be happy with him killing both of them here, but tough. Jeff had lots of acres here. He could bury them where they'd never be found. Jeff would never tell. He'd listen for a while and then surprise them. If he played his cards right, he might just screw the woman in front of Sean. He'd finally have his revenge on Football Stud. This was going to be fun.

Ben's eyes were glassy, the deranged glint evident.

Sean was standing at the front door.

"Hi, Sean, what brings you out here today? If I didn't know better, I'd say someone planned a party here and forgot to tell me."

"Can I come in?" Sean asked.

"Sure, someone you know is here."

Sean said, "You go first and show me the way."

Sean internally breathed a sigh of relief when he saw Cheryl sitting in the room.

Jeff had moved behind the bar. "Sean, can I get you a drink?"

"No, not today."

Jeff said, "Now tell me what this is all about. What can I do for you?"

"A warrant has been issued, Jeff. I've come here to arrest you."

Jeff's temper started to show, "Arrest me for what? That's bullshit. You always were a joker, Sean." Jeff, though, was not smiling.

"To start with, the recent murders of the Pinkstons."

Cheryl let out a slight gasp.

Never taking his eyes off Jeff, Sean matter-of-factly said to Cheryl, "Just sit still. Don't do anything. I have to take care of this."

"This is preposterous. You don't have anything on me. How can you arrest me for that?"

"You're a lawyer. You know I have to read you your rights."

"I don't need that shit," Jeff angrily replied.

Sean pulled out his handcuffs, "I'm going to have to cuff you, Jeff," and Sean started walking toward the bar.

Jeff said, "I don't think I'm going to let you do that, Sean."

Sean noticed Jeff moving his hand toward the underside of the bar, "I wouldn't go for that gun, Jeff."

Jeff paused and looked out the window. His focus returned to Sean, and he said, "Sean, I think you've got it all wrong. I didn't shoot anybody. It was Ben. We only went there to destroy the meth labs because of all the problems in the county, and the next thing I knew, Ben has gone berserk and started shooting the people."

Sean looked incredulous at him, "Then why didn't you tell us that?"

"And implicate myself in five murders?"

Cheryl was stunned. She never suspected Jeff of murdering the Pinkstons. She also felt responsible for what was unfolding. She knew that Sean would never have come alone to arrest Jeff if it wasn't for her being here. Jeff was like a cornered animal, which meant the odds of this resolving peaceably were not good. She knew that Sean was trying to diffuse the situation, but walking away now was not an option. Cheryl wanted to try and distract Jeff, so she asked him if he gave Missy Collins the drugs she used.

"Missy? What's this about?"

"She got her drugs from somewhere. I heard that it might have been her boyfriend that gave them to her. That was you, wasn't it?"

Before Jeff could answered, Sean asked, "Jeff, did the heroin, crack and meth come from your operations? Did you take a little off the top for your personal business?"

Jeff became noticeably shocked. He thought to himself, *"This changes everything. How did Sean know about the drug operation?"*

Sean's back was toward the kitchen, so he couldn't see that Ben had quietly entered from the kitchen. Cheryl was sitting off to the side, so like Sean, she didn't see Ben. However, Jeff saw Ben and thought with relief that Ben was there to help him. Ben had his gun out.

Jeff's cockiness resurfaced, "I think you need to put the gun and cuffs down, Sean."

Sensing the sudden change in Jeff, Sean didn't have a good feeling. "No, I'm going to take you in."

Nodding toward the back, Jeff said, "Yeah, Sean. I took a little off the top, but it doesn't concern you. I don't think Ben is going to let you do that."

Cheryl looked back and saw Ben and gave a little scream.

Sean turned so he could see both Jeff and Ben. Jeff said, "I've never been happier in my life to see you, Ben."

Cheryl thought that she and Sean were going to be killed, while Sean simultaneously was accessing how to get the upper hand or at least drag this out until the state police arrived. They both were surprised by Ben's next move.

Pointing his gun toward Jeff, Ben angrily spit his words, "You rotten SOB traitor! I've worked for you all my life and done everythin' you wanted me to do, and even what the old man told me, and you turn on me like I'm nobody."

Jeff tried to calm him. "You know better than that, Ben. I'm going to take care of you."

"How the hell can you tell Sean it was me, when you planned it all? Everythin'!" he yelled.

It was obvious to everyone that Ben was unhinged.

Jeff was starting to get nervous. He'd never had Ben question him or turn on him. He needed to get Ben calm and focused.

Jeff spoke calmly and deliberately, "Ben, let's take care of these two. That's what we need to do now. I was just trying to buy some time here with Sean, and good for us, you showed up."

Jeff was trying to get his gun out without drawing Ben's attention.

Sean knew what Jeff was trying to do and wanted to get Ben to put down his gun before someone got shot. "Ben, murder is not a solution. Put your gun down. It's not going to do you any good. The state police are on the way. You can't get away. Don't make things worse by doing something stupid."

Ben's venom pivoted to Sean. He sneered as he moved over to where Cheryl was sitting and stepped in back of her—while still training his gun in Sean and Jeff's direction. He grabbed a fistful of her hair and yanked back her head, causing Cheryl to yelp. "Sean, you can fool others, but not me. You ain't got those state troopers comin' here. Your lyin's not going to help you this time."

Ben gloated, "Killin' you is goin' to be a great solution to everythin' you've done to me. You know, Sean, I shot Mike. I know he's your best friend. I figured it was a good way to make you suffer before I killed you. Mike deserved it anyway, though. He was weak, always doin' what you told him. Your lady friend here was goin' to be next. I saw her leave your place this mornin'. By killin' her, you would suffer again, before I killed you. Sean, put your gun and handcuffs on that chair beside you. If you don't do as I say *RIGHT NOW*," wrenching Cheryl's head back even harder, forcing a shriek, "I'm goin' to put a bullet in her."

Cheryl cautiously sank a little in the chair to relieve the pressure on her neck. Sean wanted to buy some time. "Why did you two kill the Pinkstons?" Sean asked.

Ben spit his words. "It sure as hell wasn't like he said," pointing the gun toward Jeff, "me goin' berserk! Tell them, Jeff. Tell them the damn truth!" he yelled.

Jeff placated him hoping to distract or diffuse, whatever it took, "Okay, Ben. Okay. Ben had found the two labs. The Pinkston boy was selling to kids at school, and Ben found out. We knew then where to look." Jeff did not know that Ben had a gig on the side with the Pinkstons. "Anyway, destroying the labs was all we had in mind. When we went back that night to burn them, Pinkston had obviously discovered Ben had been there and put up that alarm. We had already planted the bomb at the other lab, and when Pinkston confronted us, we killed everyone at the house so we wouldn't be discovered. We knew the police would destroy the labs, and we went back over to the first place, but I guess they had heard the shooting, because they were coming out with the guns. So we had no choice but to kill them and remove all the evidence."

Sean asked, "Why do you want to destroy the meth labs? You could have had them arrested."

Jeff said, "We didn't want the State or Feds coming around."

Sean said, "You're the big fish in the area with the drug operations, aren't you?"

Jeff said, "Yeah, Sean—a very big fish. I got an offer too good to pass up. My Columbian partner offered to buy that failing paper plant and retool it. I hate that you'll never see the state-of-the art operation we have in the basement. That poly product line expansion gave us the perfect cover. You know, Sean, I knew you were going to be a problem when Mike hired you. Too bad. I always liked you."

"Well, since you're planning to kill me anyhow, tell me why you killed the Burkharts?"

Jeff looked at Cheryl and back at Sean. "What do you mean? I didn't kill them." Jeff then looked back at Cheryl, "Is that what you think? That I killed them because supposedly my dad had paid for a life insurance policy for your grandpa?"

Sean could tell that Jeff was confused about this, and frankly so was he. "The gun," Sean said, "it's the same one that we used to use for target practicing, and you're the only one who had a gun for us to use. It's the same gun that was used in the Pinkston murders and the Burkhart murders. A three-way match, Jeff."

Jeff was confused. Sean finally understood. Sean said, "It was your father wasn't it that killed the Burkharts. He used the gun he gave you for your birthday. You didn't know."

Jeff said, "I had no idea. I was in town that weekend, and there had been the murders, and I thought I should take it back to campus with me in case I ever needed it for protection. He asked me once after that if I had the gun, and I told him I did. I guess he never thought about it being traced, or either he forgot."

Sean looked at Ben, "Were you involved with Jeff's dad that night, Ben?"

"Yeah, he asked me to go. He knew he could count on me. He thought Burkhart was there by himself. It's a good thing that he took me. He probably wouldn't have made it out alive if I hadn't been with him." Ben was now gloating at Jeff. "It was after that night that he told me."

Sean asked, "What did he tell you, Ben?"

"That I was his son, too."

Jeff uttered in disbelief, "The hell you say. That's a pipe dream."

Ben smirked at Jeff, "He was proud of me. He told me though not to ever tell anyone about what happened that night. He said that many times that night. He told me to get rid of my gun. He also said for me not to tell anyone about me being his son, because they might get suspicious, that we could accomplish a lot of things together if people didn't know."

Jeff snorted, but he seemed less certain.

Sean hoped that he could keep them talking. "Ben," Sean asked, "do you know anything about the man that Mike's father was supposed to have run over one night?"

"Oh, yeah, Jeff, that's another thing that OUR dad asked me to take care of. There was a hippy who was hangin' out at Knuck's. He was just a drifter. Dad had somethin' put in old man Adams' drink after he knew I had killed that hippy. It went as smooth as silk. You see, Jeff, I'm not dumb like you think. I'm actually more helpful to OUR dad than you. You're tryin' to pin things on me and make me a scapegoat, but I'm not goin' to let that happen. Once I get rid of you three, Dad will have

411

me to help him with everythin'. I'm goin' to start with her, so Football Stud can watch her die, and then Football Stud himself, and then you, little brother. I want you to see how much better I am at handlin' things than you."

Ben was growing more unbalanced. Sean calmly said, "Don't hurt Cheryl. I'll put my gun and cuffs down. Don't do anything stupid."

Sean drifted toward the chair. Ben was focused on Sean and didn't see Jeff open the drawer. Watchful of Ben, Jeff slipped out his gun, but at the last second, Ben noticed. When Jeff raised his gun to shoot Ben, Ben shot first, and Jeff fell.

Sean moved to grab his gun, but Ben was too quick and aimed at Sean. Cheryl screamed. Before he could pull the trigger, shots rang out from the outside terrace. Ben dropped to the floor. Sean looked up and saw Danny. Sean yelled for Cheryl to call 911 and ran over to check Ben's pulse, but Ben was dead. He then ran over to where Jeff lay. Jeff was conscious, but his pulse was weak.

Sean said, "Jeff, buddy, hang on. The EMT's will be here soon. Come on, Jeff, don't give up."

With life flowing from his body, Jeff tightened his grasp on Sean's arm and wheezed, "Sean, you always were the smart one." He gasped. "Tell Mary I'm sorry."

Danny had run in and stood looking impassively at Jeff.

Sean heard the sirens in the distance. The state police arrived along with the EMTs. Jeff and Ben were pronounced dead at the scene.

Sean asked Danny how he happened to be there. Danny told him that he couldn't let anything happen to Cheryl. Danny said he got there right after Cheryl arrived. He pulled his truck off where it wouldn't be seen and went around back where he thought they might be. Fortunately, the windows were open. He didn't know why she was going there, but he had a bad feeling. He felt when Sean arrived, things were going to be okay, but then he saw Ben walk in. "When Ben aimed toward you, Sean, I was ready."

Chapter 59

About the same time in Sebring, Florida, Jack was sitting on his back patio and heard someone knocking on his front door. When he opened it, it was Randall Thompson. "Well, Randy, this is a surprise."

"Well, I was driving back to Bekbourg, and thought I'd stop in and see an old buddy. Can I come in?"

"Sure. Come in, and we'll go sit out on the patio."

"That's okay. We can stay in here. I won't be staying long since I need to get on the road."

"Sure thing. Have a seat over there."

Randall opted to stand but walked over near the window. "You're good at driving that thing," Randall said, pointing to the wheel chair.

Laughing, "Yeah, I'm entering the 5-K in the fall. How's Margaret doing? Does she like living in Florida?"

"Took to it like a fish to water. We both like it here. We don't get back to Bekbourg much, but Jeff comes down to see us."

"Is he handling things for you in Bekbourg?"

"Well, I keep my fingers in the pie, but yes. He's a good son. He's smart and tries hard. Finally quit all that partying with those women and settled down. I don't know if you knew, but he got married about two or three years ago. Her name is Mary. She had a little girl by a first marriage. Mary's the granddaughter of Theodore Zimmstein."

"You mean the former Speaker of the Statehouse?"

"Yeah, Jeff scored well on that one. He has his eye on the Statehouse and then maybe being Governor. He never told me, but I think he saw Mary as a way to make that happen—a powerful family with lots of money—great pedigree."

"Sounds like it."

Randall said, "Say, I heard you had a visitor recently from Bekbourg?"

"Well, news travels fast."

Randall laughed, "Well, actually, Jeff and I were talking yesterday afternoon. I don't know if you remember Mike Adams who became the sheriff after you retired. Anyway, someone shot him, and he's in critical condition. Jeff stopped by yesterday to visit his wife, and she mentioned that one of the deputies had come to visit you."

"Yeah. It's always good to see someone from home."

"I heard it was a deputy, Sean Neumann."

"Yeah."

"What did you tell him, Jack?"

"Everything."

This news displeased Randall. "You didn't have to do that, Jack."

"I know I didn't, Randy, but I had a chance to clear my conscience and maybe make something right for once. Mike Adams is a good man. He didn't deserve what you did to him back then, and he didn't deserve to be fighting for his life now."

"That's too bad, Jack. You crossed the wrong people."

"I've got a couple of questions, Randy. Why did you kill the Burkharts?"

"Burkhart was drawing too much attention. I didn't want the Feds or state to start snooping around. He wouldn't listen. I got word that he was a middleman on coins worth about $250,000. Roger had taken delivery of the coins on the day before July Fourth. He was supposed to deliver them two days later and receive payment and his fee. I planned to persuade Roger to see things my way. Didn't know others were going to be in the house. I was going to steal the coins.

"He was a middleman. If he lost the coins, he would have been out on a very long limb, because he wouldn't have the coins or the money. Without that, he couldn't deliver the coins or pay the seller. I was going to tell him we'd work with him on the financial bind he was going to be in, if we got the assurance from him that he would toe the line. He wouldn't have a choice, since he couldn't cover the cost of the coins.

"Roger must have heard us, and he came down with a gun. Pandemonium broke loose. Ben, like he was prone to do, opened fire—hitting Roger. Roger's wife came down the steps with a gun, and the brother and his wife came running out from the downstairs bedroom. Between Ben and me, we shot them. We found some gas in the garage, and—being a remodeled old farm house—it went up like a tinder box."

"How did Henry Willis fit in all this?"

"I couldn't take any chances. I knew Willis. He was a small-time crook in town. I offered him money to take the fall. He was up in years, and I knew he had a daughter and granddaughter. I didn't know he had cancer. When he died so suddenly, I was concerned someone might look into it, but he had confessed and was in prison, and it seemed that everyone forgot. He had insisted that I pay for a life insurance policy that would go to his daughter upon his death. Seemed like a good trade. No questions would remain on the Burkhart murders, and he had found a way to make sure his daughter and granddaughter would have something to live on."

"I'm surprised you honored the insurance policy, Randy."

Randall laughed, "Well, I can't say I didn't think about it. I figured Willis' daughter probably knew the details. I might not have paid, but Willis wasn't as dumb as he let on. I learned that when he and I negotiated the details of him pleading guilty. He might have had something written somewhere to blow the whistle if I didn't pay or if something happened to his daughter or granddaughter. So I paid. I figured that his daughter wouldn't try to blackmail me—thinking I might harm her daughter, and I would have. But, it never came to that. She moved away. I knew where she was, up there in Cleveland, but she seemed to go on with her life, and I let sleeping dogs lie."

"I see. You said, 'Ben.' You mean that goofus deputy?"

"Yeah. He wasn't the brightest around, but he was very loyal to me, Jack. I'm glad you took my suggestion and hired him."

"How did you get Ben to do your bidding like murder?"

"I didn't intend for things to happen the way they did, but the way it turned out that night, I was glad Ben was with me. You see, he is my son. His mother lived up in the northern part of the county. After Ben was born, I supported them, but after a while, she got bored waiting around. I later found out that she had been having other men come around, and some of them weren't too good to Ben. I gave her some money to leave town and told her if she ever came back, I'd kill her.

"I hired an old lady to care for him. Told her that his mother abandoned him, and I wanted to help with the charity. Didn't like to see kids not cared for. So, Jeff and Margaret didn't know that he was my son. Actually, I only took him along that night to help find the coins—not thinking anything would happen. Just figured Burkhart was stone drunk and it would be a cake walk to get the coins. Like I said, good thing Ben was there."

"What about the Burkhart kid? You killed the kid."

"Well, we didn't know for sure he was there. He didn't come downstairs."

"Why did you set up Mike's dad to make it look like he ran over that drifter?"

"Just like you, Jack. We wanted to have something to control Mike with, and Jeff had told me how close Mike was to his father. I had someone slip something in his drink that knocked him out. Ben had killed the guy. He never had any problems carrying out the messier side of the business. We drove Mike's dad to the place where Ben had put the body and ran it over with his car. By then, Ben was doing my bidding, so he was there to make sure everything went as planned. Ben was concerned about what you were going to do with the body, but he couldn't argue too much—afraid you might catch on. But, you must have buried the body, because nothing ever came of it."

Jack said, "Why did you leave Bekbourg? Why not stay there where your power base was?"

"Well, we had some operations going on down here, so I left the Bekbourg stuff to Jeff. Plus, I like the weather down here better. Hell, I can transact business offshore enjoying the pleasure of being on my boat. I'm afraid Jeff is taking a liking to doing business here, too. He recently bought a bigger boat. It comes in handy. I told him he can't leave Bekbourg though—too much going on there."

Randall pulled out a gun and aimed it at Jack. "I hope I've answered all your questions, Jack. I've already spent more time here than I planned. Sorry to have to do this, but you talk too much, and I need to get on my way."

Before he could pull the trigger, a bullet hit him right between the eyes. Jack sat there in his wheel chair and looked at Randall lying on the floor. Jack's blanket had a bullet hole in it.

Chapter 60

Gomez pushed the workers hard over night to get the drugs ready. A shipment had gone out yesterday, and with tonight's shipment, the bulk of the delivery would be made. The rest would go out in smaller quantities over the next couple of days, and then they would mothball the plant's drug operation for a while.

When the drug operation was set up in the factory's basement, Thompson purchased property to house the workers. Hispanics living in the newer part of Acorn Knoll were relocated by Gomez to work in the drug operation. They processed, cut and packaged the drugs. They then loaded them in boxes for shipping to their customers.

Not all the Hispanics living in the newer part of Acorn Knoll were involved in, or knew of, the drug operation. Some worked in Gomez' cleaning service company, a cover he used for the illegal operations, and for his recent landscape business— another cover. Others had moved there at the urging of their families and worked in legitimate businesses around Bekbourg. Even if any suspected the illegal drug operation, they would not dare talk, because they knew retribution would be ruthless to themselves and their family members.

A bus transported the workers to and from the plant. Gomez lived in an apartment not far from the Shopper's Pavilion. After the bus departed, he got in his car and headed toward home. However, after pulling onto the road, he spotted something—a dark van mostly hidden behind an abandoned warehouse.

When Gomez returned to his place, he dressed in a disguise and retrieved a hidden pre-paid phone that was unused and untraceable and slipped out the back. He walked to the Shopper's Pavilion. The employees didn't pay any attention to his passing through. Closely watching that he wasn't being observed, he walked out the back door. He pulled out the untraceable phone and placed the call.

"My favorite nephew, I am pleased with the progress. We are close to having the order filled, Si?"

"We sent the first delivery out last night and have the second delivery ready to go out tonight. Two smaller deliveries will go out tomorrow and the next day, so we are on schedule."

"Very good, Dante, but that is not what you called to tell me, no?"

"Uncle, I am a suspicious man."

"As well you should be."

"As I was leaving the plant this morning, I saw a dark van that I have never seen before near the plant."

"Mmmm, I see," said Miguel Esteban. "What are you thinking?"

"I think today I should get out as much of the shipment as possible and destroy the plant. We will not meet the entire order, but I do not have a good feeling."

Esteban was silent. Gomez waited.

Finally, Esteban said, "We have not picked up any law enforcement activity around the county or the paper plant. The DEA agents that came to town when the Pinkstons were killed have not been back. There has been no sign that they are on to our operation there."

"What you say is true, Uncle, but something does not feel right. This van was suspicious."

A long silence ensued. Esteban finally spoke, "You have never failed me, nephew. I trust your judgment. I do not like the idea of destroying the facility, but I do not want the U.S. agents to find evidence on how we operate our business. Get the shipment out today that is ready. I assume you have a plan?"

"Si."

Gomez didn't walk back through the store, but instead, walked around the side and cut through some parking lots until he reached a storage company. He opened his unit and got in a car that he kept secured. There was no chance that it had a tracking device or would be recognizable by the authorities if they were watching.

Gomez drove to a secure location and called Joe Sommers on a phone Joe kept with him at all times but had never used. "I have talked to the Señor. We are clearing out today, but first, we must load all of the supply that is ready. You need to take one of the cargo vans and arrive at 2:30 pm. Put one of the logo signs on it so nothing looks suspicious. Stan will have the employees cleared out by then. You and he are to load everything that is boxed. Forget what is in the basement. You will drive to the Pittsburg drop and secure the van. Fly out of the airport to our secure location. Clear out of the plant as soon as possible."

"I understand." Joe got busy, because there wasn't much time.

Gomez called Stan Andrews on a similar untraceable phone. When his phone rang, Stan knew something big was up.

He listened to Gomez's instructions. "At 1:30 today, you are to announce to all employees that an inspector is returning to follow up on a recent concern that was detected. They will be paid for a full day's work, but they must vacate the plant by two o'clock. No exceptions. The inspector has requested that the plant be completely empty for the inspection. Make sure that no one remains. As soon as everyone is gone, go to the basement and prepare the charges. Joe is coming with a van to load everything that is ready to go. You and he are to quickly load the van. Once he leaves, set the charges to detonate in one hour. You will fly out of the Columbus airport. We will meet in our secure location."

"As you say," Stan replied.

Years ago, Gomez had located an abandoned storage container several hundred yards from the paper plant. Inside was a perfect location for him to watch the plant and have an undetected escape if needed. He parked his car and carefully made his way to the storage container and watched to ensure his orders were carried out.

Soon after 1:30, he saw the employees driving away. At 2:30, he saw Joe drive the van through the gate and lock it. He watched and waited, checking his watch every five or so minutes. He had not seen any suspicious vehicles pass by the plant or in the vicinity, but he felt that time was of the essence. He was expecting to see the van pull out soon. Peering over at the factory, he willed that they were close to leaving.

Close to four o'clock, chaos materialized out of thin air. A helicopter swooped in. Numerous armored vehicles, SUVs, vans and cars swarmed the area. One of the armored vehicles smashed through the gate. The door located on the side of the old plant at basement level was blasted, and armored men rushed the premises. In what seemed a matter of seconds, the paper plant was breached. Gomez tried frantically to call Joe and Stan, but cell service was jammed. He had no way to reach them. He slipped out of his hiding place and made his way on foot out of the area.

Joe and Stan had almost completed loading the van when the DEA swarmed the building. Joe and Stan were caught at the loading dock. DEA agents dressed in full body armor took the elevator to the basement. Their expertise alerted them to the denotation devices, and bomb squads were brought in.

Joe and Stan were taken to a DEA facility, and the factory was secured. All drugs and equipment were confiscated.

About the same time the DEA was raiding the paper plant, agents were making simultaneous raids and arrests at the Bekbourg dealership, Gary Werner's home, the known residences of Joe Sommers, Stan Andrews and Dante Gomez, as well as the new section of the Acorn Knoll trailer park.

Chapter 61

The emptiness of the funeral home's parking lot bespoke of Jeff's fall. Mary was standing at the front beside an older man whom she introduced as her father. Sean had to give Mary credit. Her husband had died in disgrace, but she was following through with seeing him buried. Mary was pleased to see Sean. "Sean, this has been horrible for me and Rachel. I never suspected this other side of Jeff. Once I get back on my feet, I plan to come back to Bekbourg to try to make right the wrongs done by Jeff."

As Sean walked toward the back door, he saw Danny walking up the other aisle. Danny spoke to the family members, and Mary gave him a brief hug.

Sean stepped into the parlor and waited for Danny. As they shook hands, Sean asked Danny how he was doing. "I'm doing okay, Sean. I don't like to think about everything that happened. I never thought when I was improving my shooting skills, that I would ever kill someone, but I couldn't let him shoot you, Sean." Danny paused, and Sean waited. Finally, "I had no idea that Ben was Jeff's half-brother." After another pause: "That's another thing that's been on my mind. I don't know if you know. Jeff and I were half-brothers. Dad told me in high school. I never wanted it to be true, and you know that Jeff never really wanted anything to do with me. I don't think he knew, though. It doesn't matter. It's ironic, I guess, that Jeff, Ben, and their dad died on the same day. The Thompsons and Ben were bad seeds, Sean. I'm glad my dad took care of me and kept Randall out of my life, not that he ever tried to be involved. After everything that happened, I finally told Sally that Randall was my dad. She knew Norm wasn't, but she didn't know who was. We don't see any reason to tell Drew. I've been thinking about you, what it must have been like coming back to Bekbourg and running into all this mess. These were friends."

"I'm sorry, Danny, for everything you've been through. Dad told me about Randall being your biological father a couple of days before everything happened. I have to say, Danny, I never expected to run into this deadly villainy, and I sure never foresaw Jeff and Gary ending up the way they did."

"Yeah, it's crazy. I feel for Mary. She seems like a nice woman. Well, Sean, I'm moving on and putting this behind me." Danny turned and walked away.

Chapter 62
Six months later

Neither Stan Andrews nor Joe Sommers cooperated with law enforcement. Dante Esteban a/k/a Dante Gomez had not been located. The DEA busts dealt a huge blow to the money streams funding Middle East terrorists and drug supplies feeding drug sales in the U. S.

Sean and Cheryl were engaged to be married. Sean was interim sheriff. She was working on an expose on the Bekbourg corruption and drug culture. The nightmares still visited Sean, although not as frequently, but Cheryl and Buddy were there to support him.

The recording made by Cheryl's recorder at Jeff's that fateful day answered many questions about Jeff and his father's activities over the last twenty years. Cheryl was glad her grandfather's name was cleared.

Mike survived and cleared up some details about Missy Collins. Jeff was having an affair with Missy. He actually cared for her, but she had an addiction issue. To keep her happy, Jeff provided her with drugs, most of which he got from the supply being manufactured at the paper factory. They had been partying one night, and Jeff slipped off to sleep. When he woke, he found Missy unconscious. He called Ben as well as the emergency personnel. They rushed her to the hospital but couldn't revive her. Jeff was concerned about his reputation, so Ben filed a brief incident report, and Jeff convinced the judge to seal the records. Mike was kept out of the loop except for the briefest of facts. Sean tracked down Missy's mother, who lived in Granville, Ohio. She told Sean that Jeff had personally come to tell her that Missy had died. He told her Missy had worked for a paper plant that he ran. He paid for all the burial arrangements in Granville, for which she was grateful.

The car dealership was closed for several weeks as the DEA and other law enforcement authorities audited the records. After the law enforcement agencies concluded their review, its largest supplier canceled its truck distributorship. Becky had taken control from Gary of the dealership. She faced, head-on, the struggles of the dealership since Gary's arrest. She apologized to the community and customers and wanted to "earn the trust of the people and return to providing superior customer service and being a steward to our community."

Most people were unaware of Becky's knowledge in the business, but over the years, Gary had talked a lot with her about customers and financing matters, and some of their successful promotional initiatives had been her ideas. It had been difficult to process Gary's complicity in the Esteban drug operation, but she was determined to try and salvage the dealership to support her daughters in the way in which her family was accustomed.

Gary was living in a small efficiency apartment and saw his daughters when Becky allowed it. He was cooperating with the authorities as part of a plea bargain to reduce his prison time.

The murders of Jed and Brody Todd remained unsolved.

The paper plant had been closed for three months while the DEA and a host of other law enforcement searched every part of the plant and removed all equipment used in the drug operations. The Ohio governor pressured the U.S. government to quickly wrap up its investigation, because of the adverse economic impact to the local economy and to the employees. Other than Stan Andrews and the one loading dock employee, none of the employees who worked in the manufacturing operations knew anything of the drug operations. Those who worked in the drug operations in the basement were arrested or disappeared without being caught. Once it reopened, a member of the governor's economic council, who was a retired chief executive officer from a manufacturing company, took over as interim CEO. He named Stella Long as the plant foreman and Christy Finnigan as the business manager. The company was struggling to regain its footing.

Sean smiled as he recalled his visit yesterday with Tanner Bradford, his Commanding Officer. Tanner had a huge smile, "I lost so much sleep over you."

"Commander, I miss the Marines, but what I'm doing now works, too."

Tanner continued, "Yeah, Lucky called me and told me about everything that went down in Bekbourg and how the DEA credits you with that huge bust. I'm happy for you, Sean. I heard that Lucky offered you a job with the FBI. He'd be lucky to get you."

Tanner and Sean laughed at his joke.

"I'm not sure what I'm going to do. Some people around Bekbourg are encouraging me to run for sheriff. I'm giving that some thought."

Tanner said, "Whatever you decide, I wish you the best. Sean, I wish Tally could have been here, but he's in Afghanistan on assignment. He wanted you to know we got the people responsible for what happened to you and Clint that night in Kuwait. I told him I'd tell you. Your informer, Jyot Al-Nashi, didn't double-cross you. There was a Kuwaiti, Hameed Fahad, who was a middle level officer in defense. He had become suspicious of Jyot and fed him information on the two deliveries where your team missed the drug delivery. Fahad had men stationed, and they saw you, Clint and Tally rush in to thwart the pick-up, just missing the action. So, Fahad set up the fake delivery of drugs in the warehouse. There weren't any drugs there that night. Jyot was sitting off in a distance, hoping your team was going to be successful. When he saw the explosion, he knew he had been set up, and he knew he was a dead man if he didn't escape that night. His wife's people are Bedouins, and he made it to them and stayed in the desert hiding among them for several months.

"Tally told me that you had already fingered Colonel Bruce Moorehouse as the ringleader from the U.S. side, but you didn't have the evidence. I sent another team over to report to Tally. With what happened to you and Clint, the troops there were angry, and tips starting coming in to Tally. Tally's investigation eventually led to Fahad. They found that he was living well beyond what he should have and traced his assets. We didn't have the smoking gun against him to tie him to Moorehouse or enough evidence to pin him to the trafficking operation, so we were waiting, hoping for a break.

"Our big break came when Jyot secretly made his way back to Kuwait City and contacted Tally. He told Tally that he had been set up and that his life was in danger, but he wanted Tally to know he never set up you and Clint. Tally told him he had to give up the man who set him up. He was afraid, but he did. He told Tally it was Fahad.

"Tally's men moved against Fahad, and he was convinced to cooperate. He gave names, routes, logistics, everything. He gave us the evidence that directly tied Moorehouse to the operation. We found evidence that Moorehouse had bank accounts with large amounts of money. We moved on the participants and shut everything down. Moorehouse must have realized the jig was up, because he was found in the desert, shot in the head with his own gun.

"Sean, we cut the head off that trafficking ring. You, Clint and Tally made it all possible."

"Tanner, what happened to Fahad?"

"I guess he was frightened we might turn him over to the Kuwaiti's, because he was found hanging in his cell."

Sean was glad to know the end result of the investigation that he, Clint and Tally had started and to know that the criminals had been stopped and the drug operation shut down.

Sean was leaving Mike, who was convalescing at home under Geri's care. The state attorney general decided for a variety of reasons, including statute of limitations and lack of evidence, not to pursue charges against Mike.

The air was cold and crisp, but the sun magnified the beauty of the winter day. Sean stopped to open the truck door, gazed up and studied the blue sky and the white, heavy cotton-like clouds floating high above. He would never, as a young man, have foreseen the men Jeff and Gary became. Even though both were flawed, they had been Sean's close friends once upon a time, and memories of the fun times they shared were forever branded in Sean's being. So much had happened since he had returned to Bekbourg. It was ironic that two murders twenty years apart were like bookends in their adult lives. Each had written their own story, but they were bound by friendships forged during their youth. Twenty years later, the final chapter of those relationships had been written. Now, it was time to start a new book.

ABOUT THE AUTHOR

Sherrie Rutherford lives on Florida's Gulf Coast and has ties to Ohio, East Tennessee and Houston. She and Larry love traveling, hiking (especially in the Great Smoky Mountains), and playing Bridge. She is a retired attorney. Her passion for Appalachia and railroad history inspired the Bekbourg County Series.

CPSIA information can be obtained
at www.ICGtesting.com
Printed in the USA
LVHW080604300822
727112LV00001B/30

9 781734 599206